ACCLAIM FOR
ZEKE AND NED

"Captain Call and Gus McCrae of *Lonesome Dove* must now make room for Zeke Proctor and Ned Christie of the Cherokee Nation. With Diana Ossana, Larry McMurtry has created another cyclorama in words of his own richly colored West."

—Dee Brown, author of
Bury My Heart at Wounded Knee

"A grand-scale tragedy . . . recounted with a conversational authenticity and understated humor that is a McMurtry trademark . . . The authors know how to sustain a drama played out over a plate of corn and vinegar cobbler, and they do it well. . . ."

—Joyce Maynard, *Los Angeles Times Book Review*

"Tender, well-written . . . A colorful and often poignant dramatization of historical events and figures. If this isn't the way things happened and the people actually were, it's the way they should have been. . . . Perhaps one of McMurtry's best novels."

—Clay Reynolds, *Houston Chronicle*

"The novel's pleasure is in the details: the fleshly present, the interiority that turns textbook footnotes into characters."

—Laurie Stone, *The Village Voice*

"The women . . . [make] this novel a heartbreaker."
—Susan Dodd, *The Washington Post Book World*

"This is a story that certainly has the potential to be among McMurtry's best. . . ."

—Curt Schleier, *Grand Rapids Press* (MI)

"ZEKE AND NED is a dandy adventure, full of sights, sounds, scents, and a sense of place and time. We've been taken down this trail before, but it's one of our favorite rides."

—Martin F. Kohn, *Detroit Free Press*

"What gives this well-wrought tale its depth is how McMurtry and Ossana convey the era's various moral shades of gray."

—*Publishers Weekly*

"Mr. McMurtry's literary aim is as dependably true as Ned Christie's lethal marksmanship. . . . Readers . . . should be pleased by the strong heroines. . . . It is the richer emotional texture provided by the women in this work that elevates this novel from a galloping good read set on the plains to the higher plane of an insightful comment on the human condition."

—Jan Galetta, *Chattanooga Free Press* (TN)

"Larry McMurtry and Diana Ossana have created a rich epic. . . . [They] reapply the great McMurtry theme of heroic but flawed tragic characters reacting to tectonic shifts in their world at the end of an era. . . ."

—Phil Montgomery, *The Dallas Morning News*

By Larry McMurtry and Diana Ossana

Zeke and Ned
Pretty Boy Floyd

By Larry McMurtry

Dead Man's Walk
The Late Child
Streets of Laredo
The Evening Star
Buffalo Girls
Some Can Whistle
Anything for Billy
Film Flam: Essays on Hollywood
Texasville
Lonesome Dove
The Desert Rose
Cadillac Jack
Somebody's Darling
Terms of Endearment
All My Friends Are Going to Be Strangers
Moving On
The Last Picture Show
In a Narrow Grave: Essays on Texas
Leaving Cheyenne
Horseman, Pass By

ZEKE

and

NED

LARRY McMURTRY

and

DIANA OSSANA

POCKET BOOKS
New York   London   Toronto   Sydney   Tokyo   Singapore

This book is a work of fiction. Names, characters, places and
incidents are products of the author's imagination or are used
fictitiously. Any resemblance to actual events or locales or persons,
living or dead, is entirely coincidental.

POCKET BOOKS, a division of Simon & Schuster Inc.
1230 Avenue of the Americas, New York, NY 10020

ISBN: 0-671-89168-5

First Pocket Books printing October 1997

10   9   8   7   6   5   4   3   2   1

POCKET and colophon are registered trademarks of
Simon & Schuster Inc.

Map by Anita Karl and James Kemp

Cover design by Chip Kidd
Stepback photos courtesy of Phillip W. Steele, author
of *The Last Cherokee Warriors,* published by Pelican
Publishing Co., Inc. © 1987

Printed in the U.S.A.

FOR VIOLET NADINE, ULDINE LAVERN, AND
MARIAN YVONNE . . . THE ANYAN GIRLS

When the Pilgrim fathers reached the shores of America, they fell on their knees. Then they fell on the Indians.

ANONYMOUS,
quoted by H. L. Mencken

They made us many promises, more than I can remember, but they never kept but one: they promised to take our land, and they took it.

RED CLOUD
Chief, Oglala Sioux

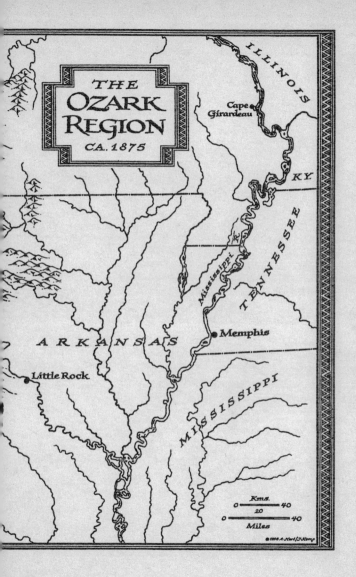

THE
OZARK
REGION
CA. 1875

ILLINOIS

Cape
Girardeau

K.Y.

Mississippi

TENNESSEE

ARKANSAS

Memphis

Little Rock

MISSISSIPPI

Kms.
0   40
    20
0   40
Miles

© 1996 A. Karl / J. Kemp

BOOK ONE

ZEKE'S FOLLY

If folly were grief, every house would weep.

GEORGE HERBERT

Cherokee Nation,
Going Snake District
Indian Territory

1

"ZEKE'S PROBABLY GOT THE ONLY DOG IN THE WORLD THAT can walk sideways," Ned remarked to Tuxie Miller as they sat astride their horses, watching the cautious Zeke Proctor and his short, fat, black dog, Pete, sidestepping along in front of the dry goods store.

Zeke's preference was to walk sideways, with a wall at his back, when in Tahlequah or any other place where his enemies might gather in strength. Pete, his constant companion, was as mean as a coon, but fatter than all but the fattest coons.

"It's too muddy here, let's go on home," Tuxie said, though he did not expect to get his way, or even to get an answer. Ned Christie liked town life; whenever he got a little ahead on his farming, he was bound for Tahlequah.

"I guess my dog could walk sideways if she practiced," Tuxie added. He had a blue bitch named Thistle who was, in his view, at least as smart as any dog Zeke Proctor had ever owned.

About the time Zeke and Pete slithered around a corner, Tuxie happened to notice Bill Pigeon's horse. The horse, a gaunt sorrel, was tied in front of Old Mandy Springston's house.

"There's Bill Pigeon's horse, he don't like me," Tuxie said. "That's another reason for getting on home."

"I didn't know Bill Pigeon's horse didn't like you," Ned replied. "I guess that's news to me."

Ned knew perfectly well it was Bill Pigeon, not his horse, that did not like Tuxie Miller, but it amused him to befuddle his friend by taking every word his friend uttered literally. It was a useful tactic, particularly if Tuxie was drunk or otherwise out of his head. The slightest criticism of how he put things would cause Tuxie to give up on human language entirely—he had been known to maintain a noble, slightly offended silence for upwards of a week. If addressed persistently, Tuxie might caw like a crow, or snuff like an angry armadillo; sometimes, at night, he would frighten the household with a perfect imitation of a rattlesnake's rattle—but he would not speak a syllable of Cherokee, much less English.

On this occasion, however, he chose to ignore Ned's remark. It was a drizzly June morning, and the wide main street of Tahlequah had an abandoned wagon sitting in it, bogged to its hubs in the thick, gummy mud.

"If fish could live in mud, we could go fishing right here in the street," Tuxie remarked.

Tuxie looked up and frowned. Across the street from where Zeke had been slinking along stood three reasons why the man kept his back to the wall.

"There's the Squirrel brothers, they don't like me, neither," Tuxie said. "We could have gone to Dog Town—most people like me in Dog Town. We could even have gone over to Siloam Springs. I've never even had a fistfight in Siloam Springs. You would have to bring me to the one town where nobody likes me—and it's too muddy to get down off my horse, besides."

Before Tuxie Miller could list any more reasons why they ought to get out of Tahlequah, they spotted Zeke Proctor again. This time, he was sidling along beside the meeting hall, the long building where the Cherokee Senate convened. Though the Cherokee Nation considered themselves separate from the rest of America, their laws, courts, and jury system were modeled after those of the whites. Lawlessness in the Cherokee Districts had been on the upswing ever since the Civil War, when desperadoes from the North and South sought to take advantage of murky law enforcement along the border between Arkansas and Indian Territory. Tuxie himself had an aversion to controversy, and was not a force in tribal government; but Ned Christie was a respected member of the Cherokee Senate, and a scrupulous one at that.

"I wonder why Zeke's so suspicious all the time," Ned

asked. "There ain't many people as suspicious as Zeke Proctor."

"Why wouldn't he be suspicious?" Tuxie inquired. "The Becks don't like him, the Squirrels don't like him, and neither does Bear Grimmet."

Zeke was short but hefty, and the coal black Pete was fat. The sight of the short, hefty man and his fat dog sidling along the wall of the meetinghouse amused Ned Christie.

"I get tickled every time I look at Zeke Proctor," he said.

He waved at Zeke, who waved back; Pete barked. Tuxie saw that Ned had a gleam in his eye, the gleam he was apt to get just before he got drunk, or fell in love. Since little Lacy, Ned's sweet young wife, had died of cholera the year before, Ned had been mighty moody. Tuxie had a feeling that Ned was nearly ready for a new wife.

"If we had a bottle of whiskey, Zeke might invite us home," Ned said. "He looks like he's thirsty for some good whiskey, to me.

"Old Mandy sells the best whiskey," he added—a pointless remark, in Tuxie's view. Old Mandy sold the *only* whiskey, at least the only whiskey available in Tahlequah. An occasional white whiskeyseller would wander through the District, peddling rotgut. But Zeke and Ned, and even the mild Tuxie, knew better than to purchase bad whiskey from a white man. Bad whiskey was known to make a man blind for days; and sometimes, for life.

"Go see if you can talk her out of a bottle," Ned said. "I ain't got no cash on me, but she knows I'm good for it."

"I ain't goin' in there while Bill Pigeon's horse is tied outside," Tuxie protested. "Bill Pigeon's been known to shoot at people for no reason at all, 'specially if he's drunk."

Ned trotted off toward the meeting hall without so much as a reply. Ned was casual about danger, particularly dangers that might only apply to Tuxie. It was partly because Ned was so handsome, Tuxie felt. Ned Christie was the handsomest man in the Cherokee Nation—women just dropped in Ned's lap, heavy and sweet as dewberries in June.

Also, Ned was a dead shot with rifle or pistol. He would often blow squirrels out of the very top of some elm tree or sycamore, and he would not spoil the meat, either. He would just shoot the limb right beside where the squirrel was resting, and the squirrel would come sailing down. Ned would pick it up while the squirrel was still stunned from the fall, and whack it against a stump a time or two to finish it off.

Tuxie himself would rarely even see the squirrel until it hit the ground. He did not like to be tilting his head up toward the sky, if he could avoid it. His Aunt Keta, who had often taken him skunk hunting when he was a boy, told him his brains would run out his ears if he tilted his head up too often. Later on, people tried to persuade him that his brains were not really that runny, but his Aunt Keta's warning had a power over him. He preferred to leave squirrel hunting to people like Ned Christie. Ned had no fear of runny brains, or of anything else that lived on Shady Mountain, where he made his home.

While Tuxie was wondering what to do about the whiskey he was expected to purchase, Pete took a sudden run at Ned's big grey horse. Pete came skipping through the mud, snarling and spitting like a badger. He ran right up behind the grey, and was able to jump high enough to get a good grip on his tail.

That horse ain't going to appreciate a thing like that, Tuxie thought; and sure enough, he was right. Ned did not seem to notice the fat, black dog hanging on to his horse's tail—but the horse noticed. The big grey let Pete hang for a moment, and then kicked him about ten feet into the air. Pete got right up and leaped for the tail again. This time, the grey kicked him sideways, into a bunch of speckled chickens who were pecking around in the mud, hoping for a wet worm. The chickens squawked and flapped their wings, running back toward Old Mandy's chicken house, feathers flying.

Zeke whistled at Pete, who trotted over to his side, as bold as if he had not been kicked twice by an animal a hundred times his size.

Tuxie dismounted, and followed the speckled chickens. It occurred to him that Old Mandy might be hiding some of her whiskey in the chicken house.

Just about the time Ned caught up with Zeke Proctor, he noticed the Squirrel brothers heading up the street. They were well spread out—Rat Squirrel rode on the west side of the street; Jim Squirrel was on the east side of the street; and

Moses Squirrel was right in the middle of the street, where the mud was deepest.

Zeke Proctor did not manifest the slightest interest in the Squirrel brothers.

"You ought to train that horse better," he said to Ned. "A well-trained mount would know better than to be kicking at Pete."

"If you had a tail and Pete was hanging from it, I guess you'd kick him, too," Ned said mildly, as he dismounted.

Zeke had a wispy moustache and goatee, though his shoulder-length hair was thick and black. He wore a big floppy hat, to avoid the necessity of squinting in the powerful June sunlight. He had three pistols and a large knife stuck in his belt, and carried a rifle.

Pete rolled on his back, hoping his master would tickle his belly, but Zeke's mind was not on tickling dogs.

Ned had a notion there was bad blood between Zeke and the Squirrel brothers, but he could not remember offhand what the bad blood was about. His deceased wife, little Lacy, had been a Squirrel herself—he did not particularly want to be shooting down one of her brothers, if he could avoid it—but here they came, plodding silently through the mud.

Zeke and Ned were both members of the Keetoowah Society, a conservative group whose main purpose was to see that the Cherokee people kept to the old ways. Their leaders believed it was important to try and work at a kind of peaceful, live-and-let-live existence with white men when possible, but not at the expense of Cherokee tradition and independence. The forcible removal of over seventeen thousand Cherokees from their native land was too fresh a memory, and the Keetoowah aimed to see that history did not repeat itself.

Zeke Proctor's father, a white man by the name of William Proctor, had married Zeke's full-blood Cherokee mother back in New Echota, Georgia. Zeke himself had come up the Trail of Tears with his mother's people when he was only seven years old. Watching many of his own people suffer and die on the long journey to Oklahoma wedded Zeke Proctor to the Cherokee way forever.

Ned Christie was a full-blood, born and raised in the Cherokee Nation. The Keetoowah Society strongly supported Cherokee governmental authority and favored their own law enforcement, especially after unscrupulous whites began crowding into the Cherokee Nation after the Civil War.

The Squirrel brothers were not members themselves, and if they were on their way down the street to kill Zeke Proctor, Ned would have to fight along with his Keetoowah brother. He did find it irksome though, that hostilities seemed to be brewing before he had even been in town long enough to procure a drink of whiskey.

He had not come to Tahlequah to fight; in fact, he had come with courting on his mind, and the object of his affections was Jewel Sixkiller Proctor, Zeke's own daughter. Young though she was, Jewel stood out as the beauty of the whole valley— tall and long stemmed like a lily flower, with huge almond eyes, blue-black hair cascading to her waist, and a comely figure beyond her years. Ned had made up his mind that he wanted to marry Jewel, and he meant to concentrate his ener- gies on persuading Zeke to let him court her: that was why he promptly sent Tuxie off to get whiskey. Zeke had a mighty thirst, and would undoubtedly be more amenable to marrying off his daughter after he had imbibed a bottle of Old Mandy's fine whiskey.

So, under the circumstances, the Squirrel brothers were a vexation, at best. Ned felt his temper rising at the mere sight of the bothersome trio.

"Are them Squirrels out of sorts with you?" he asked Zeke after he had dismounted. "They act to me like they're out of sorts."

Zeke Proctor's eyes got hard as pebbles when he was chal- lenged, but they were not particularly pebbly at the moment. Pete was still rolling around on his back, hoping to be tickled on the belly. Tuxie Miller was standing in front of Old Mandy's chicken house, looking useless.

"I'll handle the Squirrels," Zeke said. "Why'd you get off your horse?"

There was not much friendliness in Zeke's tone, and it put Ned off a little. It might mean that Zeke would have preferred him just to keep on riding, and not get into any courting talk about Jewel.

"I prefer to shoot from a standing position, if I'm called upon to shoot," Ned replied, a little stiff in tone himself.

Meanwhile, the Squirrels had arrived, lining themselves up

to the west of the meeting hall. Rat Squirrel was picking at a scab on his chin.

"Zeke, don't you be going around the mill," Jim Squirrel said.

"Fair warning, Zeke," Moses added.

Zeke looked at the Squirrel brothers with half-lidded eyes.

"You boys get along now," Zeke said mildly. "Can't you see that Ned and me are working on Senate business?"

"What Senate business?" Rat Squirrel wanted to know.

"You ain't a senator, Rat, we can't be talking to you about Senate business," Zeke said. He spoke in the mildest tones. The mild tones were a characteristic that confused many men about Zeke Proctor. He could be talking along to you in mild tones, and then between one mild tone and the next, he'd be putting bullets in you, faster than a tailor could stitch.

"Stay away from the mill then, Senator," Jim Squirrel said. "Polly's our sister, and she's a married woman. We don't want you sniffing around her, and she don't want it, neither."

"If I need to know what Polly wants, I guess I can ask her myself," Zeke said.

"You boys get along now," he said again, looking Moses Squirrel right in the eye. His tone had abruptly stopped being mild, and his eyes were pebbly.

The Squirrel brothers looked at one another, sideways looks that did not require them to completely take their eyes off Zeke.

Ned dropped his hands onto the handles of the two .44s his father had given him when he was twelve. He decided to mainly shoot at Moses, since Jim and Rat were known to be erratic marksmen, and Moses could shoot.

Zeke chose that moment to reward his dog, Pete, with a lengthy tickle on the belly. Pete wiggled in delight. Ned supposed it was a ruse; Zeke would come up firing at any moment.

Almost as Ned thought it, firing commenced—but it did not come from Zeke or from the Squirrel brothers. Three men came dashing out of Old Mandy's house, with Bill Pigeon right behind them. Bill Pigeon stopped, stood flat footed, and emptied two six-shooters at the fleeing men. One man flinched, but all three kept on running.

"Bill, he's testy, ain't he?" Zeke remarked. He walked over to his horse and climbed on. The Squirrel brothers, distracted by the gunplay, trotted over to Bill Pigeon to inquire what had been the cause of the quarrel.

Tuxie Miller was waving from a bush behind the chicken house. He was excited—he had a whiskey bottle in each hand.

"Zeke, Tuxie's got whiskey," Ned pointed out.

"I see that, let's go drink it," Zeke said.

2

WHEN JEWEL SIXKILLER PROCTOR SAW NED CHRISTIE RIDING up to the house with her father, her heart began to flutter like a trapped bird.

The sun had just come out, and she was spreading wet laundry on some red haw bushes behind the house. She wanted the laundry to get as much sun as possible. It had been so rainy lately that a few of the clothes smelled a little mouldy from never getting quite dry. The six-year-old triplets—Linnie, Minnie, and Willie—were playing nearby.

It annoyed Jewel that her heart behaved so, just because Ned was coming. It fluttered against her rib cage, like a mockingbird or sparrow that had flown in a window of the house and could not find its way back out. She wanted to stay calm and composed, and just go on spreading the laundry on the red haw bushes.

But she was not calm and composed, for the sight of Ned Christie stirred up something in her, something she could not control. Even her fingers seemed to lose their strength when Ned Christie showed up: Jewel promptly dropped two clean shirts on the wet grass, an occurrence that would have annoyed her mother, Becca, had she seen it. Linnie, the most helpful of the triplets, picked up the shirts for her before they got very muddy.

Zeke and Ned and Tuxie Miller splashed across the little creek behind the barn, and came trotting on toward the house. Zeke was carrying Pete in front of him in the saddle. Pete was too short legged to keep up with the horses when the men were riding fast. They must have ridden through a heavy shower, for the sunlight sparkled on droplets of water in Ned Christie's long, black hair. He was the tallest man Jewel had ever seen, but that was not why her heart began to flutter when he came visiting. He hardly spoke to her—no more than a "hello," or maybe a "thank you," if she offered him chicory coffee—but his eyes would not leave her alone. Mostly she cast her own eyes downward when Ned was in the house. She focused on her sewing, or on tending to the triplets. The triplets had come late in Becca's life, and were quite a handful. Jewel was almost full grown and had to help her mother keep an eye on the three feisty children. They were quick as little wildcats, and just keeping them out of the big fireplace where the women did the cooking was a hard job.

At the moment, Jewel was glad for the triplets. It made it easier for her to keep her eyes busy, so Ned Christie could not look in them. Once or twice—just for a moment—Jewel had raised her head, and Ned had looked in her eyes. In those moments, Jewel felt him take power over her; the fluttering stopped, and she felt still and helpless, like a bird that could no longer fly.

This time, it happened while she had a wet shirt in her hand, about to spread it on a bush. Ned looked at her just before he swung off his horse, and Jewel froze under his glance, motionless by her bush like a quail might be, just before it flushed. She *wanted* to flush—wanted to run in the house and get busy stirring mush, or patrolling the triplets—but she could not move. Tall Ned Christie had taken power over her again, and she could not do anything but stand by the red haw bush, until the men walked off toward the back pasture to look at a new black horse Zeke had recently acquired. They were passing a whiskey bottle back and forth. Looking at the bottle released Jewel, even though Ned did glance her way a few times while they were inspecting the horse. He glanced her way, but he was too far off for his eyes to take power over her. She finished spreading the laundry, then took the empty basket back to the house.

Zeke had slaughtered a white shoat a few days before, and her mother was frying pork chops, while Eliza, Jewel's little sister, snapped green beans.

"I thought I heard the menfolk," Becca said. "I expect they're hungry."

Rebecca Sixkiller Mitchell married Zeke Proctor seventeen years earlier, after Zeke had courted her for a mere three days.

Becca's uncle, Money Talker Mitchell, was known throughout the territory for his fine racehorses. Zeke had traveled all the way to Missouri—where Becca's family settled on their way west after Becca's baby sister, Margaret, died of the measles during the Trail of Tears—to bargain with Uncle Money Talker for a colt from his prize stallion. When Zeke laid eyes on the lively Becca, he asked her father, a Baptist preacher, to marry them right away. So, Zeke returned home to the Going Snake with a spirited colt *and* a spirited wife. Becca's father, like many Cherokees, was drawn to the river baptism and fasting practiced by Baptists. Many Cherokees welcomed rituals from the Baptist religion, since they resembled a lot of their own sacred ways. Becca herself liked to visit the little Baptist church just outside of Tahlequah whenever she had occasion to travel to town.

Becca stood a good six inches taller than her husband, Zeke. Though Becca had never fully recovered her strength after the triplets' birth, it was clear where Jewel had gotten her fine features and her willowy stature. Becca's long hair was pulled back from her face in a braid thick as a horse's tail, accenting her high cheekbones.

"They had a whiskey bottle, Mama," Jewel said.

"Men will always be having their whiskey, Jewel," Becca replied, wiping sweat from her forehead with her dress sleeve. "That don't mean they won't be hungry. Help your sister snap them beans."

3

NED WANTED TO GO RIGHT IN ZEKE'S BIG HOUSE AND START sobering up with a few cups of strong chicory coffee. That way, he could be looking at Jewel Sixkiller Proctor while he was getting over the whiskey.

Zeke, though, was still in a drinking mood, and he preferred to drink in the little smokehouse with the freshly butchered remains of the white shoat hanging above them. Once Tuxie Miller showed Zeke the place under the henhouse where Old Mandy Springston kept her extra whiskey, there had been no restraining him. He promptly crammed four bottles into his big saddlebags, an action which alarmed Tuxie Miller. Zeke showed no sign of meaning to pay for the whiskey, either.

"Old Mandy's mean," Tuxie reminded Zeke. "She'll be wanting to get somebody to kill you, if you steal that much whiskey. Bill Pigeon's her old boyfriend . . . she might get Bill to do it."

"You just saw Bill Pigeon miss three men at point-blank range," Zeke told him. "Why would I worry about Bill Pigeon?"

"I think he might have winged one of those men," Tuxie said, but his remark went unnoticed, as the three of them galloped out of Tahlequah. Tuxie considered putting his two bottles back in the hiding place, to make the theft a little less noticeable, but he knew such a consideration would be treated with scorn by his companions. He quickly drank the two bottles instead.

Ned Christie had no head for whiskey. He got thoroughly drunk on half a bottle. Zeke, however, drank two bottles and was still sober enough to open the black horse's mouth and count its teeth. The only way to tell Zeke Proctor had been drinking was to look at his eyeballs: they got red as a vulture's comb after the third or fourth bottle.

While they were sitting in the smokehouse talking about pork chops, the bright sunlight vanished, and a heavy shower rumbled over Going Snake Mountain. Jewel had to dash out of the house and snatch the clothes off the red haw bushes. To her dismay, they were nowhere near dry.

Tuxie Miller had to go outside and puke, to the great annoyance of Zeke.

"Go in the house and gobble for the triplets," he ordered Tuxie, after he wobbled back inside the smokehouse. "They ain't heard you gobble lately."

Tuxie was unrivaled in the Going Snake District for his ability to call up wild turkeys. He could also call up coyotes and bobcats, but the ability to call up bobcats was a mixed blessing, as Tuxie discovered one day when a large male bobcat jumped over a bush right on him, under the impression that he was jumping on a female bobcat.

Tuxie felt too sick to gobble, but he obediently traipsed off toward the house, leaving Zeke and Ned with two full bottles of whiskey and the remains of the shoat.

Ned was wanting to ask Zeke if he could take Jewel home with him to be his wife, but Zeke's eyeballs were almost as red as the red haws. Besides, Zeke's mind was on killing—not on marrying.

"I don't dislike the Squirrel boys, particularly," he said. "The family I hate is the Becks. There's only one good Beck on the face of this earth, and that's Polly, and she lives over at the mill with that white man, T. Spade."

"I think she's married to him, Zeke," Ned pointed out. "I believe they're hitched."

"They're hitched," Zeke said, gloomily. He had been taken with Polly Beck for over a year now, and the fact that she was already married had been a big obstacle to his happiness. It was not unusual in the Old Place for a Cherokee man to have more than one wife; Zeke himself knew men in the Keetoowah Society who had taken a second, common-law wife.

"I ain't taken a new wife for seventeen years now," he remarked.

Ned made no comment. At least Zeke was talking about marrying; it might lead around to the point where he could ask for Jewel.

"Seventeen years is a good long stretch of time to go without a new wife," he said. "My first two wives died, and Becca's too poorly now to have many more babies. I bet Polly Beck could have some fine babies, if she had the right encouragement."

"I bet Jewel could have some fine babies, too," Ned said, seizing his moment.

The minute Ned said it, Zeke got a distant look in his eye—it was such a distant look that his eyeballs even stopped being red.

"Which one of the Squirrel brothers would you have shot, if they'd showed fight?" he asked.

"Moses," Ned said, annoyed. Zeke knew perfectly well he had not ridden all the way home with him to Going Snake Mountain just to talk about the Squirrel brothers.

"I would have shot Rat," Zeke said. "How can you like knowing somebody with a name like Rat?"

"Well, but you can like knowing somebody with a name like Jewel," Ned countered. "I would be pleased to marry Jewel, if there's no objection."

"The objection is, Becca needs Jewel—she's the only one who can keep the triplets out of the fireplace," Zeke said. "I can't afford to have my triplets getting scorched."

Ned thought that was a ridiculous objection. Still, Zeke was his host; he had to at least pretend to take the objection seriously.

"Let 'em get scorched once or twice," he suggested. "It'll teach 'em to avoid fireplaces."

Although fairly drunk, Ned managed to summon his most reasonable-sounding voice. It was the voice he used in the Cherokee Senate when debating whether to put a new roof on the Women's Seminary, or some other tribal matter of serious weight. He thought he might manage to sound reasonable enough to persuade Zeke Proctor that he'd be the perfect husband for his beautiful daughter Jewel.

Zeke Proctor, though, had a teasing devil in him, even when he was drunk enough to be red in both eyeballs.

"No, that fireplace gets too hot," he said. "The women pile wood in it till you could scorch an ox. My triplets ain't as big as an ox—one of 'em could get scorched to death, if I don't keep Jewel to watch 'em."

Despite his desire to remain senatorial in his tone and his bearing, Ned began to feel like doing a little scorching himself. What right had Zeke Proctor to sit there, drunk as a goose, and think up reasons why he could not let Jewel leave home and marry? It was that kind of behaviour which caused most of the residents of the Going Snake District to get so riled at Zeke. Several men had taken potshots at him, for being so cranky. Ned was beginning to think that maybe the Squirrel brothers had a point.

"Zeke, I got to have Jewel!" Ned blurted out, suddenly. The thought of having to ride all the way back to Shady Mountain without Jewel filled him with gloom. He felt he'd almost rather jump his horse off a cliff, or drown himself in a creek. It was true that Tuxie Miller and his family lived nearby; he was always welcome at Tuxie's house, but he did not want to always be going to Tuxie's house. He wanted to be at his own house; he just did not want to be there alone. Two or three times since Lacy died, he had got so lonesome he'd even let the hounds crawl up in his bed. Once, he had pulled out his pistols and shot at his own wall, just to hear some racket.

Sitting at home listening to the owls hoot was not satisfactory. He thought he had been a pretty good husband to Lacy, but Lacy had died. Now he had set his heart on Jewel—Zeke did not need to tease him by yapping on about the triplets getting scorched.

"I got to have her, Zeke," Ned said, again. "I'm getting too lonesome up there on the hill. It's been a year since my Lacy passed away, and it's time for me to marry again."

Zeke turned a kinder eye to Ned after his passionate outburst. He himself had buried two wives, and his Becca had never quite recovered from the birth of the triplets—Jewel and Liza did most of the housework now. Zeke knew how it was to slop around all by himself, with no wife to do for him and keep him company. After his first wife, Jane, died in the cholera epidemic that had raged through the Cherokee Nation nearly twenty years ago, Zeke had grown so tired of cooking for himself that he had begun to eat his meat raw. Mostly it was venison, with a little beef now and then; he would just sprinkle a little salt on a slice, and bolt it down. He had gambled too much during his time of mourning, and lain with lewd women whom he ought not to have lain with.

"Jewel's young, Ned," Zeke remarked, but in a more encouraging tone.

"How young?" Ned asked—he had no clear notion of Jewel's age. When he looked at her, all he could think about was taking her home with him, to lay with him on his corn-shuck mattress. He could imagine how it would feel to wake up with her arms around him, and her sweet breath on his face—it would sure beat hell out of sleeping with the hounds!

"She's little more than sixteen," Zeke said. The fact was, Jewel *had* arrived at marrying age; and though Ned was quite a bit younger than Zeke, the older man had always been impressed by Ned's solid ways and kind nature. He knew Ned would not mistreat Jewel, and that he would make her a fine husband—a far better one than Rat Squirrel, at least. Rat had been sulking around lately, at times when he knew Zeke was not at home. Besides, Ned Christie was a suitor he had to respect as a man: Ned was, without question, the best shot with pistol or rifle in the whole Cherokee Nation—by the time he was ten, he could outshoot any man around, including Watt Christie, his own father.

Zeke considered that it was fair enough to tease Ned a little. He was not going to hand over a beauty like his Jewel, without making the lucky suitor sweat a bit. He knew, though, that it would be downright foolish to push Ned Christie too far. He was not dumb, like the Squirrel brothers, who had yet to realize that their own sister, Polly Beck, was so eager to leave her husband for Zeke that she had hired a witch woman to witch her husband to the point where he might lose his senses and drown in a creek.

But Zeke knew that it would be foolish to carry his teasing too far. If Ned were to get riled enough to take a potshot, there was very little likelihood he would miss.

"My Lacy wasn't but sixteen when we married," Ned pointed out. "She wasn't much older than Jewel, and she was a lot smaller built."

Zeke decided that there was no point in debating the matter any longer. Ned had his mind made up, on top of which they were running out of whiskey.

"You got my permission to ask her," Zeke said, standing up.

"Couldn't you ask her for me?" Ned said. "I've not spoken to her much. I might choke on my tongue, if I tried to come out with a question like that."

"Nope," Zeke said flatly. "If you ain't man enough to ask her, then I doubt you'll be man enough to make her a decent husband."

Ned stood up, feeling shaky. He was six foot four, and Zeke's smokehouse was not much taller than that. When he rose, he smacked right into a hindquarter of the white shoat Zeke had butchered. It hung from a hook just above him. In his eagerness to have Zeke Proctor accept his suit, he had forgotten they were in the smokehouse.

The sight of Ned smacking himself in the eye with a slab of shoat struck Zeke as hilarious, and he howled with laughter. Zeke's funny bone was easily tickled, even in the worst of times, and when he had downed a quart or two of whiskey, he found plenty to laugh about in the wild ways that prevailed in the Going Snake District.

"Dern—now I guess I got blood in my hair," Ned said, galled with himself. His old Grandmother Christie had taught him to take care of his hair. She told him there was power in it

—he ought to not let women cut it—and also to avoid barbers generally, as being of low worth.

"Don't be letting anybody barber you like a white man," his old Granny Christie told him, and he had taken the advice to heart: no barber had ever touched his hair. Now he was worried that Jewel would not want him, if he showed up to propose with blood in his hair.

"No, but you're a little salty," Zeke informed him. "We salted this pig down pretty good. Let's go get this courtin' over with, then we can eat."

"Not if Jewel says no," Ned said. "If she turns me down, I won't have an appetite for weeks."

As they walked to the house, Ned kept trying to brush the salt out of his hair, a sight which amused Zeke. He himself had always been bold with women. He preferred to walk up and grab them, a tactic that had so far won him three feisty wives and the favors of Polly Beck—a woman who was feisty, if she was anything.

Ned, though, was clearly not up to the bold approach. He was walking unsteadily, not from the whiskey but from the thought of having to propose to Jewel.

"Why, Ned—I believe you're shy," Zeke said, a wide smile on his face.

Ned heard a wild gobbling sound. It was as if a flock of wild turkeys had suddenly run inside Zeke's big house. It startled him, but when he heard the wild giggling of the triplets, he remembered that Tuxie had been sent inside to gobble for them.

"Listen to that," Zeke said. "Old Tuxie missed his calling. He'd have done better as a turkey!"

4

NED CHRISTIE SAT THROUGH A MEAL OF PORK CHOPS AND green beans without saying a word.

Once or twice, he raised his eyes to Jewel, but he immediately lowered them again. He felt he had no small words in him—just the big words he had to say to Jewel, and he had to protect the big words until the time was right. He did not even compliment Becca on the cooking, so anxious was he to hold on to the big words.

Jewel knew Ned wanted to take power over her. She felt a fluttering deep inside at the thought, but not so strongly as it had felt when she saw him riding up with Zeke and Tuxie Miller. She thought she was ready to accept it, if Ned really wanted her. Her sister Liza did not even notice. She had always been the wordy sister, and she yapped all through the meal.

Becca *did* notice. When Jewel looked at her mother for reassurance, Becca turned her eyes away, or went to the pots to dish up more food. She would not look at the daughter she was about to lose. Becca knew the ways of men and women; knew that Jewel was of an age to marry; and had known for some time that a man would soon be coming for her daughter. Now that man was here at her table. He was a handsome man, too, and from what she had seen and heard, well able to provide for a wife. Still, it made her lonely to think that her girl would be going away. She herself was not well, and Jewel's quiet good spirit had been a help to her on days when she had the megrims so badly that she could hardly do her work. Jewel was a worker, unlike Liza, who was mostly talk. Liza fussed and frittered, talking a blue streak all the time.

Becca rarely cried, especially not in sight of Zeke. He could not tolerate a weepy woman. At the first sign of tears, he would jump on his horse and leave, often for a week or more. He expected his womenfolk to be smiling when he returned, too. Becca looked at Jewel, and looked at Ned; she knew the time had come when her daughter would be going. Twice she had to leave the table to hide behind the big chimney, to wipe her eyes with her apron so as not to disturb her husband, who was eating with a good appetite—though not so good an appetite as Tuxie Miller's. Tuxie was renowned throughout the Going Snake District for his prodigious appetite. On this occasion, he ate ten fried eggs, twelve pork chops, and most of the bucket of green beans Liza and Jewel had snapped.

Zeke, who liked Tuxie, was nonetheless a little sobered by the man's intake.

"I don't think he's gonna leave us a thing," he remarked, more in awe than in anger. "He's et most of that pig, and the whole bean patch."

"Throwing up makes you empty," Tuxie remarked, without

apology. He was hoping Becca Proctor would send one of the girls out to the henhouse for a few more eggs. He seldom got such a good feed at his own house. Dale, his wife, had borne him nine babies, and she was a lot more interested in making more babies than she was in cooking up vittles. The last time Tuxie had pork chops in such quantity was when he killed a wild pig, but that stroke of luck was a good three years back.

"I can't figure out where he's putting that food," Zeke said, to Ned. "He's skinny as a fence rail . . . it must be slidin' down into his legs."

Zeke spoke mainly to take his mind off Ned Christie and his dilemma. Ned had a powerful presence, and at the moment, a troublesome presence—he was staring at his plate so hard that Zeke feared the plate might crack. He wanted to help Ned come out with his question, if only to lighten the atmosphere a little, but he could not figure out how. Ned was so gloomy, he was making everybody else at the table miserable, everybody except Tuxie, who was still forking green beans into his mouth at a rapid rate.

Jewel kept her eyes downcast, waiting. Even the chatty Liza had fallen quiet. Becca kept getting up and running behind the chimney. Outside, it got dark; a rain squall came in with a little hail, peppering the shingles above them like buckshot—but still, Ned Christie was silent. Zeke got annoyed, finally; he hated gloomy meals. It was plain to him from the way Jewel sat there, still as a doe in hiding, that she was not going to turn Ned down. Why wouldn't the man speak?

Ned was thinking maybe everybody would leave the table soon and get on with their chores. But everybody seemed numbed. Even Tuxie, now that he had eaten everything there was to eat, had a vacant look in his eye. The hail had stopped; when Ned looked out the window, he could see the white pebbles speckling the muddy lots where Zeke penned his heifers.

Jewel sat right across from him, waiting. Ned had never felt so awkward in his whole life. Proposing to Lacy had not been near such a chore. Lacy had been a friend of his sister's, and had mostly done her growing up in their house. Jewel, though, lived far from Shady Mountain, and he had only seen her five times. For all he knew, she already had a beau. For all he knew, she might turn him down flat.

He could feel everybody at the table waiting. It was as if all activity had braked to a screeching halt, while he and Jewel were resolving their future. But he could not help it. His tongue would not come out with the big words.

Then he risked a glance, and met Jewel's eye. They both risked a glance at the same time, and their glances smacked together. Both hastily looked down, then up again; their glances smacked together a second time.

Jewel wanted to smile at the tall man, but she was too afraid.

Ned felt emboldened by the two glances. Jewel did not seem to mind looking at him, at least.

"With all this rain, the creeks will be high," he said. This time, he did not drop his eyes when Jewel returned his gaze.

"If you'd like to get your things and come with me, we ought to be getting on home," Ned continued. "It's a long ride."

Jewel felt a rush of happiness—yet, he had put the matter differently from what she had expected. She looked at her mother, to see if her mother felt matters had been stated correctly.

Becca did not feel they had, but she knew men were awkward about such matters, and she did not want to blight her daughter's chances just because Ned Christie was tongue-tied.

"But Ned, what do you intend?" Becca asked.

Ned suddenly felt deeply embarrassed. He realized he had forgotten to mention marriage. In his mind, he had said the word fifty times, but it had not found its way out of his mouth. Becca was frowning, and who could blame her?

"Why, I was hoping Jewel would marry me," he said. "The preacher will be on the Mountain this weekend . . . he could marry us then. I don't think we need to wait."

"No, you don't need to wait," Becca agreed.

"Zeke, does that suit you?" Ned asked. He worried that he had annoyed Zeke by his omission. Zeke just sat there, with a mild look on his face.

It was Becca who suddenly turned on him, fierce.

"It don't matter what Zeke thinks—I'm her ma!" she pronounced. "It's what Jewel thinks, and what I think, that you need to worry about. I won't be sending my daughter off, unless she'll be married proper."

"Why, she will be—proper as a preacher can do it," Ned said. "I didn't ride all this way to ask Jewel to be no concubine. I want her to be my wife, if she'll agree."

Becca looked at Jewel again. Though Jewel was a quiet girl, there was an eager happiness in her face.

It was a hard thing: Becca knew she had to let her daughter go.

While the men went back outside to the smokehouse, to whittle and gossip, Becca took Jewel upstairs, and she and Liza helped her pack her few things. Liza chattered like a magpie, but Jewel was mostly quiet. Becca Proctor had the feeling that she herself would not be living long, but she choked down her sorrow and saw to it that Jewel did not forget anything she might need.

When it came time to leave, Jewel kissed Liza, and then she turned to her mother.

"Oh, Jewel," was all Becca could say, when she hugged her daughter good-bye.

It was still drizzling when Jewel climbed up behind Ned on his big horse. Soon they were across the creek, and out of sight in the misty valley.

Tuxie Miller was a little disappointed. He had been hoping matters might drag on until suppertime. One more hearty meal before he left the Proctors would have suited him just fine.

5

SULLY EAGLE WAS SLOW BUT SURE.

Sully, one of the oldest men in the Cherokee Nation, was known throughout the Going Snake District for his meandering pace—he moved slower than cold molasses poured. He had worked for Zeke off and on for years, and though Zeke might fault his speed, he did not fault his trustworthiness. Sully could be trusted with anything: grain, cattle, even money. He would invariably deliver whatever was put in his care, whether to a bank, to a mill, or to a pasture. Becca in particular despaired whenever Zeke sent Sully into Tahlequah or Siloam Springs for supplies, because she knew she might have to wait weeks for the supplies to arrive, even though neither town was far away. Sully was prone to side trips; he would often ramble all over the Going Snake, collecting oddments of gossip before he showed up with Becca's supplies. Zeke tried to persuade Becca that there were benefits to Sully's tendency to ramble. Sometimes he would arrive with a nice string of fish, or a couple of fat possums skinned and ready for the pot. But Becca was not mollified. The fact that Sully was old, lame, blind in one eye, and practically stone deaf did not interest her, or soften her much toward Sully. Becca wanted her supplies, and she did not countenance waiting a month for them.

So when Zeke looked up from mending a harness and saw Sully Eagle driving the wagon full tilt toward the lots, he knew something was wrong—perhaps something seriously wrong.

Sully had been sent off to the mill just three days before with a wagon full of corn to grind. Zeke had not really expected him back for a couple of weeks, and yet here he was, hitting the creek at a fast clip. Zeke did not know what to make of it. He rushed out of the work shed so fast, he stubbed his toe on the anvil in his eagerness to get the news.

His fear was that something might have happened to Polly Beck, wife of T. Spade Beck, the man who owned the mill. Maybe the witch who was supposed to be witching T. Spade had got mixed up and witched Polly instead. It was an awful thought. Zeke was counting on Polly Beck being a second wife to him, and in the near future, too, as soon as her cranky old husband, T. Spade, could be persuaded to get drunk and drown in the creek.

"Take a look at this corn, Zeke," Sully said, in his old croak of a voice. Sully had gossiped so much over the years that he had nearly worn out his voice. The team of brown mules was lathered, from the pace Sully had set.

"What's wrong with it?" Zeke asked, relieved it was only the grain Sully was in a fret about. Maybe the grind had been too coarse; if that was all, it only meant that Becca would have to cook it longer. He could grind more corn, but he would not be likely to find a woman in the Going Snake District as winsome as the lovely Polly Beck. Polly was short, buxom, and feisty. Polly's father, Joseph Squirrel, was a full-blood Cherokee; her mother was Irish, with flaming red hair. Polly's own hair, red like her mother's, hung to her waist in a wild, bewitching tangle. Becca had lost her enthusiasm for his embraces since the birth of the triplets, which made Zeke gloomy. He had not broached the subject of a second wife with Becca, though he surmised that she might welcome an extra pair of hands around the house to help out with the triplets. Since Jewel's departure, the triplets had been running them all ragged.

"T. Spade weeviled up this corn," Sully said in his froggy old voice.

"What?" Zeke asked. The ground corn was neatly sacked and stacked in the wagon, like ground corn ought to be. Sully had such bad eyes that it was doubtful he could see a weevil if one was crawling on his eyeball.

"T. Spade's got a room in that mill where he breeds up weevils," Sully insisted.

"T. Spade's a miller," Zeke said—he had never heard anything so foolish. "Why would a miller be crazy enough to breed up weevils? He'd put himself out of business quick."

"Nope, he's got a room out back of the mill where he throws rotten grain," Sully said. "That's where he breeds up his weevils."

"Breeds 'em, and does what with 'em?" Zeke asked.

"Open one of them sacks and you'll know," Sully said. "T. Spade don't like you. He don't like Cherokees, and I doubt he likes Choctaws, either. He shoveled a bunch of them weevils into your corn."

Zeke clambered up in the wagon, and began to open the sacks. He saw immediately that Sully was telling the truth: the corn meal was boiling over with weevils. Zeke kept on opening sacks, until he had opened them all. Every sack was thick with weevils. The best corn crop he'd harvested in years was ruined.

"The son-of-a-bitch," he said when he'd opened the last sack. "You should have shot him."

"I would have, but I didn't have no bullets," Sully informed him.

Zeke was beginning to steam. Sully Eagle had killed men in his day; he had killed Bear Grimmet's father, for one, in a dispute over a colt. Why had he let T. Spade Beck ruin the corn crop he had been entrusted with? It was a blot on Sully's otherwise spotless record.

"You had bullets when you left here," Zeke reminded him. "What became of them?"

"I shot 'em all at a bear," Sully said. "I jumped him over by Siloam Creek. He was a fat young bear, I think he would've made good eating."

"Where is he, then?" Zeke asked.

"He run off into a thicket," Sully admitted. "I hit him twice, but he kept on going. I guess he was too fat to die."

"This is a fine damned stew!" Zeke said. "Now we ain't got no corn, and no bear meat, either."

"You can feed the corn to your cattle," Sully pointed out. "Cattle don't mind weevils."

"I didn't work all spring to grow every bit of my corn for the dern heifers," Zeke said. "You need to unhitch those mules, they're winded."

"All right," Sully said. "I'll go back and look for that bear after a while. He would make good eating."

"Nope, I'll tend to Mr. Bear," Zeke said. "I'll tend to T. Spade, too. You stay here and help Becca with the chores."

Sully was disappointed. He had once been an above-average tracker, and was convinced he could locate such a fat little bear, given a day or two, even with his diminished eyesight. But Zeke was in a temper; it would not do to argue with him at such a time. Sully got down from the wagon, and began to unhitch the mules.

Zeke headed at once for the house to collect his guns. Now that he'd had a moment to think, he realized there might be a bright side to what had happened. T. Spade Beck had declared war when he weeviled his corn. Ruining a man's corn crop was a deadly insult; Zeke could simply go and kill him. He would not have to wait for the results of the witching.

Becca and Liza were staring into the fire when Zeke came inside to gather up his arsenal. Since Jewel left, they had both been low, so low that Zeke was sort of relieved to have an excuse to go. The triplets clung to his pants leg, but he shook them off and gave them each a kiss. He gave Becca a quick peck on the cheek, but she did not even look up.

Before Sully Eagle had much more than got the mules unhitched, Zeke Proctor was back outside and on his way down the road to do battle with T. Spade Beck.

He carried a knife, a rifle, and three pistols.

6

T. SPADE HAD NEVER BEEN A WAKEFUL MAN.

He usually slept soundly through the night, snoring out of one side of his mouth. He and his wife, Polly, slept in the loft of the mill; if T. Spade did wake up, it was only to make water. He would stumble over to the door of the loft, and piss out into the darkness. Often as not, he pissed on the chickens, which the chickens did not appreciate. Sometimes the hens would get so upset that they would squawk for the rest of the night. If it was near dawn when T. Spade got up to make water, he might come back to bed with his bladder empty, thoughts of love on his mind. Polly would have to accept him with the hens clucking and raising Cain right underneath her; then, often as not, it would be time to get up and make a fire. Polly liked her sleep. Having to accept T. Spade that early in the day left her as fretful as the hens.

She mentioned the matter to Zeke, once she started slipping off with him. Zeke listened, and grinned his sly grin.

"But you *are* a hen," he said. "You got soft feathers, like a hen should. When are you coming over to my henhouse, Polly?"

"He'll kill me if I leave, Zeke," Polly told him.

But Zeke did not want to hear that.

"Soft feathers," he said, again. "A man could get smothered in feathers this soft."

A woman could get killed for letting you act like a rooster with her, too, Polly thought. But she could not help herself. She kept slipping out to see Zeke. He had a buffalo skin he brought with him for them to wrap up in on chilly days.

She never did know what alerted T. Spade, but something alerted him.

T. Spade had been in the habit of going into Siloam Springs two or three days a week to drink and play cards, but then he suddenly stopped. He only went into Siloam Springs now if he absolutely had to. He had enjoyed hunting coons at night, and frequently went fishing with one of his cronies from town, but he gave up coon hunting and fishing, too.

One day, Polly spilled coffee on him, and he slapped her so hard she was dizzy for an hour.

The worst part of it was that T. Spade started watching her in the night. She had gotten used to sleeping with the rhythm of his snoring. But then he stopped snoring, too. If she happened to wake up in the night, T. Spade would be propped up on his elbow, watching her. She was afraid to ask him what was the matter. He might turn the question around, and ask her about Zeke. Polly was not a good liar, and she knew it. She did not want T. Spade to start asking questions—she was afraid of what might happen if he got her talking. He had not hit her often, but when he did, he hit her hard.

T. Spade soon made it impossible for her to slip off and see Zeke. He stuck close to the mill, and saw to it that Polly had plenty of chores. Even if all the chores were finished, Polly did not dare take a walk. T. Spade would just sit in his chair and look at her, sometimes for hours at a time. He even built an outhouse behind the mill. They had always just gone in the bushes, like most folks, but T. Spade dug a pit and nailed up an outhouse over it. He did not want Polly wandering out in the bushes—not anymore.

Polly knew Zeke must have come several times and waited at their meeting place in the woods. She missed him; she wanted him to touch her soft feathers; but there was no way she could slip off now.

T. Spade had been a freighter before he bought the mill. He had several times driven teams of oxen all the way from Tennessee. He still had his bullwhip, and he knew how to use it. Polly was afraid he would use it on her, if she ever weakened and admitted anything about Zeke.

Soon the tension at night began to be more than she could bear. Much as she liked being with Zeke on the buffalo robe, and feeling his wispy moustache when he kissed her, fear began to drown out memories of Zeke Proctor and their pleasures. Every day, T. Spade seemed to grow more watchful and more demanding. Once, while Polly was spreading washing on the bushes, T. Spade put several big corncobs on a stump behind the mill and started cutting them in two with his bullwhip. He did not miss a single cob—a knife could not have halved the cob any cleaner. He looked at Polly when he finished, and coiled his whip.

That night, Polly had a dream that T. Spade was lashing her. When she woke from the dream, sweating and shaking, T. Spade was on top of her. Half the night, sometimes, he was on top of her—as if to show her that, though he might be old in years, he was not old in all respects.

Polly Beck had always been one to look on the bright side. A pretty day was all it took to send her spirits floating high. But under the constant pressure of T. Spade's watchfulness, she ceased to be able to take pleasure even in the sunlight. She went to bed weary, and woke up weary; sun or cloud ceased to matter to her. T. Spade was at her so much that she could barely remember Zeke's soft moustache, or the shine in his eyes when he looked at her.

It did not take T. Spade long to make his point, and his point was that he still wanted Polly for his wife. For a time, T. Spade had shown so little interest in her that Polly convinced herself he might not mind if she went off to be Zeke's new wife. Zeke could give him a cow or two, or whatever the two men decided was a fair exchange for a woman who was no longer really young, and the parting would be amicable and in accordance with custom. Lots of men in the Going Snake District had more than one wife, even though one of them might only be common-law. The legalities of it did not matter to Polly; she just did not want the men fighting. If they fought, either Zeke or T. Spade would likely end up dead, and Polly would rather stay put and be a little less happy than to have either man killed.

But T. Spade Beck was her husband, and he reminded her of that forcefully and frequently now. His lack of interest had been just a temporary lull. He was still determined to have her as a wife, which was a thing Polly had to yield to. It might be in her to slip off and meet Zeke Proctor, to let him kiss her and touch her soft feathers, to let him lay with her on his buffalo robe; but it was not in her to deny her husband what was his. She had accepted T. Spade in marriage—he could release her if he chose to, but Polly could not release herself. Once T. Spade made it clear he had no intention of yielding any husbandly rights, Polly ceased to struggle. She accepted, again, her place as his wife. It horrified her to think she had been so silly about Zeke Proctor that she had tried to get the old witch woman, Spider, to witch T. Spade and make him drown.

One day, old Spider hobbled to the mill to beg a little corn-meal for her mush. Polly told her, right out, to forget about the witching. She no longer wanted her husband to drown in a creek. Zeke Proctor would have to find another woman to beguile with his soft moustache and shining grey eyes.

Once Polly let T. Spade know by her chastened demeanor that she was not going to wander from him, he finally became convinced of her fidelity, and ceased to watch her all night. He began to sleep soundly again, snoring out of the side of his mouth. He came to her often still, but no longer with a vengeance.

Polly thought the danger had passed. She felt a little wistful when she thought of Zeke, but being wistful was a lot better than fearing for her life.

Then one day, while Sully Eagle was waiting with Zeke's wagon and team, Polly saw T. Spade shoveling weevils into the freshly ground corn. He put a shovelful of weevily maize into every one of Zeke's sacks. Sully Eagle did not say a word, and neither did Polly.

T. Spade was red in the face. He always got red in the face when he was really angry. That night, for no reason at all, he hit her so hard she nearly fell out of the loft.

Polly knew, then, that it was not over.

7

ZEKE SET OFF IN A FURY TO GO KILL T. SPADE BECK.

The man had shoveled weevils into his corn sacks, an insult that could only be wiped out by gunplay. Once T. Spade was dead or at least shot up, he meant to lope home with Polly Beck. Then, he would send Polly, Becca, Liza, and the triplets off for a visit with Jewel, while he armed himself for a siege. T. Spade had five brothers and a small army of cousins, some of whom would undoubtedly try to avenge him. Zeke thought he might try to persuade Ned Christie to join him until the first hostilities subsided. With a marksman of the stature of Ned Christie in his camp, Zeke felt sure he could hold off any number of Becks. Davie Beck, a wild renegade, was the one most to be feared. Davie Beck had been known to steal wives

31

right out of their husbands' beds; the husbands unfortunate enough to wake up while the thievery was in progress were promptly dispatched. He was known to be shortsighted, however, and could only shoot effectively at close range. Zeke had no intention of letting him get in close range, a thing easy to prevent with Ned around. Ned could spot game in the woods quicker than a red-tailed hawk, and he could spot a target as large as Davie Beck two miles away.

It was eighteen miles from Zeke's house to the Beck mill. Despite his urgent fury, Zeke met with a few distractions on the way. He heard the thunk of an axe as he was riding along; when he went to investigate, he found Daniel Redbird and his son Charley trying to chop into a bee tree. Zeke had a terrible sweet tooth. There was no such thing as too much sweetening, in his book. He took a hand at the chopping in return for a bucket of honey. Daniel had a jug of whiskey in his wagon, and they resorted to the jug from time to time to relieve the monotony of chopping. The tree was a bois d'arc, and hard as a crowbar. It was so late when they finally chopped through to the honey that the three of them rolled up in the wagon for the night, and slept.

When Zeke woke the next morning, it was foggy, causing him to slow his start. Zeke had told the story of T. Spade and the weevils, and the Redbirds were sympathetic—but Daniel, a nervous man, cautioned Zeke to wait until the fog lifted before hurrying on to kill T. Spade.

"You could mistake your man, in fog this thick," Daniel said.

"I won't mistake my man," Zeke assured him. "Don't forget to leave my honey with Becca."

He was barely out of earshot of the Redbirds, when he jumped the same fat bear that Sully Eagle had jumped. The bear loomed up in the fog, scaring Zeke's horse, Joe, so badly that he ran away, with Zeke sawing at the reins. Zeke managed to put two bullets into the bear before Joe bolted, but the horse ran for half a mile before Zeke could get him quieted down. He dismounted and backtracked to where he had jumped the bear, but the bear had already departed.

"That bear's probably over the hill by now," Zeke said to Joe, reproachfully. "Sully didn't get him, and neither did I."

A little before noon, the fog burned off. Zeke was half a

mind to track the bear, but then he thought of Polly Beck and let the notion go. She had not been at the meeting place the last few times he had come to visit. T. Spade might have got suspicious and penned her up. T. Spade was cranky—but he was not a pure fool.

When Zeke came in sight of the mill, he was relieved to see that no wagons were waiting with grain to grind. Then he saw Polly going into the mill with an apron full of kindling. He did not try to attract her attention; if T. Spade was suspicious, he might be laying a trap. He could be in the loft with a rifle, waiting.

Zeke circled the mill, keeping well into the underbrush. He wanted to be sure none of T. Spade's lazy cousins were lounging by the cistern, or getting drunk in the smokehouse. He tied Joe to a little post oak tree, not far from the small clearing where he had often met Polly.

There were no cousins in sight, but while he was studying the situation, Polly came out the back door and stood on the porch, looking his way. Zeke was well hidden in a chinaberry thicket. Polly could not see him, but maybe she could sense him—he was not sure. While he was watching, Polly walked the length of the porch and bent over to scrape something out of a bucket—lye soap, it looked like. She was a pretty woman, light of step; he had always fancied women who were light of step. The sight of her made him all the more anxious to get the gunplay over with, so he could take her on home.

A glimpse of Polly in her beauty, after missing her so long, put Zeke in the honeymoon mood right away. Before he could even enjoy thinking about it thoroughly, T. Spade Beck stepped out on the porch, in his long johns. When he saw Polly bending over the lye bucket, he went right over and started pulling up her clothes. T. Spade had a white, pointy beard hanging off his chin, which made him look goatish, Zeke thought. There he was, trying to rut with Polly in plain sight, like an ugly old billy!

Zeke pulled two pistols, shoved his way out of the thicket, and started shooting. T. Spade looked startled. He had not gotten very far with his rutting, and when he saw Zeke Proctor coming at him with two guns blazing, he experienced an abrupt change of mood. He usually kept a rifle on the back porch for just such emergencies, but he had taken the rifle into the mill and was caught now, in his underwear, without a weapon—a damn nuisance to be sure.

Polly had been in a dreamy mood when T. Spade crowded up against her by the lye bucket. She was not in a state to discourage him. Then, to her shock, while still bent over, she saw Zeke spring out of the thicket with his guns in his hands.

I should have got word to him, she thought—I should have let him know.

She felt a horrible mistake was about to happen. Zeke might be upset about the weevils, but mainly he was coming at T. Spade because he wanted her. He did not realize she had changed, had decided to stay a wife to T. Spade.

Zeke could not be shooting her husband, Polly thought. Polly immediately jumped in front of T. Spade. She would explain the matter to Zeke when things were calmer.

"No, Zeke . . . no! Leave be!" Polly said.

As she said it, she felt something nudge her chest. To her relief, Zeke stopped shooting; the fact that she was shielding T. Spade had brought him to his senses, she thought.

Her relief was so great that it made her weak for a moment, her legs giving way. She sank down, braced against T. Spade's legs. She looked for Zeke, to see if he had put away his guns. She had a big need to speak to Zeke; there were just a few words she needed to say to him. She hoped her husband would not take it wrong.

Then Polly's eyesight began to fail her. It was as if a cloud came over her eyes, white as the mists had been in the mornings, in her girlhood in the Tennessee hills. One moment she saw Zeke standing by the woods; then she could not see him at all. When she looked up at her husband to see if he was angry, she could not see him, either. A mist had blown in and settled in her eyes.

"T., it's looking rainy . . . you better go inside and get your overalls on," Polly said. Zeke drifted out of her mind; then she lay back flat on the porch, a heaviness on her limbs and on her eyelids.

But she was worried about her husband—he was not really dressed for chilly weather, and he was prone to coughs.

"You get on inside now, where you'll be warm," Polly said to her husband, in a worried tone.

Then the heaviness became a lightness, and Polly forgot that worry, and all worries. The mist grew thicker and more white; it hid the valley and the hills; it hid T. Spade and Zeke; it was whiter than the mists of Tennessee.

The mist surrounded her. The mist was all she knew.

8

ZEKE KEPT WALKING TOWARD T. SPADE'S PORCH. POLLY BECK was still—too still. He had to find out what he had done.

T. Spade himself seemed dazed. He went inside the mill and came back out a moment later with a rifle, but then all he did was prop the rifle up against a barrel on the porch.

"Polly, wake up," T. Spade demanded. But Polly did not wake up.

Zeke kept hoping she would sit up, or at least make some movement. If she would do that much, he would be happy to go. He would just go home, and let things be. He had lost all interest in shooting T. Spade, and from T. Spade's behaviour, T. Spade evidently had no interest in shooting him.

T. Spade bent down next to Polly, and tried to lift her. Though he was a large man, the effort was too much for him. Normally, he could lift his wife easily, since she was lighter than a big sack of cornmeal. But now she seemed much too heavy to lift. He looked up at Zeke, who stood silently at the foot of the porch steps.

"Help me carry her in, Zeke," T. Spade requested. His voice was flat and dull. Zeke stepped up onto the porch, and bent down on the other side of Polly's body.

The shock had weakened both men, and it was all they could do to lift Polly and carry her up to the bed in the loft. Why carry her up? You'll just have to carry her back down to bury her, Zeke thought, as they struggled up the stairs. There was a small spot of blood on the front of her dress. The spot was right over her heart.

After they got Polly settled, T. Spade sat down in a rocking chair next to the bed and dipped some snuff. From the rocking chair, he had a good view out the door of the loft, all the way

35

across the valley and to the hills. He did not look at Zeke, nor did he have any more words inside him.

Zeke had no words, either. He stood by the bed for an awkward moment, looking down at Polly. She was as white as if she were made of snow. There were not many women in the Going Snake District so light of skin. Becca would have been jealous of that skin, if he had managed to bring Polly home with him.

Zeke felt he ought to say something to T. Spade, but he could not think what the right words might be. There did not seem to be any words right enough. A lot of things could be changed, but not death. Polly could not come back to life, no matter what words Zeke might say.

Zeke walked on down the stairs and out of the mill, so distracted that he completely forgot he had come to the Beck mill horseback. He had walked almost a mile in the general direction of his home before he remembered his horse Joe.

While he was walking back to get his horse, he jumped the same fat yearling bear that both he and Sully Eagle had tried to kill. The bear was trying to scratch out some varmint, a badger maybe, that he had cornered in its hole. The bear stopped scratching for a moment, and gave Zeke an impudent look.

But Zeke walked on by and left the young bear to its scratching. He had just killed Polly Beck—an innocent woman —a woman he had meant to marry.

The last thing he wanted to have to do on such a day was skin an impudent bear.

9

ZEKE WAS SO UPSET ON THE WAY HOME THAT HE COULD NOT think clearly. He had ridden off with every intention of bringing Polly Beck, a red-haired, light-stepping woman, back to his house to be his second wife, but instead ended up killing her with a shot meant for her husband, T. Spade.

T. Spade should have been dead by now, or at least well wounded, and he and Polly should be riding home to start their married life together. But T. Spade was rocking in a rocking chair, looking out the window of his loft—and Polly was laid out a few feet away, dead.

It was a terrible turn of events, and Zeke knew that he had no one to blame for it but himself. In the first place, he should have never tried to shoot T. Spade with a pistol. He had never been much of a pistol shot, which was why he had brought his Winchester. But when he saw T. Spade pulling up Polly's dress right there on the front porch, he had lost control of his thinking to such an extent that he had popped off with his pistols, when he should have sat down with his rifle and taken sober aim.

A worse thought was the possibility that Polly had a change of heart and no longer wanted to leave her husband. Maybe she had not cared that T. Spade was pulling up her dress; maybe she had wanted him to—in which case Zeke had killed a happily married woman—a woman he should have never been slipping off with in the first place.

It had been an accident. He had wanted to love Polly, not kill her. But what he had wanted or intended no longer mattered: he had shed her life's blood and put her in her grave. The weight of guilt on his conscience was heavy as an anvil, and he would be carrying the anvil of that guilt forever.

That was the worst of it: Polly would always be dead, and it would always be his fault. He could never make up to her that he had killed her. Instead of being with him by a warm camp-fire, on a quilt or a buffalo robe, she would be dead in the dirt —a grievous waste of a light-stepping woman, and one that should not have been.

Zeke became so distraught he did not know whether to ride on or stop, go home or go away. He knew he would have to sort out the question of the law pretty soon, but he was not up to it right this minute. Dog Town was about five miles away, and in Dog Town maybe he could find someone to give him counsel—or failing that, someone to sell him whiskey. He needed to have a few sips and brace up. T. Spade Beck might be dazed for the moment, but his dazement would pass, and he and his brothers and cousins would be taking up arms.

Polly had been half Cherokee—the same as Zeke Proctor. Zeke's mother, Dicey Downing, had been Cherokee, and his father, William, had been white. William Proctor had lived as a true Cherokee, joining his wife's family on the Cherokee

Nation in their native Georgia soon after his marriage to Zeke's mother.

T. Spade was a white man. Under the law, when a white man married a Cherokee woman, he became an adopted citizen of the Cherokee Nation, and subject to their laws. But T. Spade had not conducted himself as a Cherokee; in fact, he had resented the notion that he was supposed to become a citizen of the Cherokee Nation and had made his resentment known to Polly's family, as well as the rest of the tribes living in and around Tahlequah. He had gotten away with charging Indians higher prices for grinding grain than he charged whites, only because Polly's family was liked and respected throughout the Nation. White men got away with stealing from Indians because Indians were not allowed to testify against whites, though plenty of whites testified against Cherokees. T. Spade knew the law, and took full advantage of it.

T. Spade himself was not popular with his in-laws, either, but they tolerated him because of Polly. Knowing T. Spade, he might even try to get the white marshals after Zeke, even though it would be wrongheaded. If Zeke were tried for shooting Polly, then he ought to be tried in the tribal court. The white marshals would not be likely to care that the shooting had been a tragic accident; they would jail him and then hang him for having shot a white man's wife.

In Dog Town, the first person Zeke saw was Tuxie Miller. Tuxie was loading a keg of nails in his wagon, and it was all he could do to lift the keg.

"Dern, you wouldn't think nails would weigh this much," Tuxie said, when he finally got the keg securely situated.

"Where's Ned? I need advice," Zeke said abruptly, when he rode up next to Tuxie's wagon. He did not have time to discuss the weight of fencing nails with Tuxie Miller.

"Why, Ned's at home, I believe," Tuxie told him. "If it's just advice you need, I can sell you some for a nickel."

Tuxie was in a light mood, as he always was when he managed to escape Dale, his terrier of a wife, for even a few hours. Dale did not tolerate long absences, or laziness of any sort. In her view, the hours of sunlight were made for working. If Tuxie even felt like yawning between sunup and sundown, he had to leave home to do it.

His remark about selling advice did not amuse Zeke Proctor one bit.

"I just kilt somebody, I got to talk to Ned," Zeke blurted.

"Good Lord—was it T. Spade?" Tuxie inquired. Tahlequah and Dog Town were small communities, and gossip traveled easily between the two towns. Tuxie himself had heard there might be bad blood between Zeke and T. Spade Beck.

"No, it's worse than that. I kilt Polly. It was an accident," Zeke said. "I shot at T. Spade, and Polly jumped right in front of him just at the wrong time. She's dead."

This news knocked Tuxie right out of his jesting mood. Zeke Proctor was going to need a good deal more than a nickel's worth of advice. As soon as word of the killing got back to Judge Parker in Arkansas, the white marshals would be coming, right or wrong.

"We better go on up and see Ned, then," Tuxie agreed. "You want to get a jug?"

"I want to get a jug," Zeke replied.

The thought of Polly, white as snow on that bed, was heavy on his mind.

10

NED CHRISTIE HEARD ABOUT THE KILLING BEFORE ZEKE AND Tuxie arrived. Soldier Sixkiller, Jewel's cousin, had happened by that afternoon. Soldier had heard it from Bear Grimmet in Siloam Springs; Bear had heard it from one of T. Spade's cousins.

In the hills and flatlands where the Cherokee people lived, news traveled faster than horses. It was nearly thirty miles from the Beck mill to Ned's Mountain, but Ned had the news to chew on an hour before Zeke and Tuxie came riding up.

"Both of you men are in trouble," Ned announced when he walked out to greet his guests. "Zeke's in trouble with the law, and Tuxie's in trouble with Dale. She's done sent your oldest boy over here twice to tell you she expects you home."

Ned saw at once that Zeke Proctor was in bad shape.

"Get down, Zeke," he said. "Jewel's cooking a possum, we'll be eating pretty soon."

Zeke did not want to eat. Whiskey, confusion, and remorse were churning in him like the rapids along the Arkansas River. He was relieved to see Ned, at least. Though Ned was the younger man by more than a decade, there was something about him that was solid—in his company, people got the feeling that if things got bad, Ned could handle them. Ned Christie stayed calm in situations that would cause most people to go wild and act foolish. He had the ability to keep on doing one thing at a time, until the crisis passed.

It was his calm authority that had caused Zeke to travel thirty miles to see him on a day when life had gone terribly wrong. The fact of Polly's death would be a tragedy forever, but the world had not ended, not yet. Something would have to happen next, whether Zeke wanted it to or not. He could not crawl in a hole and give up, like a sick goat would be apt to do.

Besides the possum, Jewel had made a squirrel stew and a mess of wild greens. Tuxie kept telling himself he ought to get on home before Dale got any madder, but he was not a man to willingly turn away from squirrel stew, especially since Dale refused to cook varmints. In her view, squirrels were varmints.

Jewel was shocked to see how sad her father looked. When she was younger, he had been ingenious at making dolls for her, out of corncobs and bits of rag. Zeke had always been the jolly one of the household. When her mother was low, Zeke would make jokes or whistle tunes, until he had everyone, including Becca, cheered up.

Zeke hugged Jewel hard when he first came in, but after that, he seemed hardly to know where he was, or who he was with. He sat at the pine-slab table looking blank, saying nothing. He ate only a bite or two, although Jewel dished him up the first plate of stew.

She had heard the talk, of course, between her cousin, Soldier, and her husband, Ned. Her cousin said that Zeke had killed some woman he meant to take to wife. The news was so upsetting that Jewel would have preferred not to hear it. For one thing, she did not think her mother would have wanted Zeke to have another wife. Jewel knew men sometimes had more than one wife, but she had just become a wife herself, to a husband she loved with all her heart. What if Ned showed up one day with another woman, and told her she would have to accept the new woman as his second wife? Jewel knew she would never be able to stand it—she would not share her husband with *any* woman. If Ned tried to bring a new woman to their home, Jewel knew she would have to be strong enough to leave.

It was just a problem in her mind, of course; Ned had given no sign that he had any such intention. A few days after he brought her home to be his wife, he walked with her down to the spring and whispered to her that he wanted babies. Jewel was startled by the ways of men; she did not say yes or no. She wanted Ned to have what he wanted, and if he wanted a baby, then she wanted one, too. She wanted to be a good wife to Ned for as long as she was allowed, although the only part of being a wife that she felt confident about so far was cooking. Ned must want the baby very much, she thought. He came to her almost every night now.

Jewel fried the possum meat and cooked the squirrel stew, even though she was upset by what her father had done. In the years of her childhood, Zeke had never raised a hand to Jewel, or spoken a cross word to her. Yet, he had wanted to be with this new woman, Polly Beck, so much that he had ended up killing her. The thought of upsetting Becca had not checked him, nor had he minded taking Polly away from the husband she had married. What it meant to Jewel was that men would have their way where women were concerned, no matter what women might want.

She had just begun to experience the power of a man. There was pleasure in it, but no certainty. At times after Ned had been with her, Jewel wished she could go home and be certain of life again—home with her mother, and her father, and her sister, and the triplets.

She wished it, but she knew it could not be. She was Ned Christie's wife, and she always would be, until one of them met their death. It was enough that her husband wanted her; she wanted to live so that *only* her husband wanted her. She did not want some stranger to appear one day and want her so much that he killed her husband—or else killed her—the very thing her father had just done.

"My Jewel's the best cook on the Mountain," Ned said proudly. He could not get enough of praising Jewel. That she had learned the wifing part of life so quickly made him feel like a lucky man. His only complaint—not that he voiced it to anyone except Tuxie Miller—was that in her shyness, Jewel rarely spoke. She worked with a will, but what she felt as she went through her days, or lay with him on their old shuck mattress at night, he did not know. Jewel, so far, had been a good wife, but a silent one.

Ned had made the remark about Jewel's cooking in the hope that talk of vittles or other light matters might divert Zeke some from his grieving.

Zeke looked up briefly at Jewel, lovely and quiet. The time when he had her at home as a daughter seemed a long time lost, though she had been gone only a few weeks.

"Yes, we miss her at home," Zeke said. "Becca's too forgetful. She forgets, and burns the mush."

"Dale can cook, only she don't cook varmints," Tuxie said. "It's deer meat or cabbage at our house, mostly."

"Dale will be cooking *you,* if you don't behave better," Ned observed. He liked Dale Miller, even though she was violent. When her temper was up, which was often, she would grab whatever was handy and chunk it. She chunked accurately, too. Once, when he had teased her a little too hard, Dale flattened him with a stick of firewood, thrown from twenty feet. Ned had half meant to marry Dale himself, but he was shy about his courting. The next thing he knew, she had married Tuxie and started spilling out children. There were nine, to date. Despite being scared to death of Dale, Tuxie did manage to keep her spilling out children.

Zeke was not diverted long by mention of Jewel's cooking. The bad thing he had done was sure to have consequences, and how bad the consequences might get was the thing he wanted to talk to Ned about. Zeke trusted his Keetoowah brother completely. The Keetoowah Society denounced white authority of any kind, and were strong supporters of treaty rights of independence within the Cherokee Nation. Strong avengement would be taken against anyone who harmed a Keetoowah brother, and Zeke knew Ned would do what he could to keep him safe from the white marshals, if they came.

"It was an accident that I shot Polly, but the white law won't see it that way," Zeke said.

"Even if they believe it, they won't care," Ned replied. "You best eat that stew—you might have to go on the scout for a while, and if you do you won't be eating vittles as good as these."

Zeke found it impossible to enjoy the tasty vittles with so much trouble hanging over him. He was so upset, he could barely think at all.

"You better turn yourself in to Judge Sixkiller, him or the tribal sheriff, one," Ned said. "Maybe if you do, the white law will stay over in Arkansas. We don't need the federals in a case like this."

"Need it? We never need it," Tuxie Miller said. Then he got up from the table and shot out the door, headed home to Dale. Tuxie had to work up the nerve to face Dale. The minute he had his nerve worked up, he was gone.

Judge B. H. Sixkiller, the man Ned wanted Zeke to turn himself in to, was Jewel's great-grandfather. When Judge Sixkiller heard that Jewel had left home to be the wife of Ned Christie, he sent her a red blanket and a good stone crock. The blanket was one he himself had been wrapped in when he was a baby in the Old Place, long before he and all the Cherokees had been forced to march to the new Cherokee Nation along the Trail of Tears, more than thirty years before. It was an old blanket, soft from much use. Jewel kept it safe in a tight box where the mice could not get at it. She meant to use it to wrap her babies in, when they came.

Now her great-grandfather would be sitting as judge over Zeke. There were not many families in the Going Snake District, and most of them were related to one another, through marriages or elopements. B. H. Sixkiller was a fair man, and a busy judge. Jewel had not seen him in almost two years, and she did not know what he would think of Zeke killing a woman he wanted to take to wife. It had been an accident, Jewel felt sure of that; but still, the woman was dead.

Ned himself was not certain what action Zeke ought to take. Going on the scout—that is, hiding in the hills—would be the simplest procedure. Zeke was already in the hills. That was what most Cherokees did when they found they had run afoul of the law. The fact remained that T. Spade Beck was a white man; he would no doubt appeal to the white law in Fort Smith, Arkansas. But if Zeke presented himself to the tribal authorities promptly and admitted the accident, perhaps T. Spade would wait. If the Beck clan knew that Zeke was going to be tried properly before a tribal court, they might not take up arms against him—at least, not until the verdict was in.

After thinking about the matter, Ned concluded that Zeke ought to present himself to the Judge right away, and give an account of his actions. When blood was shed and a life lost, there had to be legal proceedings; otherwise, everybody in the District would soon be shooting at one another.

The worst element of the problem was not Zeke, or Judge Sixkiller, or the Sheriff of the District, Charley Bobtail: the man Zeke finally had to fear was Judge Isaac Parker—known throughout the Territory as the hanging judge—who held court in Fort Smith, Arkansas, a day's horseback ride away. Judge Parker had no respect for tribal law, and he did not believe that Cherokees or any other Indians ought to get to try themselves, unless the crimes in question were so low on the scale of crimes that it was not worth sending a marshal over to the Going Snake District to collar the miscreant. If the crime was more serious than stealing chickens, Judge Parker wanted to make sure that he had the criminal in his court where he would be subject to white law, which often meant the noose.

That was not the way it was supposed to be. By treaty with the United States government and approved by Congress, Cherokees and the other tribes in Indian Territory had the right to try their own criminals in their own courts. That was supposed to be the law of the land, but it did not seem to apply in Fort Smith. Judge Parker was always sending the marshals into the Going Snake District to drag back criminals. Many times, he was after the whiskeysellers, Indian or white—but if the marshals could not catch the whiskeysellers, they would grab any Indian who was handy and pretend they found whiskey on his property. Judge Parker was the reason most Cherokees preferred to go on the scout when they got in trouble. Often, Judge Parker's marshals would try to take prisoners right out of the Tahlequah jail and haul them off to Arkansas.

"Sheriff Bobtail don't like me," Zeke pointed out. "I trust Judge Sixkiller, but I don't know what Charley Bobtail might do."

"Why don't he like you?" Ned asked. It was the first he had heard of any problems between Zeke and the Sheriff.

"Because my horse beat his horse in a horse race," Zeke

said. "It was over in Siloam Springs, three years ago. I bet him ten dollars, and I won. Charley's held a grudge ever since."

"Which horse?" Ned asked. "Not that sorrel?"

"Yep," Zeke said. "That sorrel."

"I don't know why he thinks that horse can run," Ned said. "I've seen mules who can outrun that horse."

"There's the Squirrels, too," Zeke reminded him. "If I'm sitting there in jail, with no better guard than Charley Bobtail, what's to stop the Squirrels from coming in that jail and shooting me like a possum in a trap—or, if not the Squirrels, then the Becks?"

Ned had forgotten about the Squirrels. He had been wanting to get along and marry Jewel the day the Squirrel brothers warned Zeke in Tahlequah. Now it came back to him: Polly Beck had been a Squirrel, and Zeke was right to be cautious about surrender. Moses Squirrel was capable of immediate murder, in Ned's view, and Rat Squirrel was not much better than an egg-sucking dog. That left Jim, who was friendly unless he was drunk. When he was drunk, he liked to curse and strike out.

While Ned watched, Zeke's head drooped down on his chest. Jewel noticed, too. She quickly made her father a pallet by the fireplace. She did not want Ned to be worrying him about going to jail until he had a good night's rest.

Ned was of the same opinion—Zeke looked like he was about to topple into the gravy.

"Go on and rest, Zeke," Ned advised. "We can go see the Judge tomorrow."

Zeke was grateful for the pallet. He lay down, but kept his three guns handy. He had locked his dog Pete in the springhouse before he left for the Beck mill. He was afraid Pete might get barky and give him away. Now, he lacked his watchdog, just when he needed him.

"Pete's cooped up in the springhouse. I hope Becca remembers to let him out," he said, just before he fell asleep.

11

THE NEXT MORNING, THE MEN SPENT OVER AN HOUR CLEANing their guns.

On the Mountain, the only weapon Ned usually carried was his old single-shot squirrel gun, unless he was after deer, in which case he took his Winchester. This morning, though, Ned cleaned his two .44s and his Winchester, and Zeke did the same with his three weapons. There was no talk at the table. The men took their coffee and biscuits, but then concentrated on their weapons.

Jewel was used to lots of attention from Ned in the morning. He was always grabbing her, kissing on her, looking at her with eager eyes. Sometimes, he tried to get her to come back with him to the mattress, but Jewel resisted. Such things belonged to the nighttime, she felt, and besides, she had chores to do.

This morning, she felt apprehensive. Ned and her father were preoccupied with their guns. Ned asked once for more coffee, but he did not look up when he asked. Soon, both men went outside to saddle the horses. Jewel felt such a nervousness that she could not get her mind on the chores. She meant to churn butter, but had mislaid the top to the churn. She started three times to look for it, but then forgot what she was about.

Ned had not left Jewel at night since he brought her home to be his wife. She did not want him to leave her, either. She was scared of the Mountain at night. There were bears, for one thing, and wild pigs that might come at her. With Ned there to hold her in his arms, the fear was not bad, but now Ned was saddling up to go. What if he failed to get back by dark? What if there was gunplay, and he was killed? Ned was her husband now. The thought that he might not return to her alive was so upsetting that she could not keep her mind on the churning. Ned was butter crazy—the slabs he spread on his biscuits were thicker than the biscuits themselves. Anyway, why make butter if Ned was going off?

For a moment, Jewel was afraid the men were just going to ride away without telling her what to expect. Zeke had ridden off from Becca plenty of times without telling her whether he would be gone an hour or a month—but finally, Ned came back into the house to look for the whetstone.

"That whetstone must have legs, it was right here on the hearth last night," he told Jewel.

"I can't find the churn lid, either," Jewel admitted.

Then Ned gave her a kiss, taking his time about it, too. They were kissing so long that Jewel got a little embarrassed; after all, her father was standing right outside the door, with his bridle reins in his hands. What would he think of such kissing? She did not really want Ned to stop; when he stopped, he would be riding away. Ned had the power to confuse her, to make her want two things at the same time. Her heart still fluttered like a bird when he came to her, or even when he just looked at her across the table. On occasion, Jewel would go outside and cut firewood when they did not need firewood, in order to calm herself. Even when it got dark, she did not trust the fluttering in her breast, for she felt like she might be getting to love Ned too much. Becca told her it was the things you loved too much that you were sure to lose. Jewel could not stand the thought of losing Ned. Sometimes, deep in the night, when even the woods were silent, she would wake up with the fear that Ned had died. She would put her face against his chest, to feel his heartbeat; but even the feel of his strong heartbeat did not always reassure her, nor did the feel of his warm breath on her cheek. A heartbeat could stop, and breath could cease. Becca, her own mother, had two husbands die, and now Zeke was in trouble—so much trouble that Ned felt he had to take all his guns to town.

Finally, Ned left off kissing her. He looked once more for the wandering whetstone, but did not find it.

"If you see that whetstone, put it back where it belongs," Ned said. He liked things orderly. Everything in the house had a place where it was supposed to be. The churn lid was supposed to be on the churn, the whetstone on the mantel. He hated to go off with a dull knife, but with the whetstone missing, there was not much he could do about it.

Jewel went outside and hugged her father. He had the distant look he always got when he was impatient to be someplace. Ned had the look, too: they were off to do men's business.

"Let's stop at Tuxie's, he might want to go," Ned remarked, once he mounted.

Jewel wanted to ask when they would be back, but managed to hold her tongue. Ned probably did not know when he would be back, and even if he knew, he would not appreciate being asked. Men did not like to account for themselves that way.

"Don't let that pig out till we've been gone awhile," Ned instructed, as he was turning to leave. "That pig will follow horses—if it wanders off too far, it might run into a bear and we'd be out our meat."

Jewel did as instructed. She sat by the pigpen on an old bucket until the men had been gone long enough to be all the way to Tuxie Miller's. The pig grunted at her while she sat. It wanted to get out and go looking for acorns; then, when she did let it out, it stood by the back door for an hour, hoping for some slop.

Right after she finished churning, Jewel found the whetstone. It was under the pallet she had made for her father. Jewel wished there was a way she could let Ned know it had been located.

But there was no way. He was already gone.

12

DALE MILLER WAS FORCEFUL. THERE WAS A RIGHT AND A wrong, and she could tell them apart. Tuxie could not, and in fact, most men could not, which is why it was important that they marry. Single men, in her view, were just a nuisance to the community, for even if they were sober, they usually could not tell right from wrong, and single men were rarely sober anyway.

She was a white woman, married to a Cherokee man, the daughter of missionaries who had traveled the Trail of Tears with the largest contingent of Cherokees to come up from Georgia and Tennessee. Dale was born in the Cherokee Nation, raised and educated at the missionary school her parents established in the Going Snake District. She set her eye on Tuxie Miller early, though she had demonstrated a brief fascination with Ned Christie, the handsomest man Dale had ever seen.

Ned was sweet natured and shy, but strong willed; Dale knew that marriage to a man like Ned would mean a considerable amount of their married life would be spent head-butting. Ned seemed to care for her, but his pride was such that she never really knew where she stood with him. Dale herself was forceful to the point of rudeness, at times, but she was good-hearted and loyal, and her judgment as to a man's character was acute.

It was said that in 1828, gold had been discovered on a creek which ran right through the middle of Tuxie's grandfather's property back in north Georgia; that incident was what set the whites to overrunning the Old Nation and finally forcing the removal of the Cherokee people from their homeland ten years later. Tuxie was orphaned out—one of the several hundred Cherokee children who had lost their families during the worst part of the winter trek in 1838—and was raised in the orphanage just outside of Tahlequah. Tuxie Miller, mild mannered and easygoing, was the perfect mate for Dale, and she knew it.

Dale marched right out to Zeke Proctor, and proceeded to explain the right and wrong of his situation to him.

"Zeke, you need to get home and make it up with Becca," Dale informed him, without preamble.

Zeke looked startled. Like everyone else, he was unprepared for Dale's forceful way of putting things.

"Make it up for what?" he asked. "I get along fine with Becca."

"If you get along fine with her, why were you slipping off to see that red-haired slut?" Dale asked. "Now you've shamed Becca in front of the whole community."

Zeke did not answer. He felt considerably aggravated. Why had they stopped at Tuxie Miller's anyway? Dale Miller was known throughout the District for her contrary ways. All he wanted to do was get to town and settle his legal problems. The last thing he needed was to have Dale Miller lecture him on his behaviour.

Tuxie felt embarrassed—after all, Zeke was a guest. The hospitable thing to do would be to ask him to get down and take some coffee. But Dale was Dale: speaking her mind usually took precedence over the rules of hospitality.

"Becca's poorly, she needs help with the triplets," Zeke said, finally. "I had every intention of marrying Polly before the accident happened."

"Where I come from, you *hire* help—you don't marry it," Dale said.

Dale had little tolerance for the loose habits that prevailed out west. Now here sat Ned Christie, armed to the teeth, going off to do battle if need be on behalf of Zeke Proctor, though he had a young bride at home, a girl just sixteen years old who would have to fend for herself on the Mountain while her husband was gone.

"Cleave to the wife of your bosom, that's what the Good Book says," Dale quoted. She looked right at Ned when she said it.

Ned grinned. Dale was always trying to back him into a corner by quoting scripture. He got along with her fine, but he refused to back. The nine children began to slip out of the house to observe the company. They were as shy as mice. Ned was jealous of Tuxie, for having produced nine children, while he himself had yet to produce even one. He meant to remedy that, now that he had his sweet Jewel. What he did not want to do was waste half a day arguing scripture or anything else with Dale Miller. Dale had little patience, and would argue for a week once she got wound up.

"Tuxie, are you coming?" Ned asked. On the ride over, his mind had conjured up an army of Becks and Squirrels who might be waiting for them in ambush, or else in Tahlequah. Tuxie possessed a 10-gauge shotgun that would give them an advantage in close-range shooting. Tuxie had once managed to kill twenty-two ducks with only one barrel of the shotgun, though, of course, the ducks had been tightly bunched. Having him and his shotgun along might discourage a suck-egg like Rat Squirrel from trying to sneak in close.

Before Tuxie could answer, Dale turned and gestured at her children. All nine of them were now lined up in front of the cabin: four boys, five girls.

"No, he's not going," Dale said. "I'll not take a chance of having my children orphaned over some foolishness of Zeke's."

"Besides that, I've got a cow with bloat up the hill half a mile," Tuxie said. "I've got to poke a knife in her and see if I can let out the bloat. She's our milk cow, the younguns depend on her."

Dale's pique was subsiding a little. Zeke had no colour in his face; he looked tired, and sad. Dale remembered that Zeke had been a good friend to her father when her father was dying. Zeke had ridden twenty-five miles on a sleety day to get some medicines from an old healing woman. The medicines had not saved her father, but Zeke had shown himself to be a loyal friend by making that ride. Though it annoyed her when people could not always be good, the fact was, sometimes they just could not.

Zeke Proctor was no more all of a piece than most men. There was good in him, as well as bad. The older men got, it seemed to Dale, the more prone they were to making bad mistakes, particularly if they did not have a strong wife to show them the Christian way.

Ned Christie was a fine man and a good neighbour, willing to pitch in and help when there was work to do. Dale had set her cap for Ned, but then she took the cap off when she discovered how headstrong he was. Since she knew herself to be no less headstrong, Dale chose Tuxie when she decided to marry. Tuxie she could bend; life with Ned would have been one head butt after another.

"If you men are fearful of a scrap, you better eat first," she said, looking up at them and moderating her tone. "We got corn cakes."

Tuxie was relieved. Dale had remembered her manners, and just in time, too. It would have been an embarrassment if she had sent his friends away hungry. Dale mostly did remember her manners; it was just that she would have her say first. Zeke had little appetite, but Ned ate his share, and most of Zeke's.

"I don't know why he would marry a woman like that," Zeke remarked, as they rode on toward Tahlequah. "I'd just as soon marry a badger."

Ned just chuckled. He liked Dale.

13

JUDGE B. H. SIXKILLER WAS ANNOYED THAT ZEKE HAD LET twenty-four hours elapse before presenting himself in Tahlequah.

In twenty-four hours or less, one of the Becks could have ridden to Fort Smith and called for the white law. If that had occurred, there would be a squabble, at the very least, and the Judge was too old to enjoy squabbles. B. H. Sixkiller had curly white eyebrows, and had been much admired by the women in his day—four of them had married him, but they were all dead now, and the rheumatism in his joints pained him so badly on wet days that he had not applied himself to finding a new wife. When he got a little respite from his duties as a judge, he usually went fishing.

Zeke Proctor looked plenty repentant when he told his story, but the Judge was stern with him anyway. Crimes resulting from marital irregularities were a particular annoyance to him. He had gotten along fine with all four of his wives, and as a result deplored concubinage and other loose arrangements. Women's shapes might differ, but their natures did not—not in the Judge's view. Now Zeke had sown discord in the community, merely because he wanted a woman different from the one he had.

"Zeke, you're a damned reprobate!" the Judge said. "Your trial will be in two weeks. Take him off to jail, Charley!"

Sheriff Charley Bobtail's heart sank when he heard the order. "You mean I have to keep him for the whole two weeks?" he asked. As sheriff of the Going Snake District, his responsibilities were large and wide ranging. In respect to the jail, he had to function not only as sheriff, but as jailer, janitor, and cook. He did not look forward to having Zeke Proctor as a prisoner for two long weeks.

The Judge was writing up the Affidavit of Trial. If he got it posted soon enough, so that everybody knew Zeke would be held accountable for the killing, maybe the white law would leave them alone. Speed was of the essence, which was why Zeke had been a fool to waste a day before he made his report. If white law got hold of him, he'd be lucky to escape the noose.

"I'm not such a fool as to want to feed this man for two weeks," the Judge said, looking up from his affidavit. "If the marshals show up, it will probably be tomorrow. If we've got him in jail and the trial date's set, they'll have to leave without him. Then you can let him out, and he can take his chances."

Zeke was relieved by that news, and he saw the Judge's point about the marshals. If they ran into him on the Mountain, or caught him at home, they'd probably just kill him, unless he killed them first. But he still did not savour the notion of being in the Tahlequah jail for any length of time. He had been in it once or twice for minor scrapes, and knew it to be a drafty place with hard bunks. He missed Becca, Liza, and the triplets, and wanted to get home to them as soon as possible. Becca would be worried, and the triplets would be more than a handful, with only Liza to help.

Charley and Zeke went out. Ned started to follow them, but when he took a step toward the door, the Judge looked up and frowned. Ned stopped—he had great respect for the law that emanated from Judge Sixkiller.

"Are you in a hurry, Mr. Christie?" the Judge asked.

"No, I'm just here with Zeke," Ned replied. Being in the presence of Judge Sixkiller made him feel solemn, for some reason.

"I see you're fully armed," the Judge observed.

"Yes sir," Ned said.

"It's better to live in peace with your neighbours and not be shooting at them," the Judge said.

"I ain't shooting at 'em," Ned said.

"A man who carries three guns is likely to end up shooting at somebody, sooner or later," the Judge observed. "A peaceable man ought to be content with fewer guns."

"I was afraid there'd be trouble with the Becks or the Squirrels," Ned informed him.

The Judge ignored this reasoning. He looked out the window, and saw that Sheriff Bobtail and Zeke Proctor had yet to make it to the jail. They were standing in the street talking, which was incorrect procedure, and a distraction from the matter at hand.

"You married my granddaughter. Why'd you do it?" the Judge demanded to know, in the tone he might use with a felon.

Ned was so taken aback by the question that for a moment he lost his bearings. Judge Sixkiller was looking stern. Ned was at a loss for what to say, his mind having suddenly gone blank. Why *had* he married Jewel? Ned felt like he would rather be in jail with Zeke than to face Judge Sixkiller and his questions about his new wife.

He paused a moment, and took a deep breath.

"Jewel was of a marrying age," Ned said carefully. "She seemed a fine girl. I believe she'll make a good wife."

"Of course she'll make a good wife," the Judge said with a hint of indignation in his voice. "Do you think you have it in you to make a good husband, Mr. Christie? That's a better question."

Ned had every intention of being a good husband to Jewel. He had been a good husband so far, and he saw no reason why he could not continue to be one. But how was he to convince Judge Sixkiller of that? Just looking at the stern old man with the curly white eyebrows made him feel tongue-tied.

"I aim to be good to Jewel," Ned said, finally. "I believe I can be good to her."

"I hope you *are* good to her," the Judge said. "I will not have Jewel mistreated. She wouldn't have married you unless she meant to be a good wife to you, and I imagine she expects you to stay alive and help her raise your children."

"Why, I aim to stay alive," Ned said. "I aim to grow old with Jewel."

"Then stop piling on the pistols," the Judge said. "You look like a gun rack. There's too much wanton shooting in the District, and I mean to curb it. I have not felt the need to carry a weapon in more than thirty years. When I was a circuit judge, I rode all over this District with nothing on me but a pocketknife. If you do the same, you'll live longer, and my granddaughter might escape the sorrow of being a widow."

The Judge looked out the window. Sheriff Bobtail and his prisoner were still milling around in the street. Zeke seemed to be smoking a cigar, which was vexatious behaviour in a man who was supposed to be incarcerated.

"Go out there, Mr. Christie, and tell Sheriff Bobtail to proceed to the jail immediately and lock up that prisoner," the Judge said. "Who told him to lag?"

"Well, I didn't," Ned said, glad to have a reason to leave. Splitting logs with a hatchet would be preferable employment to having to address Judge B. H. Sixkiller. He did not feel that he had acquitted himself very well in the conversation, either.

"I have nothing but the best intentions where my wife is concerned," Ned said, before he went out the door.

The Judge did not reply. He was staring out the window, across the wide street, and he looked galled.

14

"YOU EVIDENTLY NEED TO CLEAN OUT YOUR EARS, MR. Beck," Judge Isaac Parker said emphatically. "They must be clogged up with earwax or filth of some kind. I've told you three times that I'd take the matter under advisement. Three times is more times than I care to repeat myself. It's time for you to head home."

Willy Beck did not budge. He was planted right in front of the Judge, and he meant to stay there until he got some firm guarantees. So far, Judge Parker had failed to produce any.

"My sister's dead and buried," he said. "Zeke Proctor shot her in broad daylight, her husband was a witness. I don't want to hear no talk of advisement. I want you to send a marshal over to get him. Then let him be tried and hung."

"As you well know, the culprit is already incarcerated," Judge Parker said. As soon as he could locate Chilly Stufflebean, his bailiff, he meant to dock his wages fifty cents for having let Willy Beck get past him and into the Judge's office. Part of the bailiff's job was to keep people with grievances as far toward the front of the courthouse as possible. Once they got back down the hall toward the Judge's chambers, they were apt to prove hard to dislodge—Willy Beck, the man standing in front of him, was a case in point.

"He's in an Indian jail, and if they bring him to trial it'll be in an Indian court and with an Indian jury," Willy said. "Our brother's lost a wife to foul play, and our brother's white. We want that damn killer tried in your court. Then we want him hung."

"Was your sister a pure woman?" the Judge asked, suddenly. He looked out the window and saw Chilly making his way back from the outhouse. Chilly's main drawback as a bailiff was his unstable gut. All too often, he was visiting the outhouse when he ought to have been keeping people like Willy Beck from interfering with the work of the court. Judge Parker was the court, and he suffered plenty of fools in the course of his work. But he did not suffer them gladly, and Willy Beck was no exception.

"What?" Willy asked, when the Judge made the inquiry about Polly.

"Was your sister a pure woman?" the Judge asked, again.

"Of course she was pure—she was my sister," Willy replied. "Zeke Proctor had no business going over to the mill bothering her. He was fair warned."

"Pure women don't let rascals bother them—I'd like to see some scoundrel try and bother *my* wife," the Judge said. "If there's botherment to a level that the wife can't handle, then it's the husband's place to chastise whoever it is that's doing the bothering. It ain't the court's place. You couldn't recruit enough marshals between here and Memphis to hold down that kind of botherment."

"But there was a killing!" Willy Beck insisted.

"Yes—a woman—your sister," the Judge replied, just as Chilly walked in the door. Chilly was shivering, although it was a warm day: thus his nickname.

"I'll take it under advisement. Now get this man out of here, Chilly," the Judge ordered. "I have several warrants to issue."

"Then issue one for Zeke Proctor, while you're issuing!" Willy Beck retorted. Judge Isaac Parker was proving a big disappointment. He was supposed to be the hanging judge, but he did not seem very interested in the fact that a murder had been committed, or convinced that Zeke Proctor needed hanging.

"Not today, sir, don't forget to clean out your ears when you get home," the Judge said. "You may experience deafness later in life if you don't swab the wax out once in a while."

Chilly was skinny but tall. The height was an advantage when it came to ushering folks out of the Judge's chambers before they had finished having their say. Few people ever got out their say with Judge Parker.

"That's what court's for, Chilly," Judge Parker frequently informed him. "If I let them have their say before the trial, what it generally means is that I have to listen to a bunch of lies twice."

"They ain't supposed to lie when the court's in session, they're under oath," Chilly reminded the Judge.

"Dogs ain't supposed to suck eggs, either, but they do," Judge Parker replied.

15

CHILLY STUFFLEBEAN, TWENTY-FOUR YEARS OLD, DID NOT intend to be a bailiff all his life.

He wanted to be a judge like his idol, Isaac Parker. The Judge had given him an old book of statutes, which he kept under his bailiff's chair, to pore over in idle moments. Chilly had been told by a local doctor that he had insufficient blood in his body, the result being that he was skinny and much prone to the shivers. He kept a blanket draped over his chair to wrap up in. The old courthouse in Fort Smith was cold and dank, but it was Chilly's home. Both his parents had died of lung infections when he was eleven, at which age Judge Parker took him in to do the sweeping and empty the spittoons.

Chilly slept on a bench in the courtroom, wrapped in his blanket. Out the window, he could see the Arkansas River; sometimes the moon shone on the water, but more often the river would be wrapped in mist.

Chilly loved the river. When his father was alive, they had a small boat to fish from, and Chilly liked to sit in the boat and watch the creatures of the river. He tried to imagine what it would be like to have a life beneath the water, as turtles did, and muskrats and snakes and fish. His father, Logan Stufflebean, had been a fine fisherman. Once he had hooked a catfish that weighed over one hundred pounds—they hung it up and weighed it on a scale at the hardware store.

Chilly had cared deeply for his father. Sometimes, Chilly dreamed that his father was still alive. When the dream ended and he had to face the fact that his father was dead, the disappointment was so keen that he wiped tears off his cheeks.

The thing Chilly liked to think about most was the law, a force he only dimly understood. The law did not exist in any one place or any one time, like the catfish his father had caught, or the mist that lay on the Arkansas River in the mornings. Judge Parker had nearly fifty books in his chambers, all of them crammed with law. The courthouse where Chilly worked and lived had been built because of the law. Judge Parker, the man he looked up to most, worked day and night, year in and year out, seeing that the law got enforced among the people. The law was everywhere, like air, but on court days it collected itself inside the courthouse, as mist collected itself on the surface of the river.

Since Chilly lived in the courthouse and had for many years, he had come to feel that the Fort Smith courthouse was where most of the law belonged. He knew there were other courts—Indian courts, for example—but he could not imagine that there could be much better law than they had in Fort Smith, or a better judge than *the* Judge: Isaac Parker.

Thus, he was a little puzzled that the Judge had seemed reluctant to send marshals up to Tahlequah to bring back Zeke Proctor. Chilly had seen Zeke Proctor twice, both times when Zeke was riding in horseraces. Zeke was a fine rider, and had won both races, but that did not excuse him from the strictures of the law. If he shot a woman, he needed to face Judge Parker and make his case. Chilly, who ushered people in and out of the Judge's chambers every day, resented the fact that people referred to Judge Parker as the hanging judge. It was most unfair, in Chilly's view: the Judge had tried hundreds of men, and only hung seventy. If people could see the riffraff that came in and out of the courthouse, day after day, they would realize Judge Parker was actually picky about whom he chose to hang.

Judge Parker liked to whittle, and kept a sharp pocketknife on his desk, just for that purpose. Part of Chilly's job was to sweep up the shavings the Judge would have under his chair at the end of the day, willow shavings, mostly. Judge Parker preferred to whittle willow sticks. He liked the way willow wood smelled, and kept a good supply of whittling sticks in his desk drawer.

In his eagerness to understand the law, Chilly would sometimes venture to ask the Judge a few questions, if the Judge had time and seemed receptive to inquiry. After ushering Willy Beck to the street, Chilly went back to the Judge's chambers to see if there were errands that needed running. The Judge, who used no tobacco, was peeling a willow stick the way a cook peels a potato.

"Are the Becks gone?" the Judge asked.

"No," Chilly replied. "They're just standing outside the

courthouse. I expect they're hopin' you'll change your mind and send a marshal off after Zeke."

Judge Parker kept on peeling. "I can't change my mind because I haven't made it up yet," he said. "You can't pay attention to family sentiment when you're doing this job, Chilly."

"No sir," Chilly agreed. In his experience, families were the most troublesome part of law work. Mainly it was wives, thinking up reasons why their husbands should be let out of jail. But if it was not wives, it was mothers—and if it was not mothers, it was apt to be brothers. Nobody wanted to admit they had plain, simple criminals in their families. Chilly supposed he would have been the same way, if he had been lucky enough to have a family. He did hope someday to have a wife, but at present it was only a remote dream, more remote, almost, than his dream of being a judge. There were no schools handy where he might learn judging, and no women who had shown the least bit of interest in being his wife. Chilly cast fond glances at a girl named June Lawton, whose father was a preacher, but so far June had not cast many fond glances back. As far as Chilly could predict, he was very apt to go through life being a bailiff. At least he had a solid bench to sleep on at night.

The Judge had peeled his willow stick. The peeling bark hung in one long curl, and then dropped to the floor.

"What families want is vengeance," the Judge told him. "But I'm not in the vengeance business."

"No sir," Chilly said, again.

"If you were the judge, what would you do in this case, Chilly?" the Judge asked. It amused him at times to test his bailiff's reasoning powers by demanding that he play judge for a little while.

"Well, I don't know the facts," Chilly answered. Having to play judge for the Judge made him mighty nervous. If he slipped up in his judgment, the Judge might think less of him, which would be a thing hard to endure. Judge Parker was the one person he had to look up to—he did not want to lose the Judge's good opinion of him.

"The facts are few, which is lucky," Judge Parker said. "I don't like cases where there's a whole passel of facts. Zeke Proctor went up to the Beck mill one day and shot Polly Beck dead. What I have heard is that T. Spade Beck, who runs the mill, put weevils in Zeke's corn. No sane individual would want weevils in his corn, and so Zeke went up there to kill T. Spade. Evidently, he was a poor shot—he hit the wife instead, and she died on the spot."

The Judge paused. Chilly held steady. There might be more facts to come. He did not want to render a hasty opinion.

"What do you think about the weevils?" the Judge asked.

"If I raised up a corn crop and somebody put weevils in it, I'd be mad, too," Chilly ventured.

"Ruining a man's corn crop is an actionable offense, but it doesn't necessarily call for murder," the Judge commented, in a neutral voice. "Mr. Proctor then went to Tahlequah and turned himself in to Judge B. H. Sixkiller, who is a respected member of the judiciary. I respect him myself. Zeke Proctor admitted the killing, but claims it was an accident, which it probably was. A trial date has been set. They're letting the man keep his dog in jail."

"His dog?" Chilly said. "Why would he need his dog, if he's in jail?"

Judge Parker had begun to whittle on the willow stick. He whittled carefully, but he wasn't trying to whittle the stick into any kind of shape—he was just whittling it away, shaving by fine shaving. He didn't respond to Chilly's question about the dog. From Chilly's point of view, the fact that Judge Parker was aware that Zeke Proctor had his dog in jail was itself a remarkable thing. The Judge spent most of his time in his chambers, speaking to as few people as possible—yet, he knew everything that went on, not only in Fort Smith and eastern Arkansas, but way up into Indian Territory as well.

"Be sound on your facts, Chilly," the Judge had told him many times. "A man who's sound on his facts needn't hesitate in his judgments."

Chilly doubted that he would ever be as sound on his facts, about Zeke Proctor or anything else, as Judge Parker. But the Judge was waiting for him to say something, and he knew he must not hesitate too long.

"I expect it was an accident, Judge," he said. "I doubt Zeke meant to kill the woman."

"Accident or not, she's dead—the question is, should I let Judge Sixkiller try him, or should I attempt to bring him here?"

the Judge asked. "The Becks want him tried in white court, and the Cherokees want to try him themselves."

Chilly did not know what to say. The Indian courts were such a constant problem that Chilly wondered why the government had ever let them be set up. It was obvious to him that their court was as good as anybody could ask for, and Judge Parker the best judge in Arkansas, if not the best judge anywhere. Why would the Cherokees keep wanting to try criminals when Judge Parker was more than willing to take on the task?

"Chilly, answer the question," the Judge said, as he whittled the willow stick into a smooth cylinder of wood. "Should I bring Zeke Proctor here for trial, or should I let Judge Sixkiller handle the matter?"

"It would be good for you to try him, if you've got the time," Chilly replied cautiously.

"You ain't looking at the matter carefully enough," the Judge promptly informed him. "Of course I've got the time— there's always time to hold court. The problem here ain't time —it's money."

"Oh," Chilly said. The Judge was always complaining that the government did not allot him enough money to run his court properly. Chilly himself was only responsible for sweeping and bailiffing and the spittoons. The money was not his province, and he had no idea what sums the Judge had in mind when he complained about the government. He himself was paid $35 a month, plus his bench. In his opinion, he had one of the better jobs available in Fort Smith at the time, and he did not intend to complain, though, of course, the Judge was free to rail against the government if he saw fit.

"This court is broke till next month," the Judge informed him. "It can't afford the kerosene to keep the lanterns burning. If it happened to be a dark day when we tried Zeke, it'd be so dark in the courthouse that we might not even be able to see the rascal. He might slip out a window and be thirty miles away eating catfish before we even noticed he was gone."

Chilly was shocked by that statement. Even if the courtroom was a little dark, he thought he was a good enough bailiff to keep a prisoner from slipping out a window.

"Judge, I'd tackle the man before I'd let that happen," Chilly said.

"Chilly, I was trying to explain to you that this court exists in a state of poverty," the Judge said, slightly annoyed by the protest. "We can't afford kerosene, not till next month, and we also can't afford marshals. The only way I could afford to send a marshal up there to Tahlequah to try and talk Judge Sixkiller out of his prisoner was if there happened to be a marshal fool enough to work for free. And a marshal fool enough to work for free probably couldn't hold his own in a discussion with Judge Sixkiller.

"I have no doubt such a man would come back empty handed," he added, conclusively.

"Oh—I see," Chilly said, confident that he now understood the Judge's position. It was dangerous work, marshaling, particularly if the marshaling involved a foray into the Indian lands. Quite a few marshals fell victim to ambushes, and most of the ambushing was done by whiskeysellers, many of whom were white men—criminals and fugitives—hiding out from the white law. Selling whiskey in the Territory was a serious crime, and a large reward was available to any marshal who brought a whiskeyseller to trial. Several marshals had been tempted by the reward to go up toward the Mountain in search of whiskeysellers. Three or four had come back badly shot up, and an equal number had never come back at all.

"Justice costs money," the Judge said, with a sigh. "If I had unlimited funds to spend on marshals, there wouldn't be a criminal within two hundred miles of here. The fact is, I can't even afford to light the lamps. It's a sad comedown."

"Lucky for Zeke Proctor, though. I guess he'll stay where he is," Chilly said.

"He'll stay where he is. Whether that's lucky is another matter," the Judge said.

"Why? Do you think Judge Sixkiller will let him off?" Chilly asked.

"No, Judge Sixkiller will give him a thorough trial, if it gets to trial," the Judge said.

"Why wouldn't it get to trial?" Chilly asked.

"There's a passel of Becks, and they're all hot," the Judge replied. "The dead woman was a Squirrel on her pa's side, and there's quite a few Squirrels. I expect they're all hot, too."

"You think they'll lynch him?" Chilly asked.

Judge Isaac Parker had finished talking. He kept whittling away on his willow stick.

16

ZEKE HATED CURBS ON HIS FREEDOM, AND JAIL IN TAHLEQUAH was a major curb on his freedom.

Having Zeke there soon proved to be a curb on Sheriff Charley Bobtail's freedom, too. Zeke was a demanding prisoner if there ever was one. Miscreants and felons rarely spent more than a few hours in the Tahlequah jail. Once they sobered up and submitted themselves to Judge Sixkiller in a spirit of humility, the Judge usually let them go, though not without levying a hefty fine.

Throughout the first night and most of the second day, there was general apprehension within the jail. Everybody expected the white marshals to show up and attempt to take Zeke back to Fort Smith. Sheriff Bobtail had strict instructions from the Judge, and the instructions were not to let the marshals have Zeke. Ned Christie stayed the night, sleeping in the Cherokee Senate meeting hall. He missed his young wife Jewel—he dreamed of her soft eyes, and sweet breath—but he felt he ought to stay with Zeke at least one day. After all, he was a senator; perhaps the white marshals would listen to him if they showed up. Most of them had little interest in carting prisoners from one place to another, and Judge Parker was not popular with them because he paid the smallest fee possible for their services and permitted no extravagance. Their real hope in taking assignments to Tahlequah was to catch a whiskeyseller and collect the handsome reward. Two whiskeysellers, if apprehended and convicted, would yield enough reward money to enable a marshal to retire.

When the second day came and went with no marshals, Ned decided the crisis had passed and prepared to go back to his wife. Zeke was annoyed with the whole arrangement. He did not want to be in jail, but if he had to be, he wanted Ned to go and bring him his dog, Pete, for company.

"Pete might still be in that springhouse. If he is, I guess he's living on bugs," Zeke said. He and Ned had been throwing dice all day, to no purpose. Neither of them had any money.

"I imagine Becca let him out," Ned said, keeping his eyes

63

on the dice. He wanted to go home and lay with his wife. He did not want to go all the way to Zeke's place, just to let a dog out of a springhouse.

"He could be a hundred miles away by now," Sheriff Bobtail said.

"Pete? Why would he be a hundred miles away?" Zeke asked, with some indignation. What right did Charley Bobtail have to be making such comments about his dog?

Sheriff Bobtail declined to follow up on his remark. He had meant to go coon hunting that evening, and was annoyed at having to stay in Tahlequah just to hear Zeke Proctor complain. It occurred to him that he might deputize Ned Christie for a few hours, just long enough to get in a good coon hunt. Ned looked restless, though; he might not tolerate being deputized. It was a vexing situation for all concerned and was made more vexing a minute later, when the wild renegade Davie Beck came stomping into the jail.

Davie took little care with his appearance. His shirt was liberally stained with tobacco drippings, and his pants were muddy. He had a long-barreled pistol stuck in his belt.

"I ought to shoot all you fools, and I *will* shoot *you,* you goddamn killer!" he said, glowering at Zeke. "I've taken a solemn vow to avenge Polly, and I'd just as soon do it now."

"I guess you would, since I'm in jail and unarmed," Zeke said. "I suggest you come to my house day after tomorrow, and we'll have at it."

"Now, Dave," Sheriff Bobtail said. "Zeke's in my custody —don't you be threatening him." Unfortunately, the Sheriff was not possessed of a weapon just at the moment. He did not like wearing his pistol, because it interfered with his posture, and he had left his rifle out by the woodpile.

"Shut up, Charley, you ain't even armed," Davie retorted. "I would rather not kill no sheriff, but I will, if I'm interfered with."

Ned Christie stood up and sidled between Davie and Zeke. Davie was the runt of the Becks, and Ned was a good foot and a half taller and considerably better armed. Davie's old pistol had part of the handle wired on.

"This man is a legal prisoner," Ned informed Davie. "Judge Sixkiller put him in jail, and the trial is set. He wants to try a live prisoner, not a dead one."

Davie Beck was prone to animal-like fits when he was enraged. His hair would stand up like a mad coon's, and he would snarl and hiss like a wildcat. In his rage, he would suck in air and swell like a bladder. Now, facing Ned Christie, his eyes got pig red, and he snorted a few times through his thick nose hairs.

"You ought to get back to your goddamn hill, Ned," Davie said. "I will shoot any man that opposes me."

"Get to shootin', then," Ned said, promptly drawing both of his .44s.

Instead of pulling his old pistol with the wired-on handle, Davie gave a snarl and jumped for Ned's throat. Ned whopped him with one of the big .44s right up the side of his head, knocking him into a corner. Davie was up in a flash and came for Ned again, trying to butt him down. Ned sidestepped, and whacked him right across the nose with the same big pistol. Everybody heard the nose crack. Blood came pouring forth, as if someone had just pulled a stopper out of Davie's nostril. He went down again, but managed to lunge from a prone position and sink his teeth into Ned's calf.

"Watch him, Ned, he bites!" Zeke warned, a second too late.

Ned did not need the warning—he knew Davie Beck bit and clawed in his rages, but he had not supposed Davie could recover from two whacks with a .44 pistol quite so swiftly.

Sheriff Charley Bobtail could hardly believe his eyes. Davie Beck was not much more than half Ned Christie's size, and Ned was far better armed—and yet there Davie was, his face and chest smeared with blood, chawing at Ned's leg as if it was a pork chop.

Ned had to whop Davie Beck three more times directly on the head and neck before Davie ceased his biting. Even then, Davie still showed signs of fight. He fumbled for his pistol, but Ned kicked his hand away and took the pistol. To Ned's astonishment, the pistol was not even loaded.

Then Davie got up on his knees and pulled a knife. It was a big clasp knife, which he promptly smeared with blood as he was trying to open the blade. Though his leg pained him, Ned could hardly keep from laughing at Davie Beck's determination to do him violence. Davie stopped trying to open the clasp knife for a moment, and spat out a bloody tooth, one jarred loose by Ned's second blow.

"Watch him now . . . watch him now, he's quick," Zeke warned, from his cell. He felt sure Ned would prevail in the struggle, but there was always a chance Davie would manage some wild move and get through Ned's guard, shoving the big knife into his liver.

If that happened, his own doom would swiftly follow. Charley Bobtail had neglected to arm himself. The bloody Davie Beck would make short work of the Sheriff, who, in Zeke's view, was a slow man in the wrong job.

Ned had no intention of allowing Davie Beck the slightest opening. He squatted down so as to be at Davie's level, and pointed both .44s directly at Davie's bloody head.

"Now, Davie, I want you to scat," he said firmly. "You had no business coming into this jail and misbehaving. Judge Sixkiller has set a trial, and it's less than two weeks away. You and your brothers will just have to wait until the law has had time to proceed."

Davie's hands were so slippery with blood that he failed to get his knife open, and Ned had his unloaded gun with the wired-on handle. He had lost all his bullets in a wager at cards, and had only brought the gun in hopes of bluffing Charley Bobtail. Had he known Ned Christie was there, he would have stopped and borrowed some bullets—but of course, it was too late for that now. Ned had the drop on him, and Ned was known throughout the Territory for the accuracy of his aim.

Besides, his ears were ringing from Ned's blows, and another tooth or two felt like they were working loose. The one thing Davie wanted to avoid was swallowing his own teeth. Swallowed teeth could grow in your stomach and puncture you fatally, his grandmother had told him when he was a child growing up in Mississippi.

He managed, with difficulty, to get to his feet. Ned Christie's eyes had a chill in them. Davie could tell the man would not be loath to shoot him.

"I have got to attend to these teeth," Davie said, once he was up. He started for the door, but turned just before he got to it.

"Goddamn you, Ned," he coughed. The blood had thickened up in his mouth.

"Scat now, I said," Ned repeated. "Just go along, or else die."

"One of these days I'll skin you and peg up your hide," Davie said, spitting out red froth. "That's my solemn vow." Then he left.

Ned holstered his pistols, and looked over at Zeke.

"It's a good thing I stayed, ain't it?" he said.

"Yep," Zeke replied. "I expect I'd be in hell by now, if you hadn't."

17

WHEN DAVIE BECK GOT HOME, THERE WAS SO MUCH BLOOD on his saddle that T. Spade's first thought was somebody had shot his horse.

When Davie dismounted, he did not seem immediately capable of speech. He began to walk around in circles in front of the mill. First one Beck brother, then another, trickled out to observe him. Sam, the eldest Beck, interrupted Davie's circling long enough to determine that he was bleeding from the ear as well as from the nose.

Nosebleeds were a common thing among the six Beck brothers. They frequently inflicted them upon themselves in the course of their many disputes. Frank and Willy, the middle brothers, had scrapped almost from birth and were subject to even more frequent nosebleeds. But it was rare for Davie to receive an injury, either from a brother or from anyone else, the reason being that there was no predicting where a fight with Davie Beck would stop. Once he passed into one of his animal fits, brother or stranger was just as apt to end up dead. The worst thing Davie had on his conscience was the drowning of cousin Simon Beck, which had occurred right after Davie's own wedding to a yellow girl named China Lee. Cousin Simon had kissed the bride a little too enthusiastically for Davie's taste. While the wedding party tippled, Simon and Davie fought their way down a hill, through a thicket, and into a creek. Davie returned to the wedding party not much worse for wear, but cousin Simon never returned. He was found two days later, with a bloody head and his lungs full of creek water.

Davie tried to claim that a Choctaw must have jumped Simon, but no one in the Beck clan believed it. No one inquired closely into the matter, either. Davie did not welcome efforts to corroborate his stories.

Davie was always the victor in his disputes; he did not stop fighting until his opponent was either dead or so damaged that he could not function. Thus, when Davie rode up, his saddle bloody to the stirrups, bleeding not only from the nose but from the ear, the assumption among the Beck brothers was that Zeke Proctor and anyone who might have tried to defend the man must be dead. The thought that someone might have bested Davie in a fight did not occur to any of them.

"So, is the rascal dead, Dave?" T. Spade asked. He knew he should have gone to avenge Polly himself, but he had suffered from an overpowering lethargy since her death and had allocated the matter of revenge to his renegade brother.

"No, but he will be, soon enough," Davie muttered. It galled him to admit failure. Bitterness at Ned Christie flooded his heart.

The news took the assembled Becks aback. It was unthinkable that Zeke alone could have bested Davie—so, what was the story?

"Well, why ain't he dead?" Frank Beck managed to inquire. He was normally fearful of questioning his brother, but in this instance, he was so overwhelmed by curiosity that he could not contain himself.

"Because that goddamn Ned Christie took his part," Davie admitted. "I didn't have no bullets to shoot the son-of-a-bitch with. Lost them at poker over in Dog Town."

"Now that was foolish," T. Spade remarked. "Ned Christie's a dead shot. How did you expect to kill him without bullets?"

"I didn't expect him to be there in the first place," Davie told him. "I expected to get in the cell with Zeke, and cut his damn throat."

"That was rash. How did you expect to get in the dern cell?" Willy asked.

"I meant to ask Charley Bobtail for the keys and if he wouldn't give 'em to me, I would have cut his goddamn throat first," Davie said. "But Ned was there with two pistols and a rifle, and he wouldn't back down. He thumped me on the head with them dern big forty-fours until I lost my reason."

T. Spade Beck was staggered, though he knew Ned Christie was a formidable man. But Davie had bested formidable men time after time—why had he not bested Ned?

"Didn't you fight back atall?" he asked.

"Bit his leg," Davie said. He was still walking in circles, dabbing at his ear with a piece of rag he found someplace.

"Dern . . . why bite his leg?" Frank Beck inquired. "You could bite his leg till it thunders, and the man could still slap you with them big pistols, or anything else that might be handy."

Willy was the thoughtful Beck. His brothers all tended to act first, and think later, if at all—but Willy had small belief in taking action without thinking about it for a few minutes first. What he had to think about now was the fact that Ned Christie, the best shot in the District, had allied himself with the murderer Zeke Proctor. It was an unexpected turn of events, made more ominous by the fact that Ned had managed to best Davie in a direct encounter, something that no one else had ever done—and had suffered only a minor injury in the process, to boot.

"We might have to kill Ned. I don't know why he interfered," Willy said.

"Well, they're Cherokees, Willy. Besides, that girl of Zeke's married him," T. Spade reflected. Since Polly's death, he had stopped trimming his beard, which was long and dank from tobacco spittings.

"That's it," Frank concluded. "Ned married Zeke's girl. That makes him and Zeke in-laws."

Sam, the silent Beck, was so moved by the spectacle of his blood-soaked brother, that he ventured an opinion, too.

"It's more than the girl," he said. "They ain't just Cherokees—they're Keetoowahs. They speak in signs to one another and such. They believe in them Little People, and witches and spells. I expect they made some Indian medicine, which is why Davie couldn't whip Ned."

"I shouldn't have gambled my bullets," Davie reflected. The fact was, once in a card game, he would gamble anything he had. The power to stop was not in him. More than once he had come home barefooted and beltless on muddy nights because he had gambled his boots and belt.

"It's probably all that saved you," Willy said. "I wouldn't be shooting at Ned Christie—not me. If you'd had bullets, I expect that old pistol of yours would have misfired and he might have shot you dead."

Stung by this criticism, Davie whirled into another animal fit, though a short one. He jumped at Willy and pounded him to his knees. Before Willy could catch his breath, Davie kicked him in the pit of the stomach. When Willy fell over gasping, Davie jumped on his head with both feet and tried to mash his teeth down his throat. He wanted Willy to swallow a few teeth, that might then grow in his stomach and puncture him. It would mean an agonizing death, just the kind he wanted his mouthy brother to die.

Nobody pulled Davie off. When Willy was unconscious, Sam Beck rendered his conclusions.

"Willy ought to know better," he offered.

"What ought we to do, T.?" Frank Beck wondered.

T. Spade dribbled more tobacco spittings into his beard.

"I expected Judge Parker to send the marshals after Zeke," he said.

"Well, he won't, the old bastard," Sam said.

"We could hire a marshal or two ourselves, then," T. Spade observed. "Billy Yopps might need the work."

Davie Beck had stopped walking in circles. Stomping his brother Willy had restored his good humour, to some extent, and he was feeling a little better. For a moment, he was tempted to shoot *all* his brothers—they were a vexing lot. But he had no bullets, and it would be a chore to borrow enough to wipe out the vexing Becks. He went over and kicked at Willy a time or two more, for good measure. Willy groaned, and then proceeded to roll partway down the slope behind the mill.

"The trial day is in about a week," Davie said. "I mean to go to the courthouse and kill every single person that's on Zeke's side."

"Davie, couldn't we hire a marshal or two to help?" T. Spade asked. "It'd seem more legal, that way."

What was legal did not interest Davie Beck in the slightest. While his brothers were trying to revive Willy, he stumbled over to the springhouse and held his head in the cold springwater until the blood stopped dripping out his ear.

18

NED STAYED TWO DAYS IN THE TAHLEQUAH JAIL, WAITING FOR the Becks to come back in force and try to take Zeke.

Zeke was in a low mood, and spoke little. When he did speak, it was to complain about Judge B. H. Sixkiller and his arbitrary ways. The Judge had led him to believe that he would be released and allowed to go home, once the threat of white marshals had passed. Then the threat did pass, but the Judge unaccountably lagged about the release order.

Zeke pestered Sheriff Bobtail unmercifully. Several times a day, Charley Bobtail had to chase all the way across the street to the courthouse to see if Judge Sixkiller had changed his mind back so that Zeke could go home.

The news of Davie Beck's fit soon spread far and wide. The common opinion was that both Zeke and Ned were dead men. All the Becks were vengeful, but Davie Beck was vengeful far beyond the norm. Men who had done Davie Beck the most trifling slight months or even years before still slept with two or three guns at the ready in case Davie, bent on vengeance, showed up. Sooner or later, he always showed up, generally with a club in his hand. Given a choice, Davie Beck would usually choose to beat on people. The knife and the bullet were too gentle, in his view.

The only person in Tahlequah who was not apprehensive about Davie was Ned Christie. He considered himself a match for Davie, no matter when he came or what he chose to arm himself with. Ned spent most of his days playing Chinese checkers with Zeke—it was one of Zeke's favourite games. Every time Ned would decide to go outside and stretch his legs, Zeke would demand one more game, and Ned usually gave in. He usually won, too. Zeke had watery vision up close and as a result was not very good at Chinese checkers.

On the afternoon of the third day, Tuxie Miller came to pay Zeke a visit and was immediately sent to the Proctor home to fetch Pete. News had come that Pete was poorly. The dog was so upset by his master's absence that he would take no food.

"Go get him for me, Tuxie, he's pining away," Zeke said.

He had said the same thing to Ned several times, but Ned turned a deaf ear. He was not going to put Zeke at risk by going to fetch his dog.

"I expect he'll eat when he gets hungry enough," Ned said.

"I doubt it," Zeke said, gloomily. "He's a one-man dog, and I'm the man. I expect he'll just die."

Tuxie had a soft spot for Pete. The little black dog's ferocity amused him.

"I doubt Pete knows how big he is," he said, several times. "He may think he's as big as a bear."

"No, he don't know how big he *isn't*," Ned corrected. His view was that Pete was a noisy little nuisance. He was beginning to be lonesome for Jewel, and he wanted to kiss her—badly. He could not keep his mind on Zeke's dog.

"Go get him, Tuxie," Zeke said, again. "Davie Beck might go take vengeance on him. He will, if the thought crosses his mind."

So Tuxie went. He was hoping Becca might make him up some taters and cornbread, but all he got when he arrived at the Proctor house was a little gravy and some salt pork—plus a lot of slobbering from Pete.

"I want my husband home. I want to know about that woman," Becca said to Tuxie.

"Why, Ma? She's dead. I'd just let it be," Liza said. She was trying to make Tuxie stay the night, but with no better grub at hand than gravy and salt pork, he declined.

"You ain't me," Becca replied, to Liza. Becca sat at the table pulling grey hairs out of her head.

Watching a sickly woman pull grey hairs out of her head took the edge off Tuxie's appetite. Dale, his wife, was secretive about all things involving her womanly appearance. Only once or twice had he glimpsed her attending to her hair, or any other part of her person. She had made it clear early on that she was a modest woman who expected to have her modesty respected. She wore thick cotton gowns and knee stockings to bed every night, no matter how sultry it happened to be.

"I've known men to get in trouble from too much looking at females," she informed Tuxie, on more than one occasion.

"I'm already in trouble. I'm married to you," Tuxie said meekly, when the subject of male and female came up.

"That's not trouble. That's your salvation," Dale informed

him crisply. "You'd be a rolling-down-the-hill drunk if you didn't have me to keep you on the straight and narrow."

Liza hated to see Tuxie go. With her pa in jail, things were so dull around the house that any company would have been welcome, though she particularly enjoyed having Tuxie around, even when her pa was at home. Liza decided she would make an effort to marry Tuxie, in the event his scrappy wife Dale should happen to die.

Becca Proctor watched Tuxie ride off with Pete, feeling bitterness in her heart—not toward Tuxie, but toward Zeke, her husband. She loved Zeke; she knew she would always love him, but she could not excuse his behaviour. He had sent a friend fourteen miles to fetch his dog, but had sent her no message. Was his dog more important to him than his wife?

More importantly, there was the matter of the woman he had killed. The killing was surely an accident, for Zeke was not a violent man. In their years together, he had never hit her, though he had cursed her several times. She herself was more prone to hitting when her temper was up than Zeke had ever been.

What also bothered her was that he had gone to where the woman lived. Maybe he had gone meaning to kill the woman's husband for some reason—or, maybe there was more to it than that. Maybe he had been slipping out with the woman.

With Zeke gone, Becca had plenty of time to think, and some of her thoughts were painful. She recalled that, more than once in recent months, Zeke had casually talked about the fact that in Cherokee society it was appropriate for a man to have more than one wife. Both times, Zeke had made the remarks while they were in bed. He had his eyes half shut at such times, but he was not asleep. Maybe he had been feeling her out; maybe he had meant to bring the Beck woman home as a second wife.

Becca had not responded when Zeke made his remarks about more than one wife. Her grandfather on her father's side had kept two wives, but that was in the Old Nation, many years ago. Zeke knew well enough that Becca had been raised Christian, her father being a Baptist preacher and all. He must have known she married him intending to be his only wife.

Probably the woman had been younger than Becca, and prettier. No doubt the woman had encouraged his rutting.

Becca had been too poorly to do much more than accept it, since the triplets were born. The thought grew in her that Zeke had meant to bring the woman home to her house—a younger woman, with a harlot's ways.

With that thought came anger, and Becca began to pace the floor. Liza saw the change in her mother, and kept out of her way.

It was a long walk to Tahlequah, but Becca thought she might have to make it. She was Zeke Proctor's wife, and she wanted answers to the questions that were rising up in her. Zeke had sent for his dog, and not for her, but he might get more than he bargained for, on a day when she felt up to the walk to Tahlequah and the jail.

Tuxie tried to carry Pete in front of his saddle the way Zeke did, but Pete was too full of beans. Twice he jumped off to chase after squirrels; once he ran right along the horse's neck and jumped off his head, which the horse failed to appreciate.

"If you're so dern full of beans, you can just trot along behind," Tuxie informed the frisky dog.

In the jail, Pete jumped up in Zeke's face, licking him and slobbering on him a while. Then he put an end to the jail's one amusement by swallowing four or five marbles right off the Chinese checkerboard. Not all of the marbles went easily down Pete's throat—he ran around in circles trying to wheeze them back up and then he collapsed, rolling on his back with his tongue lolled out and his legs kicking. Zeke got shaky. Here he had just got his dog back, and now the dog was choking to death on a bunch of marbles.

"Spit 'em up, Pete!" he yelled.

"Grab him, Ned!" Tuxie said.

"Grab him, Sheriff!" Zeke said, throwing Sheriff Bobtail a look of desperation.

"Why would a dog eat marbles?" Sheriff Bobtail asked. "They'd make poor grub, even if a fellow was hungry."

"He ain't a man, he's a dog, you fool!" Zeke said. Pete was rolling around with his tongue all the way out of his head, right in front of him, and he himself felt paralyzed. Somebody else would have to save Pete, if he was to be saved.

Ned thought the marbles would finally go down, though it was true Pete was struggling ever more weakly. He picked Pete up by the tail and pounded him a few times across the back.

Sure enough, two marbles dropped out. When Ned sat him back down, Pete coughed and staggered for a bit, but then he turned back into his old self and began to snarl at Sheriff Bobtail, who was annoyed at the dog's bad manners.

"It's against the rules to have dogs in jail," he suddenly remembered.

Zeke ignored this comment. Pete jumped up in his lap and growled at the Sheriff, who decided it might be best to let the matter drop. Old Mandy Springston had been pressed into service to cook for the prisoner, but her grub was so terrible only a starving man could have forced much of it down. With Pete in jail, there would be somebody to clean up the leavings.

When it came time for Tuxie to start home, Ned decided he would go along, too.

Zeke did not protest. He knew Ned had marital responsibilities. Besides, Sheriff Bobtail had agreed to let him keep his guns in the cell, in case Davie Beck showed up again. Even a prisoner in jail had a right to defend himself.

"I'll be at the trial, Zeke," Ned assured him. Zeke just waved. He looked a lot more cheerful, now that he had Pete for company.

"Say howdy to Jewel," he said, as Ned left.

It began to cloud up toward the west, as Ned and Tuxie rode home. It quickly came up a monsoon, rainwater dripping off the leaves.

"I miss Jewel. I guess I was needing to be married," Ned said, as they rode along.

"I expect so," Tuxie allowed.

"Do you miss Dale?" Ned asked, annoyed that it was so hard to get Tuxie to make conversation when it rained.

"Miss Dale? Why would I?" Tuxie asked. "Dale ain't gone."

"I mean if you're away overnight," Ned said. "Don't you miss her when it's bedtime?"

Tuxie thought of Dale for a moment, in her heavy gown and woolly knee stockings. Even at night, Dale insisted on her way. Still, he was loath to say anything unkind about his wife to their neighbour Ned Christie.

"It's seldom I stay out overnight," he answered, finally. "I guess I might miss her, though, if it was a long night."

Tuxie rode on a little ways, thinking about how it would be

to miss Dale. But the fact was, Dale was always there—he had no idea how it would feel to miss her, because she was never gone.

Later still, when they were at the foot of the Mountain, Tuxie began to feel that he might have inadvertently slighted his wife, by being wavery about whether he would miss her or not.

"If it was two or three nights, I'd miss Dale bad," he said.

Ned Christie was not paying Tuxie any attention. He had begun to think of Jewel. In two hours, he would be holding her in his arms. He remembered that she was young; he remembered her fearful look, as he and Zeke were riding away. Suddenly, a wave of remorse swept over him. Why had he left his young wife, just to ride Zeke Proctor to jail? Zeke was a grown man. True, they were Keetoowah brothers—but that hardly meant he had to leave his sweet wife unprotected on Zeke's account.

He had lost interest in the question of Tuxie and Dale. He had little concern whether Tuxie missed Dale or not. He wanted to get home to Jewel and lay in her smooth arms. The first thing he meant to tell her was that he would not leave her again.

It began to rain harder as they made their way up the Mountain. Soon, the horses were slipping and sliding in the thick red mud.

19

JUDGE ISAAC PARKER AND JUDGE B. H. SIXKILLER HAD ONE thing in common: they both hated expense—neither man believed in using two stamps when one would do.

Judge Sixkiller had been in Fort Smith buying a pump, when Judge Parker walked into the hardware store looking for a good axe. While he was chopping firewood that morning, the head of the axe had flown off and struck his milk cow. The milk cow had not been seriously injured, but Judge Parker considered it a close call—jersey milk cows were not easy to come by in Fort Smith. He could not afford to jeopardize the one he had, a family favourite named Belle Starr, after the notorious female bandit.

The two judges met at the cash register. Judge Sixkiller, recognizing Judge Parker from pictures in the newspaper, quickly introduced himself.

"Good Lord," Judge Parker said. "How are you, sir? I never expected this pleasure."

"Neither did I, Your Honour," Judge Sixkiller replied.

"You're the very man I need to speak to," Judge Parker said. "Providence must have sent you."

"No—it was my wife," Judge Sixkiller informed him. "The pump broke, and she says she can't tolerate being without one."

"Is that rascal Zeke Proctor still in your jail?" Judge Parker asked.

"He's in a cell in the Tahlequah jail, yes," Judge Sixkiller assured him.

"Well guarded, I expect?" Judge Parker inquired.

"No, poorly guarded," Judge Sixkiller admitted. "Sheriff Bobtail would be hard put to guard a stump—if it grew fast, it might escape him."

"They're an affliction, sheriffs," Judge Parker agreed. "Several I've known have been too dumb to count up money. Do you think your prisoner will survive until the day of trial?"

"It depends on the Becks," Judge Sixkiller observed. "Davie Beck come for Zeke once already, but a friend of Proctor's named Ned Christie happened to be there at the time. Ned stood off Davie Beck. There's not many a man could do that."

"Let's walk along to the back," Judge Parker said, taking Judge Sixkiller by the arm. He had become uncomfortably aware that the customers were staring at them. He could hardly blame them, of course. It was not often that a white judge and a Cherokee judge could be found passing the time of day in a hardware store.

Judge Sixkiller, too, had become a little nervous. If news got back to Tahlequah that he was friendly with Judge Parker, his own fate would be as uncertain as Zeke Proctor's. Not a few Cherokees had climbed Judge Parker's gallows and dangled from his noose. Most of them had been renegades who would have been hung sooner or later, but not all their relatives had accepted Judge Parker's verdicts. Friends of Judge Isaac Parker would not be likely to last long, in the Going Snake District.

Nonetheless, Judge Sixkiller followed Judge Parker to the back of the store. He was hungry for some judge talk, and so was Isaac Parker. The men found two nail kegs behind a pile of harnesses. The kegs made ideal seats, and the hanging harnesses a nice barrier. They could talk without having to bear much public scrutiny.

"I expected you to send a marshal and relieve me of my prisoner," Judge Sixkiller said, once they were settled. Judge Parker lit a stub of a cigar, which he had extracted from his coat pocket. Judge Sixkiller preferred chewing. He sat close enough to the back door so that he could spit off the porch, there being no spittoon nearby.

"No, I can't afford to waste a marshal on adulterous killings," Judge Parker said. "The truth is, I can't afford marshals, period. When I do get the funds to hire one for a few days, I try to point them at the whiskeysellers."

"I believe you have a bailiff, though," Judge Sixkiller said. "I am forced to conduct court without a bailiff, unless I can find a volunteer."

"Yes, I have Chilly Stufflebean," Judge Parker told him. "He has lived in our courthouse since he was a boy. Maybe I ought to loan him to you for the Proctor trial. I expect you'll have an unruly audience. It's hard to keep track of the evidence and the statutes if you don't have a bailiff to shush the crowd."

"I'd be grateful, sir—real grateful," Judge Sixkiller said at once. "I'll have to disarm the crowd at a trial like this. Your man could help stack the guns."

"Then I'll send him," Judge Parker said. "With the court low on money, there's not much for Chilly to do. He has not traveled that I know of. It would do him good to see a little of the world."

The judges chatted for a few more minutes, hidden by the curtain of harnesses. Funds, or the absence of them, came up several times in the conversation. If the two judges saw eye to eye on one thing, it was that the judiciary was seriously underfunded.

"The fools call me the hanging judge, but three new hang ropes came the other day, and I didn't have the funds to pay for 'em. I sent 'em back," Judge Parker confessed. "Now that's a scandal when a court can't even afford ropes to hang low renegades."

"I can barely afford the ink it takes to write up the verdicts," Judge Sixkiller told him, not to be outdone.

After a little more commiseration and a friendly handshake, Judge Sixkiller rode off toward Tahlequah with the pump strapped behind his saddle.

Judge Parker watched him go, before bargaining for another cigar. He could afford three cigars a week, but only because he struck a hard bargain.

Chilly Stufflebean was taking a short nap on his bench when the Judge walked in and informed him that he had been loaned out to Judge Sixkiller as bailiff for the Proctor trial.

"All that way?" Chilly asked. He had rarely left the precincts of Fort Smith. A journey to the Cherokee country seemed a frightening prospect.

"What if I get lost?" he asked, nervous at the thought of having to journey so far.

"Why, you won't get lost, Chilly—there's a road," Judge Parker said.

20

WHEN BECCA WALKED INTO THE TAHLEQUAH JAIL, ZEKE WAS nonplussed. It was the last thing he would have expected.

Becca rarely traveled, except by foot. As a girl, she had taken a bad fright, once; some mules ran off with a wagon her folks had left her in, and a wild, one-horned cow charged the mules and spooked them. Becca had not been hurt in the runaway, but as a result developed a fear of animal locomotion which had proven lifelong. If Becca Proctor needed to go somewhere, she walked.

"Why, Bec . . . what have you got?" Zeke asked, when Becca walked in. She wore a thin shawl, and carried a small hamper. Zeke's immediate thought was that there might be a gun in the hamper. He had stopped worrying about the Becks walking into the jail and shooting him. The Becks were biding their time. They had been biding their time ever since Ned Christie had turned back Davie Beck's recent charge.

Now here stood Becca, with a hamper over her arm. She might have got tired of being without a man. If she had a gun, she probably wanted him to take it and break jail. Becca had never been content with his strayings, which were frequent, though mostly just to horseraces, or the gambling halls of Dog Town or Stinking Water.

The trouble was, Becca Proctor had fury in her. It slumbered deep beneath her smoky grey eyes and rarely came up. But when her fury did come up, Becca struck like a snake, snarled like a she-panther, bit like a frothing sow. Once, she had got her teeth in Zeke's ear—they were in the barn at the time—and he yelled so loud the milk cow jumped the fence and left. Another time, Becca had raked at his eyes with her fingernails and only just missed scratching one of them out. He still had a diagonal scar across his eyelid from that scrape.

Now Becca was in the Tahlequah jail, having walked fourteen miles on a chill day, carrying a hamper over her arm. When Zeke had last seen her, she had been feeling particularly off-colour, but she did not look off-colour now. She had been propelled to walk fourteen miles by one of two things—loneliness or anger—and Zeke was fairly certain it was not loneliness. Either she meant to free him or she meant to kill him, Zeke could not immediately guess which. Sheriff Bobtail had wandered off to the store to buy fishhooks. He planned to get in a day of fishing before the big trial, which was in three days. The Sheriff would be no help if Becca was bent on vengeance, and neither would Pete, who was snoring under a bench.

Pete had adapted well to jail life. Now and again, he even caught a rat, but Zeke had no time to worry about Pete's rat catching, with Becca standing there. She walked over to the cell, and looked him up and down.

"You're skinny looking, don't they feed you?" she asked.

"Old Mandy does the jail cooking," Zeke informed her. Her remark had been made in a neutral tone, and so Zeke could not get a sense of how things lay with her. For the time being, he thought best to keep to the back of the cell.

Becca came closer. She put her hand in the hamper, and came out with a Bible. She looked at him a moment, and thrust it through the bars of the cell.

"I brought you this, Zeke," she said. "You need to read it. There's things in it about how a husband should treat a wife. I marked the place where it says it."

Zeke felt let down. He had primed himself for escape or

murder, and now Becca was holding out a Bible. It irritated him that the woman would suppose he did not know how to treat a wife. After all, they'd been together now for seventeen years. He knew very well how to treat a wife. If she wanted to walk fourteen miles and risk the rain, she would have done better to bring him grub.

"I will take this Bible, but I would rather have had a pork chop," he told her, taking the big book.

Becca just looked at him.

"I won't be cooking no pork chops for you until I know about that woman you shot," she said. "If you was slipping out with her, I want to know it."

Zeke was startled by the audacity of the question. Here the woman had walked fourteen miles in the rain, just to ask him if he had been slipping out.

"The Bible says not to traffic with harlots," Becca said. "I won't be a wife to a man who does. I don't care if the whore is dead."

"Becca, I'm here trying not to get hung or shot up by the Becks," Zeke informed her. "This is a matter we can talk about if I live."

"We can talk about it right now, I reckon," Becca said. "You ride off one day without a by-your-leave, and the next thing I know you've kilt a woman. I'm your wife. I want to know about it."

Zeke felt rattled. Charley Bobtail had deserted his post, otherwise Becca would not be able to stand there bringing up uncomfortable matters. She would not bring them up in front of a sheriff, but where was the Sheriff when his prisoner needed protecting?

When he tried to think how to answer what she was asking, he felt a confusion spreading in his mind, like milk spilt on a table. The whole business of Sully and the cornmeal and the weevils and the yearling bear all seemed as if they had happened to someone else—some friend of his, or a cousin, or a kinsman, or somebody he had been traveling with. He could barely remember sneaking up to the Beck mill with his three guns, nor could he get Polly Beck to stand up clear in his mind's eye. He remembered he had been meaning to take Polly home and have her for a second wife, but he no longer clearly remembered what had led up to his decision. It had all happened in another time; or, it had been a dream he was somehow unable to awaken from.

"Bec, it was an accident that I killed the woman," he said, finally. "I went to kill T. Spade because of the matter of the weevils. The woman got in the way of my shot, and it killed her. It was a plain accident . . . that's why I give myself up for trial."

"It ain't the killing I need to know about," Becca said. "It's what went on between you and her *before* the killing."

Becca paused, and looked at Zeke carefully. He looked miserable as a wet dog on a cold day. Zeke had never liked having his actions questioned, or examined in any way. If he came home with a bloody nose, or a tooth knocked loose, or a scrape on his knuckles, he welcomed no commentary or inquiry. If she asked him how he skinned his hand, he would swell up and sulk for hours—yet, she *always* asked him. She did not consider herself hard to get along with, particularly, but she had no intention of living with a man she could not question, if questions plainly suggested themselves. Now he had killed a woman, and she meant to know what lay behind it. She did not accept the weevil explanation.

Zeke hesitated, running over in his mind what he could remember, and what he wanted to talk about. The thing he remembered most clearly was the yearling bear. Though the bear had jumped out of the fog, he remembered that it had a little white spot on its muzzle. His main wish was that he could start life over just before he jumped the bear. He had gone into that fog a free man, and had come out of it a prisoner of actions he had never intended.

The last thing he needed was for Becca to be asking him questions about his relations with a dead woman. He could barely remember the relations—everything that had happened since came to overshadow any prior relations with Polly Beck.

"I was brought up to think it proper for a man to take more than one wife," Zeke said, finally. "In the Old Nation, it was the common thing."

Becca's grey eyes narrowed and darkened.

"You meant to force her on me, then," she said, after a moment.

"It's right in this Bible, somewhere," Zeke replied. "The patriarchs in olden times had more than one wife. I've heard preachers say it. In the Old Place, men could take more than one wife."

"You're a hypocrite, Zeke. Don't be talking to me of preachers, and don't be talking to me about the Old Place. If it was olden times, I could send you packing with nothing but the clothes on your back," Becca told him. "You meant to bring that harlot home with you, didn't you? You would have forced her on me—wouldn't you?"

His look was a look of guilt, Becca realized: he had whored with the woman until he decided to marry her, in order to whore with her more. The killing was an accident, she believed that part. But it was not the killing she was concerned about right this moment.

"If you want things to be like olden times, then you can pretend you don't have a wife and a family, because now you don't," Becca informed him. "I'm going back to my people, Zeke—and I'm taking the children with me. I won't live with a man that would force a harlot on me."

As a Keetoowah brother, Zeke had taken a vow to uphold the old ways of his people. Cherokee families had been mother-led clans; when a Cherokee man married, he joined his wife's family. If a Cherokee wife wanted to divorce her husband, all she had to do was pack his things and put them outside the door, since the marriage property and the children belonged to her. These were all things Zeke knew; in his heat over Polly Beck, he had somehow managed to put them out of his mind. Now here was his wife, telling him that if he wanted to live by the old ways, he had to live by *all* of them. It was a damn nuisance!

Zeke knew he better come up with a good reason for Becca to stay, and quick.

"But what about the stock?" Zeke blurted. "Charley Bobtail won't let me out, and the stock will run wild."

From the look on Becca's face, the reason he had chosen for her to stay was not convincing. In fact, it made her eyes darken even more.

"Sully can tend to the stock," Becca said. Her voice was low.

She turned to leave, but then looked back once more at the man who had been her husband for seventeen years. Her face looked like death.

"I won't be a wife to you no more, Zeke Proctor—this is the end of it," she said.

Zeke tried to think of another argument that would make her change her mind. But he could not come up with one—his mind had gone blank.

Becca waited for a comment, but she saw that Zeke was stumped.

"Good-bye, Zeke," she said. "I wish you success at your trial."

Then she left.

Zeke sat down on the hard bunk where he slept. Pete woke up and jumped in his lap, hoping his master would scratch him under the chin. But Zeke was too low to feel like scratching Pete's neck. Sully Eagle was no hand with livestock; half the cows would soon get loose from him, and go wild. The more he thought about the situation, the lower his spirits sank.

He felt a pain starting, deep in his rib cage.

He knew he'd be lucky to have a cow left, by the time he got out of the jail.

21

FOUR OF THE BECKS—WILLY, FRANK, SAM, AND T. SPADE— decided to make a trip to Fort Smith to see if they could bribe a marshal.

Judge Isaac Parker had been a terrible disappointment. With only three days to go until the trial, Zeke Proctor still rested in the Tahlequah jail, eating free food. He even had his dog for a companion. Willy Beck's view was that they needed to bribe a marshal and bribe him quick, else Zeke Proctor would be tried in Cherokee court and no doubt would escape the consequences of his murderous actions.

"We're white—he ought to be tried white," Sam Beck said, more than once. That Sam Beck took it into his head to speak at all was an indication of how serious the matter was. Sam Beck had been known to go as long as two years without saying a word to anyone, unless it was to Dickie, his mule. If he spoke at all, it would usually be to repeat something one of his brothers had just said. Within the family circle, this tendency had earned him the nickname Echo.

Now, though, Sam Beck ceased to be an echo—he was so outraged that Zeke got to keep his dog in jail, he offered to contribute $4 toward bribing the marshal.

On the trip to Fort Smith, Sam harped on the matter of the dog so much that T. Spade finally lost his temper and yelled at his brother.

"Quit your yapping about his damn terrier," he said. "If you want to yap, yap about my wife who got kilt. Now I'll have to go court some hussy I don't even know, or else do my own cooking."

Sam had not considered that aspect of the matter. When the brothers arrived at the mill, T. Spade had been subsisting on a diet of cornbread. Being a miller, he had access to abundant corn. It was obvious, once Sam thought about it, that T. Spade was right: he would have to court up a new wife. A diet of cornbread alone would soon grow boresome.

Davie Beck had been left at home. He was too volatile for the delicate negotiations that might be necessary if a marshal was to be bribed. Since his encounter with Ned Christie, Davie had spent most of his time at a blacksmith shop in Dog Town. His plan was to convert an old saw blade into a knife, so he could rip Ned Christie's guts out the next time he saw him. Davie was no blacksmith, and the work was proceeding slowly. He kept using larger and larger saw blades, in order to insure himself a fatal rip when he went for Ned Christie's guts.

On the way to Fort Smith, the Beck brothers ran into Sully Eagle. Sully was sitting by the road, thinking. When he saw the Beck brothers approaching, he regretted not having chosen another road to think by. They knew he worked for Zeke; he and Zeke were both Cherokee; and the Becks were frustrated men—what if they decided to hang him, to relieve their feelings?

"We're looking for a marshal, have you seen any?" T. Spade asked, looking down at Sully, the latter still in his thinking posture.

It was a well-known fact that Sully Eagle knew the whereabouts of practically everyone in the Going Snake District. If a bribable marshal was handy, it would save them a long trip to Fort Smith.

"Yes, Bill Yopps is in Stinking Water, visiting his ma," Sully said. "He's wounded in the shoulder, though. A whiskeyseller shot him."

"Did Bill kill the whiskeyseller?" Willy inquired.

"No, that whiskeyseller ran off," Sully said, getting to his feet. He was glad Davie Beck was not in the company. Davie Beck did not like him. Of all the people in the Going Snake District, Davie was the hardest to keep up with. Everybody knew him, but nobody could keep track of him. Yesterday, he had been in Dog Town, trying to make a saw into a knife, but today he might be riding the roads, looking for someone to beat with a club. Sully decided to walk down into the woods. He might find a log to sit on, while he thought. With frustrated people like the Becks on the loose, it was not wise to stop and think in plain sight.

"I don't like Bill Yopps, he don't pay his bills," T. Spade informed them. "Is that the only marshal you've seen, Sully?"

"Oh, I ain't seen Bill," Sully said. "The last marshal I seen was Dan Maples, and that was last week. He was north of Tahlequah, tracking a horse thief."

With that, he walked slowly into the woods, in search of a log to sit on. As he was walking, he got an uneasy feeling, uneasy enough that he stopped to look back.

Sure enough—T. Spade Beck was pointing a rifle at him.

Sully got moving, in order to take full advantage of the cover. T. Spade shot three times. One of the bullets clipped a red leaf, right by Sully's head; the other two went wild. Sully hurried on deeper into the trees. When he considered it safe to look back, the Becks were gone.

After such an experience, Sully felt nervous. He decided it was not a good day for reasoned thought. Besides, now that Becca had taken her daughter and the triplets and gone north to her people, there were chores aplenty around the Proctor home—chores aplenty, and nobody but Sully to do them. A bobcat had already got one of Zeke's geese, the turkeys were nervous, and three of the red hens had stopped laying. Sully could hardly wait for the trial to be over, and Zeke to be freed. Zeke needed to get home, and help out with the chores.

"If you needed to shoot at Sully, you should have hit him," Willy Beck complained. "Now he'll tell everybody that we're out gunning for folks. It'll make it a sight harder to hire a marshal."

"I don't recall asking your advice," T. Spade responded. "Sully's the one who told Zeke about the weevils. If that old fool had kept his mouth shut, I wouldn't be having to do my own cooking." In fact, he had not at first intended to shoot at Sully. But then rage flared at the thought of the loss of Polly, and the poor cooking he'd been required to subsist on, and he flashed off the three shots.

"I expect Zeke would have noticed them weevils for himself, T.," Frank Beck said cautiously. "*I'd* notice, if somebody weeviled up my corn."

"You can go home if you intend to yap, Frankie," T. Spade replied. "Let's go hire Bill Yopps—he might be the best we can get."

"But the man's down in the shoulder," Frank Beck said. "Dan Maples is around somewhere, and he's able bodied. I'd rather hire him."

"I'm putting in four dollars," the newly voluble Sam remarked.

"Why, Dan Maples won't bribe—any fool would know that," T. Spade said. "He's only interested in rounding up whiskeysellers. He may *like* Zeke Proctor, for all we know."

"I thought you didn't like Bill Yopps," Frank reminded his brother. "You just said the man didn't pay his bills."

"He don't, but we're in a hurry, that trial's day after tomorrow," T. Spade reminded them. "Stinking Water's a lot closer than Fort Smith—let's go sound him out."

"I'm for it," Willy said. "If the man's only got one arm, maybe he'll cut his price."

"Willy, he's still got two arms hanging on his body," Frank said. "Sully only said he was crippled in the shoulder."

Still, the economic argument had strong appeal to Willy—it always did.

"It won't hurt to ask," he said, as they headed off to corral Bill Yopps.

22

WHEN JEWEL SAW NED CLEANING HIS GUNS, SHE BEGAN TO shake.

Zeke Proctor's trial was the next day, and it meant her husband would be leaving again. Jewel did not know if she could stand it. Ned had been away four nights when he rode with Zeke to Tahlequah to see the Judge. For Jewel, they had been nights of loneliness and fear. The sounds of the woods, sounds she scarcely noticed when she lay warm in Ned's arms, became sounds of danger and menace. Bears, wolves, panthers—all lived on the Mountain. She knew that wolves and panthers were shy and rarely seen, but she had always feared them anyway.

Bears, however, were her prime fear. Her mother had once told her to stick close to the house and lots when she was in her time of the month, for bears could smell the blood. Long ago, during the time of the Trail of Tears, Jewel's old grandmother had known of a woman who was taken by a bear during her time of the month. No one could remember the woman's name. Her grandmother had known the woman, though her name had been forgotten.

Ned laughed, when Jewel spoke to him about her fear of bears. He traded for a good rifle, and gave Jewel a few shooting lessons, but he did not take the talk of bears seriously.

"If a bear shows up, just bang the frying pans together," he said. "Bears don't like loud noise."

"Maybe I ought to have waited till you grew up to have married you," Ned told her, one of the times when she was trying to explain how scared she got when he was away. He tried to make her laugh by saying it, but it only made her more nervous.

Jewel gave up trying to make Ned understand her fear. She knew he would only laugh that much louder if she tried to tell him that the wood sounds—the owls, and coyotes, and other varmints—scared her when he was gone.

Jewel's worst fear went so deep she never talked about it with Ned: that was her fear of men. Her father had told her that bad men sometimes changed themselves into owls, so they could travel under dark cover and commit their evil deeds at night, when no one could see them. Rough men, most of them white men, traveled on the Mountain—whiskeysellers, bandits, men on the run from the law. Some of them knew where Ned lived, and some of them probably knew he had married. They might spy on the two of them; they might know when Ned was away from home. What if they came, in the night? Tuxie Miller's house was three miles away. She could not run for help, if a harmful man showed up. She would have to fight alone. What if two or three whiskeysellers or a few bandits came at her, all at once?

Jewel was a wife now, and she knew what men wanted of women. She belonged to her husband, and the thought of another man being with her that way made her feel sick and shaky. It was just such a worry that made her shake when she saw Ned cleaning his guns. What if rough men came while her husband was gone? Once or twice a week, some hungry traveling man would show up at their door, wanting a little grub. With Ned around, it made no difference—but with Ned gone, Jewel could hardly be trusting enough to offer a stranger grub.

The fear built in her for a week. Finally, the night before the trial, it filled her so full that she could not contain it.

"Take me with you to town, Ned—I fear to stay alone," Jewel blurted out, when they were getting ready for bed.

"I'll ride the mule," she added. "I'll even walk. I'm a fast walker, I can keep up."

Ned looked at her with astonishment. They had a farm—chickens, a pig, two heifers, a mule, a garden to tend. Did Jewel think they could just walk off from a farm? Zeke Proctor was her father; Zeke had livestock and poultry and a farm. Jewel must know there were responsibilities that could not be shirked, once a man took a mate and began to live the married life.

"Jewel, you've got to stay here and tend the place," Ned said, trying not to sound angry. Jewel was but a girl, just sixteen. He ought not to expect her to be a forceful woman on the order of Dale Miller; in fact, he was sure he would never want her to be *that* forceful. But he did want her to recognize that she could not merely follow her whims. She was married now, and her place was at home. He could not be letting her traipse off to Tahlequah, even if she could walk fast.

Jewel knew that was what Ned would say, and yet, disappointment hit her like a blow. It meant she would have to miss him, and he had no notion how painful that missing would be. Even before he was out of sight, it would begin—and it would not relent until she saw him walking up the path to their door.

Despite herself, tears flooded out, so copiously that they wet the front of her old gown. She cried silently. Ned had already blown out the lantern and could not see her tears. It was only later, once they lay down, that Ned felt the wetness on her gown.

"Jewel, honey, did you spill something?" he asked. Then he touched Jewel's wet cheek, and realized the wetness was tears. Jewel did not cry often, but when she did her eyes got as big as cups, and the tears fell down in a flood.

"Why, what is it?" Ned asked. He had already forgotten her desire to accompany him to the trial. He thought she might be sick.

Jewel did not answer him for a while. She was torn between her need to tell her husband the truth, and her conviction that he would not like it if she *did* tell him. She started to lie, to tell him the tears were tears of homesickness. The fact was, she often did pine for news of her mother, and Liza, and the triplets.

But her tears, this time, were tears of sadness and dread. Without meaning to, she had come to love Ned too much, so much that it hurt not to have him with her, not to have him touch her. She knew that people came and went in life; men, particularly. Errands had to be run, and visits made. Ned was a senator, too—he had told her on the ride home, that he would have to be going to Tahlequah from time to time to sit in the Senate and have his say about tribal matters. At the time, Jewel paid little attention to his words, she was so filled with her feelings about going home with him to the Mountain, and being his wife.

Now, her caring and her need were an embarrassment to her. They were feelings too strong to hide. She had not meant to become so attached, and yet she had.

Ned was peering at her, but could not really see her. The

night was moonless, and the room was pitch black. He felt a certain fear himself. When women took ill, they often died, and died quick. Lacy, his first wife, had only been ill for a day and a night when she passed on. Jewel looked healthy, but then so had Lacy up until the infection took her. What if Jewel had taken ill? What if she died?

"Are you sick, Jewel?" he asked, his voice full of concern. "If you're sick, I better fetch Old Turtle Man."

Old Turtle Man was an ancient Cherokee healer, with long white hair and a crouchlike walk. He had come along the Trail of Tears from Georgia in 1838, at the same time as Zeke Proctor and his family. He lived in a dirt house five miles from Ned's place. He was called Turtle Man because he caught turtles and terrapins and kept them in his cave. He even had a snapping turtle in a washtub. It was said that he used the liver of his turtles in his potions, though no one knew for sure. The healing knowledge the old man carried around in his head was considered sacred, and the mixing of potions and such was done in the privacy of his cave.

Old Turtle Man could follow animals when they were old, or sick and on their way to die; he would speak to the animals, whether dog or deer or bear, and take organs from their bodies once they had passed on to the other side. When Lacy got so sick the old man had been away on a journey, gathering roots and spiders. He had been seen in Stinking Water with a jar full of spiders and a big bundle of roots and leaves on his back. Ned had the notion Old Turtle Man might have saved Lacy if he had not gone on his journey just when she took ill.

Jewel had seen Old Turtle Man only once. His old hands were twisted from having spiders bite him. He had come to Becca, when she was sick; his voice was low, like the voice of a frog, and he smelled like wet weeds.

"I ain't sick," Jewel told her husband, conquering the desire to lie. "I just get scared when I know you have to go away."

Ned relaxed at once, though he was a little vexed. Jewel was young, but she ought to know better. He would have no place to board her, even if she did go; he himself meant to bunk under a shed. Besides, if Zeke got acquitted and the Becks decided to make a fight of it, the last thing he needed was his wife in the middle of a shootout.

"Dern it, Jewel, I told you to bang the pans if you see a

bear," he reminded her. "What else is there to scare you, way up here on the Mountain?"

Jewel did not want to tell him about her fear of men. He would scoff at her, probably—Ned's marksmanship was feared throughout the District. He felt that the mere fact she was his woman would scare off any ruffians that happened by. He had told her once, after their passion, that he would kill any man who offered her insult.

Jewel had no doubt that Ned meant what he said: he would kill any man who offered her insult. But the killing would come later—it would not spare her the insult. She knew, too, that there were men traveling through this country who had little fear of Ned Christie; there were men who had never even heard of him. A man might come from Missouri or Tennessee or even farther away, and all he would see was a woman alone.

"Leave me some bullets, Ned. I need to practice with that rifle," Jewel said, in the morning. Ned was saddled up and ready to leave, and Jewel was determined not to cry until he was out of sight. She could ill afford to talk much at such a time. The sadness might get into her voice and ruin her plan not to cry.

Ned counted out twenty bullets and gave them to Jewel in a little pouch. He was pleased that she meant to practice, but he was in a hurry to leave. The trial was bound to be lively, and he was excited to be heading for town.

After he rode away, Jewel climbed up in the loft and cried herself out. Some crows settled in the big sycamore tree behind the house and set up a violent cawing, while she cried. Jewel's great-grandmother Sixkiller had told Jewel how the Cherokee people were all descended from seven clans, and that her own people were part of the Bird clan. By the time Jewel was ten, she knew the names of all the birds in the Going Snake District, and could identify each one of them just by hearing their songs.

Today, though, Jewel was in such a low mood, she began to grow irritated with the cawing crows. She did not want to listen to their cawing all day, not when she was sad.

When Jewel was a little girl, she had been prone to bad dreams. Once, when she was not quite six, she woke from an awful nightmare. Her father tried to comfort her with a story about how the doves and the whippoorwills flew dreams from one place to another. Then he lit a candle, and put it on her windowsill, saying that the light would draw the birds close and bring her sweet dreams.

That night, before she went to bed, Jewel lit a candle and put it in her bedroom window.

23

MARSHAL BILL YOPPS WAS IN A SHOCKING STATE OF DISARRAY when the Beck brothers finally found him, though not much worse disarray than the muddy community of Stinking Water itself.

Two cows had died in the street of Stinking Water the month before, and nobody had bothered to remove them, unless one counted the four turkey buzzards, who were removing the cows piecemeal.

Marshal Yopps himself had been removed, in a sense. His woman, Belle Blue, a notorious whiskeyseller, had removed him from the shanty where she lived to the chickenhouse behind it. Belle Blue had a white mother and a Cherokee father, both of whom had come from the Carolinas up the Trail of Tears. She was Old Mandy Springston's major competitor for the whiskey market in the Going Snake District. Belle's main occupation was madam, and so it was in her best interests to serve decent whiskey to the men who came to call. It was a known fact that women made the best whiskey, in the Going Snake.

Marshal Yopps had been in a near perpetual state of drunkenness for several years. Belle Blue told the Becks frankly that she could not have Marshal Yopps any closer than the chickenhouse. He was too prone to making inroads on the corn whiskey she had to sell.

"Pouring whiskey into that man is like pouring water into a posthole," Belle informed the Becks. "He just soaks it right up."

Belle herself was plump and uppity.

"T. Spade could marry *her*," Willy suggested, as they were walking toward the chickenhouse.

Frank Beck, who considered himself a good judge of

women, was appalled by the suggestion—it showed how naive his brother Willy was, when it came to matters of the flesh.

"That woman would make short work of T. Spade," Frank said. "She'd finish him before the wedding bells even stopped ringing."

Sam Beck thought that one over, but was puzzled by the reference to wedding bells. So far as he knew, T. Spade owned no bell of any kind.

"Davie, now . . . Davie might hold his own with her," Frank added.

Marshal Yopps was snoring when they found him. He had white chicken feathers in his brown beard, and the wound in his shoulder had leaked a dark rusty stain down one sleeve of his shirt.

"He looks played out to me, boys," Willy said. T. Spade had lagged a bit behind, far enough that he had not heard the conversation about Belle Blue making short work of him.

"Wake up, Bill, we want to hire you to kill Zeke Proctor!" T. Spade announced in a loud voice, whereupon Marshal Yopps promptly woke up and looked around.

"Zeke? I'll kill him for thirty dollars," he replied. "I don't like that rascal anyway."

"Why not?" Frank wondered.

"He's got that snappy little dog, that's why not," the Marshal said. "That dog's charged at me more than once."

"You're free to kill the dog while you're at it," Willy told him. He thought making the dog available for slaughter might prompt the Marshal to lower his price.

"You'll have to work quick," T. Spade warned. "The trial's tomorrow."

Marshal Yopps did not like the sound of that. It was a sunny day in Stinking Water, a good day to lay around and drink. Perhaps the bright sunshine would cause Belle Blue to be a little cozy with him. In any case, he wanted to move slow until he was fully awake and had his wits about him. The process of collecting his wits often took half a day, and he could not start it properly until he had several swigs of whiskey. Now here were the Beck brothers, looming over him and trying to hurry him. He did not appreciate it. He crawled out of the chicken-house, and began to brush the feathers off his person.

"Why, I'd rather not hurry, T.," he said. "I can kill him just as dead after the trial."

"No, he might get acquitted, and we don't want that," T. Spade informed him. "He's just sitting there in Tahlequah, and it's only a ten-mile ride. Go get him and bring him back to us. We'll soon give the scamp what he deserves."

Marshal Yopps quickly foresaw complications with that plan.

"What if Charley Bobtail won't give him up?" he asked. "It's a dern sight harder to take a man out of a jail than it is just to ambush him while he's watering his horse or having a shit behind a bush.

"More expensive, too," he added, after a pause.

Willy Beck got rubbed the wrong way by that information.

"Thirty dollars is enough to pay for a killing," he said firmly. "It'll only cost you one bullet, if you shoot straight. That's profit enough, whether you take him out of jail or not."

Bill Yopps looked disgusted. Amateurs were always quick to ignore the legal complications when they wanted some scoundrel killed. Zeke Proctor was Charley Bobtail's prisoner —Charley would have to be handled skillfully, else he might refuse to give him up.

"You could say you're from Judge Parker," T. Spade suggested.

The mere mention of Isaac Parker's name was enough to cause Bill Yopps's blood to boil. He kicked irritably at a speckled hen that was following him a little too closely, looking like she might be ready to peck him.

"That goddamn Judge Parker, he's too goddamn tight," he said. "I won't hunt up prisoners for him."

One reason he was sleeping in the chickenhouse behind Belle Blue's was because Judge Parker had dismissed him from the marshaling force over a quarrel concerning expenses—a fact he did not volunteer to the Becks. Bill Yopps had engaged a blacksmith to shoe his horse and had sent the bill to the court. The bill was for seventy-five cents, which Judge Parker considered profligate. He called Bill Yopps into his chambers, and looked him in the eye.

"Marshal Yopps, do you understand the procedures involved in horseshoeing?" the Judge had asked. He was not asking friendly, either. He had a raspish growl in his voice.

"Why, of course—do you take me for a child?" Bill Yopps replied, indignant. "I can shoe a horse."

"That's what I expected," the Judge said. "You look able bodied to me, although you smell of whiskey. Why would you put this court to the expense of a blacksmith, when you could have shod the animal yourself?"

"I was in a hurry," Bill Yopps replied. In fact, he hated shoeing horses, and always engaged a blacksmith if one was sitting idle.

"Did you imbibe liquorous spirits while you were waiting for this work to be done?" the Judge inquired.

"I don't recall," Marshal Yopps said, though in fact, he had drained the better part of a jug while the smithy was at his work.

"Dismissed then, for a poor memory," the Judge had said. "I won't employ a marshal who can't remember what he's done."

Bill Yopps was stunned. Marshaling was his only source of income. He had been planning to arrest a skillful whiskeyseller within the next few days, and earn a big reward in the process. Now the Judge was asking for his badge.

"What if I pay back the money?" Bill Yopps asked, a feeling of desperation coming over him. If the Judge made good the dismissal, he soon would not even be able to afford Belle Blue, who demanded the same fee as the blacksmith.

"Too late for that," the Judge answered. "This is a poor court. I won't have able-bodied men hiring out work they can do themselves."

The Judge had stood firm—so firm that Marshal Yopps soon pulled himself together and entered into serious negotiations with the Becks about the matter of Zeke Proctor. The plan was to wait until the trial was about to start and take Zeke as he was walking from the jail to the courthouse. The opinion of the Becks was that Marshal Yopps ought to engage a few deputies.

"Zeke's got friends," T. Spade reminded him. He made no mention of Ned Christie. Men with stiffer backbones than Bill Yopps might waver if they thought the task meant taking on the best marksman in the Going Snake District.

"He ain't the only one with friends," Marshal Yopps said.

He had interrupted negotiations long enough to persuade Belle Blue that he would soon be prosperous again.

"Thirty dollars, Belle," he said. "Now think of that. We can do some horseshoeing when I get back from town." Since discovering that Belle Blue and the blacksmith cost the same money, he had started calling what he wanted to do with Belle horseshoeing. Belle was not won by the term or by the man, but she did like the sound of $30.

"Maybe we can, and maybe we can't," she told him. "I'd prefer to save it till I'm paid, but you're still welcome to the chicken house."

She also allowed him access to her whiskey. The Becks were tough negotiators. She knew if she allowed Bill Yopps to grease himself up a little, he might accept a lower wage.

Bill Yopps conceived a notion that was too good to share with anyone. Instead of killing Zeke while he was on his way to trial, he'd kidnap him and spirit him off to Fort Smith. It was well known that Judge Parker did not particularly approve of the Cherokee courts. If he and a few deputies could snatch an important prisoner such as Zeke Proctor and rush him to Fort Smith, Judge Parker might be inclined to restore him to marshal status.

The Becks were nervous. Despite his brushing, Bill Yopps still had a good many feathers stuck to his person. Also, the wound in his shoulder was leaking down his sleeve again. The sight disgusted Sam Beck to the point that he was sick at his stomach. Bill hardly looked like a man who could defeat much opposition.

Bill asked for an advance of $10 toward expenses, but Willy Beck was adamant: he was not to have a cent until the prisoner was delivered to the bar of justice—Beck justice—or else killed.

"What do you aim to do about deputies, Bill?" T. Spade asked. He, too, lacked confidence in Bill Yopps, but time was running out, and he doubted they could find another man to attempt the job.

"I'll go up to the Cave," Bill Yopps assured them. "There's always a few killers resting up by the Cave. I guess if I can deputize three or four, we can take your man."

The Cave was a ledge of overhanging rock on the ridge of

the Walk Back Mountain. It was a favourite resting place for outlaws and renegades—white and Indian alike—and a far piece from any sheriff's office. The way there was all uphill. Rattlesnakes liked it, too, because of the abundance of rocks on which they could sun themselves. One bearded outlaw named Rolly Dan had become fond of snake meat. He had strung a line between two trees to peel snakeskins on. There would usually be two or three peeled rattlers hanging from it. Rolly Dan would smoke them like hams.

Without further discussion, Marshal Yopps saddled up and headed toward the Cave. The Becks watched him go with skeptical faces.

"We ought to have started looking for a marshal sooner," Willy observed. "If you wait till the last minute, you have to take draggy help."

"I think we ought to go cart Zeke off ourselves," T. Spade said. "If we all go in a bunch, I doubt Ned Christie could stand us off."

The remark was greeted with silence. Neither Frank, nor Willy, nor Sam wanted to think about what Ned Christie might do.

"If it's fight Ned Christie or stay home, I plan to stay home," Willy said, finally.

T. Spade took offense at the remark.

"A fine bunch of brothers *you* are," he said.

"Why, we're fine," Sam said. "I'm putting up four dollars toward the marshal, and it wasn't even my wife that got killed."

"No, and it never will be, because no woman would be foolish enough to have you," T. Spade said bitingly.

Sam regretted that the discussion of wives had ever begun. His bachelorhood was a sore trial to him, and T. Spade knew it. He longed for a woman and had proposed to several, but with bleak results. His brother's words were cruel, but true: no woman would have him.

"You oughtn't to be hard on Sam about women, T.," Willy admonished, when they got home. Sam was so depressed, he neglected to unsaddle his horse. He had wandered off toward the creek, to brood about his bachelorhood.

"Shut up, Willy, or I'll start in on you," T. Spade said.

24

ON ZEKE'S LAST NIGHT IN JAIL, HE BEGAN TO MISS HIS FAMILY.

Once the missing began, it soon got bad. The morrow—indeed, his whole future—was uncertain. The jury might find against him; or, the Becks might take advantage of the fact that Judge Sixkiller planned to disarm the crowd. They might storm the courthouse and finish him. Ned Christie, the one man he could count on to protect him, was late showing up. Zeke knew that Ned, his Keetoowah brother, would not flatly desert him, but Ned had a ways to travel, and accidents could always happen along the road.

It was chilly in the jail. Pete was whiny, demanding more attention than Zeke was in the mood to give him. Pete kept trying to jump up in Zeke's lap, and Zeke kept pushing him off. The last time he did it, Pete got annoyed and nipped at Zeke's hand. In a mood of tit for tat, Zeke tried to kick at him, but Pete was too quick, and he missed.

It was so lonesome in the jail that Zeke even missed Liza and her constant babble. He missed the triplets, too. The triplets could never get enough of their pa; they crawled all over him whenever they got the chance and sometimes slept on top of him, like little possums. Minnie liked to tickle his ear and play with his moustache.

Mainly, though, Zeke missed Becca. In his worried state, he began to remember the earlier, livelier Becca, the one he had been with three times in one night. They were both convinced that passionate night had produced the triplets. It might be that Becca was too old to produce any more triplets; it might be that he was too harried with worries to be with a woman three times in one night; but he and Becca could still do well enough, and it was saddening to him that he could not be with her on what might be his last night alive. He felt alive, too—he felt the need of his wife Becca—and yet, because of his foolishness with Polly Beck, a good woman had left him and gone back to her people.

About midnight, Sheriff Charley Bobtail came in to check on his prisoner. Men had been known to do desperate things on the night before they had to face Judge B. H. Sixkiller across a courtroom. One foolish young bandit had cut his jugular with a pocketknife. The Sheriff found him dead, in a pool of his own blood.

Zeke Proctor had not taken matters that far, but he did look mighty unhappy.

"I wish you'd just let me go, Charley," Zeke said.

"Zeke, what would you do if I did?" the Sheriff asked, surprised by this unorthodox petition. "The marshals would just hunt you down, if I let you go."

"I've wronged Becca," Zeke said. "Now she's left me. I need to go make it up to her before I submit to trial."

Sheriff Bobtail was so surprised by this development that he was struck silent.

"I've known trials to be put off," Zeke said. "It's a family matter I need to settle. Once I get it settled, I'll come right on back. I'll give you my Keetoowah oath, if that will help."

Charley Bobtail wished he'd stayed in bed. Now Zeke had gone and reminded him they were Keetoowah brothers, a fact that put him under a certain obligation. How much obligation was the question on Charley Bobtail's mind.

"Good-bye, Zeke, it's late at night for conversation," the Sheriff said. He hastened out the door, into the fresh night air.

Walking home, he happened to pass Judge Sixkiller's house. There was a light in the Judge's window. Charley Bobtail peeked in and saw the Judge sitting at his little rolltop desk, reading a law book. On impulse, Charley went to the door and knocked.

The Judge had a law book in one hand when he finally opened the door.

"Zeke's wanting to go make it up with his wife before the trial," the Sheriff said. "He says he'll come right back, once he's got the matter settled."

"You didn't let him out, did you?" the Judge asked.

"No, he's still in jail," the Sheriff replied.

"Go home, Charley," the Judge told him. "I'll visit the prisoner in the morning and discuss the matter with him myself."

"Are we still having the trial, then?" Charley asked.

"Nine o'clock," the Judge replied.

Then he shut the door.

25

WHEN NED CAME UPON CHILLY STUFFLEBEAN, THE MAN WAS sitting on top of his mule with his feet out of the stirrups, upstream a little ways from the normal crossing of Little Boggy Creek. The Little Boggy had just demonstrated how it got its name, because Chilly's bay mule was bogged nearly to its haunches.

The man on the bogged mule was wearing a black coat and a black necktie. Ned thought he might be an undertaker—maybe he had the mishap of getting bogged on his way to arrange a funeral, or lay out a corpse.

The puzzling thing was that the man was stuck twenty yards downstream from the usual safe crossing. Why cross a creek with a name like Little Boggy and not stick to the tried-and-true ford?

"Howdy," Ned said. "How'd you come to be in that shape? Most people cross right here, where I am."

"I was aiming to," Chilly informed him. "There was a snake there, though—a big ugly cottonmouth. I was raised not to disturb snakes, so I came downstream. Now I'll be late for the trial, and probably get fired, to boot."

"Oh, I'm on my way to Tahlequah, if that's the trial you mean," Ned said. "Wade on over here and I'll carry you in myself. It ain't but three more miles to Tahlequah. We won't miss that trial."

Chilly did not relish the prospect of wading. For one thing, the fat water moccasin might still be around, and he would be easier pickings wading than he would be on his mule.

For another thing, there was the matter of dress. He was expected to be the bailiff at Zeke Proctor's trial, and he had on his only suit of clothes. In fact, the suit of clothes had belonged to him for one day. Judge Parker had insisted that he buy it, and had helped him get a bank loan to pay for it. The banker had been skeptical and so had the merchant, but Judge Parker considered the matter of attire so important that he accompanied Chilly first to the bank, and then to the dry goods store.

Chilly was very proud of his suit—it had given him the

confidence to make the long ride through the hills from Fort Smith to Tahlequah. He felt sure that bandits and hooligans would be likely to respect a traveler in such a suit.

Now his mule was bogged in the mud, three miles shy of the trial, and the only way to get out of the situation was to wade in the same mud, which would surely not improve the condition of his new suit. If he came in to the trial muddy, Judge Parker would be sure to hear about it, and the consequences might be dire.

Chilly decided his best option was to undress, a tricky thing to do on a bogged mule. Cautiously, he raised one leg at a time, and pulled off each shoe. Then he very carefully stood up in the saddle, as an amused Ned Christie watched. Using great care not to spook the mule, Chilly managed to get his new pants off. The shirt and coat were easier, and the necktie was no trouble at all.

"Now that's smart," Ned said. "Why muddy up your good clothes?"

At that moment, he saw the water moccasin Chilly had been talking about. It lay partly hidden behind a rock, and it was big and ugly, just as Chilly had claimed. Without giving the matter much thought, Ned took one of his .44s and blew the moccasin's ugly head off.

The gunshot spooked the bogged mule, who lurched forward in a violent attempt to free himself. Fortunately, Chilly was agile—he managed to get off the mule just as it lurched, his clothes held in a bundle high above his head. The only casualty was a shoe, which slipped out of the bundle and started floating downstream. It floated right down to Ned, who reached over and picked it up. He poured the water out of it, and followed Chilly to shore.

"I thought that mule was bogged too deep to spook," Ned said. "Most mules just give up and die when they bog that deep."

Chilly, who was hastily dressing, looked horrified at the thought of the mule dying.

"That mule can't die," he said. "That mule belongs to the court back in Fort Smith. Judge Parker would probably hang me if I let anything happen to that mule."

"You're as good as hung, then," Ned advised him. "I ain't

got a rope to pull him out with, I expect he'll sink on down in the mud and drown about the time the trial starts."

He was mostly pulling Chilly's leg. It would take the better part of two days for a mule to bog deep enough to drown. Once the trial was over, Chilly could come back with a rope and a winch, and if he could find a stout tree to fasten the winch to, he could winch the mule out.

Chilly was unaware that Ned was teasing him, and was soon in an agony of indecision. Should he miss the trial and save the mule, or save the mule and miss the trial? On top of that, he had no idea how to tie his necktie. Once he got dressed again, he stood there, staring at the tie dangling from his hand.

Ned Christie saw his plight, and got down to help. He had never tied a necktie, either. On formal occasions, he contented himself with a clean bandanna. Though tying a necktie looked easy—there were professional men who managed it every day —in practice, it proved to be impossible. Ned tied several knots, but none of them looked acceptable. Chilly tried several knots, with the same result. One end of the necktie always came out too long, and the other end too short.

Before they knew it, time had slipped by. The mule was still bogged, and the necktie still untied. Ned happened to cock an eye at the sun, his only timepiece, and when he did, he grew alarmed: it was just short of nine o'clock.

"Get on, we'll have to lope it," Ned said, and Chilly obeyed. He held his wet shoe in one hand, and his necktie in the other. Ned had understated when he said they'd have to lope it to Tahlequah, and soon had his big grey gelding in a flat-out run. He knew Zeke counted on him being there. He might get blue if the trial started with Ned not around to take his part in case of trouble.

Chilly Stufflebean grabbed the saddle strings as best he could. He managed to stuff the necktie into the wet shoe, and then held the wet shoe between his teeth. He, too, had an interest in being on time. The bailiff had to be there well before the judge, in order to see that there was water in the judge's pitcher, and spittoons handy both for judge and jury. He knew carrying a shoe in his teeth was not orthodox behaviour, but it was, in his view, better than being late.

When they came down the hill to Tahlequah, Ned slowed the gelding. They came to the courthouse in a high trot. A considerable crowd was milling in the street. It was mostly just curiosity seekers, but the Becks were part of it—all except Davie, who was not in view. The drunken marshal, Bill Yopps, was astride his horse over by the dry goods store, a number of ruffians with him. Charley Bobtail was not to be seen, but Judge B. H. Sixkiller was on the steps of the courthouse, dressed for court in a black frock coat a good deal more worn than Chilly's.

Chilly hastily jumped off Ned's horse, and slipped on his other shoe. In his haste, he forgot that he had stuffed his necktie in it. His foot was muddy, and so was the necktie, once he pulled it out. With the Judge looking at him sternly, he made no attempt to knot the necktie.

"I expect you're the bailiff. Didn't Judge Parker supply you with a mount?" the Judge inquired.

"He did, Your Honour—a mule," Chilly admitted. "It bogged in a creek. If this fellow hadn't come along and give me a ride, I doubt I would ever have got here."

"I expect a bailiff to be on time, whatever the circumstances," Judge Sixkiller said. "In ten minutes, you would have been late. I prefer to start my court promptly, and I'm sure Judge Parker's the same."

"Yes sir," Chilly said. "I'll go in and set out the spittoons."

"That won't take long," the Judge informed him. Though an Indian, Judge Sixkiller differed very little in his behaviour from Judge Parker, Chilly observed. Both men had a stern way of speaking; both of them made Chilly feel that he was not trying hard enough.

"How many spittoons do you set out?" Chilly asked. "We got six, in Fort Smith. One for the Judge, two for the jury, and three for the crowd."

"I allow one for the jury, if it's a long trial," Judge Sixkiller told him. "I don't chaw myself, and I don't encourage it in the crowd. If they must chaw, they can walk outside to spit, or else sit near a window."

Chilly went behind the Judge's bench and retrieved the single spittoon, setting it in a spot convenient to the jury box. It looked to be a busy day for a bailiff, if there was only one spittoon for the whole courtroom. He would have to be up and down every hour or so, just to keep the spittoon empty.

He would be thankful when Zeke Proctor's trial was over.

26

THE SQUIRREL BROTHERS WERE NEARLY LATE GETTING TO THE trial because Rat had carelessly left the gate unlatched when he did the evening chores. The horses got out, and spent the night eating crabapples in a crabapple thicket nearly two miles from the house. It was an awful inconvenience, one that caused Moses Squirrel to curse his brother roundly.

"I have never left a goddamn gate unlatched in my life," Moses pointed out.

Rat Squirrel, feeling surly and picked on, made no reply.

The horses were eventually caught and ridden hard to Tahlequah. They stopped in the high woods for a moment, to survey the scene.

"Why, there's Bill Yopps. He's got Slow John with him," Jim Squirrel observed. "I ain't seen Slow John in a while."

It was just about time for the trial to start. They were about to ride on down the hill, when Moses Squirrel spotted Ned Christie, sitting on his horse in front of the courthouse.

"Uh-oh—there's Christie," Rat remarked. "Do you see him, Mo?"

"I ain't blind, 'course I see the man," Moses said. He was still out of sorts about the horses, and seeing Ned Christie did nothing to improve his spirits.

After some cogitation, he spoke again.

"Let's don't go to the trial," Moses said, finally.

"What?" Jim said, startled. "Not go to the trial? Why not?"

Though he had no intention of saying so to his brothers, Moses Squirrel had a powerful dread of a gun battle with the most expert marksman in the Going Snake District. The mere sight of Ned, sitting on his horse in a Tahlequah street, was enough to awaken this dread. Moses knew there had to be a more sensible way to revenge themselves on Zeke Proctor than to meander into a gunfight with the deadly Ned Christie.

"I don't want to," Moses told them. "I don't like being in stifling rooms."

"Then why did we ride so fast to get here?" Rat inquired, puzzled.

"Because I hadn't thought of a better plan yet," Moses informed him. "Now that I'm here, I've thought of a better plan."

"What would that be?" Jim asked.

"Let the Becks fight first," Moses said. "I expect Ned will kill most of 'em, but one of 'em might get lucky and kill Ned. If Zeke gets off, he's got to go home sometime. We can ambush him, and blow a hole in his gut."

The Squirrel brothers all looked around at one another. Although they had been eager for days for the big trial to begin, the thought of Ned Christie and his marksmanship put a serious damper on their enthusiasm. They remembered the day Ned had stood by Zeke in the street, when they were warning Zeke to stay away from Polly. Ned had made it clear that he would fight with his Keetoowah brother. Only the shootings at Old Mandy Springston's had got them out of that little scrape without loss of life—or at least, loss of blood.

"Ned's a two-handed shooter," Rat observed. "He rarely misses, whether he's shooting with the left hand or the right."

"I don't much like stifling rooms, either," Jim Squirrel allowed.

"There's a passel of folks waitin' to go into that trial," Rat said. "There won't be no place to spit, unless you get near a spittoon."

"Well, I ain't too good to spit on the ground," Moses said. "This is as close to that trial as I want to get. There's plenty of good places to ambush Zeke, if it comes to that."

"I spit on somebody's leg once, chawin' in a crowded room," Rat mused. "The fellow didn't like it none, neither."

With that, the Squirrel brothers dismounted, tied their horses, passed a thick, black plug of tobacco around, and sat down under a good shade tree to await developments.

"I'd be a fool to risk spittin' on somebody's leg agin," Rat added, after a moment. "Next time, it might be fatal."

27

NED HAD NOT DISMOUNTED, AND WAS LOOKING OVER THE crowd.

The Becks stood together, and Marshal Yopps was still across the street with the three ruffians. Ned thought he recognized one of them, a bandit named Slow John. Slow John took an inordinate amount of time searching his victims, once he decided to rob them. He required the men to undress, and insisted that women take off their shoes. It was his belief that precious jewels were most likely to be concealed in ladies' shoes. He was known to murder at will, should a victim become impatient with his lengthy searches. The other two ruffians Ned did not recognize, but they looked like the sort of men that were likely to be found at the Cave on the ridge of Walk Back Mountain. Ned tried to observe the Becks to see if they were signaling Bill Yopps or the ruffians, but the Becks were just standing by the hitch rail, waiting to be admitted to the court.

Judge Sixkiller ushered Chilly Stufflebean inside so that he could be lining up chairs. Then he came back, and spoke to Ned.

"If you plan to attend this trial, I'll make you foreman of the jury," the Judge said. "I know you are friendly to the defendant, but I believe I can trust you to rule fairly, once the evidence is heard."

"I accept, but the Becks won't like it," Ned said, slipping off his horse.

"I do not run my court to suit the Becks," the Judge informed him. He could see the Becks—they were already exhibiting signs of displeasure from the mere fact that he was holding a conversation with Ned Christie. They were frowning, and he had no doubt that curses were on their lips.

But Judge B. H. Sixkiller had more important concerns to voice. He stepped a little closer to Ned Christie so that what he had to say would not carry into the crowd.

"This is a Cherokee court," he said. "It has the right to be independent, and I aim to keep it independent. But the federal government wants it—they don't want us to try our own crimes. I mean to see that this is a fair trial conducted in a professional manner. We cannot afford to give the federal government any excuse to come in here and interfere with our system of laws."

"I agree, Your Honour," Ned said. "They've got no business interfering."

"Judge Parker has been good enough to loan me his bailiff," the Judge said. "I want him to disarm the crowd. He's not known in this community, and I expect the Beck faction to balk. There may be others that balk, for their own reasons. I want you to stand at the door with the bailiff and see that the firearms are handed over."

"Yes sir," Ned assured him. "I expect that will thin out the crowd a little. There's people here who feel undressed without their weapons."

"They'll have to come naked of armament, if they want to spectate in my court today," the Judge said.

He turned to go inside, and then looked back at the crowd in the street.

"I hope a few of them do go home," he said. "It's more crowd than will fit in my courtroom. You stack them guns neat now, and advise the bailiff to do the same. We don't want to damage anyone's weapons."

There was a stirring in the crowd. Heads turned back toward the jail, as Sheriff Charley Bobtail, using two of his sons-in-law as deputies, walked Zeke over from the jailhouse. The sight stopped conversation for a moment; in the silence, Pete could be heard, barking furiously. He had been left in the jail, and he made his displeasure clear. Zeke was handcuffed. He walked right past the Beck brothers without even turning his head. Then he looked up and saw Ned, his face brightening. Ned nodded at him as he passed, and Zeke nodded back.

Once Zeke had passed safely into the courthouse, Chilly came out and stood next to Ned.

"This is a fast judge," he said. "He's already got his robes on. We better hurry up and seat the crowd."

"Come on, folks, it's time to have this trial," Ned said, in a voice that carried well down the street. "The Judge wants this to be a peaceful trial. Every man of you will have to check guns when you come through the door—and that means boot guns, too."

"Boot guns?" Chilly asked. "We don't have such as that over in Fort Smith. If I had to carry a gun in my boot, it would blister my ankle."

Several rowdies turned red in the face upon being told they would have to check their pistols.

"What about you, Christie?" a man named Fry Morgan yelled. Fry was a brawler who had once wrestled a three-hundred-pound catfish out of the Arkansas River with his bare hands. He was round as a barrel of nails, and almost as heavy.

Ned had expected the question. Everyone in the District knew he carried two .44s. He immediately took the pistols out of his pockets and handed them to Chilly, who looked surprised.

"There, now, I went first," Ned said. "Mine are checked. Get yours out and hand them over if you want to come in."

To his surprise, the Becks were the first to comply. T. Spade, Sam, Willy, Frank, all calmly handed Chilly their weapons and filed in, followed by two of Polly Beck's sisters, the only women to venture into the court. They were countrywomen, subdued by the unfamiliar setting. Ned felt sorry for them—he had lost a sister himself, to pleurisy.

The arms check went rapidly, so rapidly that Chilly was hard put to keep up with the crowd. Judge Sixkiller had cautioned him twice not to damage the guns he was handed. His court could not afford bills for gun repair. Chilly arranged the pistols carefully along two benches in the foyer. Ned had to help him, since some of the men handed over as many as five pistols. Fry Morgan himself had a gun in each boot, two in his pockets, and one in his belt.

Fry was a man of high temperament; the fact that Ned had checked his own .44s did not completely mollify him.

"This is a damned nuisance. The Becks are the only ones mad at Zeke," Fry said. "I say disarm the Becks and let the rest of us stay comfortable."

"It was the Judge's rule, not mine," Ned pointed out. "He's strict, and this is his court. Let's get a move on, so we can get this trial started."

After a moment's reflection, a disgruntled Fry Morgan yanked off his boots and handed over the last of his pistols.

28

BILL YOPPS AND HIS RUFFIANS MADE NO MOVE TO COME IN, A fact that worried Ned considerably. Bill Yopps stood beside his horse, but the other men were mounted. All had rifles as well as pistols, and Bill Yopps had a shotgun, to boot.

Ned quickly went inside the courtroom, and spoke to the Judge.

"Your Honour, you need to post a guard while this trial is going on," he said.

"Why?" the Judge asked. "A guard would just be expense."

"The Sheriff's done called up two deputies," Ned reminded him. "Make 'em stand on the porch. There's some men over by the dry goods store that I don't trust. I expect the Becks have hired a few killers."

Ned Christie's apprehension struck him as sound. The Becks themselves were behaving suspiciously well. As a clan, they were not noted for correct behaviour; what was even more suspicious was that the wild one, Davie, wasn't even present.

Judge Sixkiller laid his pocket watch on the table. It was already ten past nine, an affront to his sense of punctuality. To make matters worse, Zeke's lawyer had not arrived.

The Judge motioned to Sheriff Bobtail, who stood at the back of the room with his two sons-in-law.

Just as he was about to order the Sheriff to ask the two deputies to stand guard, peace with the Becks suddenly came to an end.

"Who's running this goddamn trial, B.H.?" T. Spade asked, standing up. "Is it you, or is it Ned Christie?"

T. Spade had got to his feet to speak. He began to shake as if he had the palsy, and his face was as red as if he'd been stung by bees.

"Sit down, sir, and control your profane language," the Judge admonished. *"I* run this court, and I will not tolerate profane bluster in my courtroom. Mr. Christie is merely a juryman."

This was too much for Willy Beck—he popped up, just as T. Spade sat down.

"Juryman? Why, if he's a juryman, I ought to be a juryman, too," Willy proposed.

"Sit down, Mr. Beck!" the Judge ordered, annoyed. "I will *not* have spectators jumping up and down. The jury will be fairly chosen once Mr. Proctor's attorney arrives."

"Hell, Your Honour, start without him," Zeke said.

Zeke was suffering from stomach cramps. He wanted to get the trial over with so he could go try to persuade Becca to come home. He wanted to see Becca so badly that he had even considered paying the Becks blood money to square with them, if possible, about Polly Beck. But Snelson Alberty, a lawyer from Arkansas, had come by the jail one day and persuaded Zeke to engage him as counsel. Snelson was a small man with a fast mouth; Zeke decided to hire him mainly because of his fast mouth. A lawyer who could talk lickety-split might make the trial go faster, which was the only thing Zeke cared about. The quicker the trial was over, the sooner he could get his family back home.

The Judge, though very annoyed by the late start, knew he owed the defendant some good advice.

"You're charged with a serious crime, which is murder, Mr. Proctor," the Judge reminded him. "It could be that your attorney's horse went lame. And it may be in your best interests to wait a few more minutes."

"No, get her started, Judge," Zeke said. "I'll take my oath and tell the truth, and we'll leave it to the jury."

Sheriff Charley Bobtail had started forward two or three times and then stopped, as the Judge and the Becks were wrangling. Finally, he approached the bench to see what the Judge wanted.

"Post them deputies on the front porch," the Judge ordered. "Tell them not to admit intruders."

Ned Christie stood back a few steps, just to the left of the Judge. He was beginning to experience a powerful disquiet. Many a time in the summer, he had watched clouds build up in the great western sky, and grow darker and darker—all he could hear at such times was the low rumbling of thunder that was soon to come. The animals would tense up at such times, and so would the humans. Then came the storm: first a few splatters of rain; and then, within moments, limbs would be snapping from the wind and thunder would break and crack, like a mountain falling apart. Lightning would flash, and hailstones the size of apples would pour from the clouds.

In the courtroom, looking at the silent crowd, Ned felt the same tension building. Something was about to happen—something violent. He began to wish for his guns. A step at a time, he began to walk back to the benches where the guns were stacked. He felt a fierce need to have his .44s in his hands.

Another factor which contributed to his potent apprehension was that Tuxie Miller had not yet arrived, and Tuxie had promised him faithfully that he would be at the trial. Once a promise was extracted from Tuxie, even Dale could not force him to break it. Tuxie Miller was a man of his word. Yet the trial was under way, or about to be, and there was no sign of Tuxie.

It crossed Ned's mind that the Becks might have set an ambush along the trails to Tahlequah. Davie Beck was known to be skilled at ambush. The fact that Davie was nowhere to be seen might account for the absence of the lawyer—it might account for the absence of Tuxie, as well. Tuxie was a careless traveler. His mind wandered, he sang hymns that popped into his head, and he would be unlikely to notice an impending ambush, particularly if it was set by an ambusher with the wiles of Davie Beck.

Ned quickened his step. He wanted his .44s, and this fact was not lost on the Beck brothers—all of whom promptly leaped to their feet.

"Watch that damn Ned, he's headin' for the guns," T. Spade announced. A moment later, Frank Beck shot at Ned with a derringer he had managed to conceal in his hat. The little bullet hit a spectator named old Tom Alston on the very tip of the nose. Old Tom had not heard the pop of the gun, and was surprised to discover himself with a profuse nosebleed. Frank Beck quickly fired his second barrel; this bullet grazed Ned's hand, but did no more damage than a hen peck.

In two more strides, Ned was at the bench and had his pistols. For a moment, he considered turning back to the courtroom but was deterred by the sound of three horses outside, coming at breakneck speed. He jumped out the door so fast that he knocked one of the newly appointed deputies flat on his face and into the street.

Sure enough, one of the racing riders was Tuxie Miller. Ned saw at once that he had been wounded—one pants leg was red with blood. Two men were pursuing him, about fifty yards to his rear. One of them was the maniac Davie Beck, and the other an old man Ned could not immediately identify, with long, white hair and no hat. Davie Beck was not shooting, but the old man was popping at Tuxie with a six-shooter. Davie was waving what looked like a saw as he rode, and the old man with the streaming white hair was holding a big bowie knife between his teeth.

The deputy Ned knocked over had dropped his Winchester. Ned picked it up, and immediately shot Davie Beck's horse. The fatally wounded animal went down in a heap, with Davie underneath it. Ned thought that would stop the old man, but it did not—the old fellow ran right over Davie, just as Davie was trying to struggle out from beneath his fallen mount. Tuxie Miller reached the courthouse and spilled off his horse, almost into Ned's arms.

Tuxie was white as a ghost, from loss of blood or fear or both, Ned reckoned.

"Shoot, shoot, it's White Sut Beck!" Tuxie gasped, before stumbling into the courthouse, his wounded leg pouring blood.

Ned remembered then that the Beck clan had a patriarch somewhere. Ned had heard no mention of the old man in years, and supposed he was dead. White Sut was said to live in a shack under a tree in an obscure spot west of the Mountain—he was said to keep a bear and a buzzard as pets, and among his many eccentricities was a fondness for hunting wild pigs barefoot, armed only with a knife, probably the very knife he was now gripping between his teeth as he bore down on the courthouse, white hair streaming. Davie Beck lay run over in the street beside his dead horse. He was not moving a muscle.

Ned had to act quick. The easiest thing was to shoot the old man's horse out from under him, which Ned did. But his horse, a stout sorrel, did not die clean and immediate. Instead, it began to run in circles, pouring blood from behind a foreleg and nickering a wild, high nicker of distress. Then, to old White Sut's extreme annoyance, the sorrel quit circling and went off in a dead run back toward where it had come from, the old man cursing and sawing at the reins all the while.

That'll fix *him,* Ned thought, keeping an eye on Davie Beck, who had still not moved a muscle since being run over by old White Sut. It struck Ned as odd that Davie had ridden in carrying what looked like a saw, but he had no time to brood on the matter.

Bill Yopps and his ruffians had suddenly vanished.

29

NED RAN BACK INSIDE THE COURTROOM, JUST AS SHOTS erupted. As he passed the bench with the guns on it, Ned scooped up two or three more pistols.

When he jumped into the courtroom, he was not surprised to see Bill Yopps climbing through a window, his shotgun cocked. Without delay, Ned shot him. Marshal Yopps fell backward, discharging the shotgun directly into the chest of quiet Sam Beck, who had been helping him get through the window.

The ruffians who had been with Bill Yopps were handing pistols and rifles inside to the Becks. As soon as he could get his pistol cocked, T. Spade turned and fired at Zeke, who had been on the prisoner's bench. But Zeke was no longer on the prisoner's bench, and T. Spade's bullet took Judge B. H. Sixkiller in the throat.

The Judge did not feel the bullet at first. He stood up, and tried to rap his gavel. It was a court of law he was conducting, and a court of law had to be conducted with propriety. Men were not to be climbing in windows and using firearms in his court. Ned Christie had been right about the deputies, but now the deputies were outside, when the Judge needed them inside. He tried to rap for order, but dropped his gavel.

When he bent to pick it up, he noticed blood on his hands; worse than that, the bending did not quite work. He could not reach the gavel, which lay right at his feet. But the gavel moved, or he did—one moment it was below him; then suddenly, it was at eye level. Judge Sixkiller got his hand on it, and began to rap it on the floor. It made him feel better to be rapping the gavel. He meant to rap it until people stopped clambering about and put away their firearms and settled down and behaved, like people in a courtroom ought to. When he turned his head toward the crowd, all he could see was feet—

feet in farmer's shoes and feet in boots. He saw a body laying not far away; it looked like one of the Becks, but he had never known the Becks well, and could not say which Beck it might be. He rapped the gavel again, and began to wave for the bailiff Judge Parker had so kindly loaned him. He wanted the bailiff to wade into the crowd and get them seated. Because Zeke Proctor's lawyer had been late, the trial was already well behind schedule.

It was a thing that bothered the Judge grievously, too, for throughout his career he had insisted on punctuality. He meant to explain to Judge Parker the next time he saw him the chain of circumstances that had led to the trial slipping off schedule. Above him there was shooting and shouting, but the Judge, watching the feet, occasionally rapping his gavel, slipped beneath the racket into a place of quiet. He was the judge; he still had his gavel; and the gavel represented the law he had long tried to serve. He was confident he could eventually bring the trial to order and see that the matter before him was judged in a dignified manner. He loved the dignity of the law and always had, even when he had to do his judging in a plank schoolroom somewhere in the District and hand down rulings involving milk cows and goats. All the shouting and clambering going on around him would have to stop—and it would stop, he knew, once people heard the rapping of his gavel. It was a good gavel, oak wood, solid; he had ordered it special from a law store in Chicago, Illinois, and had waited six months for it to reach the District. Once they heard it rapping, the crowd would respond.

But now, just for a moment, it was good to rest, in the quiet place beneath the clambering and the shouting. He needed to rest, just for a moment—it might be a long trial.

"My God, T. Spade just shot the Judge!" Ned said. He could see no sign of Zeke. Maybe Marshal Yopps's ruffians had dragged Zeke out the window and cut his throat, or taken him off to hang. But there *was* sign of Tuxie, who sat scrunched up in a corner, trying to get his leg to stop bleeding.

"Where'd Zeke go?" Ned asked. Then he took a shot at Slow John, whose head had just appeared in the window. Slow John disappeared, though Ned had shot high, nervous about hitting some innocent in the crowd, most of whom still sat on benches, bewildered.

"Zeke ain't passed this way," Tuxie said. "Loan me a weapon, I'm unarmed."

115

"You stay down like you are," Ned said. "They can't hit you if you're down. I got to find Zeke."

Meanwhile, the Becks—all except Sam, who was dead—had equipped themselves with the firearms handed in through the window.

"Give up, Zeke, you're surrounded," Willy Beck yelled. "There'll be innocent folks killed if there's too much shooting in this courtroom!"

Then Willy saw a man about the height of Zeke and immediately shot him, only to realize when the man fell that it was not Zeke at all—it was a skunk trapper named Bully Lanham, a fellow he knew only slightly. Oh, Lord, I should have waited till he turned around, Willy thought. He realized that he had just fulfilled his own prophecy. Bully Lanham was a man with few friends who had probably just wandered into the trial out of curiosity.

Slow John made the mistake of trying to hand another gun through the window, this time to Frank Beck, who already had so many guns in his hands that he was having a hard time figuring out which one to shoot. Ned saw Slow John out of the corner of his eye; he jumped on a bench so as not to risk firing across the crowd at too low an angle. Slow John saw him and ducked, but not quickly enough or far enough. His hat fell off, and Ned's bullet hit him dead center in the top of his skull. Slow John fell back out the window and was seen no more until after the battle, when the bodies were counted.

It was Tuxie Miller, trying to keep low in the corner, who first spotted Zeke Proctor. Zeke, still handcuffed, was inching along on his belly, well protected by a forest of legs and feet.

That Zeke, he's sly, Tuxie thought. He waved at Zeke, but Zeke had his head down, trying to avoid notice.

30

CHILLY STUFFLEBEAN HAD BEEN IN THE MIDDLE OF AN AISLE when the shooting started.

He had been trying to persuade an old man with a face so weathered that it looked rusty to move closer to the window so he could do a tidier job of getting rid of his tobacco juice. The old man had spat on the floor twice, a thing that would have earned him immediate expulsion from Judge Isaac Parker's courtroom, for Judge Parker supplied spittoons in adequate numbers and expected them to be used. The old fellow was resistant to Chilly's polite suggestion that he move over to a window. In fact, he ignored Chilly so rudely that Chilly had a notion to grab the old man by the scruff of his neck and carry him outside.

He was attempting polite suggestion, when he looked over and saw a man handing guns through the window to T. Spade Beck. That was highly irregular and would have to be stopped at once, but before Chilly could move to stop it, Ned Christie shot Bill Yopps, who discharged his shotgun square into Sam Beck. The blast knocked Sam in among the spectators, one of whom fell backwards onto Chilly's legs, knocking him down.

As he fell, Chilly saw Judge Sixkiller put his hand to his throat. From that moment on, Chilly's main effort was to avoid being trampled. He heard more gunshots—a lot more gunshots —so many, in fact, that he soon concluded being knocked over might be a blessing in disguise. He was close to the Beck side of the courtroom, and when he risked looking up saw that all three of the remaining Becks were firing steadily across the courtroom. He could hear their bullets thunking into the walls, which indicated to him that the Becks were inexpert marksmen. They were firing point-blank in a crowded area, and all they were able to hit was the other side of the room.

Ned Christie stood boldly on the bench he had jumped upon, and drew the same conclusion. The Becks were shooting hell out of the walls. Zeke was nowhere to be seen; Tuxie was losing too much blood; the Judge was down, though not necessarily dead; one Beck was finished; and he himself had accounted for Bill Yopps and Slow John. He needed to get a tourniquet on Tuxie's leg before the man bled to death. It was time to end the bloodshed.

"Here, now!" he yelled, leveling both pistols at T. Spade Beck. "You Becks give it up, or I'll kill every damn one of you!"

At that moment, there was a wild howl from behind him. Ned turned to see Davie Beck, his forehead bloody, trying to fight his way through the crowd. Davie was still waving the saw blade in front of him like a sword. A crude effort had been made to shape it into a long knife, but it nevertheless looked like a saw blade to Ned.

"Let me through, you goddamn pullets!" Davie yelled. He was practically frothing at the mouth, in his frustration at not being able to plow a path through the gaggle of spectators.

"Ho, Davie—ho, now!" Ned cried, leveling a gun at him.

"I've come for your liver, Christie, and I'll take your damn balls while I'm at it!" Davie bellowed, pushing two frightened muleskinners aside.

"You won't saw me, Davie!" Ned replied, cocking his pistol. He raised his gun to shoot, but before he fired, Zeke Proctor suddenly rose out of the crowd just behind Davie Beck. He threw his handcuffed arms over Davie's head, and sank his teeth hard into Davie's right ear. When Zeke's teeth bit into his ear gristle, Davie screamed like a banshee. He tried to turn and saw at his attacker, but Zeke began to choke him with the handcuff chain, still biting hard on his ear. The two men went down in the crowd, rolling over and over, not far from where Tuxie Miller sat—looking far too pale, and feeling increasingly faint.

"Here, Christie, take this to hell with you!" T. Spade yelled, leveling a long-barreled Winchester rifle at Ned.

Ned swung his pistol toward T. Spade, but then saw that T. Spade did not know how to work the rifle. In his haste, he jammed a shell halfway in the chamber, a fact that frustrated him so that he began to pound the stock of the rifle onto the floor. The third time he struck, the gun went off—the bullet struck Thelma Grimmet, Polly Beck's older sister, who was trying to squeeze past her brothers-in-law and run away. Like Sam Beck, Thelma was hit at point-blank range and was dead before she hit the floor, a fact that horrified Frank Beck. Here they'd come in force to the courthouse to kill Zeke Proctor, having gone to the expense of hiring Bill Yopps and three ruffians, and so far they had only managed to kill two members of their own family. If they did not manage to get their wits about them, there'd be no Becks left at all.

"Hell, we're only killin' off one t'other!" he told his brother. "Let's jump out that window while some of us are alive!"

"I'm willin', but what about T.?" Willy Beck ventured.

Frank Beck had developed a sudden and powerful urge to live. Before anyone could stop him or offer him argument,

Frank Beck jumped out the window, landing right on top of the two remaining ruffians from the Cave, both of whom were squeezed up against the building awaiting developments. The one development they had not expected was to have Becks raining down upon them. Willy Beck, his pistol empty, took only a moment to follow Frank's lead. Willy landed right on a thin ruffian named Eli Ross, damaging Eli's spine so badly that he was never able to walk fully upright again.

Ned thought the fact that T. Spade Beck had been flagrantly deserted by his brothers might cause the old man to give up. But in that assumption, Ned was wrong. Exasperated by the Winchester which had caused him to slaughter a harmless sister-in-law, T. Spade grabbed two of the pistols that had been handed in to him and began to fire in the direction of Zeke and Davie, who were still rolling around on the floor locked in mortal combat. T. Spade knew he might hit his brother, but thought the risk well worth it. He disliked Davie only slightly less than he disliked Zeke, though Davie was his own blood.

Ned started to shoot him, but the crowd was on its feet by this time, and even from the bench he could not fire without considerable risk to the spectators.

"Ned, I'm dyin', take the news to Dale if you get time," Tuxie Miller requested.

Ned knew better. Tuxie was merely wounded in the leg, but Tuxie had gone ghost white and did need attention. While Ned hesitated, hoping for a clear angle that would allow him to put T. Spade down before he killed more spectators, Chilly Stufflebean struggled to his feet. Just before he left Fort Smith, Judge Parker had lent Chilly a small pistol—a .32-caliber, with a three-inch barrel.

"I doubt you'll need this, Chilly," Judge Parker told him, "but feel free to use it if you find yourself in a desperate situation."

Chilly figured this was what the Judge had meant by a desperate situation. T. Spade Beck stood not ten feet away, firing point-blank into a crowded courtroom. Any moment, he could swing the gun in Chilly's direction. But Chilly knew it was his duty as a bailiff to try and stop indiscriminate manslaughter, whether T. Spade pointed a gun at him or not. Judge Parker had never permitted slaughter in his courtroom.

"Put down your gun, Mr. Beck," Chilly said. His voice could barely be heard over the din.

Chilly stood firm, knowing that Judge Parker would expect firmness. T. Spade shot twice and missed twice. Both bullets whizzed under Chilly's arm; one of them nicked his black coat, and then struck Lotte May Grimmet, Polly Beck's other sister. Lotte May and Thelma had both married Grimmets. Chilly heard Lotte May gasp and fall, but he could not afford to turn and look: T. Spade was moving toward him, cocking the pistol for a third shot. Chilly saw from T. Spade's red-veined, demented eyes that he was beyond reason. The man was not going to stop shooting until his gun was empty. He had missed so far, but he might not keep on missing.

Chilly lived a moment that seemed like a year—at least there was autumn in it, and winter—for he was going to have to take a life, or else lose his own.

"Mr. Beck . . . ," Chilly said; then he broke out of the other end of the moment that had stretched on through the seasons, pulled the trigger, and shot T. Spade Beck just above the left eye. T. Spade died with a look of wild rage still on his face. He lurched back a step, and then fell right at Chilly Stufflebean's feet.

Chilly immediately stuck the .32 pistol back in his pocket. He had an overwhelming urge to have Judge Isaac Parker step into the courtroom and take charge. He was sure Judge Parker could stop the carnage and get the trial finished in an orderly fashion, if only he were there.

But it was a hopeless wish. Judge Parker could not be there, and Judge Sixkiller was either dead or dying. Chilly himself had just killed an old man he had never even properly met, an old man driven crazy by the death of his wife. Chilly had not intended to kill, when he rode over to Tahlequah at Judge Parker's request; in fact, the thought had never crossed his mind. Yet, now he *had* killed. He himself felt so relieved to be alive that he could hardly gulp air into his lungs fast enough. He had not quite realized what a precious thing life was, until he saw people all around him losing it and felt T. Spade's bullets pass just beneath his arm.

Ned, across the room, thought the death of T. Spade would probably mark the end of hostilities. Several more men were down, injured, or killed in T. Spade's last burst of shooting. To his surprise, he saw Lotte May Grimmet, the woman he had bought his pig from the year before, get up, climb over T. Spade's body, and start to crawl out the window her two brothers-in-law had leaped through. One of her arms was dripping blood onto the floor. Ned liked Lotte—she raised fine shoats—and called out to her as she was halfway through the window.

"Hold up, Lotte, don't jump out that window," he said. "You're dripping blood, you may be hurt bad."

Lotte turned briefly.

"I oughtn't to have stood so close to the boys. Now Thelma's dead, and I'm shot," she replied, before climbing on out the window. Though wounded, she dropped to the ground and walked the nine miles back to her farm. Ned was not to see her again until the next summer, when he bargained with Lotte for two more shoats.

The spectators, most of whom had been jumping up and then sitting back down throughout the shooting and attempting to stay at the safest elevation, got up silently and began to hurry out of the courtroom. Many of them had to hop over the struggling bodies of Zeke Proctor and Davie Beck in order to get out the door. Zeke held the advantage, due to the fact that he had his handcuff chain tight against Davie Beck's Adam's apple. Davie's face was purple, and his eyes rolled back in his head until only the whites were visible, from having his airflow choked off so long.

Ned quickly knelt by Tuxie Miller, and cut the pants off his bleeding leg. When he did, he saw that Davie Beck had not shot Tuxie; he must have attacked Tuxie with the saw blade. Tuxie's leg was sawed to the bone, just above the knee. Ned took his own bandanna and quickly made a tourniquet, twisting it with his pistol barrel.

"Zeke's about got Davie choked to death," Tuxie observed. Even half fainted, Tuxie was amazed at the fury in Zeke's face as he tried to choke Davie, who, taken by surprise, had been unable to employ his saw blade in his own defense.

"Tuxie, I've got to get this bleeding stopped, or you'll be dead and I'll have to answer to Dale," Ned informed him. "This gunfight has been bad enough. I don't want to have to ride up there and tell Dale I let you bleed to death in order to stop Zeke Proctor from choking Davie Beck."

Tuxie understood that. He was nervous himself about having to explain to Dale how he had ridden into an ambush and got one of his legs half sawed. Dale expected him to keep both legs healthy for the plowing, Tuxie was certain.

Chilly Stufflebean, looking dazed, walked over to Zeke, who was still astraddle Davie Beck, choking him hard.

"I think you've kilt him, Mr. Proctor. His eyes have turned up in his head," Chilly observed.

"Unlock these handcuffs, I got a cramp up my arm," Zeke said. As far as he was concerned, the ornery Beck clan was responsible for his worst problem, which was that his wife had left him. Becca was a good sixty miles away, if she was an inch. When Chilly got the handcuffs unlocked, Zeke bounced Davie's head off the floor a couple of times for good measure and started out of the courtroom, only to be met by an indignant Pete, who came charging in. Pete had managed to wiggle out a window in one of the cells and jumped at his master, expecting to be picked up and scratched. Pete was badly disappointed in this; his master did not even glance at him.

Most of the spectators had managed to get out of the courtroom by then. With the room almost empty, Zeke got his first good look at the scene of carnage. The moment he had seen Bill Yopps's face appear in the window and saw the shotgun in his hand, Zeke had hit the floor and begun to crawl in amid the crowd. It did not surprise him that the Becks had hired Marshal Yopps, or that they soon armed themselves and began to shoot. He had expected trouble to break out some time during the trial, and had decided in advance that his best bet was to stay low.

Now, looking around, he knew that he had been wise: bloody bodies lay everywhere. The only man left in the courtroom other than Ned and Tuxie was old Tom Alston, who had evidently had the end of his nose shot off. Old Tom sat quietly on a bench, still under the impression that he was merely suffering from a nosebleed.

"Zeke, go see about the Judge," Ned requested. "He may be bad hurt, I think T. Spade got him in the neck."

"He's worse than bad hurt—he's dead," Chilly said, squatting for a moment by Judge Sixkiller.

"The man's right. B.H. ain't drawin' his breath no more," Zeke said. "Now the goddamn Becks have killed our judge."

"I wish Dale was here . . . I wish Dale was here," Tuxie said, with alarm. The sight of all the blood that had trickled out of him convinced him he was dying. He might never see his nine young-uns again, or watch Dale put on her heavy socks prior to getting in bed.

"You ain't dyin', Tuxie, you just need to be still till we can get you to a bed," Ned told him. "Why'd you let Davie get close enough to saw on you?"

"He fell on me out of a tree," Tuxie said. "I thought he meant to steal my horse, but then he started sawing my leg with that saw blade. If the horse hadn't reared and pitched him off, I guess I'd be one-legged now.

"I doubt Dale would put up with a one-legged husband," he added, reflecting that it took him all day to get the chores done, even with two legs.

"Dale would stay with you even if you was blind and deaf and foolish," Ned assured him. "Dale's your wife, and she plans to stick with you."

Tuxie sighed heavily. He was not so sure.

31

NED WENT TO WHERE THE JUDGE LAY, AND PUT HIS EAR against the Judge's chest, hoping for a heartbeat. But Ned was disappointed: Judge B. H. Sixkiller, his own wife's great-grandfather, was stone dead.

Zeke was looking out the window.

"There's a pile of bodies under the window, Little Eli's on the bottom," Zeke said. "He's movin' like he ain't quite kilt."

"I didn't shoot Little Eli," Ned said. "I imagine somebody fell on top of him. I shot Yopps, and I shot Slow John. If there's others dead, then I didn't kill 'em."

"Dammit, here comes old White Sut," Zeke said. "He's got his bowie knife between his teeth. We better get ready."

Ned jumped to the window. Sure enough, White Sut Beck was charging back through Tahlequah on the big sorrel.

"I shot that horse, I would never have expected him to run

at such a pace," Ned said. "He run off with the old fool, but I guess White Sut finally got him turned."

Chilly stood at the window, too. He had never seen such a wild sight as the one he faced at the moment: an old man with long, white hair and a flopping coat racing at them on a bloody horse, a huge knife between the old man's front teeth.

Watching the crazy old man race toward them on the wounded horse gave Chilly the sad sense that he was in the wrong place. Somehow, while trying to do his duty as a loan-out bailiff, he had come to a place so wild that the law had no chance of prevailing. Dead bodies lay all around him. Now and then, he heard a groan from someone wounded, but not yet dead. He himself had killed a man, a man maddened by grief for his dead wife. Somewhere back in Little Boggy Creek, Judge Parker's favourite mule was slowly drowning. Chilly had intended to take Ned Christie's advice, borrow a winch, and go save the mule. But with so many dead to lay out, and then the wounded to attend to, he knew he would probably have to let the mule go. He longed deeply to be back in Fort Smith, and he wished the day he was living had not really happened. He wished he could be waking up on his bench in Judge Parker's courtroom, ready to carry the spittoons down to the Arkansas River and let the river water wash them all clean.

There were disputes in Fort Smith, to be sure—there were even gunfights—but they seemed mild things, compared to the bloodbath he had just witnessed and survived. Tahlequah was a place of wild men, wild like the old man who was racing toward them at the moment on the bloodstained horse.

Zeke Proctor had only met White Sut Beck once in his life. He had accidentally stumbled on the old man while he was brewing whiskey, and the old man had tried to set a sow bear on him. He had the sow bear chained to a tree, but White Sut unchained her and sicced her on him. Zeke had to put spurs to his mare and make a run for it. Even then, he might not have made it if he had not been to a horserace in Dog Town. He had happened to be astride his fastest filly, who had better wind than White Sut's sow bear.

Zeke had supposed the old man was dead, though occasionally he would hear tales of a wild old hermit who lived on Raw Rock Mountain with a bear and a buzzard. He supposed the tales were hyperbole, a not-uncommon thing in the Going

Snake District. Now he was forced to realize that not only was White Sut still alive, he was feisty and bent on mayhem and murder—his lifelong interests, so far as Zeke could discover.

"Shoot that dern horse, Ned, or we'll have to choke that old fool down like I choked Davie," Zeke said. "He's killed eight or ten men with that big knife of his. I don't know how many he's killed with guns.

"He set his sow bear on me once, I don't want to mess with the old lunatic," Zeke added, annoyed that Ned was merely watching the old man descend upon them. Ned ought to be shooting, Zeke thought.

Ned finally lifted his pistol and aimed at the big sorrel horse again. But before he could shoot, Davie Beck himself, clutching his mashed throat but clearly far from dead, staggered into the street and tried to wave White Sut down. While Zeke and Ned had been watching the spectacle of his old kinsman, a badly choked but still alive Davie Beck had managed to crawl out the courthouse door, unobserved. He was staggering and stumbling, sucking air for all he was worth. He still had his saw blade in one hand, and he was bent on escape.

"Why, dammit, I thought I had Davie choked all the way dead," Zeke said, amazed to see a man he had just spent ten minutes strangling rise up and wander down the street.

"Davie must have learnt that trick of rolling his eyes up in his head," Zeke reflected. "Usually when a man's eyes roll back like that, he's thoroughly kilt."

"The Becks are hardy," Ned observed. "They're like cockroaches—you might think they're dead, and then before you know it, they've done crawled off. You have to keep checking once you have 'em down, to make sure they're dead."

Ned watched as White Sut Beck slowed long enough to pull Davie up behind him on the bloody horse. The sorrel was beginning to favour her wounded leg, but she still managed a crooked lope as the Becks turned and headed out of town. They passed in easy pistol range, but Ned did not shoot. He knew they were dangerous men, men he might have to reckon with again. But for the moment, they posed no danger.

"Shoot, you can still hit 'em," Zeke said, but Ned shook his head, and put his guns back in his pockets.

"I've done enough killing for one day, Zeke," he said.

"We've got the wounded to attend to, and the dead to lay out for their kin. Then we need to get on home to our womenfolk."

Ned looked around at the carnage, shaking his head.

"There'll be hell to pay on the Mountain, because of this," he said.

32

ZEKE SAT DOWN ON A BENCH IN THE COURTROOM, WEAK ALL of a sudden—so weak he could not have held a pistol straight enough to shoot if his life had depended upon it.

What Ned had just said was true. There would be hell to pay on the Mountain and throughout the Going Snake District because of what had happened in Tahlequah that day: a judge was dead—the most respected judge in the Cherokee Nation.

Zeke had survived, but surviving had momentarily sapped his strength. He stood up briefly, and tried to help Ned and Chilly turn over the bodies that lay facedown so the dead could at least be identified. But he was too weak to even turn a body. He felt drained, and it was all he could do to sit upright. If one of the Becks came charging back through the door bent on vengeance, he would be able to put up no resistance. Ned or the skinny bailiff from Fort Smith would have to stop them, if they were to be stopped.

"Zeke, this is terrible," Ned said. He had tried to help a wounded man named Jackson Lowry sit up, and the man had coughed lightly and died, as Ned was holding him.

"How many dead?" Zeke inquired. He had once herded stock with Jackson Lowry. They'd had much trouble with a brindle cow on a trip back from Kansas with some beeves.

"I make it eleven, counting Jackson," Ned said. "But there's three wounded, one of them bad. I expect it will be a dozen dead folks before the dying stops."

"Dale didn't want me to come," Tuxie said, in his weak, bled-out voice. "I ought to start listening to Dale, she knows what she's talkin' about."

Chilly had been dragging the body of Sam Beck over to the line of dead that Ned Christie was arranging along one wall of the courtroom. Sam Beck was the worst shot up, for his guts were exposed. Chilly's stomach came up, suddenly—he had to drop Sam Beck's legs and run to the window to vomit. Then, once the heaving stopped, the same weakness that had hit Zeke Proctor hit Chilly, too. He sat down by the window, numb and stunned. It seemed impossible to him that he would ever recover enough strength to make it home to Fort Smith.

Judge B. H. Sixkiller's felt hat was hanging on a peg behind the bench. Ned took it down, and placed it over the Judge's face. He would have to go home and inform Jewel that she had lost her great-grandfather. It would be a sad, sad task, not merely sad for Jewel, but for the community and the District. Judge Sixkiller had been their best man, indeed the *only* man with authority to turn back the white marshals when they came looking for Cherokees they wanted to hang.

Outside the courthouse, more people were leaving than were staying. Ned looked out the window and saw little groups of men mounting up and riding slowly out of town, toward the hills. Some were in wagons; a few walked. Several men stood in the street, not talking, just waiting. A few women stood together by the church. It was a bright day, the sun shining on the hills without the interference from so much as a single cloud. The whole courtroom smelled of gunpowder and human blood, and yet, the hills were bright with sunlight.

While Ned was looking, another of the wounded men died. He was a skinny fellow with a hole in his pants. Ned noticed the odd fact that he wore one boot and one shoe—maybe he had been in such a hurry to get to the famous trial that he had not been able to locate the correct footgear before he left home. It did not matter now; he had left home forever. Being as the day was hot, the skinny man would probably have to be buried wearing a boot and a shoe, unless his womenfolk lived close and could get the matter corrected while the graves were being dug.

Ned looked at Chilly Stufflebean, who still sat by the window, a blank look on his face.

"When you feel better, would you go out and see if you can persuade some of those men to get started with the buryin'?" Ned asked.

"But I don't know 'em," Chilly replied, weakly.

"Sir, it's a chore for the bailiff," Ned told him. "And you're the bailiff. Zeke and me have got to go. If I can free that mule when I go back across the creek, I'll leave it tied there for you."

"I expect it drowned during all this killing," Chilly said.

He felt a hopelessness take him. He had failed at the job Judge Parker had sent him to do. Probably no bailiff during the long course of the law had ever failed worse. Despite his best efforts to disarm the crowd and keep the peace, twelve people, at the very least, were dead. It was an awful thing to have to go tell Judge Parker, and he would likely have to walk all the way to Fort Smith. Chilly had a wish that he had never been orphaned, never been allowed to sleep on a bench in the courthouse. What it had all led to was a hot courtroom that stank of blood.

In spite of his weakness and his hopeless feeling, he had no trouble, once he went out to the street, in finding men who were willing to go in search of a doctor for the wounded—and willing, even eager, to dig graves for the dead.

In fact, he soon had more gravediggers than there were spades. Ned Christie himself walked over to the hardware store and borrowed three shovels so the digging could go quicker. Once equipped, the men fell to with a will—Ned even dug for a while. After all, it was common work, the work that all mortals would need to have done for them, someday. It took Ned's mind and the minds of the other men off the killing they had witnessed. Turning over the dark earth, lifting out spade after spade of dirt, was a relief.

Yet, it was not proper to simply drop these people in the ground without their wives, husbands, and kinfolk being summoned to weep over them and pay final respects. A minister was found, but some of the dead had trekked to the trial from as far as thirty miles away, and the day would not be long enough for runners to scour the Mountain and bring the kin to Tahlequah for the burial, too.

Zeke Proctor, after sitting with his hands limp and his head drooped on his chest for many minutes, finally found enough strength to walk outside and sit on the steps in the warm sun. He did not take part in the grave digging; even if he could hold a shovel, he knew he did not have the strength to dig. Neither did Chilly Stufflebean, who got a long case of the dry heaves. Over and over, in the shelter of the bushes south of the courthouse, his stomach tried to crawl up and out of his throat. He knew he was too weak to attempt Fort Smith that night. He might bog in that treacherous little creek, and drown, like Judge Parker's mule.

Once the graves were dug to a decent depth, Ned came back and loaded Tuxie Miller onto his horse. Tuxie had been dozing fitfully on a bench in the courtroom. He felt feverish to Ned—the cut was deep, and Davie's old saw blade might have been rusty. Ned knew that he had best get Tuxie home to his resourceful wife, Dale, as quickly as possible. The doctor who finally showed up had tried to disinfect the wound, but he was an old doctor, and not as competent as Dale Miller—not in Ned's view.

"I got to be going, Zeke," Ned told his friend. "If Tuxie was to get blood poisoning, it would be touch and go if he'd live."

Zeke sat looking toward the hills to the west, where the sun was just beginning to dip. Pete, subdued by his master's lack of interest, lay comatose at Zeke's feet.

"Do you have a horse here still?" Ned asked. "You'd best come with me."

"No, I'm goin' to get Becca now," Zeke informed him. "I need my wife."

"Go get her, but hurry and come to my place," Ned suggested. "You know how fast news travels in these hills."

Zeke *did* know, and being reminded stirred him enough that he immediately got to his feet. Already, the runners and the riders would have crested the hills with the news. A fast horseman might, even then, be nearing the Arkansas River. By morning, one or more men would be at the courthouse; by the afternoon, an army of marshals might be on their way to Tahlequah. One thing was certain: nothing, now, would stay Judge Isaac Parker's hand.

"I guess my horse is still in the livery stable," Zeke said. "Go on, get Tuxie home. I'll be fine."

To Ned, Zeke still looked pale and slow. He did not look like a man who was fully able to take care of himself.

"Don't linger now, Zeke. Go get Becca if you want, but then you come and find me. We're going to have to go on the scout."

"On the scout," Zeke repeated, with a nod. Then he and

Pete started walking slowly toward the livery stable, passing the twelve narrow graves as they went.

It occurred to Zeke, then, that though a dozen people were dead, he had still not been tried. Zeke counted the gravediggers and found that they numbered thirteen—an adequate number to make a full jury, plus one.

Ned Christie was just about to leave, when Zeke called out to him.

"Ned, you're a senator. Can't you pick a jury?" Zeke asked.

Ned was taken by surprise. He wanted to get Tuxie home to Dale before blood poisoning set in his wound. He did not wish to concern himself with judicial matters.

"A jury to do what?" he asked, still horseback.

"To try me. I need to be tried, and there's enough men here to make a fine jury," Zeke said.

"I'm a senator, but I ain't a judge, Zeke," Ned reminded him. He was taken aback by Zeke's unorthodox suggestion.

"It's the jury that decides to convict or not. That ain't the judge's job," Zeke said. "I want to be tried right now, otherwise the marshals will never let me rest."

They won't anyway, Ned thought—but he decided he might as well humour his friend. Besides, when the white marshals did come, it would not hurt to be able to say that judgment had been rendered in the matter of Zeke's crime, even if it was a judgment handed down by a bunch of gravediggers.

"Well? Are you men willing?" Ned asked, looking at the gravediggers.

Nobody spoke, either to agree or to object. Ned was irritated at having to take the time to prompt them, when his friend's life hung in the balance from his bad wound.

But Zeke Proctor would not relent, or withdraw his request. He wanted to be tried, then and there.

"Swear them in, Ned," he insisted. "Scratch off old Tom, he's got part of his nose shot off. The rest ought to make a decent enough jury."

"All right, raise your hands," Ned said. "Swear to render a fair verdict on Zeke Proctor and the matter of Polly Beck.

"You don't have to, Tom," he added to the old man, the end of whose nose occasionally still dripped blood. "You ought to head on home and patch up that nose."

The other men raised their hands. Though they had been digging with a will, the heavy weight of judicial responsibility seemed to weigh their arms—a few could barely get their hands higher than their elbows.

"All for acquittal, raise their hands again," Ned said, hoping that his instruction bore some resemblance to proper jury procedure.

All twelve jurors raised their arms.

"Be sure, now," Ned urged. "We want to tell the whites we done this right."

Nobody said a word. Two or three men went back to their digging. Ned thought of asking them to vote one more time, just to be on the safe side, but after a moment, he decided against it. The whites probably would not take the vote anyway—not without argument.

"Acquitted, then," Ned said. "Go on now, Zeke, and get Becca."

"I thank you," Zeke said. He shook hands with each of the jurors, before proceeding to the livery stable.

Zeke pondered the events of the day as he walked, the arbitrariness of life weighing heavily upon him. Who would have thought that his wanting Polly Beck for a second wife could have turned into so much bloodshed? He guessed that the patriarchs had been wrong about the matter of more than one wife; he guessed that Becca had been right to bring him a Bible to the jail, instead of a pork chop. He shook his head, as he approached the livery stable, at his own folly.

Ned made sure Tuxie Miller was secure in his saddle, and went at an easy pace out of Tahlequah. Tuxie's leg had stopped bleeding, and he did not want bumpy traveling to make the bleeding start up again.

"Oh, Lord, it's been a bloody day, ain't it, Ned?" Tuxie remarked.

"Hush talking, Tuxie. It's still a long ways home," Ned told him. "You need to be quiet now, until I get you to Dale."

Ned kept the easy pace, until darkness closed over them. As he was crossing Little Boggy Creek, his horse nickered—so did Tuxie's. There, not far from the creek, was Judge Parker's mule. It had freed itself somehow, and was grazing peacefully beside the trail to Fort Smith. Ned tried to catch it, so he could leave it for the bailiff as he had promised, but the mule was skittish from its ordeal in the mud. It would not be caught.

Ned was forced to leave it. He hoped it would stay close to the road as it grazed, so the tired deputy, Chilly Stufflebean, would not have to walk all the way back to Arkansas.

BOOK TWO

ON THE SCOUT

Now you have covered her over with loneliness. Her eyes have faded, her eyes have come to fasten themselves on one alone. Let her be sorrowing as she goes along, and not for one night alone. Let her become an aimless wanderer, whose trail can never be followed.

CHEROKEE HYMN

1

A FERRYBOAT MAN NAMED LONNIE VONT WAS THE FIRST PER-
son to bring Judge Isaac Parker news of the massacre in
Tahlequah. Lonnie had awakened to find a muddy mule nosing
around his ferryboat—Judge Parker's own brown mule, in fact.
He had ferried the same animal to the east side of the river two
days earlier, when it was on loan to Chilly Stufflebean. Chilly
Stufflebean, though, was nowhere to be seen.

Lonnie Vont thought Judge Parker might want his mule
back, with or without his young bailiff. The Judge might even
want it back bad enough to offer a tip. But just before he
started across, two wagoneers traveling from Memphis took
passage to the west bank of the Arkansas. In the course of the
trip, not a long one, the more voluble of the two men mentioned
that there had been a terrible massacre in a Cherokee town up
in the hills. Forty men had been killed, in a shootout in a
courtroom. They had heard about it from an old coloured man
who farmed a small spread on the flats near the Greater Boggy
River, a stream that sometimes flooded and washed out his
crops. The coloured man had once been a slave to one of the
chiefs of the Choctaw Nation. The chief had freed him out of
consideration for long and loyal service.

"Forty men? Are you certain of the number, sir?" Judge
Parker asked, when the news was conveyed to him later that
morning. He looked at Lonnie Vont sternly. Lonnie chewed
leaf tobacco, uncured; he had just crammed a leaf in his mouth
about the time the Judge put his question to him. He hastily
removed the chaw before answering.

"Forty, Your Honour, that's what the old nigger told the wagon boys," Lonnie Vont said, more than a little unnerved by the Judge's stern look. The likelihood of a tip for mule return seemed to be getting slimmer by the minute.

"It would take a Gatling gun to slaughter that many men, and I doubt Judge Sixkiller would permit a Gatling gun in his courtroom," Judge Parker said.

"Why, I don't know about that, Judge. I wasn't there," Lonnie told him. "Forty's the nigger's figure, not mine. I just thought you might want your mule home quick. I don't usually ferry this early."

"So now you want a tip, is that the reason you're standing there like you're planted in the ground?" the Judge asked.

Lonnie Vont was so taken aback by the tone of the question, let alone the content, that he stood with the half-chawed tobacco leaf in his hand, unable to phrase a reply.

"I consider tippage wasteful economics. The fact is, that mule can swim faster than you can winch your boat," the Judge said. "I would not own an animal too incompetent to find its way home. I thank you for the information, though I doubt its accuracy."

Judge Parker's doubts about the accuracy of the death count had to be voiced several more times during the course of a long day, as a stream of enthusiastic informants poured out of the hills and into his courtroom to tell him about the great gun battle in Tahlequah.

One man, a giant German named Dieter DeBrugge who traded in hides, assured the Judge solemnly that a Cherokee woman had told him the dead numbered over fifty.

"Fifty? Why, we'll be up to the Gettysburg figure before long," the Judge remarked. "If it was much more than ten, I'd be surprised, and ten's bad enough. I've held court on this frontier since I was twenty-three years old, and I've never had a fatality in my courtroom."

Dieter DeBrugge was not too interested in the massacre. He thought the Judge might appreciate a change of subject.

"Skunk hides make good muffs," he announced, to the Judge's surprise. "I've got plenty of skunk hides. Does your missus need a muff?"

"If she does, she can catch her own skunk," the Judge

informed him. "I don't waste money on the hides of common varmints."

Dieter felt a little hurt. He had some excellent hides in his wagon, and at the least he had hoped to sell Judge Parker enough of them to make a muff.

Once Dieter—gloom in his face—left the courtroom, the Judge shut his door and spent a few hours looking out the window. Though he did not believe fifty men were dead in Tahlequah, or forty men, either, he was firmly convinced that something had gone very wrong at Zeke Proctor's trial. Even if two or three men had been killed, it still ranked as a calamity of major proportions for both Judge B. H. Sixkiller specifically, and local law in general. For a court trial to be interrupted by violence was a terrible, terrible thing, whether it was one person killed, or a hundred. Judge Parker wanted no more exaggerated gossip. He wanted to hear the story from Chilly Stufflebean, or someone equally reliable.

The fact that the mule had come back without Chilly was a troubling thing. It might mean that Chilly himself was among the dead. The mule arrived muddy to the shoulders, and the Judge could not recall whether Chilly knew how to swim. If he had not been shot, it might be that he drowned. It was worrisome indeed. The Judge chided himself for having sent an inexperienced young man on such a difficult mission. The Judge's wife, Martha, doted on Chilly. Mart would chide him worse if the young man failed to return.

Outside the courthouse, a knot of men gathered to discuss the bloody news. As more and more of the curious or the frightened rode into Fort Smith, the knot grew and grew. The Judge's muddy mule was scrutinized for clues, and though none were found, it did not stop the more imaginative members of the crowd from concocting wild theories about what had happened at Tahlequah.

A mountaineer named Cracky Bolen, a man who lived largely on pine nuts and squirrels, said he had a dream about an uprising of the nations a night or two before. In his dream, hundreds of Cherokees and Choctaws and Creeks and Seminoles had painted themselves up with war paint, like warriors of old, and they had come pouring down from the hills and into Tahlequah, yelling battle cries as they came, wiping out everybody in the courthouse there.

Cracky Bolen's theory was so popular that other members of the crowd took it up and expanded on it. Soon, the common view was that the Cherokees had completely wiped out Tahlequah and several other communities as well. Talk arose of a general uprising that threatened the whole of Arkansas. The talk became so urgent that several of the men hurried over to the hardware store and bought new rifles.

Judge Parker stayed in his chambers all day with the shades pulled. When he walked out of the courthouse to go home for supper, he was highly annoyed to see a mob filling up the street. The mob was armed to the teeth, and ready for battle.

"Here, now—what's this? Why are you crowding up the street?" the Judge asked, impatient. "I need to walk this mule home, and I don't need a hundred people to help me!"

"But Judge, there's Indian trouble," one skinny fellow said. "We've heard the Cherokees have wiped out Tahlequah."

"That's a peculiar statement," the Judge answered, staring at the man without warmth. "Tahlequah is a Cherokee town. They own it. They people it. Why would they suddenly take a notion to wipe themselves out?"

The Judge's plain statement immediately took the steam out of the crowd. Somehow, most of them had managed to lose track of the fact that Tahlequah *was* a Cherokee community. The skinny man who had spoken up looked at Cracky Bolen accusingly.

"Well, Cracky said it. I don't know where he got his information," the skinny man said.

"I had that bad dream, and then there was news of the shootin'," Cracky said, his voice falling off at the word "shootin'." Judge Parker had caught his mule and was proceeding up the street with him. He clearly did not expect a horde of Indians to sweep down on Fort Smith. Cracky felt foolish—and he was not alone in the feeling.

Then the Judge stopped, and turned to the mob again.

"Don't you men be causing the spread of foolish rumours," the Judge said. "The truth of this is something I don't know, but I will know it by tomorrow, I expect. Is anyone heading up in the direction of the Blue Hills?"

Cracky Bolen himself lived in the Blue Hills.

"Why, me, Judge," he said. "Would your missus like some squirrels?"

The Judge thought it odd that his wife Mart had been offered both skunk hides and squirrels in the same afternoon. It annoyed him. If Mart had a desire for varmint hides, she could soon be well supplied.

"My missus can catch most of what she needs herself. I can supply the rest personally," the Judge replied tartly. He did not like a common mob making reference to his wife. "What I need is for somebody to contact Marshal Dan Maples. I need to see Marshal Maples, and I need to see him soon!"

"Why, Dan's my neighbour," Cracky said. "I'll go by and tell him in the mornin'."

"If it's on your way home, tell him tonight," the Judge said bluntly. "Much obliged."

With that, he led his mule on up the wide street, wondering what had become of his young bailiff, Chilly Stufflebean.

2

THE MINUTE DALE MILLER FELT TUXIE'S HOT FOREHEAD AND looked closely at the red, ugly wound in her husband's leg, she turned white. She even smelled the leg, putting her nose right down against the wound.

"I told you not to go off. But you went off, and now you're dying, Tuxie," Dale said, a quaver in her voice. Neither Ned nor Tuxie could remember when Dale's voice had quavered so.

She glanced once around the room at her nine silent children, and immediately took off her apron and put on her old blue raincoat.

"Put my saddle on your horse, Ned. I got to go," Dale ordered.

"Go where, honey?" Tuxie asked, startled. It was night, and pitch black. Where would his wife be going, on a pitch black night?

"I've got to find Old Turtle Man," she said. "He's our only chance."

Ned had every intention of rushing right home and spending the night in Jewel's warm, smooth arms, but Dale's look stopped him. She looked wild in the eyes, like a panicked cow. Ned knew a saw wound was bound to be dangerous, yet Tuxie did not appear that sick to him, just feverish. He had even made a certain amount of conversation with Ned, on the way home.

Now Dale was proposing to seek out Old Turtle Man, a task not easy to accomplish, even in bright daylight. The old man wandered the hills and creek beds, returning only now and then to his hut on the highest ridge on the Mountain. Dale Miller might be forceful, but that was no guarantee she could find Old Turtle Man very quickly.

"Why, let me go, Dale," Ned proposed. "It's over ten miles to that hut of his, and it's black as pitch out. That old man wanders. You might ride all that way, and still not find him."

Dale tied a rough shawl over her head, and was ready to go.

"Just saddle the horse, Ned—don't be objecting," she told him. "I'll find that old man because I have to. If I don't, I'll lose my husband."

"It's just a fever, Dale," Tuxie protested. But his wife did not bother to answer.

"If somebody has to go, it ought to be me," Ned insisted. "I know the Mountain about as good as anybody around."

"No," Dale replied, firm. "Tuxie is my husband. I'll go. You wouldn't know what to ask if you found Old Turtle Man. He might ask you questions you don't know the answers to and send you back with the wrong potions."

"And he might even ask you a question you don't know the answer to," Ned said, irritated by Dale's conviction that she was the only one in the world with any sense.

Dale found a hamper to take with her so she could bring back whatever wild medicines Old Turtle Man might gather for her. She looked at her children again, and saw that they were frightened. In this instance, she could be of little help to them, for she was frightened, too.

"There ain't no question about my husband I don't know the answer to," she told Ned Christie. "The only thing I don't know is how to save his life. If that fever goes much higher, you'll have to take him down to the creek and lay him in the water. It's the only thing that might cool him."

She looked once more at Tuxie, but she did not let the look linger. Knowing that he might die before she got back would only make it harder to leave.

"Build a fire down by the creek, Ned. Put Tuxie on a pallet," she said, once the saddle had been switched and she was mounted. "When his fever gets too scorching, put him in the creek. Leave him in the water till his teeth start chattering, then wrap him up again."

"My place is right on the way," Ned reminded her. "Could you yell to Jewel when you pass by to let her know I'm here? She might want to ride over tomorrow and help me nurse Tuxie."

Dale Miller had already whirled the horse, and put it into a lope.

In a moment, the darkness swallowed her up.

3

"I BEEN SEEING HORSE TRACKS AROUND HERE THAT DON'T belong," Sully Eagle told Zeke the minute Zeke rode up to his own house and jumped off his horse. Since his home was on the way to where Becca was, Zeke thought he'd spend a night in his own bed and maybe clean up a little before going to get his wife back.

His days in the Tahlequah jail had been so boresome that he had completely lost interest in his appearance. He'd let his whiskers grow; he'd failed to trim his moustache; his long hair was tangled; his long underwear was filthy; and there might even be a louse or two about his person—none of which would help him with Becca, a woman to whom cleanliness was truly next to godliness, as she had so often pointed out to him.

On his way to the house, he made a hasty tour of the lots and determined that at least some of his livestock were still alive. The mule was present; a few shoats had been born; and the milk cow was jingling her bell from somewhere in the meadow. Sully Eagle had done a reasonably good job of keeping the place in order, it seemed, despite which Zeke was in no mood to listen to Sully's theories about horse tracks. All he wanted was to spend the night, change his underwear, trim his moustache, and be off to see Becca as soon as it was light.

"What's the grub, Sully?" he asked, ignoring Sully's remark about the horse tracks.

"Corncakes," Sully replied, a little hurt that Zeke was so

abrupt. "I been fryin' up that weevily corn. It's that or hunt, and I'm not goin' off huntin', not with the Becks on the loose. T. Spade shot at me once, and he didn't miss me by enough. I won't take the risk again."

"There'd be no risk, T. Spade is dead. A bailiff shot him," Zeke informed him.

"A what?" Sully asked.

"A bailiff, he's a person who works for the court," Zeke said. "I had hoped for better grub than weevily corn. Surely there's pork in the smokehouse."

"No, there ain't. Didn't you hear about the whirlwind?" Sully asked.

"I been in jail," Zeke reminded him. "News was sparse from up this way."

"A whirlwind hit the smokehouse and blew it away," Sully said. "I hid in the root cellar, or it would have got me."

Zeke, devastated by this news, dashed out the door and ran up the slope, only to discover that for once Sully Eagle was not exaggerating: his smokehouse was certainly gone. Sully ambled up, just as Zeke sat down on a stump to collect his wits.

"What about the meat? It might blow the smokehouse away, but surely the meat's somewhere," Zeke reasoned. Not only had his wife left him, but his smokehouse was gone, too. It was a poor homecoming.

"A bear got the meat," Sully said. He did not comment further.

"Why didn't you shoot it, Sully?" Zeke asked. "There was two pigs in that smokehouse, and a full quarter of beef. That's too goddamn much meat to give to a bear."

"It was dark, and I was still in the root cellar," Sully told him. "I don't like to shoot at bears when it's dark, it's apt to rile them up."

"Well, this has riled *me* up!" Zeke announced. "I lost my smokehouse, and all my meat, too. If you'd just banged the frying pan, that bear would have gone away."

Sully concentrated on frying up the corncakes. There was no point in trying to reason with Zeke Proctor when he was out of sorts. Zeke's temper was erratic, which was why he had got in trouble in the first place. Now he had shown up at home, expecting everything to be perfect, despite the absence of his wife and the prevalence of such things as whirlwinds and bears. Sully decided that the best thing he could do was concentrate on his cooking, and pick as many weevils out of the corncakes as he could before passing them to Zeke.

"I thought there'd be grub here, I hate losing meat," Zeke said several times, as he was consuming the corncakes. Though anxious in the extreme to get Becca back home, he nonetheless felt out of sorts with her suddenly, for going off to her people and leaving the farm management to strange old Sully Eagle —a man who, it appeared now, could not be counted upon to take even the most rudimentary steps toward the upkeep of his farm—steps like shooting a bear that was making off with all the pork.

"Once I get Becca home, I intend to track that goddamn bear and kill it," he said, his annoyance growing as he attempted to choke down the tasteless corncakes. The corncakes were so dry that he had to soak them with molasses in order to make them palatable.

"One of them shoats is growin' fast," Sully ventured. "It'll be big enough to butcher in another month."

"I doubt it," Zeke said. He was in a mood to disagree with everything the old man said, just on principle. Sully, a dependable man when Zeke was right minded, became more and more undependable in Zeke's mind, as Zeke became more and more irked.

Since Zeke was almost as testy as a bear himself, Sully decided to abandon any attempt to make conversation for the evening. He wandered off to his shed, over by the livestock lots. It was filled with cornshucks and made a comfortable resting place. Occasionally, he heard the rustle of a big rattle-snake, from somewhere down in the shucks, but he had never been an enemy of the snake people and rested at ease, despite the proximity of the large snake. Once in a while, on warm days, he would see it resting on a flat rock by the cistern. Pete would trot down and yip at the snake sometimes, but Pete knew better than to go for it. The old snake was tolerant, but not so tolerant as to put up with much insult from a fat black dog.

In the morning, Zeke hauled a couple of buckets of water up from the well and set about cleansing himself. He had intended to heat the water and indulge in a proper bath, but when the time came his impatience was such that he skipped the heating and just bathed cold, shaved cold, and did not even bother to trim his moustache. Sometimes, if she was in an especially good mood, Becca liked to trim his moustache herself. Perhaps she would be pleased that he had left it for her to trim.

As Zeke was saddling up, Sully wandered down the hill carrying a possum he had cornered in the outhouse. It was a fat, young possum; Sully had already skinned it and had it ready for the frying pan. Zeke decided the day was young enough so that he could wait and have a bite of possum before setting off.

"I'm seeing too many horse tracks that don't have any business being around here," Sully remarked, as they were finishing the possum meat. Zeke had grease on his moustache from his greedy approach to the possum.

"You said that last night," Zeke reminded him. "Don't be worrying me about horse tracks—half the Becks are dead. Don't be lazy about hunting, either. The Becks that are left have better things to do than shoot at you."

He then favored Sully with a quick report on the courthouse massacre.

"Twelve kilt? Why, that's half the community!" Sully exclaimed. "I am sorry to hear that White Sut Beck escaped. Davie's bad, but White Sut is worse."

"Ned could have killed him, I don't know why he didn't," Zeke told him.

"White Sut lives way over by Salt Hill, with his bear and his buzzard," Sully said. "They say he sleeps in the salt. Maybe that's why he's crazy.

"I think the Squirrel brothers made them horse tracks," Sully added.

Though Zeke was impatient with more mention of horse tracks, Sully thought it best to remind him that the Squirrel brothers were still on the prod. They were nowhere near as mean as the Becks, but Moses Squirrel was a fair shot, capable of putting a bullet in Zeke, mean or not.

"I have no interest in the Squirrels, and I'll tell 'em so if they attempt to interfere with me," Zeke said, as he mounted to leave. "I want you to sweep out this house and mop it down. Becca won't like it if she has to come home to a dirty house."

"What if she don't come back, Zeke? Who will you wife with?" Sully inquired.

Zeke was so annoyed by the question that he rode off without a reply. What grounds did Sully Eagle have to suppose that Becca might not consent to come back home? He was putting himself out to the extent of riding forty miles to see her; why would she not return with him? He was a wanted man, too. He should be putting distance between himself and the white marshals who would soon be showing up to look for him. Surely Becca would want to come back, once she realized what a risk he was taking for her.

She might not, though—that was a fact Sully Eagle had been impolite enough to remind him of. Women could do what they pleased, and he could not force Becca to come back if she did not want to come back. He remembered her last look in the jail: her look had been cold and steely as a gun barrel. What if he rode all that way and Becca met him with the gun-barrel look? What would he do then?

Zeke's worry increased, as he rode north. The fact was, Becca had metal in her. She could stiffen like steel in response to offenses he had not intended. Mainly, she had been a dutiful, hard-working wife—she kept a tidy house and was a fair cook when she put her mind to it, and she had never refused his embraces. Past a point, though, Becca felt free to ignore orders she did not like, and would not be told what to do. He had been raised to believe that a wife ought to love, honour, and obey her husband. He knew Becca loved him and supposed she probably honoured him; but when it came to obeying, she felt free to walk her own trail.

Zeke hated courting women. He was too busy for it. If Becca refused to come back home with him, he would be in a pickle. He had accidentally killed the only other woman he fancied— Polly Beck—and he would be hard put to know what to do for a female if Becca showed him her gun-barrel side.

He was not a man to sleep well in an empty bed, either. The sap rose too strongly in him at night, and the thought of having no companion at the supper table except old Sully Eagle did not please him in the least.

As Zeke rode off, he could hear Pete flinging himself at the walls of the springhouse, where he had locked him. Becca was not fond of dogs and was particularly short of affection when it came to Pete. If she saw him riding up with Pete in front of his saddle, it might prejudice his case before he got to speak to her.

Sully had orders to let Pete out in a few hours; no doubt Pete would fling himself at the springhouse wall the whole time. Pete never stopped trying to get his way, not until he was completely exhausted.

Zeke had saddled his big bay gelding for the long ride up toward Missouri. The bay had an easy lope, a gait he could sustain for miles without slacking. Zeke was loping along working over in his mind what he was going to say to Becca, when he came atop a little ridge and had to pull up to keep from plowing right into the Squirrel brothers, the three of whom were planted squarely across the trail. All three had their guns drawn and were no more than twenty yards away, killing distance even for poor pistol shots such as the Squirrels. To make matters worse, Rat Squirrel was aiming a Winchester rifle at him. Though Rat might have missed with a pistol, Zeke regarded it as unlikely that he would miss with a Winchester rifle—not at that distance.

Zeke stopped the bay, looking a good deal chagrined. He realized he should have listened to Sully, who though old and boresome, was capable of telling which horse tracks belonged on the property, and which did not. Still, it was just the Squirrels. He had bluffed them in the past, and he felt confident he could bluff them again. His desire to get Becca back home gave him even more brass.

"You boys don't be pointing weapons at me," he said. "The trial is over, and I'm acquitted. Get out of the way and let me pass."

"The only place you're passing to is hell, Zeke," Moses Squirrel said. "Disarm him, Rat."

"You disarm him, Jim," Rat Squirrel replied. "I have to keep him covered with this rifle."

"Just throw your guns down, Zeke, and that'll be that," Jim Squirrel said politely. Jim had always been a good deal more pleasant than his brothers.

"No, I was acquitted proper, and I won't give up my arms," Zeke countered. "I am going to get my wife, and I need my weaponry. You boys know there's always bandits up Missouri way."

He was considering what his chances were of busting through the Squirrels and making it to a chinaberry thicket not more than a quarter of a mile away. Once in the chinaberries, he felt sure he could outshoot the Squirrels, though it was a damn nuisance to have to take the time to do it on the day he had an urgent need to reclaim his wife.

"You may have got a passel of gravediggers to hold up their hands, but you ain't acquitted in our book," Moses said. "We intend to hang you in the name of our sister. We'd rather not shoot you first, but we will if we have to."

Zeke felt a red-eyed anger coming on. Here were the damn Squirrels, making a nuisance of themselves over Polly Beck, whom he had killed entirely by accident. It was an outrage to him that they would block him on a public trail at a time when he sorely needed to see his wife. Without further delay, he put spurs to the bay and charged straight at Rat, drawing a pistol as he came.

Unnerved, all three of the Squirrels fired and missed. Rat's shot knocked a crabapple off a tree fifty yards behind Zeke, who bumped Rat and nearly knocked his horse down as he came busting through the line of men. Zeke fired a pistol right at Rat Squirrel's head, but missed due to rapid movement.

The Squirrels recovered quickly from their surprise at Zeke's sudden charge. In a moment, Zeke heard their horses behind him, but was not greatly worried about being overtaken before he made the thicket. A factor in his favour was that the Squirrels were notoriously cheap when it came to purchasing horseflesh: they had no mount to match his bay.

He was almost into the woods, when he felt a jolt in his ribs —a strong jolt—as if a post oak limb had whacked him. But it was a chinaberry thicket he was approaching; there were no post oaks in sight. The jolt caused him to lose a stirrup, an unfortunate thing, since the bay charged right into the thicket as if it were merely shrub, breaking limbs and jumping fallen logs.

"Whoa! Whoa! You've got to slow down now," Zeke said to the horse. The command came too late: the bay jumped a tangle of logs and underbrush, causing Zeke to lose the other stirrup. A moment later, a limb took him in the chest and swept him off the gelding as cleanly as if he had hit a wire. Zeke grabbed for his rifle as he went off, but missed. He came crashing to the ground on his back, armed only with a pistol. When he rolled over, he saw a smear of blood on the grass and felt a warmth on his right side. That jolt had most likely been a bullet smacking into his ribs, he thought. The bay stopped when Zeke fell off, and stood a few feet away. Zeke knew he ought to mount and get a little deeper into the copse of trees, deep enough that he would be safe from the Squirrels while he took his shirt off and assessed his wound. But to his dismay, a weakness like that which had come over him in the courtroom assailed him again. He sat up, but could not seem to get his legs under him. There was not much blood on the leaves, and Zeke did not suppose himself to be badly hurt—but the weakness slowed him so that he was losing time. When Zeke looked up, his head began to swim. One moment he saw his gelding, and the next moment he did not. The trees seemed to be circling him, pulling in closer and closer. When he looked up at the sky, it was only a pinpoint. He heard footsteps and knew it must be the Squirrel brothers, moving in to kill him. But the fact that the trees were circling closer and closer, and the sky receding higher and higher, worried him more.

While he was waiting for the spinning to stop, he felt something cool pressed against his temple. It was cool as Becca's hand, when she came in on a winter morning from drawing a bucket of well water.

But it was not Becca's hand: it was a gun barrel, and Moses Squirrel, a cheerful look on his face, was holding it to his head.

"You're caught now, you son-of-a-bitch," Moses said affably.

Zeke had never enjoyed being cursed. He started to make a sharp reply, but found he was too tired to get sharp words out.

"You boys go home and don't bother me," he said, in a weary tone. "It feels like you've kilt me anyway."

"No, you ain't kilt, Zeke—it's just a flesh wound," the polite Jim Squirrel informed him. "You might have a broke rib, that'd be about the worst."

"Truss him up, Rat. We need to carry him out of this thicket so we can hang him proper," Moses said. He had not withdrawn his pistol barrel from Zeke's temple, not yet. Zeke Proctor was known for his abilities at escaping desperate situations, and Moses Squirrel meant to see that he did not escape this one.

"What with? I ain't got no twine," Rat replied.

"Why, I told you to bring plenty of twine, Rat," Moses reminded him. "How can we hang a man proper if we can't tie him up first?"

"I lost the twine back on the road when Zeke run through us," Rat admitted. "I had it out, all ready to tie him, but then he took that run at us and I ain't seen the twine since."

Moses was nonplussed. Here they had their man down—dazed, bleeding, and weak—and they did not have the necessary equipment to securely tie him up long enough to get him to a hanging tree.

"Tie him with your suspenders, then," he suggested, looking at Rat.

"My suspenders keep my pants up," Rat reminded his brother, looking at Moses indignantly. "If I take 'em off, my pants will fall down."

Rat had always hated to expose his legs, which were so white in color that they reminded him of a fish belly.

"Just take one of 'em off," Moses suggested. "Zeke's shot anyway. One suspender's plenty for keeping your dern pants up."

"I won't be tied with suspenders," Zeke said. "I have not sunk that low. Pull that trigger, Moses, if you're determined to have me dead because of an accident I didn't intend."

Moses wanted Zeke dead, but he did not pull the trigger. In their youth, he and Zeke had hunted coons together, and gone to many a horse race. Now the man sat before him, weak and bleeding. If they could have killed him in the heat of battle, that would have been one thing; but now that he was captured, it seemed to Moses that Zeke's death ought to be accomplished with the correct ceremony, which meant a hanging.

The only question was how to secure the prisoner until they could get him to an adequate tree. Most of the chinaberry limbs were either too skinny to hold a hefty body like Zeke's, or were too high off the ground to get a rope over. It was vexing, and the vexation was not diminished by his brother's reluctance to remove his suspenders.

"Cut a string off your saddle," Moses said, impatient. "A good leather saddle string would hold him."

Rat greeted that command with even greater reluctance.

"If I do that, I won't have nothin' to tie my slicker on my saddle with," he said.

"Goddammit, Rat, quit your whinin'—I'm losin' my patience with you," Moses said. "You was supposed to keep up with that twine, and now you've lost it. We got us a prisoner here who's gettin' weaker by the minute. He'll bleed out and die, if we don't hang him quick."

Rat realized that he had better compromise. Moses was not a man whose patience could be trusted.

"I'll take off one suspender if you'll take off one, Jim," Rat suggested, looking at his mild brother. "That way won't neither one of us have to go naked so's to hang Zeke."

"Well, but mine are stretchy," Jim Squirrel said. "If Zeke was to twist hard enough, I expect he could squirm loose, and then where would we be?"

At that moment, Zeke did squirm loose—not from bonds, but from the strange, enervating weakness that had seized him moments before. He felt his strength surge back, and with it his anger at being harassed and detained by the Squirrels. Moses was looking off for a moment, listening to his brothers discuss the suspender issue. The cocked pistol was not pressed against Zeke's temple, but was just hanging from Moses's hand. Zeke grabbed it suddenly and twisted it straight up, squeezing Moses Squirrel's hand until the pistol fired.

Moses fell backward, most of his jaw shot away. Zeke twisted the pistol loose and shot twice at Rat, who immediately turned and ran. Zeke's second shot nicked Rat in the hip, but Rat managed to get into the underbrush. Only then did Rat realize he had left his rifle propped against a stump while they were trying to think of a way to tie up Zeke.

Once Zeke saw that Moses was shot in the face and out of action for a while, he turned the pistol on Jim Squirrel, who just stood there holding his bridle reins, a disturbed look on his face.

"I didn't think this hanging would work," Jim said. "I told the boys that, but Mo's stubborn, and Polly was his favourite."

Zeke had been in the mood to shoot down all the Squirrels and put an end to the continual vexation they caused him, but Jim Squirrel was too polite to just shoot in the midst of a conversation. Zeke contented himself with disarming the man, an action which seemed to relieve Jim considerably.

"I guess you done for Mo, looks like," he said, squatting down by his brother.

Zeke took a quick look, and formed a different opinion.

"Moses ain't dying," he said. "He's just lost a piece of his jawbone. He'll have to chew his vittles on the right side of his mouth. I hope it will teach him to think twice about putting himself in my way when I'm in a hurry to get to Missouri."

Zeke got up, caught his horse, and swung quickly into the saddle. He wanted to be mounted in case the strange weakness came over him again. Once safely in the saddle, he pulled up his shirt and inspected his wound. He saw at once that Jim Squirrel had been accurate—the bullet had made a furrow in his side, probably smacking into a rib in the course of its travels. The bullet had gone out the other side, and the bleeding had almost stopped. He felt confident he could make it to Becca without serious inconvenience.

"I wonder where Rat's run off to?" Jim Squirrel inquired, looking around for his brother. "He's going to have to help me get Moses on his horse, or Moses is apt to lie here and bleed to death."

"Now Jim, it's just a shot-off jaw," Zeke repeated. From the vague look in Jim's eye, he thought the man might be suffering a spell of weakness himself. "I've done stopped bleeding, and Moses will too, after a while."

Jim Squirrel continued to squat by his brother, a faraway look in his eye. Though still annoyed at Moses, Zeke could muster no rancor toward Jim Squirrel. If it had not been for his great need to get to Becca, he might have tried to help the man put Moses on a horse.

"If I see Rat, I'll tell him to get on back here," he assured Jim. "He was pretty scairt. He's probably run on up the road by now."

"Well, if you see him, Zeke, tell him to get on back," Jim said. "I need his help. Moses is going to be fractious once he comes to and notices he's lost one of his jawbones."

Zeke was nearly to the trail when he noticed Rat Squirrel hiding behind a red haw bush. It was not much of a bush; Rat was in plain sight.

"Rat, can you walk?" Zeke called out.

"Yes, and I can run, too," Rat informed him. "If you try

shootin' at me again, I mean to run faster than I run the first time."

"I wanted you to leave off trying to hang me, you fool!" Zeke told him. "If you can walk, get on back to that clearing and help your brother."

Rat, confused for a moment, looked at Zeke as if he could barely remember he *had* a brother.

"Jim's tending to Moses," Zeke told him. "Your brother needs your help—now get on back. I have no more time for palaver."

Rat stood up without another word and trudged on back into the thicket. He had a bloody pants leg where the bullet had nicked his hip, but otherwise, he looked fit.

Zeke put the bay gelding back into his long, easy lope and got along toward Missouri. Annoying as it was that the Squirrels thought they had the right to interfere with him on a public trail, it occurred to Zeke that being wounded slightly might not be a bad thing. It might help his case with Becca. After all, not every man would ride all the way to Missouri after being shot in the ribs. He even began to regret that the wound had stopped bleeding so soon. If he arrived drenched in blood, Becca could hardly turn him away. He thought he might stop a mile or two from the farm where she was staying and try to squeeze some fresh blood from the wound. Becca had always hated for him to be sick; the slightest ailment brought out the nurse in her. She would brew up teas and soups and other healthful concoctions, until his health improved. Zeke did not believe she could harden herself when faced with his injury, particularly if he could make it drip some just when he arrived at her door.

It amused him to think what fools the Squirrel boys were. They set out to hang him, and ended up doing him a favour instead, besides which Moses Squirrel would be eating one-sided for the rest of his life. He could hardly wait to tell Ned Christie the story.

Ned would laugh and laugh.

4

"HIS BREATH'S BARELY COMING, DALE," NED SAID, LOOKING down at the white, silent body of Tuxie Miller.

All the children were outside crying. Jewel was there; Ned had brought her over to help Dale with the nursing. But Jewel was just staring, like her husband Ned. Tuxie's fever had raged for five days, and they were all tired from fetching springwater in their attempts to keep Tuxie cool at night.

Old Turtle Man had come personally, at Dale's insistence. He was down at the barn by himself, making a poultice out of some weeds and thistles he had gathered on the Mountain. Ned's view was that Dale and Old Turtle Man had got there too late. The wound had too much of a start, and now Tuxie Miller was dying as a result.

"You best give up on him, Dale," Ned said, gently. "I expect he's lost the struggle."

Dale did not even look. She would sit for hours, not taking her eyes off Tuxie. She preferred it when the others left, so that there was no racket in the room—nothing that would keep her from hearing her husband's faint breathing. As long as she could hear his breathing and Tuxie could hear hers, a sign that his wife was right there with him, she was convinced that Tuxie would not die.

Old Turtle Man came and went frequently with fresh potions. Tuxie was so ill that Old Turtle Man was gone a day and a night, traveling to the next district in order to trade with another medicine man for more powerful concoctions. Dale's job was to see that Tuxie kept on breathing until the potions gained on the infection.

Dale meant to do it, too. Tuxie would not die, unless she allowed it, and she did not mean to allow it. Ned Christie could think what he liked.

Ned drew Jewel aside, so he could whisper to her without arousing Dale.

"I'm gonna go dig the grave," he told Jewel. "It'll save time."

"But he ain't dead," Jewel said, shocked by Ned's decision.

153

"He's barely drawing his breath," Ned whispered. "I expect he'll go by nighttime. I'd rather do the grave digging in the daylight. That way, I can make a tidier grave.

"Don't tell Dale," he added. "I'll dig it 'round behind the barn, where she can't see what I'm doing."

With that, Ned slipped out the door and walked off toward the barn. Jewel did not try to stop him, though she did not agree with what he was doing. Dale had not given up on her husband; Ned ought to let her fight her fight before he started digging graves.

When Ned came racing home to get her, Jewel was so glad to see him that her heart fluttered in her breast, like it always did at the sight of her tall husband after his leave-taking. She was so excited that she was more talkative with him than usual. But sitting by Tuxie's bedside watching him fight for his life was an experience that frightened Jewel so badly, she had barely spoken. She did her best to stir up mush now and then for the children's meals, but all she could think about was how lost she would be if it were Ned who was sick and dying—and he *could* be sick and dying, what with all the fighting in Tahlequah. Jewel knew that she did not know as much as Dale; she might not be able to do the right thing to save Ned, under the same circumstances. Dale had ridden over the Mountain, on a dark night, and found Old Turtle Man; she had even persuaded the old man to follow her home and treat Tuxie personally. Without Dale, Tuxie would already be dead—Ned was right about that. Jewel knew she needed to learn as much as she could from Dale, in case she had to nurse her own husband back from a serious wound someday.

She did not like Ned's determination to get the grave digging started. To Jewel, it seemed like giving up. If someone tried to dig a grave for Ned while he was still breathing, she would resent it bitterly, even if the act was kindly intentioned.

Jewel was with child now, a fact she had not revealed to her husband. Watching Ned stride down toward the Millers' barn, Jewel felt hot tears well up in her. It was such a hard task, keeping men alive, what with all the fighting and wounds and sickness life could produce. Now she had a baby within her, a new life that she had to keep alive as well. She wanted to be as strong as Dale Miller, strong enough to keep a man alive who rightly ought to be dead—strong enough to carry nine children and keep them alive and healthy, too. But she knew she was not as strong as Dale, not yet. She was fearful when Ned was away from her, so fearful that she could scarcely sleep. She needed Ned as much as Dale needed Tuxie, yet all Dale's skill and force was barely enough to keep Tuxie breathing. Thinking about it was so worrisome that it gave Jewel a shivering feeling, deep inside her. She wanted to be strong for Ned's and the baby's sakes, but with the shadow of death hanging over the Millers' cabin, she could not feel strong. All she felt was the coldness of fear, deep inside.

Dale sat by the bedside, holding one of Tuxie's hands. Once in a while, she would press one of his fingers, and Tuxie would respond, pressing his finger against hers, just enough so that she could feel it. In Dale's mind, the fact that Tuxie still pressed her finger was a signal that he did not want her to let him go. She knew death was near, and it might be that Tuxie would get so sick that he would have to leave her, but as long as he pressed her finger, Dale knew there was a chance that he would stay. Although Tuxie was so weak that his breath came only faintly, the wound itself looked a little better to her. Old Turtle Man had mixed up a few hard blackberries he had found on the Mountain with some squeezings from the glands of a toad. He had smeared the mash into the wound as deeply as he could get it, and it seemed to Dale that it had leeched some of the poison out of the ugly red gash. She knew she had to keep the closest watch she was capable of; her eyes went constantly to Tuxie's face. She knew her husband was walking a thin fence rail between life and death, and she did not want to withdraw her attention for a second, lest he tip to the death side while she was looking off.

Ned Christie had walked off somewhere; maybe he had left to go kill Davie Beck. Ned had told her several times that he meant to put Davie Beck in his grave for what he had done to Tuxie. He spoke of vengeance while they were considering taking off Tuxie's leg. Dale had weighed carefully the matter of amputation and rejected it on instinct, but she had paid little attention to Ned's talk of revenge. Ned could worry about vengeance if he wanted to—Dale had to devote her attention to keeping her husband alive. She had nine children, and she would not desert them or skimp on their raising. Tuxie was the man she had pledged herself to, and Dale knew she faced a long, bleak widowhood, if he died. Tuxie was a good man, and she needed him. She knew she would wither without Tuxie.

She pressed Tuxie's finger again, her heart in her throat, and waited for Tuxie to press back. For several long seconds, he did not. Then Dale felt the faint pressure of his finger against hers, and her heart lifted.

Old Turtle Man arrived with a cup of bitter herbs he had been brewing in springwater. At first, Tuxie seemed too weak to swallow the black potion, but Dale got behind him and lifted his body. Finally, Old Turtle Man got a few drops in him. Dale saw Tuxie's Adam's apple move when he swallowed, and was grateful that the old healer had persisted.

Then Old Turtle Man went out the door, and began chanting one of his healing songs, while Dale wiped Tuxie's forehead with a cool rag.

"Where did Ned go to?" Dale asked, when Jewel came timidly back to the bedside.

"He went off," Jewel replied. She did not want to blatantly lie, but neither did she want to reveal that Ned was behind the barn with a shovel and a pick, digging Tuxie's grave.

Dale liked Jewel, but a low feeling came to her when she looked at the girl, so young and timid and scared. She knew Jewel had no sense yet of the power that would be hers some-day, as a grown woman—no girl could know much of that power, until it arrived. It was not the natural fact of her inno-cence and ignorance that troubled Dale when she looked at Jewel; it had more to do with things Dale did not really know herself, apprehensions that rose in her when she thought of Ned Christie. Ned and Tuxie had been friends from boyhood, and Dale knew there was no separating them. She knew, too, that Ned was as true and loyal a friend as Tuxie would ever have. Dale cared for Ned and might have married him herself, if he had been forthright enough to come to her with his need. But Ned had held back, pretending he was not needy of her. Tuxie had walked right past Ned and plunked his longing in her lap as if it were a bushel of snap beans. Before they had ever touched, Tuxie had made her feel that his need for her was so great that he might die if she refused him, so she let all thought of the handsome Ned go and opened herself to Tuxie. She had not regretted it, either, for all Ned's handsomeness and dash. Tuxie was the more gentle man, a man she could be sure of.

There was even more than that to Dale's concern. Ned seemed to be making Jewel a decent husband; he might have made a decent husband to her as well. Dale's disquiet was not about Ned Christie's character—it was about his fate. She thought it unlikely that Ned and Jewel would ever know the kind of peace she felt with Tuxie and their children. Ned would not know peace, and now young Jewel would not, either. The killings in Tahlequah merely confirmed something Dale had always felt about Ned Christie: bloodshed was his fate— bloodshed and death. Now the blood had begun to flow in the Tahlequah courthouse. Ned had killed some of his enemies, but he had not killed them all, nor had the white law from over the Mountain been heard from just yet.

There would be more battles, of that Dale felt certain. Young Jewel would have to grow into womanhood quick if she was to guard and protect her husband, and pull him out of conflict before it was too late.

Dale was lost only for a moment in her apprehensive thoughts. While she was looking at Jewel, Tuxie suddenly squeezed her hand. It was such a surprise that Dale jumped. When she looked back at her husband, Tuxie's eyes were open. Not only that, they had a faint light in them.

"What's the grub, Dale?" he asked. "My belly feels like it ain't got nothing in it."

"It don't have much, hon," Dale said. "You've been too ill to eat."

Tuxie turned his head slightly, and looked out the window. The day was bright, and the sun was vivid in the afternoon sky.

"I have never liked to be in bed in the daytime," he said. "I'd try to cut some firewood if I didn't feel so lank."

Then he noticed Jewel, and looked at her in surprise.

"Why, Jewel," he said. "When'd you come to visit?"

Then, having said his little say, Tuxie sank back into deep sleep. His breathing came so regularly that Dale did not have to listen for it. She shook her head, and dripped tears of relief onto the quilt that covered Tuxie's legs. It had been a hard struggle, harder even than childbirth, and related, she felt. As she sat through the five nights holding Tuxie back from departure with her will and the strength of her body and her love, it had been her children's birthings that she thought most about. Getting a child to come—keeping a man from going—those were the poles of her struggle. It was a grim struggle, one that required her to reach into the deepest center of herself and find the strength to prevail against Tuxie's illness. Listening to Tuxie's calm breathing made Dale wish it was nighttime. She wanted to lay down with him and rest, from all the straining. Her insides had got so knotted up with worry that she felt a good night's sleep beside her husband was what she needed to put her right.

Dale looked out the window and saw that Old Turtle Man was gathering up his pouches and his materials, getting ready to leave.

"Hurry, Jewel, go stop him," Dale said. "I'll be out in a minute. I need to thank him, and the children need to thank him, too. He come all this way and saved their pa."

Jewel went out quickly, but not quickly enough. The Turtle Man, so old that he was frail and bent with age, nonetheless had slipped away into the forest. When Jewel asked the children, now playing by the woodpile, where the old man was, they all looked blank. None of them had seen Old Turtle Man leave.

Jewel hurried to the barn. She was apprehensive that Dale would somehow discover what Ned was doing. Sure enough, he stood waist deep in the grave he was digging, his blue shirt as wet with sweat as if he had been dipped in a creek.

"Ned, stop—you don't have to dig any deeper," Jewel said.

"I do, too," Ned said. "I've only got it about three feet. A good grave needs to be six feet, at least. There's varmints that can dig down three feet, if they're hungry enough."

"No, that ain't what I meant," Jewel told him. She felt a little vexed with Ned for being so quick to disregard her advice. There were times when he just did not seem to hear what she had to say.

"Tuxie ain't going to die," she told him. "He just opened his eyes, and he's breathing better. Dale's up there crying, she's so glad."

Ned was stunned—and more than a little abashed. Jewel had tried to keep him from hasty digging, but he had not listened. Now he was standing three feet down in a half-dug grave, with no corpse to put in it.

"Are you certain?" he asked, remembering the white, silent Tuxie he had left scarcely more than an hour before.

"He opened his eyes," Jewel repeated. "And he asked for grub."

"I guess he's well, then," Ned told her. "Food's always the first thing on Tuxie's mind."

"Come back with me, you'll see," Jewel said. "Old Turtle Man left. I guess he knew Tuxie was well."

"I can't come back yet," Ned said. "I've got to spade all this dern dirt back in this hole. I need to do it quick, too. If Dale finds out I jumped the gun on Tuxie's grave, she'll be at me about it for the rest of my life."

"Ned, you shouldn't have given up so soon," Jewel said.

"Soon? It's been five days since I brought him home," Ned responded, annoyed that Jewel thought he was a man who quit too easily.

"You shouldn't have given up so soon!" Jewel repeated. They were the first words of criticism she had ever spoken to her husband, but she was too upset inside to keep herself from saying them and then repeating them. What if the child inside her got as sick as Tuxie had been? Was he going to give up on their baby and start digging a grave?

Ned was surprised. Jewel had never spoken so sharply to him before. He was too shocked to respond.

Jewel, suddenly afraid of how Ned might take her moment of anger, turned and hurried back to the house.

5

As SOON AS CRACKY BOLEN SHOWED UP WITH THE NEWS THAT Judge Isaac Parker wanted to see him, Marshal Dan Maples got ready to go. He rolled his bedroll and cleaned his gun, his mood improving by the moment. There had been no marshaling to speak of for three months now, which meant there had been no cash money for three months, either. Wilma, his wife, had not even been able to buy seeds enough to plant an adequate garden, which meant victuals would most likely be scarce before the next winter was over.

Dan was soon ready to go—Wilma had even packed him a

little cold pork and a roasting ear to eat on his travels—but then had to delay his departure because Cracky Bolen settled down at the kitchen table and showed no signs of being eager to go on to his own farm, just five miles into the Blue Hills.

"Fifty people were killed over there in Tahlequah. That's the figure I heard," Cracky said, salting a cold roasting ear Wilma had offered him.

Dan Maples did not believe that figure for a moment, and he also did not believe it was the death figure that really interested Cracky Bolen. The figure that interested Cracky was Wilma's figure, a generous, womanly figure by any standards, and particularly so by Cracky's standards, since his own wife, Myrtle Lou, was skinny as a weed, and about as unfriendly.

Dan did not blame Cracky Bolen for admiring Wilma's figure, and he did not distrust either his neighbour or his wife. Nonetheless, he was not about to ride off on a long errand and leave Cracky Bolen sitting there eating roasting ears and directing his long, lonesome gaze at Wilma's figure.

There was such a thing as courtesy, though, and Dan Maples tried to practice it. Cracky had been a reliable neighbour over the years, if tiresome in his adoration of Wilma. Dan sat patiently while Cracky ate three roasting ears, some bacon, and a tasty plate of cobbler; but that was all the patience manners demanded. After all, he was not the only unemployed marshal in the Arkansas hills. While he was watching Cracky gaze at Wilma's figure, swifter lawmen might already be riding into Fort Smith. In the wake of such a crisis, Judge Parker might hire whoever got there first.

The minute Cracky consumed the last mouthful of vinegar cobbler, Dan stood up and hefted his rifle.

"I've got to be going along and you best traipse on up the road too, Cracky," Dan said. "I expect you've got chores to do and some of them probably won't keep till dark."

Cracky was a little put out by the brusque tone in Dan Maples's voice. He had ridden out of his way to deliver important news and did not feel it quite neighbourly of Dan to rush him out before the last bite of cobbler had slid down his gullet. Still, he had to admit that if he had happened to marry a woman with a figure like Wilma Maples's, he, too, might be reluctant to go off and leave a neighbour sitting at his table. In any case, Dan Maples had never been overly friendly, Wilma or no Wilma. He seemed to feel that it was wrong to get too friendly with his neighbours, since at any moment one of them was apt to commit a crime that might require him to hang them, or at least arrest them. It was an attitude Cracky had come to resent over the years. He had helped Dan Maples slaughter pigs; helped him put up a barn; and had returned quite a few stray livestock to him, livestock that might have been lost forever. It was irksome to be treated as if he were going to take up banditry on the roads, by a man he had known for at least twenty-five years.

"No, Dan. No chores today," Cracky said. "That's why I had younguns, so I wouldn't have to do the damn chores every day of my life. I intend to take the biggest jug of whiskey I can find and go fishing, when I get home."

"Well, I hope you catch a nice, fat catfish then," Dan said. "Many thanks for bringing me the news from the Judge. I can use the marshaling, if there's any left to do."

"If there was fifty dead in Tahlequah, there'll be plenty of work for marshals for a while to come," Cracky informed him. "Many thanks for the roastin' ears, Wilma, not to mention that cobbler."

"Oh, you can mention the cobbler, all right," Wilma said. "You can compliment my cookin' all you want to. Dan's forgot how, I reckon. If he was to accidentally say something nice about a dish I cooked, I'd more than likely drop dead from surprise."

Dan Maples made no reply to his wife's remark—an unwarranted remark, in his view. He considered the best compliment a man could make about his wife's cooking was to eat it. He cleaned his plate at every meal. That was comment enough.

Wilma was annoyed with Dan for being so stiff with Cracky, a good-hearted man who meant no harm. Cracky just happened to be cursed with a mean wife, Myrtle Lou. It was Wilma's opinion that any man married to Myrtle Lou needed all the kindness he could get from his fellow man. She knew Cracky fancied her; it was the kind of fancying that was flattering to her as a woman without threatening her as a wife. Dan was often gone for a month at a time, when he was marshaling. It was reassuring to have a neighbour who would stop by once in a while. If he looked at her with some appreciation while he was taking a meal, then so much the better, in Wilma's view.

Dan Maples might not see it that way, but Wilma did not care. Dan had explained to her several times that it was his job as a lawman to be suspicious of everybody. A lawman could not be too suspicious, not in his book.

Wilma Maples lived by a different book, however. It was her opinion that Dan would have been suspicious of everybody, even if he had been just a blacksmith and not a marshal. Several times during their marriage, he had infuriated Wilma by accusing her of selling eggs, a suspicion so foolish that it made her wonder if she had been wise to marry the man. Their farm was five miles from a road—who would she sell eggs to, even if she *wanted* to sell eggs?

"Why would you think that, Dan?" she asked him, each time he accused her.

"We keep a dozen hens," he reminded her each time. "A dozen hens ought to be producing more eggs than I ever see. I expect you're selling them to get money for bonnets or ribbons. You *do* like bonnets and ribbons, Wilma."

"I like bonnets and ribbons. And skunks and badgers and plenty of other varmints like to eat hen's eggs," Wilma pointed out. "Besides that, we got nervous hens—they know they'll get eaten by a varmint themselves if they ain't careful. Half of them don't lay regular as it is."

Dan usually desisted, but Wilma knew that did not mean he was convinced. He still suspected her of selling eggs, and nothing she said ever really convinced him otherwise. Sometimes when Dan was not busy, he would wander around the place looking for hen's nests. He meant to chart their laying places so he could check for himself as to whether a given hen was laying or not. This annoyed Wilma to no end. She had been a loyal wife to the man for fifteen years, and he still suspected her of selling eggs!

Sometimes, at night, laying in bed thinking about his accusations, Wilma would get so mad it would be all she could do not to leave Dan. Once, in the night, she got in such a state of anger that she jabbed Dan with her elbow and woke him from a solid sleep.

"What would you do if it was true?" she asked.

"If what was true?" Dan mumbled—he was a sound sleeper.

"True that I sell eggs," Wilma replied. "Is it such a crime

that you'd feel you had to divorce me? Or would you just report me to the Judge?"

"Why, I . . . uh . . . I guess I'd divorce you," Dan said, after a moment's foggy consideration. "I wouldn't be able to tolerate it."

Wilma became silent, more silent than Dan could ever remember her being. Her silence was so deep that it seemed to have a weight to it. He could not remember a time when his wife's silence felt so heavy to him. She was silent the next morning, too.

They got through the next three days with very few remarks passing between them. Dan felt that Wilma was wanting him to take back his remark about divorce, but he did not intend to take it back. After all, she had awakened him from a solid sleep to ask the question. If she was not going to like the answer, she should have left him asleep. What would any man do if he caught his wife stealing eggs? All he had done was render an honest opinion.

To his puzzlement, married life had changed the night Wilma woke him up and asked him her question. Wilma did her wifely chores well enough, and was mostly cheerful in speech; but it seemed to him that she kept the heavy silence between them from then on. She did not complain—Wilma Maples was no complainer, never had been—but she did not confide in him, either. Only once, at breakfast, did she turn to him with a flash of anger and say a thing that badly startled Dan Maples.

"If I was to want to sell eggs, I'd do it and you'd never catch me," Wilma informed him. "You can wear that marshal's badge till it rusts to your shirt, and you'd never catch me."

"This badge is nickel, Wilma. Nickel don't rust," Dan replied. Wilma looked at him scornfully and went on about her business. Dan was never able to puzzle out why she took the whole matter of the eggs so severely. He had not said he would arrest her; it was not exactly a crime to sell eggs. He had only said he would divorce her, which was proper, in his view. A wife who went against her husband's commandment could expect no less.

For some reason, Wilma's remark about him not catching her if she wanted to sell eggs came into Dan's mind as he was tying his bedroll onto his saddle. Wilma walked out of the house to see him off. Cracky came out, too, and hitched himself up on his old red mule for the ride home.

While Dan was waiting for Cracky to ride off so he could give Wilma a kiss in farewell, a rather odd thing happened. A big crow had been cawing from atop a sycamore tree, down by the barn. The bird took off and circled around a few times, still cawing. Dan Maples paid no more attention to the big crow than he would to any other bird, though this particular bird commanded an exceptionally loud caw, a caw loud enough to grate on the ear. The big crow flew over the house and then dipped suddenly, landing on the chimney and cawing for all he was worth.

Dan had yet to mount. He was fingering his girth, hoping Cracky would hurry up and leave, but what slowed Cracky down was that his big red mule decided to empty its bladder before departing. That mule must have a bladder the size of a barrel, Dan thought, for the emptying went on several minutes, the large black bird cawing all the while.

The mule finally finished; Cracky waved; and Dan started toward his wife, stepping carefully over the yellow stream of mule piss that was coursing down the hill. The crow's caw was so irritating that Dan was tempted to shoot it, just to shut it up. But before he could pull his gun, the crow left the chimney, flapped once, and coasted down over Cracky, the red mule, and Wilma, heading straight for Dan Maples himself. At first, Dan thought the crow must be going to light on his saddle, though he had never known a crow to do such a thing. But it was not the horse the big crow meant to land on; it was Dan Maples's shoulder he was aiming for. Before he could so much as flinch, the big crow landed on his right shoulder and cawed in Dan Maples's face, his two black eyes not six inches from Dan's own eyes.

"Pshaw, crow . . . git!" Dan said. He reached to knock the brash bird off his shoulder. But before he could, the crow flew straight up, up and up, into the sky, high as a hawk would fly, or even an eagle. The crow went up and up, until it was almost out of sight—just a speck, in the bright morning sky.

Dan Maples was so disconcerted by what had happened that for a moment he doubted his senses. Was he awake and about to ride off to Fort Smith? Or was he still in bed, dreaming about giant crows landing on his shoulder? No bird had ever landed on him before in his life, though now and then a chimney swallow might come down the chimney and be unable to find its way out of the house.

But a chimney swallow getting lost and confused was not the same order of thing as having a big crow land on his shoulder and caw right in his face. Dan looked to see if either Cracky or Wilma had noticed the occurrence, and saw at once that they were both as astonished by it as he was. Cracky Bolen had stopped his mule and sat on it with his mouth gaping like a grain chute, looking up at the sky where the crow had disappeared. Wilma stood not ten feet away, a dishrag in her hand, looking pale as a ghost.

"Well, now, that was a sight, I guess," Dan said, walking over to his wife.

"It's an omen, Dan," Wilma said suddenly. "You mustn't go." Seeing the black bird land on her husband's shoulder upset her so deeply that she had begun to shiver. The hairs on her arms stood up, and a bad feeling clutched her stomach.

Dan was surprised by the look on Wilma's face. She was a resourceful woman who rarely looked frightened, but there she stood, looking scared as a cornered jackrabbit.

"I have to go, Wilma, I have a living to make," he told her.

"No, Dan—it was an omen," Wilma insisted. "Don't you see?"

"An omen of what?" Dan asked.

"Death!" Wilma cried. "An omen of death! Crows know when a person is about to die, don't you know that?"

"Pshaw," Dan said, again. "It's a fine sunny day, and I ain't about to die. I'm just goin' off to Fort Smith to do a little marshaling."

Cracky came trotting over on his mule to join the conversation.

"Dan, you're a pure fool if you go riding off into the fighting after you've had a sign like that," Cracky told him.

"I expect it was a pet bird that got lost from its owner," Dan said, annoyed that both his wife and his neighbour were suddenly trying to persuade him to neglect his duties. He was particularly annoyed with Cracky, the very man who had passed Judge Parker's request on to him. A lawman who expected to make his living marshaling did not lightly disregard Judge Isaac Parker's requests.

Cracky looked upward as high as he could look, but he saw no sign of the big crow.

"It wasn't a pet bird, it flew right up to heaven," he told Dan Maples. "When a dern black bird sits right on your shoulder and caws at you and then flies straight up to heaven, it means your hour is close. If I were you, I'd stay right here at home and keep my gun cocked for a few days."

"Nope. I'm due in Fort Smith, and I've wasted enough time already," Dan said. "That crow must have got loose from a circus. I heard there *was* a circus, over in Little Rock."

Wilma did not say more. Dan had set his jaw, and when Dan set his jaw, argument was useless. Cracky Bolen knew it, too. He turned to Wilma with a look of sympathy, and then rode off on his red mule. The moment they had privacy, Wilma came close to Dan and hugged him tight. Though she was cold with fright, she held Dan close, and even tried to tempt him with a soft kiss. Tempting seemed her only hope of keeping her husband. Despite his suspicious nature, he was a decent man, and she loved him as deeply as she had when she came home with him as a bride. Now the bird of death had marked him. If she lost his touch now, she would lose it forever. He would die in the mud in some Cherokee village, and she would be a lonely widow with a farm to keep, no joy in her days, and no pleasure in her nights. There were no children between them; she had not been able to conceive. If she let her man ride off to his death, she would have no one.

"I don't want you to go, Dan!" Wilma insisted, clutching him tight. "I'll beg you to stay with me if I have to."

But Dan Maples had set his jaw. He stepped back from Wilma and mounted his horse. Wilma was not crying, but she had a look of anguish on her face as she looked up at him. It was vexing to him, the way Wilma had of getting upset just at the wrong time. He had hoped for a swift departure, and yet an hour had passed and he was still at home. First it had been Cracky; now it was because a big black bird had upset his wife.

"Now, Wilma, go on back in and tend to your chores," he said. "We can't be losing money because of a crow."

Wilma did not respond. She did not even say good-bye. When Dan turned at the foot of the hill and looked back, she was still standing right where she had been, the dishrag in her hand.

Dan Maples waved, but Wilma, his wife, did not wave back.

6

LONG BEFORE CHILLY STUFFLEBEAN FINALLY STRUGGLED back into Fort Smith, a week and a day after the courthouse massacre, Judge Isaac Parker and everyone else who knew Chilly had given him up for dead. Several witnesses had seen him leave Tahlequah the morning after the massacre, but no one in the vicinity of either Tahlequah or Fort Smith had seen him since.

"Ambushed, probably," Marshal Maples concluded, as he sat talking the matter over with the Judge. "I expect one of the Becks waylaid him, or else one of the Squirrel brothers."

"I ought not to have sent him into such a hostile situation," Judge Parker mused. "He was too young for the job."

The Judge had reproached himself a good deal in the matter of Chilly Stufflebean, and his wife Mart had chipped in a healthy measure of reproach herself. The Judge felt so bad about the young man that he was considering offering a reward out of his own pocket for information about Chilly's where-abouts or his fate, as the case may be. Five dollars was the sum Judge Parker was thinking of offering, though he realized $5 might seem puny in relation to the large rewards available for the capture of whiskeysellers. He was not a wealthy man, however, and $5 was all he felt his budget would allow.

He was working up to mentioning the reward to Marshal Dan Maples when he happened to glance out a window and see none other than Chilly Stufflebean himself, walking toward the courthouse. Chilly was still some fifty yards away, but it was evident to the Judge that his bailiff was in a bedraggled state. For one thing, he was barefoot—a surprising thing, since the Judge had staked him a new suit and a sturdy pair of shoes just prior to sending him off to do the bailiffing for Judge Sixkiller in Tahlequah.

"Well, I guess he wasn't ambushed. Or if he was, all they got was his shoes," the Judge said to Marshal Maples. He found that his sorrow at the contemplation of Chilly's possible demise was rapidly turning to vexation at the thought of the young man's carelessness. The Judge's temper was not soothed by the thought that he had just been about to waste $5 hard-earned cash as a reward for information about a young scamp so careless that he could not keep track of shoes he had been given as a gift.

"Lost 'em in cricks," Chilly said, when he finally straggled into the Judge's chambers. His reception was mixed. Dan Maples greeted him amiably and congratulated him on surviving the big shootout. But Judge Parker was more interested in the fact that he had a a bad rip in his new suit of clothes, and had also lost his shoes.

"Lost them how? Talk English," the Judge demanded.

"In cricks. That's the worst part of traveling, cricks," Chilly repeated. "There was about twenty of 'em, and they all had that sucky mud underneath the water."

"Creeks—why didn't you say so?" the Judge said, finally. "That's why you were lent the mule, so you wouldn't have to wade creeks in your good clothes. I expected you to keep firm control of that mule. What happened?"

Chilly talked for an hour about what had happened, how he had wandered hopelessly through the hills for a week, following one twisty little track and then another, hoping all the while that one of the little cow paths would somehow bring him to the road to Fort Smith. He had asked directions of several travelers, all of whom must have been as lost as he was. The harder he tried to follow their directions, the more lost he became, the deeper the woods, the deeper the hills. He had five shells in his pistol when he walked out of Tahlequah, and by the exercise of careful marksmanship managed to kill one rabbit and two possums—otherwise, he would have starved on the trail.

"Possums are easier to hit than rabbits, they're slower," he informed Judge Parker and his wife, Mart. By the time Chilly got that far along in his recital, the Judge had closed the courthouse for the day and walked Chilly home with him so Mart could clean him up and give him a good meal. He was also hoping Mart would mend the rip in Chilly's new suit, though she could do nothing about the shoes, which were lost forever in a creek somewhere between Fort Smith, Arkansas, and Tahlequah.

"I know the difference between a possum and a rabbit, and Mart does, too, Chilly," the Judge said. "We've all had hardships to bear. What I need from you now that you're back is a good account of what went on in that courtroom, and I need it soon."

"Now you wait, Ike," Mart said. "Chilly's walked a far piece. Let him finish his supper before you go worrying him about all that shooting."

Mart did not exactly have her dander up, but she looked as if she could get it up quickly if handled wrong.

Chilly was Mart's pet. Over the years, the Judge had found that it was best to do whatever correcting was needed—and a lot had been needed—out of earshot of his wife Mart. That way, he only had one problem to deal with: Chilly himself. If Mart got it in her head that her pet bailiff was being dealt with too severely, her temper might flare up like a prairie fire. The Judge had been scorched by Mart's temper many times in the years of their marriage, and he saw no reason to risk it on a day when he had already borne the unnecessary loss of a costly pair of shoes.

Chilly remembered that there had been a big shootout in the courtroom in Tahlequah, but the truth was he had been so terrified on his eight-day walk through the mountains that he no longer remembered the circumstances of the shootout very clearly. What he remembered all too clearly was huddling under bushes when it rained; losing his shoes in a boggy creek full of water moccasins; and trying to find a place to sleep at night where scorpions would not be crawling underneath him and snakes would not be crawling over him. He disliked creatures with fangs and stingers. Twice on the walk, he had been badly stung by yellow jackets. One had stung him in his sleep and left its stinger in his eyelid, the result being that he had to bumble along with one eye puffed shut for two days. By that time, Chilly was carrying with him a sense of doom so heavy that he could barely lift his bare feet. All the mountains looked alike; all the trails; all the trees.

Probably a good, safe road that would lead him quickly to Fort Smith was not more than five miles away. He dreamed about the road at night, and daydreamed about it during the day, but he could never find it. He was down to his last bullet when an old man with one arm came down the trail, leading a brown ox to market. The old man was named George Nails.

When Chilly asked him what the nearest town might be, old George Nails looked at him as if he were daft.

"Why, Tahlequah, it ain't but a half mile off," old Nails informed him. "See that there smoke?" he said, pointing with a shaky hand. "That's from the chimney of the hardware store."

At the time of his encounter with George Nails and his brown ox, Chilly had been walking for five days. He was not ready to confess, to old Nails or anyone else, that he had walked for five days and was only half a mile from his starting point. By discreet inquiry—George Nails was by now wary of him, convinced that the young man was crazy—Chilly managed to discover that Mr. Nails was taking the ox to Fort Smith to be sold. Chilly considered that he was saved, though old Nails did not offer to travel with him, or even to show him the way. Chilly followed the brown ox over the hill and down to the Fort Smith road that he had longed for so intensely.

Under the stern gaze of Judge Parker, a gaze that had sought out the truth and found in it many a hardened criminal, Chilly discovered that he had powers of invention whose existence he had not even suspected. He told the Judge that he had hitched a wagon ride with an experienced drover who was on his way to Fort Smith. But then, due to drunkenness, the drover took a wrong turn and was forty miles to the west of Fort Smith before he discovered his mistake. Trying to cross an especially rocky ravine, the drover broke the rear axle on his wagon.

"That's when I decided it would be quicker just to get off and walk home," Chilly said, keeping his eyes on his plate, which was heaped with Mrs. Parker's tasty grub.

"I see," Judge Parker said, a skeptical expression on his face.

"I ripped my suit helping the man fix his axle," Chilly said, when in fact, he had snagged it on a thornbush high in the hills.

"I see," the Judge said, again. "That's when you began to wade them cricks."

"Yes, sir—they was boggy," Chilly said meekly. "That sucky mud got my shoes."

He knew he had better not try to push his lies any further. The Judge had got out a whittling stick and was sharpening his old knife on a whetstone. The Judge had sharpened the knife so much that the blade on it was thin as a fingernail. He considered the stick he had chosen, and began to whittle thoughtfully.

Chilly knew it was when the Judge seemed most absorbed in his whittling, that criminals were apt to make their greatest mistakes.

"I'll pay you back for the shoes, Judge," Chilly said.

"If you can give a clear account of what happened in Tahlequah, I'll forgive the loss of the shoes," Judge Parker informed him. "I need a clear account of that gunfight before I go sending marshals off into Cherokee country."

"Let it wait till morning, Ike," Mart suggested bluntly.

The Judge was taken aback. Mostly, he was tolerant of Mart and her ways. But at this point in time, which was a late point in time so far as he was concerned, he saw no reason to let her interfere in matters that were within the province of the court, such as questioning witnesses to the Tahlequah gunfight. He had a major witness sitting right at his dinner table, eating free grub, and saw no reason to delay his questioning.

"It can't wait till morning," the Judge informed his crisp spouse. "I intend to have a federal marshal on the road by morning, and I need to tell him who to catch.

"That's what I say," he added, noting that Mart was edging closer to having her dander up.

"Chilly's tuckered out. You ought to let him get a good night's sleep before you start questioning him about that mess," Mart insisted.

The Judge felt his own dander begin to gain altitude. Mart was too prone to interfere in matters that were none of her business—she always had been. He had been waiting eight long days for Chilly's account of the trouble in Tahlequah. Why in the devil would his own wife insist on having him wait through another night?

"Mart, you ought to go knit a rug," he suggested. "I'm the Judge. I know when I need to question a witness."

"No, you don't," Mart told him. "You may have the job of judge, but if you can't see that Chilly's too exhausted to be answering a bunch of questions, then I wouldn't want you judging me, I guess."

Chilly began to get the nervous feeling he always got when he happened to find himself in a cross-fire between the Judge and his wife. In some ways, it was worse than being in the cross-fire in Tahlequah. In that situation, things happened so fast that there was not much time to be scared—you ducked, and hoped for the best. But here at Judge Parker's dinner table, there was no place to duck. He had to sit and pretend not to notice that the Judge and his wife Mart were glaring at one another—and the glaring was because of him.

He thought maybe the best thing would be to give a quick recital of events in Tahlequah. Maybe that would satisfy the Judge for a few hours, long enough for him to catch some sleep.

"I'll just tell it quick," he said, avoiding Mrs. Martha Parker's eye when he said it. "I was nearly late because the mule bogged in a creek. Then a fellow named Ned Christie came along and gave me a ride into town. We got there just in time for me to collect the guns. Judge Sixkiller didn't want no guns in the courtroom. I offered to put out spittoons, but he didn't have but one, so that was an easy job. Then they brought Zeke Proctor in, and he barely got sat down good before somebody put a gun through the window and started shooting at him. Ned Christie shot that fellow, but another fellow pitched some guns in to the Becks, and they started shooting, too. I think one of them kilt the Judge. Then the Becks shot some of the people in the courtroom, and Ned Christie shot some of the Becks. I even shot one of them myself—I think his name was T. Spade."

"What? You shot a Beck?" the Judge asked, startled. "That's a piece of news I hadn't heard."

"Well, I shot one," Chilly repeated. "He shot at me twice and missed. I didn't know if he'd miss again, so I shot him."

"Was he kilt, or just shot up?" Judge Parker inquired.

"Kilt," Chilly admitted. "Zeke tried to strangle one of them Becks, but the man crawled off into the street and an old fellow with long white hair rode up and rescued him."

It was at this point in his recital that Chilly realized Mart Parker was right: he was too tired to be telling such a complicated story.

His head began to droop; he had the urge just to put his cheek in his plate and snooze a little, right there at the table. He knew he better not do it, for it would probably finish him with the Judge. But he felt a powerful urge to go to sleep. Despite himself, his chin tilted down toward his chest.

"Ike, he's noddin'," Mart said briskly. "Why don't you let up?"

Judge Parker saw that, indeed, his witness was fading. It was vexing, since very few facts had been accurately established, but there was not much he could do about it. He thought if he hurried, he might get in two more questions before Chilly was out cold.

"Chilly, did you see for a certainty that Judge Sixkiller was dead?" the Judge asked, determined to have a solid answer to that question.

"He was dead as a brick," Chilly told him.

"What was the count of the dead, then? Can you remember?" the Judge asked.

Chilly tried to get his brain to come up with a figure—after all, he himself had helped Ned Christie line the bodies up on the floor. He remembered that all the while one of Ned's friends had been scrunched up in the corner, bleeding from a deep wound in his leg. In his mind's eye, he could see the bodies lined up in the courtroom; he could even see them laying by the graves that the volunteers had dug. But, though he thought hard, he could not be sure of the count.

"It was ten, at least," he said finally. "I think it might have been eleven. Then another fellow died while we were turning him over . . . I guess that would have made it twelve."

"I see," the Judge said, soberly.

The Judge was silent for a moment, when he heard the count. From all the accounts he had received, he had concluded that the figure would probably be as high as ten. Now, Chilly made it twelve.

It was a sobering thing.

"I doubt twelve people was ever killed in a courtroom before," he said. "We've made a poor kind of history, I guess, up here in our hills."

When he looked at Chilly again, the young man's eyes were closed. He helped Mart ease the young bailiff down on a pallet she had made for him on the back porch, and then he followed his wife upstairs to their bedroom, a little uneasy as to what her bedtime mood might be.

Mart did not like being crossed, and yet he had crossed her to the extent of getting a hasty story out of Chilly. But Mart seemed sobered, too, by what she had heard.

"Twelve's a passel of people to die—and it was over a woman, too," Mart said, when she had put on her blue gown.

Judge Parker had a knot in one of his shoelaces. It took him a while to untie it; he could not bend as easily or reach his shoes as handily as had once been the case.

"It was over a woman, wasn't it?" Mart repeated.

"A woman, or some weevily corn—take your pick," the Judge offered.

"I pick the woman," Mart said.

Later, in bed, they each read a verse of the Bible before Mart blew out the light.

"I doubt that story about Chilly catching a ride in a wagon and ending up forty miles west," the Judge said. "That sounded like a lie to me. What do you think?"

"It was a lie, but don't you pester him about it, Ike," Mart said. "I expect he was just lost and scared, somewhere in the hills."

"Yes, but it's no excuse for losing the shoes," the Judge said. "If I had on new shoes and I came to a creek, I think I'd have sense enough to take off my shoes and hold them over my head. That way, there'd be a lot less chance of a loss."

"Well, but what if you stepped in a hole and got swallowed up?" Mart suggested, with mischief in her voice.

"Dern it, Mart, why would I step in a hole and get swallowed up?" the Judge asked.

"Because you don't know everything, that's why," Mart replied tartly. Mart was slow to get to sleep. She would keep up a conversation as long as she could. The Judge, an easy sleeper, found that characteristic trying at times, and now was one of the times.

"You think you know everything, but you don't," Mart added.

"Dern it, Mart, I have never claimed to know everything," the Judge replied.

"You may not claim it, but you think it," Mart answered.

"I do think I know enough to decide when it's time to go to sleep at night, and it's time to go to sleep," the Judge said.

"Go to sleep, then. Who's stopping you?" Mart said.

7

THE MOMENT BECCA CAME TO THE DOOR OF THE CABIN AND looked at him, Zeke got the feeling that it was not going to be easy to persuade her to come home—at least it was not going to be as easy as he had hoped it would be.

Becca had a kind of November look in her eyes, grey and chill. The fresh blood he had squeezed out of his rib wound just before he rode up did not fool her, or move her, either. In fact, it did not appear to interest her at all.

"Hello, Bec," he said, in a quiet tone. "I'm wounded in the side."

"If you're wounded, you ought to have found a doc," Becca told him. "I ain't a doc."

"But you're my wife," Zeke ventured, still talking quietly.

"I *was* your wife," Becca corrected. "How do you know what I am now?"

Zeke was disappointed in the comment, and perplexed as to how to proceed. He thought maybe the direct approach would be best.

"I'm wounded, Bec," he said. "One of the Squirrels shot me. Where else would a man go when he's wounded but to his wife?"

"That's a scratch, Zeke," Becca said, guessing. *You wounded me,* and I had nowhere to seek help, she thought. In the distance, she could hear the triplets shrieking down by the pond. In her discouragement of spirit, she had lost control of her three tots. They spent most of their days by the pond, in a thicket of reeds. They caught tadpoles and minnows and cooked small frogs over little campfires they made. Some days, she scarcely saw them from dawn until dark. As long as she could hear their voices, she did not worry much.

"I rode sixty miles to find you," Zeke pointed out. "I see your ma's cabin has lost what little chinking it ever had."

It was a rough cabin Becca was living in. Her preacher father had been content to live off what game he could shoot or trap, and whatever his congregation donated to him and his family. He had promised Becca's mother he would build her a snug

175

frame house, but the promise went unredeemed for thirty years. The old man died without ever hitting a lick, or sawing a board. Zeke could see holes between the logs where the chinking had fallen out. It was a sorry place, and it made him realize what an anger Becca must be holding against him if she would leave their well-built home and come to such a poor domicile. The cabin was not the whole of it either—there was Old Ma, and her crippled brother, Lem. A wild mule had knocked an anvil over on Lem when he was still a boy, and his left leg had been bent ever since. He had weak lungs, too, and right this minute Zeke could hear him coughing from somewhere in the cabin.

"Becca, I'd appreciate a bite of grub, if there is any to be had," Zeke said. "I went home expecting to make a meal, but a whirlwind busted up the smokehouse and Sully let a dern bear get away with the meat. All I've had since the big gunfight is some weevily corncakes Sully cooked up."

Becca remained where she was, in the doorway of the cabin. She looked at Zeke and she listened to him, waiting without being quite sure what she was waiting for. He was dirty, distraught, and hurt. The wifely thing would be to take him in, clean him, feed him, and dress his wound. Yet, the only wifely feelings she could muster were old and cold and sluggish—thick, like the boggy mud in the creeks near her home—not sudden and liquid, as they had once been.

Often, since coming home, Becca had dreamed of her life with Zeke, dreamed that they were together again. Sometimes, doing a chore, she would daydream about happy moments they had when they were younger people. Sometimes her own memories made her weep a little—it seemed that all such happiness was behind her, now that she was back home. Old Ma took snuff all day, and she was vague in her mind, calling her daughter Margaret instead of Becca, the name of her sister thirty years dead. Her brother, Lem, had a pet skunk that snapped at the triplets if they abused it. Even without the skunk, Lem was a trial to live with. He had long been afflicted with the bloat, and made wind constantly. Day in and day out, he hardly left his chair by the fireplace. Lem had been waited on by his mother his whole life, and now that his sister was back, he expected to be waited on by her as well.

Becca had not come home with hope, nor was she happy to be where she was. It was only that she had to go somewhere, in view of Zeke's behaviour; go somewhere, or rise up some night and kill him.

She left, but the leaving brought her no peace. Despite her anger, she could not stop worrying about her husband. He had made too many enemies with his vain, reckless behaviour. Probably one of the Becks would kill him, or one of the Squirrels. It occurred to her often that she might never see Zeke Proctor alive again, in which case she would have to live out her life feeling all the bad feelings she had in her breast the day she left the farm and walked to the jail.

"I hear the triplets," Zeke said, to break the silence. He was becoming a little vexed at Becca, for keeping him standing outside for such a long time. It was drizzling, and he was hungry.

"Where's Liza, then?" he asked.

"She's gone to Ned's and Jewel's," Becca told him.

Becca felt annoyed with Zeke for coming to where she was and stirring up her feelings. The feelings were so heavy and muddy it made her tired just to carry them inside her. It was hard even to stand there and talk to him, with her feelings so heavy and sloughlike.

"How's Old Ma?" Zeke asked, endeavouring to hold his temper so as not to make a bad situation worse.

"Her brain's clouded up," Becca said, looking at the fresh bloodstain on Zeke's shirt. There was old blood beneath the new blood, which made her wonder if maybe she was guessing wrong. Maybe the wound was serious; her own Uncle Perry had died of a gut wound, incurred in an argument over hounds. Zeke's wound might fester; he might even die, in which case she would have a load on her conscience even heavier than the load of feelings in her breast now.

He was her husband, after all. There he stood—filthy, hungry, and shot—wanting and expecting that she would be a wife again. He looked so weary and so pitiful that her feelings quickened a little. She had not yet lost the habit of having him for a husband. Such a habit was hard to break, though she believed she ought to break it. Zeke Proctor had too strong a will. She could live with him, or leave him, but she could never change him. If she gave in and went back to him, there might be a little happiness come from it; the triplets would have their father at home again, and there might be some possibility of getting them under control, too. Liza would come back, and they could live in their own house. Perhaps with luck, she could even conceive again and feel the joy of fresh motherhood once more. Zeke wanted more children. He told her that over and over, in their private moments. Even with the triplets, Zeke and Becca were well behind Zeke's father, who had fourteen children in all.

"Let's fan the fire," he said, when he came to her. "Let's fan the fire and get us some more tots." It was one of the things that had made her start feeling hopeless. Becca was nearly forty, and she had almost died giving birth to the triplets. She feared she might never really recover from the birth of the triplets, as it was. Zeke must know she would be lucky to have one more baby, let alone a dozen.

But Zeke only knew what he wanted. He did not know how tired she felt, or how hard it was to drag herself out of bed at night, if one of the triplets had a nightmare, or ran a bad fever. Her body might accept one more child, but if Zeke Proctor really meant to match his father, he would have to do the matching with another woman.

Zeke would find them, too, once he got what he wanted of her for a few months, or a few years, at best. He would go on being vain, and reckless; he would find willing women to slip off with; there would be more of the same hurts she had already felt. Only she would be older when they came, and even more tired than she was now.

Becca would share chores and duties, but she did not intend to share her man. If it came to a point where she had to leave again, she would be doing it with such a weakened spirit that she might give up the ghost before her triplets were full raised.

"Bec, it's drizzling, I'd like to come in, if you don't mind," Zeke proposed. "I would not have thought you'd keep me standing out in the wet like this."

Becca heard the throb of anger in his voice. But she had a throb in her, too, and she immediately let him know it.

"Don't crowd me, Zeke. I was not expecting to see you today," Becca told him. "I have to think a minute about what's right."

"Dern your goddamn thinking, and dern you!" Zeke said, his temper bursting. "We're man and wife, that's what's right. We took vows!"

"Yes, and you broke them!" Becca reminded him. "I doubt you reminded yourself of them vows when you slipped off with that woman you went and killed."

"Shut up about her, she's dead and that's that," Zeke said. "I've done been tried and acquitted for that."

"By a jury, maybe, but you ain't married to a jury," Becca told him. "I'm your wife, and I ain't acquitted you."

Zeke raised a hand, with thoughts of slapping Becca for her insolence. But then his strength suddenly left him, as it had in the courtroom and again when the Squirrels ran him down. He dropped his hand and tried to make it over to a stump a few yards away, but his legs went rubbery before he made it to the stump. The best he could do was sit down on the ground, although the rain was making shallow puddles all around him.

Becca had just put up her hand to ward off the smack, when Zeke suddenly went white. To her amazement, he took a few steps back and then sat down in the mud. Anger had been rising in her, but the sight of Zeke getting his pants all wet in the mud turned it to concern, a concern her better judgment could not smother. She ran to him and felt his forehead, which was clammy.

"Zeke, is it a chill?" she asked.

"I don't know, honey . . . I been getting spells . . . ," he said, in a confused state.

Becca reproached herself for being so stiff, but before she could say anything more, she heard the triplets shriek. They had caught sight of their pa and were racing up from the pond, yelling like little banshees.

"Why, here come the tykes," Zeke said, weakly. "I wonder if I could hire a buggy somewhere around here?"

"Why a buggy?" Becca asked. Then Lem's old hound came dashing out of the cabin, and headed for the woods.

"Where's that hound off to?" Zeke asked, surprised.

"He don't like the triplets, they've been tryin' to set him on fire," Becca said. "If they can catch him asleep by the fire-place, they stick his tail in the coals."

Zeke had a chuckle about that. The triplets' tendency to mischief had always amused him. A moment later, the triplets themselves swarmed over him like three puppies. Becca had put clean clothes on them that morning, but in no time they were muddier than their father. Zeke seemed to recover a little energy, and with her help he was able to stand and hobble to the cabin. He held Minnie in his arms; she would not be put down. Becca helped him, but she felt confused and distant— she almost wished Zeke had smacked her before he got weak. He probably wants a buggy so he can take us home, she thought. Now the children were part of it, and there was no easy way she could draw back, though it was not finished. She had made no promises. The sight of little Minnie, so happy to see her father, made Becca want to cry. The two girls were digging their hands in his pockets. Zeke had promised them each a penny when they got inside.

As soon as they walked in the cabin, Old Ma began to cackle.

"Sam Houston's come," she said to Zeke. "Howdy, Sam."

"Ma, it's Zeke," Becca said. Long ago in girlhood, her mother had ridden in a wagon with Sam Houston. Now she had got Zeke muddled up with him in her cloudy old mind.

They had been getting by with firelight in order to save kerosene, and as a result it was rather dim in the cabin. Becca got the lantern and lit it; then she stirred up the cookstove. She needed hot water and better light so she could clean her husband's wound.

Zeke saw Lem, sitting in his chair by the fire, his pet skunk in his lap. Lem was pale from staying indoors all his life. He was a huge, clammy man who did not seem to belong either to the daylight or to the dark.

"Hello, Lem. I see you still got your skunk," Zeke said, in an effort to make a little conversation. Lem did not answer. He kept on stroking his skunk.

Lem did not trust Zeke. Once he had a dream, and in the dream Zeke stole his skunk and sold it. He knew Zeke was not Sam Houston, which was what Old Ma thought, and he meant to keep an eye on him. The triplets were hard enough on his skunk. He did not mean to get friendly with a man who had stolen his skunk and sold it, even if it did happen in a dream.

8

WHEN JEWEL TOLD NED A BABY WAS COMING, HE WAS OVER-joyed. They were in bed when Jewel shyly broke the news. Ned immediately embarrassed her by pulling up her gown and looking at her belly, though so far there was not much to see.

"At least I can listen, I might hear him move," Ned said, putting an ear against her belly, which embarrassed Jewel even more, mainly because it was broad daylight and her sister Liza was visiting.

"You don't know that it's a him," she said, trying to make him get his head off her belly. "It might be a her."

"Nope, it's a boy," Ned said, wishing Liza were not down-stairs making corncakes. He would have liked to stay abed with Jewel for a while, to celebrate the big news, but he knew she would not allow it—not with her sister apt to call breakfast at any moment.

"It *could* be a girl," Jewel said again. In her own secret thinking about the child inside her, she had only seen it as a little black-haired girl. She had even imagined her big brown eyes. But Ned immediately pronounced it to be a boy. It damp-ened her happiness for a moment, mainly because it reminded her that she and Ned did not always want the same things. Now if she did have a girl, it would mean she had disappointed her husband. It reminded her that nothing was really simple in life, not even having a child by your own husband.

Ned saw a cloud pass across Jewel's expression. It occurred to him that he might have been too blunt in expressing his conviction that the child would be a boy, though he had only said what he believed. In his mind, the child was already a boy —a lively little boy who would soon be hunting squirrels with him, or helping him snare wild turkeys. The business seemed simple to him: first a boy, to carry on the name, and then some girls to help Jewel with the chores, if Jewel wanted girls.

"It's just our first one, Jewel," he said. "We can keep on and have a few girls, too, if you're set on girls."

"Get your head off my stomach, Liza might come in," Jewel said. The first little cloud across her happiness had swiftly been followed by another, the second cloud being the knowledge that she and Ned were not properly married yet. Ned had thought that Preacher Williams would be preaching on the Mountain the Sunday he brought Jewel home to live with him, but Preacher Williams had grown a tumour in his stomach and gone west to the Choctaw lands in search of a famous healer who was said to be able to coax out tumours.

She and Ned had gone along from week to week and month to month, expecting either the old preacher or a new one to show up at the little log church on the Mountain. But then word came that Preacher Williams had gone too late to the Choctaw lands. Despite the Indian healer's skill, the tumour had killed Preacher Williams, and so far no new preacher had replaced him on the arduous Cherokee circuit.

It was not a case, either, of Ned Christie simply taking for granted what was already his—he was anxious as Jewel for them to be formally married, in front of proper witnesses. After all, he was a senator, and he had both his reputation and Jewel's to think of. He spoke often of going to find a preacher, but the violent business with Zeke had intervened. Jewel did not hold it against him; the fact was, they lived in a place where preachers were scarce. But now that the child was in her, she felt they had to hurry and marry properly. She did not want to be one of those women who simply rode off one day with some man who wanted her to spend a lifetime having children by him. It was the lot of many women in the Going Snake District, but her mother had taught her better—and she expected better.

"The corncakes are cooked," Liza yelled up the stairs. "You're near out of molasses, did you know?"

"Why, I could just lick you, you're sweet as molasses," Ned whispered to Jewel. He still had his face on her belly, pretending to be listening for the baby.

"Stop it, Ned—get up!" Jewel said. "This baby's gonna be coming by winter. We got to work harder at finding us a preacher."

Jewel rolled out of bed. It was the only way to stop Ned, once he was feeling private about her. She skipped on down the stairs before he could grab her, as he was prone to do when in such a mood.

Ned felt Jewel had drawn away from him because of the baby in her, though it could have been because of Liza, who had already been visiting three days and ought to be getting on back home—at least in his view, she ought to. He realized that Jewel got lonesome for her folks and needed a visit now and then. Three days was a long enough visit in his book; a husband and wife needed the house to themselves. His own father had discouraged lengthy visits on the part of relatives, and he meant to do the same in his home.

What Jewel said about the preacher was true. It had occurred to him at times like this morning that the reason Jewel was often so shy with him, not willing to be private with him in the daylight, was because they were not properly married. A good marriage ceremony might correct that, and it was the right thing to do, in any event.

He got up from the bed and reluctantly put his pants on, wondering what to do about the preacher. Of course preachers were thick in Arkansas; he could always put Jewel on the mule and head for Fort Smith, where a marriage could be accomplished promptly. The problem with that was he might end up getting arrested before he got married. There had been no response from the white law to the shootout in the court-house, though everyone knew a response would come, and very soon. Rumour on the Mountain had it that Judge Parker was assembling a posse of marshals to descend on Tahlequah and arrest everybody connected with the shooting. A visit to Fort Smith to get married might end with a hanging, if he was not cautious.

The word from Tuxie Miller, who had seen Zeke after he returned home with Becca, was that Zeke was so apprehensive about the arrival of the white law that he planned to go on the scout the very next day.

"Tuxie said Zeke was coming here to see me," Ned told Jewel, after they sat down at the breakfast table. "He said he thinks I ought to go on the scout, too. He thinks the white law will be showing up soon, and I expect he's right."

Jewel had been sitting at the table staring out the front door, a cup of chicory coffee steaming in front of her. When Ned said the part about going on the scout with her father, Jewel came to attention.

"No. I can't spare you, Ned, not with the baby coming!" she blurted, with such exceptional vehemence that both Liza and Ned were startled. Jewel was glaring at both of them, the anger in her eyes as exceptional as the force in her voice.

"Don't jump on me, Jewel, I'm just trying to do the sensible thing," Ned explained. "I won't be no good to you or the baby, if I'm hung."

"You ain't going on the scout. Pa can, if he wants to," Jewel said. "I won't be staying up here on this hill alone no more than I have already."

Ned hardly knew what to think about Jewel's little outburst. He had no immediate plans to go on the scout, but the fact was it often seemed the most sensible practice when the white law was aroused. He himself had never been required to do it, but for many Cherokees occasional periods on the scout were an inconvenient fact of life. Though he did his best to keep Jewel well cared for and happy, it was not for her to tell him what he could and could not do in cases where self-preservation was the issue. His own father had to stay on the scout for six months once, as the result of an accidental killing.

"There's nothing to fear on this hill, Jewel," he said, trying to keep his tone mild. "We've got good bars on the doors. I doubt even a bear could break in, unless it was a mighty big one."

"I won't have you going, Ned!" Jewel burst out again, so upset at the thought of him leaving that she could not subdue her feelings. She was not going to have him leaving, not with the baby coming.

"That business in the courthouse was not your fault," she added. "We've got a child coming—I've got to have you home!"

Ned was astonished by Jewel's bold defiance. It was bad behaviour, made worse by the fact that her sister was sitting there hearing it. Liza was a blabbermouth, too. Soon it would be all over the District that Ned Christie's wife would not let him loose from her apron strings. He wanted to get up and give Jewel a good shaking, but he restrained himself.

"Jewel, you hush that talk, and hush it now!" Ned demanded. "The baby ain't due for six months. I can't be staying home every minute of my life just because you're going to have a baby once the frost falls."

Ned thought his command would cow her, but instead, it seemed to make her more defiant. Jewel was so mad he scarcely recognized her. The mild, shy eyes that he had come to love were blazing at him. Before he could move, or try to calm her, Jewel grabbed the full cup of chicory coffee and flung it at him. Most of the coffee splashed on Liza, scalding her.

"Ow, Sis, you've burnt me!" Liza yelled, jumping up from the table in order to shake the hot coffee off her clothes.

Ned realized he had a wild woman on his hands. His quiet Jewel had suddenly become a wildcat. He leaped around the table, meaning to shake her until she came to her senses, but Jewel was so angry she started to punch him. Ned would have laughed, if she had not looked so crazy. Instead of shaking her, he swept her off her feet, and carried her back upstairs to the big loft room where they slept.

When he put her on the bed, Jewel began to shriek and kick at him. She shrieked so loudly that he could hear the shrieks echoing off the Mountain. With Jewel shrieking every time she could catch her breath, Ned felt at a loss for what to do. He had heard of instances in which women suddenly lost their minds for no reason, and wondered if he was witnessing such a case in his wife. Why would Jewel throw a cup of coffee and scald her sister? She might not want him to go on the scout, but that was no reason for wasting good coffee. He remembered, then, that his father, Watt Christie, had told him women sometimes went crazy when they were with child, losing their tempers and having savage crying fits—all for no reason that he could ever determine. Lydia, Ned's mother, had made biscuits one morning while she was carrying Ned, and Watt had merely mentioned that the biscuits seemed a bit heavier than usual. Before Watt had even got all the words out of his mouth, Lydia had started picking up the rest of the biscuits, heaving them hard and fast at Watt before running out the door of their cabin, crying like she had been beaten with a stick. Looking at Jewel, Ned understood now what his father had been talking about.

After a few moments, rattled by Jewel's wild shrieking, Ned knelt beside her on the bed and gave her three good shakes. The strength went out of her then, and she stopped shrieking and lay on the bed looking at him, her hair a wild tangle. Her eyes gradually came back to being the eyes he recognized: his wife's eyes. And yet, though Jewel grew quiet, he had the feeling that she was still defiant.

"I hope you feel silly now—you went and scalded your sister," he said. "I expect she's packing to go home, before she gets injured worse."

"She ain't going home," Jewel said.

"What?" Ned asked, hoping he had misheard.

"If you're going, I want Liza to stay," Jewel informed him. "I ain't staying here alone, I told you that."

Ned suddenly slapped her—not a hard slap; one just hard enough to let her know he would not have his wife defy him. But Jewel took the slap, and hardly changed expression.

Ned began to feel futile. Maybe he had brought home a madwoman to be his wife. Nothing he said or did seemed to affect her. He had given her a shake and given her a smack, and she still seemed set on having her way.

"What if the white law comes?" he asked, to remind her of what they had been talking about before she threw the coffee.

"It was Pa they would be wanting to try. You didn't do nothing wrong," Jewel said.

"That's how *you* see it, that don't mean the white law would see it that way," Ned told her. "I guess you wouldn't like it if they put me in jail for a year, or hung me so I'd be dead forever. Then you'd be alone for sure."

Jewel knew well enough that there was reason in what he said, but there was more to this than reason. Sometimes Ned wanted to go, whether there was any particular need to or not. That was the way of men, and that was what had driven her to anger. Usually when she got a little annoyed with Ned, or expressed a criticism as she had the day he was too hasty about digging Tuxie's grave, she felt abashed later at her own behaviour. But in this instance, she felt no regret, just sadness at knowing she and Ned were different. They would always be different. He wanted a boy and the right to go when he felt like it. She wanted a girl, and a man who would always be by her side. She could not make him understand that he could go off someday and be gone forever. Every time he left, she had to live with the fear that she might never see him again. But Ned did not fear like she did, and she knew it was foolish of her to expect him to—maybe men did not feel bad things the way women did.

Jewel saw that Ned was looking at her with puzzlement. He probably wanted her to say she was sorry for throwing the coffee. She did not feel sorry, though, just a little surprised at herself that she had got so angry with him. She had thrown the cup, and even tried to punch him, though he was nearly twice her weight.

Ned did not quite know how to get life back to normal, now that Jewel had practically gone crazy. She had a few tears on her cheeks, but she was not crying, nor did she appear to be angry anymore. He was still kneeling above her, on the bed; but the woman he was looking down at did not seem to be the woman he had awakened with only an hour before. She was there, but they were separate—a troubling thing. He wanted his woman close to him, not separate; he did not want Jewel to be willing one thing, while he willed another.

He thought if they could be private, it might help pull them back close. But when he touched her, Jewel did not stir. She closed her eyes and kept them closed, until he saw it was no good and took his hand away. Then she looked at him again—calm, but separate.

"What are you scared of, Jewel, if it ain't a bear?" Ned asked, hoping to get some notion of why she wanted so badly to keep him home.

"Some man might get me," Jewel said. "I fear it all the time."

Ned was profoundly startled. It never occurred to him that Jewel feared such a thing. After all, she was his wife. His name would protect her.

"I doubt there's a man who wants to die bad enough that he'd interfere with my wife," Ned said, a quiver in his voice. Now that Jewel had told him what she really feared in his absence, he was outraged at the mere possibility of a man offering her abuse.

"I fear it all the time," Jewel said, again. "There's men coming across the Mountain that don't even know who you are."

"Why, Jewel—I never supposed that was your worry," Ned told her.

Jewel frowned slightly, though she could tell Ned was thinking about what she had said, at least.

Ned, once he thought about it, had to admit that Jewel's

worry had some merit. His reputation as a marksman did not extend much past the District. Rough men did come over the Mountain, too, men who would have no more mercy on Jewel than they would on a chicken they might want to eat. He had been vain, he knew now, to think that no man would bother his wife just because she was *his* wife.

Suddenly, the thought that he might have to go on the scout worried him in the way that it worried Jewel.

He sighed, and lay down beside her to give the matter some thought. The consequences of the courtroom battle took on a different weight. It made him annoyed with Zeke, for if Zeke had not insisted upon slipping off with a woman who was not even available, he himself would not be facing the prospect of going on the scout and leaving his wife to the whims of strange men wandering over the Mountain.

Jewel saw that Ned was anxious now, too. What she had said about some stranger getting her had upset him. When she saw the anxious look on his face, the last of her anger died. She put her hand on her husband's arm; she did not want him to be scared.

"Maybe the white law won't come," Jewel ventured. "Maybe they'll take the Becks, and you can just stay home."

"Maybe," Ned said. But he did not believe it.

The one thing he could count on about the white law, Ned knew, was that sooner or later, day or night, winter or summer, they would come.

9

AFTER MUCH COGITATION AND A CAREFUL STUDY OF THE court's finances, Judge Isaac Parker finally decided to send two marshals to Tahlequah to bring in the perpetrators of the courtroom massacre, an event that had made the papers as far away as Tennessee. To the Judge's great vexation, and before he had even dispatched the marshals, a newspaper fellow from Memphis showed up in Fort Smith and made so bold as to knock on his door.

The man was tall and had a squint, which did not excuse the

fact that he had arrived at the house so early that the Judge had yet to snap his suspenders.

"How many do you expect to hang this time, Judge?" the fellow asked. He had not bothered with the formality of an introduction.

"Who are you, sir?" the Judge asked.

"I'm G. M. A. Dogwood, *Memphis Sentinel,*" the tall fellow said. "This massacre's hot news. I'd like to send off my story as soon as the telegraph office opens today."

"Send off any story you like," the Judge said. "The court ain't in session, and it's time for my breakfast."

With that, he shut the door in the reporter's face and sat down to a substantial meal of grits and eggs. Chilly Stufflebean had been invited to breakfast and was eating with a will. The Judge's hope was that if Chilly was kept fed to capacity for a few days, his memory would improve. Though the Judge had probed and questioned, he had so far failed to extract from Chilly or anyone else an accurate account of what had happened in the Tahlequah courthouse. The Judge thought food might help, but he had applied that theory for three days now, with disappointing results. Chilly was vague on even the most basic of details, such as who had fired the first shot.

"It might have been T. Spade Beck," Chilly said, well aware that the Judge was disappointed in his reporting. On his second day back in Fort Smith, after a good night's rest, the Judge had taken him into his chambers and sat him down for serious questioning. The Judge got out a tablet and a pen, and prepared to write down details of the event as Chilly supplied them.

"We'll do this orderly, Chilly," the Judge told his bailiff. "We'll do it an item at a time. Who fired the first shot, and who did it hit, if it hit anybody?"

Three days and two solid breakfasts later, there was no clear progress made on item one, or any other item, except the final body count. Chilly was willing to vouch that twelve men had been buried in Tahlequah, but that was the only thing he was certain about.

The battle had been like a dream. Chilly had kept hoping that it *was* a dream, so that he could just wake up and find himself somewhere else; but he was not somewhere else, and it was not a dream, either. The noise of the guns in the close room was deafening; he could smell the gunpowder, and later, the blood that spilled out of the dead and wounded onto the courtroom floor. The fighting had seemed to go on for most of the morning, and yet other witnesses who had found their way to Fort Smith assured the Judge that it had all been over in two or three minutes, which to Chilly did not seem possible.

He felt sure that if he had kept to the right road and come straight home, he could have done a better job of reporting. As it was, the Judge got so discouraged with Chilly's faulty memory that he put his pen back in the inkwell and stuck the tablet back in a drawer.

"The human memory is a dull instrument," the Judge said, as he sat at his kitchen table watching Chilly Stufflebean getting fuller, but no smarter.

"Speak for yourself, Ike," Mart told him. "My memory's as sharp as a tack. I can remember every rude thing you ever said to me."

"That may be true, but the fact is, I never meant to marry a tack," the Judge said. "That newspaper fellow had an odd name—it had three initials in it."

Later, on the way to the courthouse, the Judge saw the same newspaperman talking to Dan Maples and Buck Massey, the two marshals he was preparing to dispatch to the Going Snake District. The sight was unwelcome. He did not approve of marshals spouting off to the papers. Several good lawmen of his acquaintance had been ruined by getting their names in the papers too often. Usually it made them vainglorious, which led to recklessness. The next thing you knew, they were shot, or else they turned into politicians and ran for the legislature.

"I'd like your name again, sir," the Judge said to the newspaperman, as he approached his two marshals. "You spewed it out so quick I didn't catch it on the first pass."

"G. M. A. Dogwood, at your service," the fellow said. "I'll repeat my question, too. How many of these Cherokees do you expect to hang?"

"That's a passel of initials you're sporting, Mr. Dogwood," the Judge said, ignoring the question about hanging Cherokees.

The Judge waited politely a moment, hoping the fellow would say what the initials stood for. But he did not.

"What, are you ashamed of your own name, sir?" the Judge asked, only to see the tall, squinty fellow turn beet red.

"The fact is, my mother was religious," Mr. Dogwood replied.

"Religious how?" the Judge inquired.

"Religious enough to name me God Moses Abraham Dogwood, that's how," Mr. Dogwood answered. Then, deeply embarrassed, the newspaperman turned and walked off toward the saloon. The two marshals, Maples and Massey, were left to explain themselves to the Judge, who eyed them pleasantly.

"That fellow was a newspaperman," he told them. "What was he telling you?"

"Just that the folks in Memphis are hot about the Cherokees," Dan Maples said. "There's a fellow named Christie they say is a prime outlaw."

"I've heard the name. Chilly met him," the Judge said. "What kind of outlawry does he practice?"

"Why, I don't rightly know, Judge," Dan Maples replied. "I've heard he's the best shot in the whole District."

"I'm a pretty good shot myself, but I ain't an outlaw," the Judge informed him. "Mr. Christie could be a law-abiding citizen, for all you know."

Buck Massey, a young man without schooling, planned to pay a quick visit to a whore before setting off on the long trip. The whore he had in mind was named Mary. She had a small room behind the saloon. Buck was hoping the Judge would not detain them long with idle questionings. He had been thinking of Mary all morning, and lust had him in a painful state. He had asked Dan Maples whether there were whores in Tahlequah, but Dan did not volunteer an opinion.

"There might be a whore there, I have not made such an inquiry," Dan said, in an aloof voice that annoyed Buck a little.

In Buck's view, the ready availability of whores was a factor that always had to be considered, in marshaling. He was not married, and being in a lustful state for too long was apt to affect his aim, or even his judgment. If he was going among dangerous Cherokees, he needed a steady aim, which was why he was impatient to get down the street to Mary. It vexed him that the fat old judge had detained them. What did the old fool want, anyway? Buck could see the saloon just down the street, and imagined Mary in her little room with the low bed. He was hard put to curb his impatience, as Judge Parker reviewed their equipment. The Judge even went so far as to lift a foot on each horse, to be certain the animals were properly shod.

"You men can go, now. Watch yourselves," the Judge said. "When you get to Tahlequah, see if you can locate Sheriff Bobtail and ask him what happened. I want you to be polite."

"Polite? I thought you wanted us to catch killers," Buck Massey said.

With that, Buck mounted, and to the Judge's astonishment rode his horse across the street, dismounting at the saloon. It was scarcely thirty yards from where they had been standing and talking.

"Your Mr. Massey's hasty, I see," the Judge said. "There he goes into the saloon. Is he a drunkard?"

"No, sir, a whorer," Dan Maples said, painfully chagrined. He had chosen Buck Massey to go with him, and now the young imbecile had embarrassed him in front of Judge Parker.

"I see," said the Judge, looking after Buck as the young marshal practically ran inside the saloon. "Be careful, Dan. There's folks up in those hills that don't scruple to shoot for ambush."

"I know, Judge—I intend to be watchful," Dan assured him.

Later, through the window of his chambers, the Judge watched the two marshals ride off. Before they were out of sight, the newspaper fellow, G. M. A. Dogwood, stumbled out of the saloon and fell down dead drunk in the mud in the street, where he lay for some time, snoring.

That evening, the Judge told Mart about the newspaperman, thinking she might be curious.

"Why, his ma stuck too much religion on his name," Mart said. "I'd drink, too, if I was named God. Wouldn't you, Ike?"

The Judge did not answer. He was thinking about the two marshals, and the long ride they had to make, over the hills to Tahlequah and the Cherokee Nation.

10

BECCA DID NOT SAY MUCH ON THE RIDE BACK HOME, BUT ZEKE was not about to let her reticence worry him.

Becca observed, too, that Zeke was on his best behaviour. He had even helped her on the horse he had purchased for her, a rare departure from his usual practice of riding off the moment he got his own horse saddled and mounted, leaving the womenfolk to trail behind him as best they could. Watching Zeke, Becca felt alterations of cold and heat. She knew that forgiveness was the Christian way, but it was a way she was not able to comfortably walk in—not just yet. The anger she felt when she thought about the adulteries Zeke had committed with the dead woman was indelible within her, and helping her catch her stirrup once or twice was not going to wipe it out.

The moment she got in the house—it seemed like a palace, compared to Old Ma's cabin—Becca went upstairs and transferred all her garments to a cedar trunk that stood at the foot of the bed in the little room under the roof where Liza slept. It was the same place where Jewel had slept, too, before she went off with Ned Christie.

Becca spread two quilts and a blanket where her eldest daughter had once spread her pallet. She put her Bible and a candle beside the quilts and blanket. Becca's Bible was a copy of one of the Testaments of the Holy Bible, printed in the Cherokee language. The book had been a wedding present from her Grandmother Sixkiller, who had brought the Bible all the way from Georgia. It was the only thing the army had allowed her grandmother to take from her home when they came and carted her family off to the prison stockades, before the long march away from their homeland. Reading her grandmother's Bible gave Becca comfort. She liked to pore over a page or two of the Lord's words before she went to sleep.

Then she searched carefully through the roomy bedroom where she and Zeke made their marriage bed, to be sure that none of her possessions remained. All she found was a hair ribbon, and a sock that had fallen behind the bed.

Becca felt a sadness growing within her, as she removed her things from the big room where she had come seventeen years before. Though Zeke had been a raw fellow then—apt to dribble tobacco juice on the sheets; prone to cursing when he was drunk; and given to lusts that were apt to come on him at inconvenient times, such as when she was mending a shirt, or trying to tend a child—she had accepted his rawness and impatience, and had found moments of happiness with him. In the mornings, he was generous with his affections, and he never tired of telling stories to the girls, or to the triplets, when they came along after a time.

But now he had shamed her. She could not forget it, and the happiness was lost to her. He was her husband, and she felt it her duty to cook for him, care for his house and his livestock, and see that he stayed well, so far as that was in her power. But from now on, she would make her sleeping place in the room under the roof, with her younger daughter. Christian or not—that was the way it had to be.

Once she had arranged her few possessions, Becca went downstairs, inspected the larder, which was close to empty, and visited her garden. The garden was so choked with weeds that she felt she must immediately give a week's effort to it, or else lose the whole growing season and face a bleak winter with nothing but potatoes and pork to feed her family.

The triplets—all three of them had piled on with Zeke for the ride home—were running wild down in the livestock lots, shrieking as they tried to catch the two spotted shoats and the thin calf. The old milk cow's milk was drying up from lack of milking, and the calf was only skin and bones.

Yet, the state of the place did not worry Becca. It was only suffering neglect, and she could alter that. She could even get adequate work out of Sully Eagle, if Zeke would only hold off sending him on useless errands. Even now, the place looked better than it had looked years before, when she had come home with Zeke as his new bride. She and Sully and Liza would just have to get to work—Zeke, too, if he was of a mind to stay home.

That evening, Becca made a potato soup, with a little of the corn in it, after she had carefully picked out the weevils. There was a full moon that night. The moonlight that came through the open door and the windows was so bright, they scarcely needed candles. Zeke sat by the fireplace, telling yarns to the triplets, until one by one, they went to sleep in his lap or at his feet.

Becca went quietly up after a time, leaving Zeke to sit late by the fire. Sully had walked off to his little shed, to sleep amid the cornhusks. Zeke had gotten up and arranged the triplets in a big chair by the fire, and covered them all with a little blue blanket.

She went to her pallet under the roof and took her Bible, not bothering to light her candle. She merely held the Bible in her hands. It was late when she heard Zeke on the stairs. She heard his footsteps go into the room that had been theirs, and saw the flicker of the lamp he lit by the big bed.

Then there was silence. Becca could imagine his puzzlement. Again, she felt the sadness: it was hard that things had changed, and yet, they had.

In a minute, Zeke came and tapped on the door to the little room under the roof.

"Bec?" he said, quietly.

"I'm here," she said.

Zeke pushed the door open. She saw his puzzlement in the light of the lamp.

"Bec, what's this?" he asked. "Why ain't you in the bedroom?"

"This is where I'm sleeping now, Zeke," she said. She looked at him, but did not raise her voice.

"What?" he asked, as if he had misheard, his puzzlement increasing.

"I'm sleeping in Liza's room now," Becca said, in the same even tone.

"For how long?" Zeke asked.

Becca did not respond—she did not know the answer to that. She saw him flush with anger.

"I'll be goddamned if you are, Bec!" he said. The next moment, he grabbed her thick hair with both hands, and proceeded to drag her over Liza's bed and down the two steps to their big bedroom. Then he pulled her across the floor and hauled her up on their bed, letting go of her hair when he was finished. As soon as he let go of her hair, Becca got up and without even looking at him, went quickly out the room, up the two steps and back into the little room under the roof, shutting the door behind her. She had splinters in both knees from being pulled across the rough floor.

As she was settling back on her pallet, Zeke came to the door again. He was panting heavily, but he had left the lantern and she could not see his face.

"If you drag me again, I'll leave you, Zeke," Becca said. "I'll leave, and I'll stay gone."

In a moment, Zeke was crashing down the stairs. She heard him stomp off toward the springhouse, where he kept his whiskey.

All night she waited, her scalp hurting from the pulling Zeke had given her hair. She wanted to get the splinters out of her knees, but she was afraid to light the candle for fear he might be watching. The light might provoke him again.

At dawn, Becca heard a horse loping away. She ran down the stairs in her gown, to find Sully by the woodpile. He had caught a grey field mouse by the tail, and was holding it up high enough so that Pete could not get at it. Pete was jumping as high as he could, but Sully held the field mouse out of reach.

"Where did Zeke go so early?" Becca asked.

"Zeke? He went on the scout," Sully said. He tossed the field mouse away, and Pete went dashing after it.

Becca sighed. She wished Zeke had stayed, but he had left. Her knees were aching from the splinters. She needed to get a needle and ease them out, before they festered.

"Come and eat breakfast, Sully," she said. "We've got to get to work on that garden today."

The field mouse had got in a hole. Pete was barking at it frantically, as Sully followed Becca back to the house.

11

WILLY BECK WAS ON HIS WAY TO TAHLEQUAH WHEN HE SPOTted the two marshals, who seemed to be proceeding in the same direction. Willy had never met either man, but he deduced they were marshals from the fact that they carried heavy sidearms and two impressive rifles apiece. Few people not financed by the government could afford that much expensive weaponry. Also, the two men, both dressed in dark coats, were riding at a high trot—a sign that they were on official business.

Willy himself was on his way to Tahlequah to resume a courtship that had been brutally interrupted by the courthouse massacre. He was in love with a young woman named Roberta Kunkel. Except for a harelip, Roberta was a perfect specimen of womanhood, in Willy's view. An added advantage was that being the daughter of a blacksmith, she was handy with tools. Willy was pursuing the courtship with his brothers' encouragement. What farm equipment the Becks owned was prone to frequent breakage, and having a woman handy who could fix a harrow or put a new handle on a spade would be a useful thing.

The only drawback to the arrangement was that so far, Roberta had shown no interest in marrying Willy. He had his horse shod seven or eight times in the last few months, just to have an excuse to be around Roberta. Roberta was stout, and could shoe a horse as quick as her father, but she rarely indulged in conversation while she was working. As yet, Willy had no idea what she thought of him, or whether she would consider being his wife.

"I'll marry you," he had said several times, lounging by the forge.

"Hand me that horseshoe, Willy," Roberta replied—and that was all she said.

Still, Willy took it as a good sign that she would let him help her a little with her work. He cheerfully rode the sixteen miles from the Beck mill to Tahlequah once a week to get his horse shod and pursue his courtship. Since T. Spade's death, the surviving Becks had made the mill their home—all, that is, except White Sut, who still preferred to live in the wilds. The old man had gotten so strange that Willy was nervous around him—Frank, too. Davie did not mind the white-haired brute, but then Davie was just as scary as White Sut, or almost. White Sut had taken to following his pet buzzard around. He would even steal food from it, if the buzzard located a dead varmint that White Sut liked the looks of. His bear had got loose from him, but would still show up at the mill from time to time, looking for his master, who sometimes slept on the back porch if it was rainy.

When Willy saw the two marshals, he jumped off his horse

and lifted one of its front feet, pretending to be studying the horseshoe for signs of damage. Of course, this was just a ruse, since Roberta, his beloved, had put the shoe on the horse not a week before. Willy's thinking was that the marshals would be less likely to bother with him if they thought he was burdened with a lame horse. He had decided, in any case, to lie about being a Beck, but he had not been able in the brief moments since he spotted the marshals to think what his new name should be. He thought he might use Robert for one of the names, but was mulling over a second name when the two marshals clopped right up to him and stopped.

Neither of them looked friendly, and Willy already regretted that he had not made a run for it. The older marshal, particularly, had cold eyes.

"Hand up your weapon, sir," Dan Maples said.

"Say, is there a whore in Tahlequah?" the younger marshal asked, before Willy could think what to do.

"Buck, let me do the talking," Dan Maples said, annoyed with his colleague. Buck Massey's incessant preoccupation with whores had already become wearisome to Dan.

"I'm the senior man," Dan reminded Buck. He wanted there to be no doubt in the younger marshal's mind as to who was running the Tahlequah operation.

"Hand up that gun," he repeated. "You can answer Marshal Massey once you're disarmed."

"I need my gun, I'm scared of bears," Willy pointed out.

"You'll have nothing to fear from bears when we put you in a sturdy jail, Mr. Beck," Dan said. "Besides, you'll soon have your brothers for company, if you've got any brothers left after that shooting."

"I've got Frank, and there's Davie, too," Willy said. "How'd you know I was a Beck?"

"I have seen my share of Becks, and you look like the ones I've seen," Dan informed him, though the truth was, he'd only ever laid eyes on the mild Sam Beck, once several years before. "Do you take me for such a fool as to suppose I don't know a Beck when I see one?"

Willy was cowed by the man's surly tone.

"Oh . . . all right, then," Willy said, meekly. He surrendered his pistol to Marshal Maples.

"Handcuff him, Buck," Dan said. "You should have done it

already. We can't afford to be slow, not when we're arresting Becks."

"He don't look wild to me, Dan," Buck ventured. But he dismounted, and did as he was told. As soon as Buck had Willy handcuffed, he drew back a fist and knocked him flat.

"Speak up when I ask you about whores," Buck told the dazed man.

"Now, Buck, behave," Dan admonished. "I won't have you beating the prisoner right here on a public road."

Willy's head was spinning from the blow he had been dealt, and Dan Maples was looking at him coldly. Willy began to wish he had waited a day or two before riding over to Tahlequah to continue his courtship. He hastily got mounted before the hot young marshal got a chance to knock him down again.

On the ride into Tahlequah, Dan Maples tried to interrogate Willy about the shootout in the courtroom, but Willy's response did not shed much light on the event in question.

"There was such a passel of shooting that I jumped out a window and run off," Willy told them. "My brother Frank did the same. I do know that Ned Christie shot Bill Yopps . . . that's how it started."

"Bill Yopps? Why, I marshaled with Bill. I heard he took to drink," Dan said.

"I told the Judge that rascal Christie was an outlaw," Buck Massey said. "The old fool wouldn't listen."

"Buck, you were not consulted about this detective work," Dan Maples said. "That's one thing. The other thing is that if you make one more disparaging remark about Judge Parker, you're fired."

"Fired? For calling a fool a fool?" Buck said, his pride affronted.

"That's one more. You're fired," Dan said. "I'll take this prisoner to jail. You can go on home to your whore."

Buck Massey was not used to rebuke—Willy could see that right off. The young marshal's face turned purple with rage. In a moment, he yanked out a big pistol, at which point, since he was directly between the two marshals, Willy thought it wise to ride a few steps ahead.

"Put the gun away, Buck, or else suffer your death," Dan Maples said, in a voice so cold Willy felt a shiver run down his spine.

"Bold talk, Dan," Buck said, cocking his pistol. "It looks to me like I've got the drop on you. I won't be fired for calling that old judge what he plainly is."

"You'll be fired if I say you're fired!" Dan Maples insisted. "Put the gun away, or suffer your death!"

"You are a sight, Dan," Buck Massey said. Then he noticed that Dan, too, had somehow got his pistol out and up.

Willy's horse began to crow-hop, for some reason. By the time he got him under control and looked back at the marshals, there was only one marshal to look at—Marshal Dan Maples. Buck Massey was flat on his back on the ground, his sightless eyes wide open. He was stone dead.

"I didn't hear no gun go off," Willy said, astonished.

"You must have stoppers in your ears, then," Dan said. "My gun went off, how else do you think Buck got dead?"

Willy stared, dumbfounded, and more than a little afraid. This fellow was scarier than his wild brother Davie. Davie *looked* crazy, at least. Marshal Dan Maples's behaviour was more unpredictable, and more frightening. Willy felt he ought to be real cautious while in the company of a man prone to such sudden, unprovoked violence.

"I warned him, the fool," Dan added. "You heard me."

"I heard you," Willy agreed quickly.

"What a damn nuisance the man was, and now we've got to bury him on top of it all," Dan said. "I would have done better to leave the young fool to his whore."

Willy helped Dan Maples get the body of the dead marshal across his horse. It was decided that the best thing would be to bury him in Tahlequah, where there was a fair-sized cemetery.

Willy grew sad, as they were riding in. A man was dead, and he himself was handcuffed. Now that he was a prisoner, there would be scant opportunity for courting.

"I doubt I'll ever get me a wife," Willy said, thinking out loud.

He had hoped for a glimpse of his beloved, but in that he was thwarted, too. Roberta did not happen to be at the forge, when they rode past.

"Oh, now, you're young yet, Mr. Beck," Dan Maples said, speaking in a less indifferent tone. "I expect if you behave yourself, you'll still have time for a wife."

12

"Jewel's gotten bad about me leaving home," Ned said to Tuxie. "She dern near had a fit the other day. Is Dale bad to have fits, when you leave?"

Tuxie's leg had healed to the point where he felt strong enough to pay his friend Ned an occasional visit.

"Dale used to be bad about it," Tuxie admitted. "Since I've been laid up with this poison blood, I ain't been able to leave home. I guess Dale's tired of me now—she didn't even look up when I said I was going to see you."

"Jewel ain't tired of me. I feel like I got a log chain on," Ned said. He could see Jewel down by the barn, milking a big, smelly nanny goat. Her ma, or somebody else, had told her goat milk was good for her, if she was expecting a child. Liza was with her, chattering away as usual. Liza was supposed to be slopping the pig, but so far, the slop was still in the slop bucket. The pig was looking at Liza impatiently, and Ned could not blame the pig.

"Does Dale have any sisters?" he asked. Since Liza had come to stay with them, he had begun to realize what a hard thing marriage was. For one thing, it involved tedious and boresome in-laws, such as Liza.

"Yes—Dot," Tuxie informed him. Ned had given him some tobacco, and he was enjoying a chaw, something Dale had not permitted him during the time of his illness.

"Does she talk much?" Ned asked.

"Oh, no, she never talks, Dot's dead," Tuxie said. "I get plenty of conversation from Dale."

"Jewel's not a talker," Ned admitted. "That don't mean she's easy to live with, though."

"Why, where'd you get the notion that women are easy to live with?" Tuxie asked. "Women are a passel of trouble, though I need my Dale."

"I wish Jewel would let up about my leaving," Ned said. "I need to go to town once in a while. It's boresome, getting drunk at home."

"Ned, it's no time to be going to Tahlequah," Tuxie reminded him. "Old Judge Ike Parker's got marshals on the roads."

"I don't have to travel the roads to get to town. I can keep to the high paths," Ned said. "Anyway, the marshals got no case on me. All I did was shoot in self-defense."

Ned was not really interested in what Judge Ike Parker thought—not at the moment. What interested him was relieving the constricted feeling he got in his throat, when he was wanting to leave and could not because of his young wife. He had lived a free life all his years so far, even when he was with Lacy. He was not disposed to give it up because Jewel had a baby inside her. Sometimes, he liked to drink whiskey with the boys, any boys who happened to be available for a drinking party.

Tuxie Miller was still weak from his illness, and needed frequent naps. There was a good cane-bottomed rocking chair on the porch that had belonged to Ned's grandfather and had been carried all the way from the Old Place. Tuxie made himself comfortable in it, and was soon nodding. Just before he nodded off, he remembered that Dale had pointedly reminded him to ask Ned if he had made arrangements with a preacher to marry him and Jewel proper. Dale was firm in her conviction that Ned and Jewel ought to be married before a preacher, and soon, before the baby inside Jewel grew large enough for the general public to notice.

Tuxie asked his question, and Ned said no—he had not located a preacher as of yet.

"I don't know what general public Dale is talking about," Ned said. "Jewel don't ever leave home. Nobody from the general public could see her, unless they had some good spyglasses, and then they'd mostly have to spot her through a window."

Tuxie accepted that answer, and went quietly to sleep. Then, while Ned was brooding about the impertinence of Dale Miller for presuming to tell him what was proper, as if he did not know himself what was proper, it occurred to him suddenly that Dale's impertinence might have provided him with a key to his freedom—or at least, to a trip away from home. He needed to find a preacher; why should he not go look for one?

Ned sprang up, ran to the lots, and within minutes had his horse caught and saddled. Jewel had just finished milking her nannies, and she looked alarmed when she saw him saddling up. Ned, though, had his story ready.

"I got to go, Jewel. Tuxie says there's a preacher living over at Stump Town now," Ned told her.

"What? Where's Stump Town?" Jewel asked. Though apprehensive about him leaving, she was pleased at the thought of a preacher. It thrilled her that Ned was still on the lookout for one.

"Ain't you been to Stump Town? It's over by Mule Water," Ned said, lying rapidly. "Stump Town's not much of a place, but they do a lot of preaching there."

"Why, if it's not much of a place?" the nosey Liza inquired.

"Because it's on the flats, Liza. It's easier for preachers to get to places on the flats," Ned said. He was aware that he had just created two places that did not exist, but he was so eager to get to Tahlequah and hear some town talk that he felt little guilt about the lies. Before mounting his horse, he strode over and gave Jewel an ardent kiss, ardent enough that it left her a little flustered. Since their quarrel about his absences, Jewel had been more welcoming of ardent kisses, and had even given him a few of her own. She was aware that Ned had a powerful restlessness in him, so in their private moments, Jewel was as sweet as syrup now. She wanted Ned to be happy, and considered that the only thing she had to give him was herself. She gave him what he wanted, when he wanted it, even if it meant making excuses to Liza, or leaving Liza with no one to chatter at in the early morning or the afternoon.

"Will you be back by dark, Ned?" Jewel asked. Even her desire to be married proper did not cancel out all her fears about staying on the Mountain without Ned.

"I doubt it . . . it's a far piece to Stump Town," Ned said. "Maybe Tuxie will stay the night. The way he's snoring in the rocker, he might not wake up till then, anyway."

"I'll cover him with a quilt, if that's the case," Jewel said. Before she could say more, Ned was loping away. Despite her knowledge that he was going on an errand which would officially join them as man and wife, Jewel's heart sank at the sight of Ned leaving. It sank and sank, until she was close to tears, standing there by the livestock lots. She lost interest in the foaming goat milk she had just taken from their smelly old nanny. Jewel felt so low for a few minutes, that she wondered if it had been right of her to have ever left home. She was so bound to Ned Christie that she could not be happy an hour unless he was there. She knew that kind of strong feeling could not be right, for men had to have their times to roam. But the desire to keep Ned with her every day was the strongest feeling she had ever felt, and she found herself helpless before it.

Once, during a haying time, a wild bull had burst out of the forest and knocked over three wagons in its charge. Jewel felt that her feeling for Ned was as strong as that bull had been. She could not stop it, or even direct it—the feeling raced through her with an awful force, dragging her this way and that. She knew there must be something wrong with her that she felt so much and was so helpless with feeling; she also knew she would have to moderate it somehow, once their child came, in order to give the baby decent mothering. But at the moment, there was nothing she could do about it. Ned, her husband, was not even out of sight, and she already felt desolate with missing him. As for Tuxie, he was welcome to stay, but having him as a guest was not the same as being able to sleep with her husband's strong arms around her.

She sat the milk bucket down, grabbed the slop bucket from Liza, and went to slop the pig. At least it was a moment of something to do. Ned expected her to keep up the place and not neglect the chores. Doing the chores meticulously and thoroughly, and seeing that all the animals were well were the only things that gave her any consolation when Ned was away. She might be bleak in her heart and too fearful to sleep at night, but she kept up with the chores and was a good wife, even if extraordinarily lonely.

"Are you going to have Ma over to the wedding?" Liza asked. "Ma's spirits might pick up if she could come to your wedding."

"Ma's way over past town," Jewel pointed out. "I doubt I could get her here in time. If Ned shows up with a preacher, I guess we better just do the wedding as soon as we can."

"I'll be here, at least," Liza said. "I wish Ned had a brother, so I could marry, too."

"What if his brother didn't want to marry you?" Jewel posed. "He might not like your yapping."

"I guess I could be quieter, if I was married," Liza said. She had given up her notion of marrying Tuxie Miller, if his wife should pass away. Getting wounded so severely had aged Tuxie, and to Liza he looked too old now to be her husband.

"I doubt it—you're a born yapper," Jewel said, a little unkindly. She was annoyed with her sister for being so neglectful of the pig.

13

WILLY BECK'S STAY IN THE TAHLEQUAH JAIL WAS BRIEF— just as long as it took him to walk in the front door, through the jail, and out the back door. Sheriff Charley Bobtail was so upset at having a dead white marshal presented to him for burial by a live white marshal that he merely told Willy to go inside and put himself in a cell, while he discussed legal arrangements with Marshal Dan Maples.

Willy, seeing that the back door of the little jailhouse was unlatched, simply walked through it, strolled into the woods, and went home, a walk that took him a brisk nine hours.

Now he was high on the Mountain, watching his fierce brother Davie try to drag some wolf cubs out of a den they had located. They had ridden up on the Mountain with White Sut, who was looking for his runaway bear. White Sut had taken to sleeping in the fireplace at night. He was covered with soot and ashes, and had singed his white mane of hair in several places by resting his head too close to live coals. He meant to kill the bear for desertion if he found him, and also to recover the good log chain the bear had taken with him in his flight. A black she-wolf, recently whelped, crossed their path on the Mountain, and Davie killed her, not twenty yards from her den. The notion of having a pack of pet black wolves immediately took hold of Davie.

"If I had a black wolf pack running with me, I doubt any man would oppose me," Davie said.

"Don't but one man oppose you now—Ned Christie," Willy reminded him.

It was not ten minutes after he said it, while they were both on their knees trying to reach in the wolf den, when they heard a horse loping along the high trail to Tahlequah. Willy stood up, thinking it was probably White Sut in pursuit of his bear. The old man had muttered when Davie had asked him to help them dig out the wolf cubs. When White Sut muttered, his kinfolk, including Davie, left him strictly alone, for the old man's mutterings were usually a prelude to violent fits. But the rider Willy glimpsed loping along the old narrow trail through the post oak thicket was none other than Ned Christie himself—the one man living who had bested Davie Beck in a fight.

The old trail was twisted through a post oak thicket with abundant underbrush. Not many people knew of it, and very few chose to use it. There were several easy roads in the District. If Ned Christie chose to make his way to town by such a difficult route, it was probably to avoid the very fate which had fallen Willy Beck himself: arrest.

"Davie, it's Ned, he's going to Tahlequah on the old trail," Willy said, excited. Maybe they could get ahead of Ned. If they hurried, Davie might be able to ambush Ned, and avenge his disgrace.

But Davie had his arm so deep in the wolf den he did not understand what Willy was saying, at first. He extracted one wolf pup and stuck his arm in to get a second, when he suddenly gave a wild shriek and jerked his arm out, a full-grown badger attached to his hand. The badger had come in the other entrance to the den and was about to feast on black wolf pups, when Davie grabbed him—a mistake he instantly regretted. The badger bit clean through Davie's hand with eight sharp little badger teeth. Davie jumped up and began to run in circles, trying to sling the badger off his hand. But the badger held on grimly, until Willy finally clubbed him with a pistol butt. Then, before they could kill it, the badger scuttled back into the wolf den, spoiling Davie's plan to accumulate a pack of black wolves. He had to be content with the one pup already captured, which Willy secured with twine and put in his saddlebag.

The badger also spoiled any hope they might have had of ambushing Ned Christie. Davie's hand was pouring blood; soon, his pants and all his gear were bloody. When he finally realized he had missed a chance to shoot Ned Christie in the course of being badly chewed on by a badger he could not even manage to kill, Davie Beck's fury was so extreme that he picked up a stick and began to beat his horse—though his horse was blameless in the whole affair.

"Why are you beating your horse?" Willy inquired. The inquiry was a mistake, as Willy soon discovered. A second later, Davie knocked him flat with the same stick, breaking it in the process. In Willy's view, the fact that he was being beaten with a weak stick was all that saved him from a first-class beating.

Later, when Davie was calmer, they began to speculate about Ned Christie. The old trail that Ned was using ran along a shoulder of the Mountain that early settlers called Idiot Ridge. It was said that the first woman to settle on the Mountain had lost her mind from loneliness and had become an idiot, wandering on the ridge and eating berries and nuts, until a black wolf killed her. That at least was the story; it had all taken place long before, when White Sut was a young man. At the time, White Sut worked for a slaver, who brought slaves over the Mountain from Mississippi. When questioned about the idiot woman, White Sut was not forthcoming. He had been an adept slaver, and knew the old mountain trails better than anyone alive, unless it was Old Turtle Man. But unlike the healer, White Sut was seldom in the mood to impart useful knowledge to his many nephews and grandchildren. White Sut had sown his seed liberally throughout the District and beyond, but he had no interest in the human crop that resulted.

"You sure it was Ned?" Davie asked, as they rode back toward the mill, the wolf cub whimpering in Willy's saddlebag.

"It was Ned," Willy said. "He was headed off the Mountain. He don't want to go the regular roads, for fear he'll get arrested, like I done."

Davie agreed with that assessment.

A mile or two later, they came across White Sut. He was sawing angrily at his saddlehorn with his big bowie knife. White Sut paid no attention to his vagarious descendants. He lived for himself, and rarely responded to human inquiry. He had mashed his balls on the saddlehorn when his horse jumped a creek, at which point he decided that the saddlehorn was a dangerous obstruction which could not be tolerated. It was a well-set saddle-horn, and was not coming off easily, although he kept the bowie knife sharp as a razor.

"You ought to use my saw knife, White, if you want to get shut of that saddlehorn," Davie said. "What you need is a saw."

But the old man muttered at him, and Davie knew he better let matters be. Then Willy and Davie loped off toward the Beck mill.

"Let's round up the boys and go kill that goddamn Ned," Davie said to Willy, as they rode.

"Why round up the boys? I thought you'd want to kill him yourself," Willy said.

By way of answer, Davie rode up next to Willy and back-handed him hard, promptly knocking out one of his front teeth. Davie did not like to be asked questions, not by his brothers, or anyone else. He had not forgotten that Willy and Frank had deserted him in his hour of need—that is, when Zeke Proctor had been strangling him—by jumping out the courtroom window, in view of which Willy should not get to keep all his teeth, or any of his teeth, for that matter.

What Davie did not want to say was that he only had two shells for his pistol. Two shells could well be an insufficient number to bring down an opponent as nimble as Ned Christie.

When Davie and Willy reached the mill where most of the Beck clan had been housing themselves since T. Spade's death, they noticed that White Sut's bear had returned and was sleeping on the back porch. White Sut was walking toward the porch carrying a thick fence post, and upon reaching the bear immediately began to beat him with it, causing the bear to howl like he was being murdered. White Sut's molty old buzzard sat on the roof of the mill, pulling feathers out of himself. It watched the bear get his beating, as did Frank Beck.

When the prospect of ambushing Ned Christie was presented to Frank and Little Ray Beck, neither brother proved enthusiastic about the opportunity. Little Ray had recently arrived from Dog Town with a slut named Edna, whom he had cajoled away from Belle Blue's establishment. He excused himself from ambush duties, complaining of severe cramps in the legs, the result of too much time spent in lustful exercise with Edna. Frank Beck, for his part, had been promised a turn with Edna, and was looking forward to some lustful exercise of his own.

Even old White Sut might be enlisted in the campaign. The big sorrel horse that Ned had shot eventually died, and now White Sut had nothing but a scrawny black mare to carry him on his wanderings. In his youth, White Sut had done some scalp hunting in the Texas territory. Once, they had all happened on a dead whiskeyseller on the trail to Dog Town, and White Sut had scalped him, on a whim. Perhaps he would scalp Ned Christie, once they killed him.

"Ned Christie's going to town, White," Davie said. "Now's our chance to kill him."

He had to repeat the remark three times before White Sut heard him. White Sut was beating the bear for all he was worth, and the bear was howling so loud that no one could hear anything else.

When White Sut finally wore out, the bear crawled under the porch, driving out four hounds that Frank Beck kept.

White Sut Beck normally refused on principle any request from anyone for help of any kind. When Davie mentioned that Ned Christie was in town, White Sut looked at him out of his old, red, demented eyes and did not answer. He had worn himself out beating his bear and did not want to be bothered with errands.

"White, he's the goddamned rascal that shot your horse," Davie reminded the old man. The sorrel had got them home to the mill, but was dead by morning. "I thought you had in mind to cut his head off."

"You cut it off. I'm going hunting," the old man announced. "Pay you a dollar for the head, when you get back with it."

With no further ado, he picked up a rifle and walked into the woods. A little later, the buzzard rose off the roof and flew away, in the direction his master had gone.

In the end, all Davie managed to get out of his family was six bullets, and he had to steal those. Little Ray Beck had carelessly left his pistol outside the room where he had cramped his legs through lustful exercise with Edna. Davie took the six bullets out of the pistol so that he would have a full gun at least, when he challenged Ned. He gave one of the bullets to Willy, instructing him to shoot Ned Christie in the back if he got the chance. The other five he kept for himself.

On the ride to town, they encountered White Sut, sitting on

a stump next to the trail, chewing acorns. White Sut was so wild that Willy sometimes forgot the old man was nearly a hundred years old—or maybe it was only ninety—White Sut had always been vague about his age. But there he sat, looking mighty old, on a stump eating acorns as if he were a squirrel.

"You ought to have shot that foul old bear, White," Davie said. "You've whupped it and whupped it till you're worn out."

White Sut made no reply. He had passed beyond much conversation, years before. He was thinking of a black-skinned girl he had brought over the trail from Mississippi, in the slavery days. She had been slender, with a tight, wiry braid almost as long as she was tall. He had thought at the time that maybe she had been a queen where she had come from, somewhere in Africa; her eyes had been wide set, and slanted up at the corners. She was the most winsome woman he had ever sold, winsome enough that she had stayed in his mind for sixty years.

As Willy and Davie rode on toward Tahlequah, a shadow crossed the road. When they looked up, they saw it was White Sut's molty old buzzard—he landed in a post oak tree nearby.

"If White don't outlive his buzzard, I 'spect the damn bird'll eat him," Willy said.

Davie looked up at the buzzard, sitting on a limb, its head sunk into its shoulders. It looked like it had no neck.

"I 'spect," he replied.

14

ZEKE HAD FORGOTTEN HOW HARD LIFE WAS, ON THE SCOUT. In his youth, he had gone on the scout several times, to escape legal harassment for little irregularities in his behaviour. He had once been given to much rowdiness and gambling; he had even run with the wild Davie Beck for a short while, pursuing whores they had heard about in remote regions beyond the District. In those days, of course, there were no fences in the District, and disputes over stray livestock were frequent and sometimes reached the courts.

Those times on the scout were not much more than extended picnics. Zeke would ride up to the Cave and carouse for a week or two with whatever ruffians were there. Sometimes, a few of them would ride up to Kansas or over to Arkansas and rip through some little town at night, racing their horses and shooting their guns like real desperadoes. Other times, Zeke and a companion would go deep into the forest on a big hunt. Several times he had taken a bear, and once had even killed a panther.

Sleeping out had not bothered him then, even if it was wet or sleeting. He would roll up against a big rock with his feet to the fire, sleep a few hours, and wake up ready to hunt.

The day he left his home, stung by Becca's refusal to be a wife to him, a cloud bank settled over the District and a slow, heavy rain began. Zeke had rushed off in such high dudgeon that he had neglected to bring either a slicker or a tarp. He was soon soaked, and he lived soaked for a week, for the rain continued with few breaks for seven days. He sent word to Sully Eagle, asking the old man to bring him the slicker and the tarp, but a week of hard rain followed, and the old man did not appear.

Zeke rode over to the Cave only to find it so crowded with ruffians that he could scarcely find a dry spot large enough to allow him to spread his bedroll. A sizeable gang of bank robbers were there, led by a noted killer named Slick Tom. Slick Tom boasted a scar that ran from the bridge of his nose straight up the center of his forehead, and into his hair. The scar was as red as a centipede; it throbbed when Slick Tom grew agitated, which was often. The rest of the bank robbers were mild, by comparison, except for a huge fellow named Doak, who wore only an undershirt, pants, and brogan shoes. Doak had once been shot in the stomach, the result being that his innards rumbled continually, like low thunder in July.

The only fugitive in the cave whom Zeke knew well was a local named Raw Sheed, a once-respected farmer who had first disgraced and then bankrupted himself by his wild passion for Belle Blue, the madam in Dog Town. Belle's power over Raw Sheed was so complete that she had begun to send him off on robberies, a task for which he was ill suited. He had recently botched a robbery in a little town near Fort Smith, and had been wounded in both legs by a shotgun blast from the storekeeper.

Zeke spent his first drizzly day in the Cave digging #2 shot out of the backs of Raw Sheed's legs. He even had one or two pellets in his backside, and a few as low as his heels. Zeke had to work with a penknife, his bowie knife being another one of the useful items he had left at home during his flight from Becca. The extractions took four hours, and resulted in a total of sixty-three pellets of #2 shot being gouged out of Sheed. Raw was a stoic fellow; he chewed tobacco and read his Bible during the whole operation, emitting only an occasional snort when Zeke dug particularly deep into his backside.

Raw's devotion to scripture reminded Zeke that he had recently been presented with a Bible by the woman who was now refusing to be with him as a wife.

"If you believe the Bible, why would you let a whore send you off to rob stores?" Zeke asked, while digging pellets out of Raw's left calf.

Raw considered the question, but did not answer immediately. It was his mother's Bible he was reading. She had been a religious woman, and his own pa had even preached occasionally when a regular preacher was unavailable. Raw had read the Bible, day by day, throughout his life. It relaxed him as nothing else did. Beyond that, though, Zeke's question seemed beside the point. Reading the Bible was reading; being with Belle Blue was living. If Belle Blue wanted him to rob a store, then he had best try and do it. To him it seemed simple—he could not quite figure out why Zeke Proctor was pestering him about it.

"The Bible says, 'Thou shalt not steal,' " Zeke quoted. "It also says you ain't to traffic with harlots. Now you've stolen, and you've trafficked with harlots, too. I expect it's the Hot Place for you, Raw, when you die."

"That'll be all right, then," Raw said, pulling up his pants. He meant to go back to Belle Blue as soon as his wounds scabbed over, and was not much interested in the theological points Zeke was trying to make.

The bank robbers from Kansas had been watching closely the operation Zeke was performing. Every time he extracted a pellet, he would dip it in water and lay it on a piece of buckskin. Big Doak, particularly, regarded the growing pile of pellets with interest.

"Are you plannin' to keep them pellets?" he asked Zeke finally. "If you ain't, I'd be obliged if I could have them."

Doak seemed a mild fellow. On the other hand, he was awfully large. Zeke felt it wise to be polite.

"Why, yes, I dug 'em out of Mr. Sheed here. I believe it's finders keepers," he said. "I might load them pellets in my shotgun and shoot a fat goose. A nice fat goose would be tasty."

Slick Tom had a laugh that sounded a good deal like a caw. The red scar lit up along the bridge of his nose.

"I think Doak wants them pellets," he said, with a hint of threat. "He's a big 'un. He might twist your head off, if he don't get what he wants."

"I doubt it," Zeke said. "The fact is, if he approached me right, he could arrange to purchase the pellets. I ain't seen a goose recently, anyway."

"Doak don't have a cent," Slick Tom observed.

"I thought you boys robbed several banks," Zeke said. "Why's he so broke?"

"I don't let him keep money, that's why," Slick Tom informed him. "He's too dumb to be trusted with money. Why don't you just give him the pellets—they've done been used already."

Zeke reached over with his knife and scraped the pellets into a neat pile. Then he folded the buckskin into a pouch, and tied the pouch with a little piece of rawhide string.

"I dug 'em out, why should I give them to anybody?" Zeke said bluntly. "It's not my fault you don't trust this gentleman with money."

"You could consider them rent," Slick Tom said, his scar beginning to throb noticeably.

"Rent?" Zeke said, puzzled. "What would I be renting?"

"This here place you spread your pallet," Slick Tom said, gesturing at Zeke's spot. "We was here first. We don't have to share this nice dry cave with just anybody that happens along —particularly an Indian."

Zeke stood up, and casually stuffed the little pouch of #2 shot in his hip pocket.

"I've been staying in this cave now and then for twenty-five years," he told Slick Tom. "I won't be paying no rent on it to a bunch of travelers from Kansas. This cave's for the use of anybody who's on the scout. You're a goddamn impudent fool to try and impose yourself, sir."

Slick Tom looked a little startled, when Zeke addressed him in such a tone. He had six boys with him; most of them looked startled, too.

Zeke then looked at Doak, who seemed slightly puzzled by all the talk.

"I'll sell you the pellets for five cents," he informed the large man. "I think that's a fair price. You could kill a fat deer with that many pellets, if you get close enough and aim good."

"What if he'd rather twist your Cherokee head off than pay?" Slick Tom inquired.

Zeke immediately came out with both his pistols. He pointed one at Doak, and the other at Slick Tom.

"If he wants to twist my head off, he's welcome to get to twisting," he said. "I'll give him something worse than a thundering stomach, if he tries it. And I'll give you something worse than a red scar, if you don't shut your damn trap. This cave ain't yours, and I won't be paying rent."

"Why, the man's brash," Slick Tom said, reaching into his pocket. "I guess I'll pay your nickel for you, Doak." He handed Zeke the coin.

There was no more comment. Zeke put away his guns, and spent the afternoon playing cards with Raw Sheed, who had to squat most of the time because of his injuries.

Even so, the atmosphere was tense in the Cave. Zeke did not trust the Kansas company, and it was still drizzling, too. Being on the scout was a damn nuisance, he felt; he was bitter at Becca for forcing him out with her standoffish attitude. Besides, he was too old to be forced to endure such hardships as sleeping out every night, and cooking his own meals. When he was a young man, it had been more of a high adventure. Now, it was just a damn nuisance.

The next morning, he saddled up early and left. Ned Christie had a nice, dry house, and Jewel, his daughter, was a fine cook. He thought he would go visit the Christies for a bit. Maybe Jewel would cook another possum. This time, without the trial hanging over him, he could eat with a more hearty appetite.

15

N ED SAW SMOKE RISING ABOVE THE TREETOPS WHEN HE WAS still two miles from Tahlequah. Not long after he saw it, he smelled it. Something was burning in town, and from the size of the smoke cloud, he judged it to be something big.

He urged his horse down the twisty trail off the Mountain as fast as he thought prudent. The old trail was not much used now, and vines and dense underbrush had grown across parts of it, necessitating frequent detours. Ned proceeded rapidly but cautiously, for he did not want to risk crippling his best horse —not with the white marshals on the roads. Whatever it was that burned in Tahlequah would probably be pretty well burned up by the time he got to town.

The largest frame building in Tahlequah was the building where the Senate met. Ned had the fear that some rascal who did not like the way a vote had gone might have set fire to the structure as an act of spite. But when he raced into town, he discovered that the explanation was simpler. It was the Senate building that had caught on fire, but the cause of the fire was a whirly little dust devil which had somehow whirled up sparks from the blacksmith's forge and dropped them on the shingled roof of the Senate House, igniting a couple of the old, dry shingles. Fortunately, a bucket brigade had formed quickly; even more fortunate was the fact that a good well stood not twenty feet from the back door of the building. By the time Ned raced up and dismounted, the fire was mostly out, although several men were still passing oak buckets of water up a ladder to the men on the roof, who doused the water on the smouldering spots.

Ned jumped down and ran inside the building. As one of the senators, he felt he should do his best to make a thorough inspection. He knew there would have to be a Senate session called soon to assess the damage and make arrangements for the speedy repair of the roof.

Quick as Ned was, Chief Luke Bushyhead, President of the Senate, was quicker. The Chief was kneeling down under one of the holes in the roof, a yardstick in his hand. He was already measuring the areas where he could see open sky, though some of the shingles around the open patches were still smouldering.

To Ned, the damage did not look too bad. A patch of roof not more than six feet by ten feet seemed to have burned away. A good, stout tarp would stretch over a hole that size. The senators might have to scrunch together a little, if the Senate convened on a rainy day, but to Ned, who had been afraid the whole building had burned to the ground, the damage seemed modest.

Chief Bushyhead thought otherwise. He was annoyed with the elements. The blacksmith's shop had been just down the street from the Senate House for more than twenty years without anything irregular happening. Now, because a capricious little dust devil had insisted on meandering right down the main street of Tahlequah, picking up sparks from the blacksmith's forge, he was missing a good many square feet of roof from the building where he worked. It was vexing!

Of course, such things *did* just happen, knowledge that did not mitigate the Chief's vexation one bit. Now, to top it off, here was Ned Christie, standing where he had no business standing. The Chief looked up at Ned, and scowled. He had been President of the Senate for fifteen years, a position that had accustomed him to the efficient use of authority. Luke Bushyhead was not slow to express his displeasure when things did not go to suit him.

When Chief Bushyhead looked up and scowled at him, Ned was taken aback. His father and the Chief had been good friends, and he himself had always enjoyed good relations with the old man. When he had been a boy of about six, the Chief had taken him into the woods one day and patiently taught him how to make snares—small, delicate snares, just adequate for the snaring of quail, or squirrels and other small, tasty varmints.

"Where's your horse, Edward—and is he fit to ride?" the Chief asked, without preamble. Chief Bushyhead did not believe in nicknames or diminutives; he always called every person he dealt with by his correct given name, which was Edward, in Ned's case. Men and women deserved the dignity of full names, the Chief believed, and he did not truck with jollity or abbreviation where proper names were concerned.

"Why, yes ... of course he's fit to ride, I just rode him here," Ned said, a little hurt by the Chief's curt approach. Of course, the damage to the roof had probably annoyed the old man considerably, but Ned, after all, had not set the fire. Instead, he had hurried in, ready to do his duty as a senator and help assess the damage.

"Then get back on him, and get back home," the Chief said. "I don't want to hear any extra talk about it, either. There's a white marshal down at the jail right now with a warrant for your arrest. If you don't get out of here promptly, you'll be riding off to Fort Smith with a pair of handcuffs for bracelets."

That said, the Chief knelt down, squinted up at the jut above him, and carefully took a measurement. As soon as he was convinced he had the measurement accurate, he wrote the figure down on the back of an envelope, taking time to write the figure clearly and legibly. Always a methodical man, he had once possessed a remarkable memory, brilliantly demonstrated by his fluency in both spoken and written Cherokee and English. In 1827, back in the Old Nation, Chief Luke Bushyhead had worked for the *Cherokee Phoenix,* the first Indian newspaper published in the United States. After a few years, he was finally made editor. Chief Bushyhead had been one of the tribal leaders who voted to adopt the Cherokee syllabary created by Sequoyah—a Cherokee hunter who spoke no English, but who was impressed with the way whites communicated by making tracks on paper, or "talking leaves." It took Sequoyah a mere twelve years to create the new syllabary. The *Phoenix* was published in alternating columns of Cherokee and English, the result being that Luke Bushyhead's memory had stayed sharp as a tack. But that was long ago, and he had been a much younger man. Now that the Chief had entered his eightieth year, his memory was not reliable enough to be trusted with even complex figures—or simple figures, for that matter. He tried never to be without an envelope and a pencil stub, so that he could give his memory a little written support.

Ned was stunned. On the spur of the moment, he had told his young wife a lie about a preacher and raced to Tahlequah for a short holiday from marital responsibilities, only to be ordered back home by the President of the Senate before he had been in town two minutes—all because a white marshal thought he had the right to arrest him and take him back to Arkansas.

"Can't I just go talk to the marshal?" Ned asked. "It's poor behaviour just to run from him."

The Chief had knelt down to take his next measurement, and did not appreciate young Edward Christie's interruption.

"Your father is a man of sense. Evidently you ain't," he said. "When the white law is after you, the smart thing to do is avoid it. In fact, that's the *only* thing to do. Go home now, and look after your wife. If this marshal wants you bad enough to follow you up on the Mountain, then you can try talking to him there."

Ned looked out the window. Half the citizens of Tahlequah were milling around in the street, talking about the fire. There was lots of company available, which was exactly what he had come to town to enjoy. Week after week on the Mountain, he saw no one but Jewel and her yappy sister. If he did happen to get a guest to chat with, it was invariably Tuxie Miller. Now here he was, being ordered out of town before he had a chance to visit with a single soul.

It purely and simply did not seem fair.

"All I done during that shootout was defend people in the courtroom," Ned said. "I was a juryman, appointed by Judge Sixkiller. If I hadn't made a stand, the Becks and those rowdies they hired would have killed practically everyone at the trial."

Chief Bushyhead ignored him. He carefully took one last measurement, wrote the figure down on the envelope, and stood up. Even standing, the Chief was bent from age.

"Maybe the marshal would change his mind about arresting me if I talked to him honest," Ned said. "Defending people ain't a crime. I hate to ride back home without even buying vittles."

Chief Bushyhead had never enjoyed protracted conversation. Ned Christie had been a good senator, but he was not yet old enough to have particularly good sense where the affairs of the rest of the world were concerned, the world outside of Indian Territory and the Cherokee Nation: the irrational world of the white man. Though the Chief was in a hurry to go down to the lumberyard and order the lumber needed to fix the roof, he paused for a moment longer, and looked up at the tall young man who had shown up in town on the wrong day.

"That marshal that's down at the jail just killed his own deputy in a dispute," the Chief informed him. "He's here to follow orders, and his orders are to arrest you. He'll do it or kill you, if he knows you're in town."

"I doubt I'd let him kill me," Ned said, his pride offended.

"Then you'd kill him, and the fat would be in the fire," the Chief said, blunt. "All the whites would see is two dead marshals. They might send an army in here and move us off, like they done in the Old Place. All you boys need to stay home until this thing cools off. Go home now, like I told you, and look after your wife."

With that, Chief Bushyhead turned and left.

Before Ned could move, he got drenched. Some fool had heaved a bucketful of cold well water right through the hole in the roof.

"Hold it up there, do you want to drown me?" Ned yelled. "Pour that water on the dern shingles—when I want a bath, I'll ask for it!"

The response from the roof was not friendly. The local butcher, whose name was Orvel, looked down briefly through the hole in the roof.

"We're trying to put out a fire," Orvel responded.

"Well, I ain't on fire, the roof is!" Ned said.

"Move out from under the hole if you don't want to get wet, then!" Orvel advised.

"I'm a senator, I'll stand where I please," Ned said. "I count five shingles that are still smouldering. Pour that dern water on them."

He walked over to the chair he usually occupied when the Senate met, sat down in it, and looked out the window again. The crowd was still milling in the street; abundant company was available. But down the street, he could see the marshal's black horse, hitched in front of the jail. He decided to sit in his chair for a while and wait. Maybe if he waited, the marshal would get on his horse and leave; maybe the man would head out of town and arrest some Becks. They were the people the white law ought to be after, anyway.

An hour later, he was still sitting, and the marshal's black horse was still hitched in front of the jail. The fire was out, and the crowd had thinned. People had drifted off, back to their lives. Ned kept sitting. Part of him knew that he ought to do what Chief Bushyhead told him to do: go. But another, stubborn part of him did not want to go. He had ridden all this way for a drink of whiskey and some company. Now that he was here, he meant to have it.

When Ned finally did move, it was to slip out the back door of the Senate House and into the fringe of woods that bordered the town. Old Mandy Springston's house was not far. By slipping through the woods, he could reach it without being seen by anyone in the street.

If he could not have company, at least he would have whiskey, before he started for home.

16

DAN MAPLES WAS SO MAD AT BUCK MASSEY THAT, HAD THE man still been alive, he would likely have killed him again.

He was almost as mad at Sheriff Charley Bobtail for his inept handling of the one culprit so far apprehended: Willy Beck. Because Buck Massey had been so rude and belligerent that Dan had to shoot him, and because Sheriff Bobtail had failed to lock Willy Beck securely in a cell, Dan had spent a day and a half in Tahlequah with nothing to show for it—except a dead deputy. His efforts to obtain precise information about the shootout in the courtroom had been frustrated at every turn. The fact seemed to be that no one knew for sure who had fired the first shot, or why. It was generally agreed that the Becks had come to the trial meaning to see Zeke Proctor dead, and it was also clear that they had hired a number of ruffians to help them effect that purpose. But beyond that, the facts were few and cloudy.

In Fort Smith, preparing for the trip, Marshal Maples had formed the impression that most of the Becks had been killed by Ned Christie. Though he knew it was his duty to arrest the man if he could find him, Dan's private view, expressed to no one, was that this Mr. Christie had done the court a considerable favor by killing off a number of the Becks. Rounding them up would be troublesome; trying them would be expensive. The fewer left loose, the better. He himself had caught one of the survivors, only to have the man escape while he was making funeral arrangements for Buck Massey.

Marshal Maples ended up spending the night in the jail cell that should have been occupied by Willy Beck. During the night, bedbugs attacked him so fiercely that he arose in a foul temper, his entire body covered with red bites. The bites itched badly; the marshal's only recourse was to plaster himself with mud from a big mud puddle just back of the jail. He had so many bites that he was feverish. During the night, tossing, turning, and scratching, he had a dream in which his wife Wilma flew toward him and became a cawing crow in the course of her flight.

When Sheriff Bobtail showed up, bringing him a big mug of coffee, Dan Maples was still in his underwear, hoping the mud he had plastered on himself would cool the bites somewhat.

"If I can catch that Beck fellow again, all we'll need to do is stick him in this cell for a night or two," Dan said. "The bedbugs will eat him alive, and spare Judge Parker the expense of a trial.

"You ought to burn that old shuck mattress," the marshal added. "It's nothing but a bedbug nest. I'd rather sleep on nails and staples than to snooze on it again."

Sheriff Bobtail had no intention of burning the jail's only mattress. He considered the white marshal uppity, finicky, and extravagant for suggesting such a thing.

"I believe I'll go after the Becks today," the marshal said. "I understand Mr. Christie killed most of them off. How many should I look for, Sheriff?"

"No, Ned didn't kill no Becks," Sheriff Bobtail informed him. "Bill Yopps killed Sam Beck with a shotgun, and that young bailiff from Fort Smith did for T. Spade. So far as I know, the rest of them are still alive and fit."

"What?" Dan Maples said, unpleasantly startled. "I was assured that several were dead."

"Nope—just them two," the Sheriff reiterated. "One of Polly's sisters got kilt, but she was just a Beck by marriage. All the rest of the boys are still up at the mill."

"All the rest? How many is that?" Dan asked.

"Why, Willy, Frank, Little Ray, and Davie—that's four," the Sheriff said. "Then there's White Sut. He keeps a bear."

"He keeps a bear?" the marshal asked. "Who is this White Sut? I ain't never heard of him."

"He's the grandpa of the Becks," Charley Bobtail said. He was surprised to see that the marshal had covered himself with mud. The ways of white people were strange; he himself had never found the slightest use for mud.

"You mean there's five grown men up at that mill?" Dan Maples inquired. Though adept with his gun, he did not suppose himself capable of arresting five grown men without assistance. Thanks to Buck Massey's behaviour, he felt he would be forced to telegraph Fort Smith for reinforcements.

Upon reflection, Dan decided that Sheriff Bobtail was more than likely lying about the number of Becks left alive. Though the Becks were white men, perhaps they were his in-laws; or, perhaps they owed the Sheriff money, a sum sufficient that he did not want to see them arrested and hanged before he could be paid. On the other hand, the Becks were a contentious group. Sheriff Charley Bobtail might not care to be bothered with having the unruly bunch in his jail for the time it would take to arrange transport to Fort Smith.

After all, the marshal reflected, most people lied often, if not constantly—at least that had been his experience. His own wife, Wilma, he was convinced, had been selling hen's eggs for fifteen years and lying to him about it for the same length of time. If his own wife would lie about selling eggs, then Sheriff Bobtail might well lie about the Becks. Dan Maples decided to stroll around Tahlequah for a while, to see if other citizens believed there were as many as five Becks left alive.

The stroll did nothing to calm his sense of alarm, however. The blacksmith informed him that White Sut Beck's bear was so strong, it had killed the largest bull in the District with one whack of its paw. Then, two fellows at the hardware store assured him that Davie Beck was so skilled at mayhem that he had sawed an enemy's leg completely off without even dismounting from his horse.

"He's got this saw knife," one of the fellows told Dan. "He rode right up on Tuxie Miller and sawed one of his legs off before Tuxie could get shut of him."

"I think I could manage to shoot a feller who was sawing

off my leg," Dan Maples conjectured. "At least I could shoot *at* him."

"Tuxie didn't have no gun," the marshal was told. "He's not one to go around armed."

Before long, Dan Maples had collected a dozen or more stories about the Beck family, all of which stressed their extreme ferocity. Somebody remembered that they had a room in the mill filled with millions of weevils.

"Weevils? Why on earth would they want millions of weevils?" the marshal wondered.

Bunt Boree, the proprietor of the hardware store, saw that the white marshal was an unusually credulous man, a man who could not tell a yarn from a fact. He decided to keep yarning —it would give the young marshal something to think about.

"They tie folks up and throw 'em into the weevils," Bunt said. "The weevils go in their ears, and fill up their brains."

Bunt's friend, Stoke Brown, drew the same conclusion about Dan Maples, and decided to join in the fun.

"What the weevils don't eat, White Sut saves for his buzzard," Stoke said.

"His buzzard?" Dan Maples said.

"Yep. That bird minds him, too—follows old White Sut wherever he goes," Stoke added.

"I ain't never heard of nobody keeping a buzzard," Dan Maples said. "What a dern old fool he must be!"

The more Dan Maples inquired, the more convinced he became that a lone strike against the Becks had little chance of success. He would have to telegraph for help, he now admitted. But when he located the telegraph office, in a shed behind the barber shop, it was unoccupied.

Retracing his steps to the hardware store, the marshal asked Bunt Boree where he might find the telegrapher.

"Oh, I ain't seen Ben this week," Bunt said. "Ben likes to go off wandering for a few days now and then. He has relatives among the Choctaw."

"I have no interest in his relatives, I need to find him promptly," Dan Maples said.

"Well, he was in last week . . . he may be in next week," Stoke Brown said, politely.

"Next week?! I can't wait till next week. I need men by

223

tomorrow!" Dan said. He was beginning to feel desperate. He was facing a second night among the bedbugs, unless he slept outdoors, and sleeping outdoors in damp weather made his hip hurt. Mr. Boree and Mr. Brown were polite fellows, but the news they imparted with such casualness was shattering.

"The man that runs the telegraph can't just go wandering off," Dan protested. "He needs to stay put. A community this size needs to keep the telegraph available at all times."

Bunt Boree looked vague, and so did Stoke Brown. Neither of them seemed in the least disturbed by the inactivity at the telegraph office.

"I caught a gar yesterday, out of my creek," Bunt said. "Ever caught a gar, Stoke?"

"I caught one, but I didn't eat it—too bony," Stoke confessed.

Dan Maples grew impatient. He often grew impatient when dealing with Indians, no matter what the tribe. Indian time, an ephemeral concept—devoid of the necessity of timeliness or urgency—had always confounded Marshal Maples. It was impossible to keep Indians concentrated on the important things, such as the necessity of ready access to a working telegraph. They'd rather talk about fishing for gar, a fish of no importance whatsoever. It was vexing to a white man, particularly a white man with a mission.

"I need to send word to that man—what's his name?" Dan inquired.

"Ben's his name. I guess he's wandered off," Bunt Boree speculated again. "He's got a shack about four miles west of here. He might be there, I don't know."

"But I need to send word . . . he needs to get back to work," Dan Maples insisted. His sense of desperation was coming back, stronger than ever.

"Well, I'd take it, but I don't live in that direction," Stoke Brown volunteered, in the same friendly spirit. "I live in the other direction."

"Who does live in that direction?" the marshal asked.

"Oh, quite a few people, I expect," Bunt Boree said. "Ask the Sheriff—he might know where Ben went. The Sheriff's his cousin, I believe."

"Just a second cousin," Sheriff Bobtail corrected, when the young marshal rushed up in a lather, wanting to know the whereabouts of old Ben, who worked the telegraph—at least he worked it when he took a notion to, which seemed to be on an all too random schedule, to Dan Maples.

"The best thing to do is just write down your message and your name," the Sheriff informed him. "There's a tablet in the shed there. People write down their messages and Ben will telegraph them off, once he shows up."

"But I can't wait!" the marshal demanded. "I can't wait! I need to send this message to Fort Smith now!

"Now!" he added, a moment later. He spoke so loudly that it hurt Sheriff Bobtail's ears, causing the Sheriff to cringe slightly. The young white marshal's impatience was an irritant, like a clock that ticked too loud. It was hard to feel calm, either with a clock ticking too loud, or an impatient marshal. White people, in their way, might be smart about some things— but very few of them were good about taking things in their time. They seemed to think that time itself was like a sheep, or a cow—a thing they could own, and herd around at their whim.

Sheriff Bobtail knew better. Nobody could own time, or herd it around like cattle or sheep. He had tried, over the years, to discuss the matter with some of the more intelligent whites, so that they might be more relaxed and not use up their lives so quickly. But he did not try to go into the question of time with Marshal Maples, who was acting as if the world might end if he did not locate old Ben, the Sheriff's own second cousin, to get him to send a telegram so that he could get help in dealing with the wild Becks. He would need help with the wild Becks, of course, but that did not mean the young man could go herding up time like a milk-pen calf.

Dan Maples's desperation got worse, as a drizzly gloaming settled on the hills of the town. He did not think he could stand another night with the bedbugs, but neither did he relish a night out in the wet, for it was sure to seriously aggravate his hip pain. Dan got so desperate he felt like crying, or getting drunk. He even began to regret the death of the licentious Buck Massey. He missed his wife, Wilma. He longed for the saloons of Fort Smith. He would have liked a beefsteak. He felt beside himself with annoyance that the old telegrapher had wandered off so inconsiderately. Dan felt that if he knew he had help on the way—a white man, one who understood the work of the white law—he could endure the wet, and even the bedbugs. But the knowledge that help was *not* on its way, that it might be days before the authorities in Fort Smith were aware of his dilemma, wore at his spirit—hacked it, like the saw knife Davie Beck was supposed to wield so savagely.

Finally, Dan Maples's mood sank so low he could not stand it. He knew there must be whiskey to be had in Tahlequah, and he wanted some, quick. As a lawman, he could not buy liquor directly from whiskeysellers; but then he remembered seeing several bottles and a jug or two sitting on a shelf in the jail-house—liquor, no doubt, that Sheriff Bobtail had confiscated from drunken rowdies he had had in his jail.

Dan went back in the jail, and sniffed at the bottles. One bottle smelled a good deal like hair tonic, but the others smelled liquorous. He uncorked one of the jugs, and poured a little of its contents into a tin cup he found on a shelf. The liquor from the jug did not have much of an odor, or much of a taste, either—not unless you could say that fire had taste. By the second swallow, Dan Maples had lost all feeling in his legs. It was as if he had *no* legs. Sparks seemed to rise from his belly, as if someone had lit a pile of kindling inside him. Dan did not disdain the feeling; having sparks inside him was a good change from the desperation that had been churning there. He wandered outside with the jug, and thought he saw stars—odd, since it was drizzling rain.

He walked along a ways, tipping back the jug from time to time, enjoying the sparky feeling that rose from his belly. The sparky feeling brought his confidence back; perhaps he would not need help from Fort Smith, after all. There might be five Becks, but that did not necessarily mean they could all shoot accurately. The tales he had heard about saw knives and pet bears were probably exaggerations. Perhaps the best thing would be to find a dry shed to sleep in, a shed with hay, if possible. With a good night's sleep, he might feel like rounding up the Becks himself. Judge Parker would appreciate the economy of his plan, too.

While he was walking and tippling, Dan realized that the stars he had seen were lanterns. Two men were up on the roof of the Senate House, trying to nail a tarp over the new hole in the roof.

"Say, where can I get a beefsteak?" he asked the men up on the roof.

But the men were hammering and did not answer—or, if they did answer, Marshal Maples did not hear the reply. His legs, which he had lost all sense of, had carried him away from the building that had nearly burned up that very day. While it was burning, he had been so disgusted with Cherokees and their ways that he had not even walked outside the jail to watch the spectacle. If a building wanted to burn, then let it, was his view.

Now the legs he could not feel took him beside a little creek, which trickled along above the town. The creek was not more than two steps wide, and appeared to be shallow. But to the marshal's surprise, somebody had laid a log footbridge across it. Dan's belly was sparking hotter now. It came into his mind that there might be a whore somewhere around. Although the late Buck Massey had gone whore crazy, whores themselves were not to blame. Dan would rather have had a bed visit with his warm wife, Wilma—but Wilma, of course, was a far piece from Tahlequah.

The marshal conceived the notion that there might be a whore across the little footbridge. A whore would probably not be expensive in such a place; even in Fort Smith, whores were seldom pricey.

Dan Maples started across the footbridge with the notion in his mind that there was probably a whore somewhere on the other side of the creek. In most communities, whores conducted their business a little ways out of town. But he had scarcely gotten two steps onto the log footbridge, when something pushed him off it. Before he knew it, he was knee deep in the little creek.

At first, he thought it was merely that the whiskey had robbed him of the control he normally enjoyed over his legs. The footbridge was slippery from the drizzle; maybe he had slipped, which was why he found himself knee deep in cold water. But then something pushed at him again, causing him to stagger back against the footbridge.

It was then that he noticed the men—two of them—standing by a tree about twenty feet away. In the gloaming, with the whiskey sparking and smoking in his belly, he had failed to see them. The moment he did see them, he recognized one of them as being Willy Beck: the very man he had arrested on the road from Fort Smith.

"Hold on, you're arrested!" Dan Maples said. "You rascal. This time, I'll handcuff you to the bars!

"If that's your brother, he's arrested, too!" he added.

But the men were no longer where they had been. He thought he glimpsed them higher up the hill, slipping through the trees. He pulled his pistol and shot three times, but without result. The men he had seen in the deepening dusk were gone.

Dan was vexed—very vexed—to have let the men escape. Then the two carpenters who had been nailing the tarp on the roof ran up and convinced him he was shot.

"No, it's the whiskey. I slipped off the logs," he said, allowing the men to help him out of the creek. Then he coughed, and felt a tearing pain. A second later, he began to cough mouthfuls of blood. Not until then did Dan Maples realize he *was* shot. The Becks had laid a clever ambush, if it was the Becks.

While carrying Dan Maples to the jailhouse, the two had to stop several times in their carry, to let him spew blood. They put him on the bunk with the bedbugs. He felt the wounds with his fingers, and discovered that all three bullets were in his lungs. Dan Maples knew he would not have to worry about bedbugs that night, because he would be dead.

By the time Sheriff Charley Bobtail got there, the young marshal, Dan Maples, had emptied out most of his lifeblood into a bucket. The Parsley brothers, Tim and Ted, had brought him in. They sat on stools in the jail, spitting tobacco juice into an old can. The Parsleys worked at the sawmill, and were rarely heard to speak.

"Who shot him?" the Sheriff asked.

Ted Parsley did not move. Tim just shook his head.

" 'Tweren't us," he said. "It was near dark, and he was way up by the creek. I was hammering. It was Tim heard the shots."

The Sheriff looked over at Tim Parsley, hoping for more information, but none came. Tim just sat there, looking back at the Sheriff with a simple expression on his face.

Then Charley Bobtail looked at Dan Maples, who lay on the bunk, pale as a sheet. Every time he drew breath, he blew red, frothy bubbles out of his mouth. Though the Sheriff had not really liked the young marshal very much—a man who thought, in his impatience, that he could pen up time like a heifer—he did feel sadness for him. His body was still plastered with the mud he had stuck on himself. Of course, the mud had dried, in the course of the day; some of it washed away like sand in the rivulets of blood that trickled out of the young marshal's wounds. Time—that elusive element which Marshal Maples had foolishly expected to control—was slipping away from him, as was his life spirit. But time would still be around, like the hills and the air, after the young marshal was gone; after he, Charley Bobtail, was gone; after the Parsley brothers were gone.

"I'll send for the doc, Marshal," he told the dying man. Sheriff Bobtail had an impulse to offer the man hope, although he knew there was none.

Dan Maples shook his head. He had a sense that he had been inconsiderate, and had probably caused the Sheriff considerable anxiety in the matter of the telegraph.

"No, I'd rather you didn't trouble him," he replied. "It would be a wasted trip."

"All right," the Sheriff said. Tim Parsley made a move to leave, but the Sheriff shook his head at him. Let the man have a little company as he died, the Sheriff thought.

Dan Maples's breath grew weaker; he was not blowing the frothy bubbles anymore.

Then the young marshal touched Sheriff Bobtail's hand.

"Sheriff, I'd be obliged to you if you'd take a message to my wife," Dan asked.

"Why, yes sir, what's the message?" Sheriff Bobtail wondered.

"Tell her she was right about that crow," Dan Maples said.

Then the air got heavy; he was about to sleep, when he thought of Wilma again.

"Sheriff, it's one more thought for Wilma," he said, in a whisper.

"Yes sir?" the Sheriff asked, bending close.

"Tell her not to mind about them eggs," Dan Maples said, a moment before he died.

17

NED SECURED A FULL BOTTLE OF WHISKEY FROM OLD MANDY, even consenting to pay her for the bottles Tuxie Miller had stolen out of her henhouse a few months back. Old Mandy was toothless, but talkative. She had been a whiskeyseller for many years and did not let the presence of white law, in the person of Marshal Maples, dampen her enthusiasm for her chosen trade. She kept three copperhead snakes in a box on her back porch, a fact she never ceased to remind Ned of, though he could not see what bearing the possession of three copperheads had on any question under discussion.

"I've got them serpents," she told Ned every time. "Them are venomous serpents."

"Oh, the copperheads," Ned said. He did not know what other comment to make.

"I don't fear the law as long as I've got my serpents," Old Mandy told him. Bill Pigeon was laying on the back porch dead drunk, when Ned slipped up to the door to purchase his whiskey. Ned had to step over him to get into the house, and step over him again in order to get out with the whiskey.

As he was going out with the whiskey bottle stuck in his pocket, Bill Pigeon, heavyset and dirty, sat up abruptly and tried to bite Ned's leg. Ned had his Winchester with him, and quickly whacked Bill Pigeon with the barrel. He whacked him hard—hard enough that Bill Pigeon went back to sleep. Ever since the day when Davie Beck had sunk his teeth into his leg, Ned had been particularly disturbed by human biting. He did not allow dogs to walk up and bite him; why should he tolerate it in human beings?

"You ought to tell that damn Bill Pigeon to sleep somewhere else," Ned advised Old Mandy. "Who would want to pay good money for a bottle of whiskey with a fool like Bill laying there ready to bite you?" he said.

"It's just Bill, he don't mean no harm," Old Mandy said. She could never be harsh with Bill Pigeon; he had been her last boyfriend, only fifteen at the time, fat and sweet. Mandy would make him scour the woods for persimmons, for she loved persimmons and clabber milk. Bill had grown up and gone on to be unfaithful to her with a number of smelly sluts, but she retained her soft spot for him and let him bunk on her porch when it was rainy. She did not like the fact that Ned had whacked him with a rifle barrel, but then Bill was rather in the way, and he had tried to take a chunk out of Ned's leg. She meant to make a vinegar poultice and put it on Bill's lump, as soon as Ned was out of sight.

Ned took the whiskey, crossed the creek, and crept into a thick bunch of bushes to do his tippling. He would rather have been in some saloon with a few boys to talk to, but under the circumstances he did not dare use a saloon. If he went in a saloon, Chief Bushyhead would hear about it and be displeased. The whole point of the trip had been to drink a little and yarn a little with the town boys, but that plan was spoiled. He would have to do his drinking alone and in a thicket. His trip to town was turning out to be not much fun. People in Tahlequah were nosey, and they also had good eyes. Ned knew he better content himself with drinking the whiskey in a thicket. If Chief Bushyhead got wind that he was still in town in defiance of his advice, the Chief might go so far as to ask for a vote to throw him out of the Senate, a thing that Ned did not want to happen.

Ned enjoyed whiskey as much as the next man, or so he considered; but he knew perfectly well he could not imbibe it in the quantities that were common around the District. Tuxie Miller was permitted whiskey only on rare occasions, those occasions being when Dale was absent on some family errand. But if permitted, Tuxie could drink for three days, the only noticeable effect being that he would sometimes jump to his feet and utter a good oath.

Tuxie could drink a large amount of whiskey with little visible effect, and so could many men of Ned's acquaintance. Ned himself could not do it. Drinking three swallows of whiskey made him feel light headed; drinking half a bottle made him feel happy and talky and warm, or at least it did if the whiskey was good; and drinking much more than half a bottle invariably put him to sleep. Sometimes it was a comfortable sleep, but always, after drinking for a while, Ned slept.

So it was the evening after the roof of the Senate building caught fire. Ned hid himself so well that no friend of Chief

Bushyhead's could see him, even if the man could see in the dark; uncorked the whiskey bottle; and drank.

He was thinking over some points he meant to raise with the Senate when they met to consider the matter of a new roof, when he felt his head go vague. He soon lost track of those points, as it began to drizzle in his head—a soft, warm drizzle to match the weather outside. Ned had some feisty thoughts of Jewel, and began to think of things they could do together when he got home. Coming to town had been a disappointment, mainly because the presence of the white marshal had prevented him from seeking jolly companionship, the thing he liked most about town life.

Ned kept drinking, sampling the whiskey a swallow or two at a time. After the warm drizzle, thoughts began to buzz around in his head like a swarm of bees. He wished he could just have a talk with Marshal Maples and settle things openly; he wished Chief Bushyhead had not been so adamant about sending him home. By the time the bottle was half empty, the buzzing slowed in his head, and the swarm of thoughts began to settle down. Far away, he heard a hammering, muffled by the rain. Probably the Chief had assigned some carpenters to cover the hole in the roof as best they could until permanent repairs could be made. He could barely hear the hammering, for the drip of the raindrops from the leaves and the bushes around him was lulling him to sleep. Once he started to lift the bottle to his lips, dozed for a moment, sat the bottle down, and had to start all over trying to get it back to his mouth. He yawned, and then arranged his hat brim so that the raindrops would not drip down into his shirt. Then he carefully corked the bottle of whiskey and put it in his pocket. A time before, he had spilled most of a bottle of whiskey through a failure to cork it properly before he drifted off to sleep. So he took one more drink before corking the bottle. The warmth in his belly would make for a cozy snooze, despite the drippy weather.

Ned dreamed of a child in a pigpen, wailing. It seemed that a little boy had crawled through the railing into the pigpen and then bogged himself in the deep muck in which the pigs liked to roll. The little boy was wailing, fearful of the pigs. Then a white goose came floating down from the barn; but then the white goose turned into Jewel, and pulled the squalling little boy out of the muck. There was a mule braying from a distance; Jewel got her legs muddy past the knees wading out of the pig muck with the little boy.

When Ned awoke, it was near morning and the rain had stopped. The dream was still vivid in his mind. He remembered Jewel's muddy legs, and the mule braying, and the little boy's wailing—he wondered, yawning, if it could be their own little boy, due to be born in a few months, that he had dreamed about. Although the child had been in no danger, even in the dream, it occurred to him that he ought to build a better fence around the pigpen, one with rails close enough together that a child would not be able to crawl through and bog itself.

The stars were clear above the hills in the distance. To the east, it was just beginning to be light. Ned had eaten nothing the day before, and he was hungry. He knew the Sheriff was an early riser, and Eula Bobtail, his wife, happened to be an excellent cook, for Eula had fed him tasty meals on many occasions. He thought he might stroll over to Sheriff Bobtail's house, and if there was a light in the window, planned to knock and petition breakfast.

As he walked off the hill, Ned felt a little stiff in the joints. He reached in his pocket for the whiskey bottle, meaning to take a small swig to loosen him up, but to his dismay, all he came out with was the top of the whiskey bottle. His pocket was wet, and it was full of broken glass—somehow, the whiskey bottle had broken, in the night. Ned took off his coat and carefully picked the shards of broken bottle out of his pocket. While he was about it, he noticed a hole that had not been in his pocket when he left home. Jewel kept his clothes in fine repair; if a hole had appeared in his pocket, or anywhere else in his coat, Jewel would have immediately sewn it up.

Meanwhile, the bottle was thoroughly broken, and half a bottle of whiskey lost for good. It vexed Ned, that he had gotten only half value for his money and would have to go home with a hole in his coat besides. Unless he was lucky, Jewel would smell the whiskey on the coat and conclude that he had gone after liquor rather than a preacher. It was sure to make her mad as spit.

All in all, it added up to a disappointing trip, rather than the jolly time he had been hoping for. He still meant to salvage breakfast if he could, and went tromping through the weeds and wet grass to the Sheriff's house.

Then he noticed a buggy at the jail—Chief Bushyhead's buggy, with his grey mare hitched to it. That struck Ned as odd, for it was not even all the way light. What was the Chief doing at the jailhouse so early? When Zeke Proctor had been locked up, it was uncommon for anybody to be at the jailhouse this early. Sheriff Bobtail usually fished a little, or shot a squirrel, or paid some attention to his pigs and chickens, before showing up at the jail.

Seeing Chief Bushyhead's buggy in town so early made Ned apprehensive. Something bad must have happened; Ned wondered if it had anything to do with Zeke. Ever since he had watched Zeke ride off after the big shootout, Ned had been worried about him. He was afraid the shock of the massacre might have caused Zeke to lose his fire. Zeke had always been stout in his own defense, and cautious to a fault. He had even trained his dog, Pete, to walk sideways with his back to the buildings, just as Zeke did, in order to keep a sharp lookout for enemies.

But if Zeke had lost his fire, he might have stopped being alert in his own defense. Maybe the Becks had ambushed him and killed him; or, if not the Becks, then the Squirrels. Zeke had far too many enemies to be wandering around in a low state. Zeke needed to sidle through life for a while, with his hackles up, ready for trouble. Otherwise, some wild fiend like Davie Beck would get the best of him, and cut his head off.

Ned considered slipping away from the jailhouse, back into the woods, before anyone spotted him. Chief Bushyhead had ordered him out of town and would not be pleased to find that his order had been disobeyed. Besides—slipping away was the smart thing to do in most cases. The news, whatever it was, would not take long to climb the Mountain. If it was bad, he would have the safety of the woods. He could take his wife and vanish, if need be.

But this morning, with the sun just burning off the mists in the valleys to the east, Ned did not feel like slipping away. He was a member of the Cherokee Senate, and a Keetoowah brother—if the Chief was out this early, the matter at hand might be one that would affect the whole community. He did not want to sulk off like a coyote, when important business was being conducted or important councils held. He was not a coward, and besides that, he was a free citizen of the Cherokee

Nation. Despite his considerable respect for Chief Bushyhead, it had annoyed him to be ordered to leave, when he had just got into town. He had stayed, and that was that. If the Chief did not like it, he would just have to put up with it.

Ned knocked, and boldly went into the jail. He had to stoop to get through the low door. Twice, while waiting with Zeke, he had neglected to stoop and had bumped his head.

Chief Bushyhead and Sheriff Bobtail stood by the bunk in the one little cell, looking at a body covered by a sheet. Sheriff Bobtail looked startled when Ned appeared; Chief Bushyhead just looked annoyed.

"Who's that?" Ned asked, nodding toward the body under the sheet.

"Dan Maples—he was the marshal that was looking for you," the Chief said. "Did you kill him?"

Ned thought he must have misheard.

"Did I what?" he asked.

"Kill him. I'm asking you," the Chief repeated. He pulled back the sheet a little. The dead man had no shirt on. There were three bullet holes in his chest.

"No, Chief, I didn't kill him," Ned said quickly. "I never laid eyes on the man, until this very minute."

"I believe him," Sheriff Bobtail said. "Ned ain't a killer. I expect it was the Becks."

The Chief was silent for a moment. It aggravated him deeply that young Edward Christie had ignored his order to leave town. He was not in the habit of simply ordering people out of town on a whim. Edward Christie, and for that matter, everyone with any sense in the District, knew how touchy things were with the white law. Avoiding contact with a marshal who was bent on arresting him only made sense, and Edward Christie was certainly intelligent enough and old enough to grasp a simple point of that sort.

And yet, here he stood, still in town, and the marshal who had come looking for him was dead of three bullets well placed in his chest cavity. It was a bad luck day for everyone concerned. Now the white marshals assuredly would come again —and this time, they would come like an army.

It all could have been avoided, the Chief knew, and yet it had not been avoided. He wondered what it was in people— what stubbornness or contrariness—that prevented them, time

235

and again, from doing the plain, the intelligent, the practical thing.

He did not know, and the judges did not know, and the wise men and the healers and the preachers did not know; yet, it was there. Over and over again, sensible and responsible people who knew clearly what the right thing was went stubbornly ahead and did the wrong thing.

"Are you sure you didn't shoot this man?" he asked Ned Christie again.

"No, I did not shoot him, Chief," Ned repeated. He had begun to realize that he had made a big mistake in not obeying the Chief's order to leave. The Chief, who had known him since his birth, had just asked him twice if he had killed the white marshal. If Chief Bushyhead thought it possible that Ned had killed the man, then what would the white men think? He had quickly landed himself in the thick of trouble, and had not a bit of fun in the process. All he had done was drink a half bottle of whiskey under a bush in the rain.

"Somebody shot him—that's plain," the Chief said.

"I figure it was the Becks," Sheriff Bobtail repeated.

The Chief looked at him sternly.

"Why do you figure that, Sheriff?" he asked.

"Well, he was looking for them, too," Sheriff Bobtail reminded the Chief. He was wishing he had kept quiet. Conclusions that seemed sensible enough when he uttered them had a way of seeming absurd, once the Chief inspected them in his stern manner.

"I've had no reports that the Becks were in town yesterday," the Chief said. "Have you had reports of their whereabouts, Sheriff?"

"No, but they're sneaky. They could have slipped up on the marshal while he was looking for old Ben."

"Did you see any Becks yesterday, Edward?" the Chief asked Ned.

"No, but I was drunk," Ned admitted. He saw no reason to hide the fact now.

"I didn't wake up till about daybreak," he added. "I slept under some bushes up past the creek."

The Chief and the Sheriff looked at one another.

"Near the bridge?" the Sheriff asked.

"Not too far from the bridge," Ned said. "Why?"

"The marshal was crossing the bridge when he was shot," the Sheriff said. "He slipped off into the water. He shot back at whoever killed him—shot three times. He might have wounded the killer. We don't know."

"I ain't wounded," Ned pointed out. Then he remembered that he had a bullet hole through his pocket, and a broken whiskey bottle inside that pocket.

"The man was shot about dark, and it was rainy," the Chief said. "I doubt he hit anybody. Where is your friend Mr. Proctor?"

"Why, I don't know, Chief," Ned said. "I believe he's on the scout."

"You didn't see him last night?" the Chief asked.

Ned suddenly got exasperated. Why was the Chief hammering at him so? Of course he had been foolish to disregard good advice and stay in town, but then he had no reason to suppose a marshal was about to be murdered.

"I told you twice I didn't have nothing to do with this killing!" he said loudly. "I wanted to go see the marshal and talk to him honest about what happened in the court, but you told me not to yourself. I ain't seen Zeke since the day of the trial."

He realized then that he was nearly shouting, and made an effort to lower his voice. He had a sudden, strong urge to be on his horse and gone.

"I ain't seen Zeke since the day of the trial," he repeated, in a more moderate tone.

"All right, Edward. Get along," the Chief said quietly.

"Do what?" Ned asked, surprised.

"Get along," the Chief repeated. "Go do what I told you to do yesterday—I expect now you wish you'd taken my advice," the Chief said.

"I do wish it," Ned agreed. "I just wanted to be helpful about that roof."

The Chief said no more. Sheriff Bobtail pulled the sheet back up over the dead marshal's face. Ned, careful not to bump his head, stooped and went out the door. He wished he had never had the notion to come to Tahlequah in the first place. He meant to take the good roads and ride as fast as his horse would carry him.

He had a great urge to get home and hold his young wife Jewel in his arms.

18

A MILE AND A HALF OUT OF TAHLEQUAH, WHERE THE ROAD forked, Ned changed his plans about rushing home. He decided to rush to Zeke's place instead. The death of the marshal was not a good thing; it was likely to have hard consequences for them both. Sheriff Bobtail had informed him, as he was saddling his horse, that in fact two marshals were dead. Dan Maples himself had shot the other marshal, in a dispute of some kind. Ned did not doubt the information, but he had a feeling that the white law might doubt it. They were going to be so upset by the news that two marshals were dead that they might overlook the fact that Dan Maples himself had killed one of them.

Ned's notion was to talk to Zeke about these events, and as soon as possible. If an army of white law came riding over the hills, Zeke would be affected, too. It might be that the two of them would have to go on the scout together, which would be a great vexation to Jewel, and to Becca as well.

When Ned was about a mile from Zeke's place, he was startled to see Sully Eagle suddenly fall out of a tree beside the path. Old Sully was known to do odd things, and to turn up in odd places, but Ned had not expected him to fall out of a sycamore tree on a bright morning. Though Sully had not fallen very far, he was an old man, and slow to get up. Ned got down to help him. He thought old Sully might have broken a bone.

Sully Eagle was embarrassed by his fall. The fact was, he had gone up in the tree to shake down a coon, but the coon was quick and got past him. Since he had gone to the trouble to climb up, Sully thought he might rest a moment. In the process of resting, he got sleepy and took a nap with his head against the bole of the sycamore tree. In his sleep, he dreamed that an eagle was looking for him. The eagle flew low over the hills, calling for him. It was a startling dream, for it could be either good or bad, depending on what the eagle wanted. But before the eagle found him, Sully woke up.

The eagle dream was powerful, so powerful that it caused Sully to forget he had climbed a tree after a coon. His mind seemed to have split off from his body because of the dream. In his mind, he was on the ground, but in his body, he was in a sycamore tree. By the time he was awake enough to realize his mistake, he was falling. When he hit the ground, his mind came back to his body, and came with clear information: he had fallen out of a tree. No bones were broken, but Sully was embarrassed. Ned Christie was bound to think it odd, that he was so daft that he could not remember whether he was on the ground or up a tree.

Under the circumstances, Sully thought it best to immediately change the subject, or in this case, get a subject going that might interest Ned and deflect his thoughts from the embarrassing thing he had just witnessed.

"You best watch for the Becks," he told Ned. "They're on the move."

"On the move where?" Ned asked. "I ain't seen them."

"I saw two of them headed to town yesterday," Sully informed him. "It was Davie and Willy. I hid. The Becks shot at me once, and I don't want to give them no second chance."

"Willy and Davie—are you certain?" Ned asked. It was important information, if true. If Willy and Davie had indeed been in town, then there was at least a likelihood they had shot the marshal. But he himself had been in town most of the day, and he had not seen them. Sheriff Bobtail had given him no reports of Becks being in town.

"You sure it was yesterday you saw them, Sully?" Ned asked. It was well known that Sully Eagle was not particularly reliable when it came to dates. He had been known to confuse a day with a year, to move things forward or backward in time to make them conform with spirit time. Ned's own father, Watt, was developing tendencies such as Sully's. He was mostly interested in spirit time now—he might claim that an event had happened only the month before, when in regular time it might have occurred many years back.

For himself, Ned respected spirit time. It was the way the Old Ones had lived, the way they protected the gods and their beliefs. But the matter at hand allowed for no flexibility in the way of spirit time. White law ran on white time, and in white time, yesterday meant yesterday, a rainy day in July—it did not mean the long, open yesterdays of Sully's spirit time.

Sully felt annoyed. He knew that people did not trust him

with dates or other daily information. He had to pursue what was important to him in life, and the immediate thing of importance to him was what the eagle had wanted, when it screamed at him in his dream. Had it wanted him to go along to the Other Place? Or was it merely screaming because he wanted to shoot a bear, or catch a big fish? When he had the meaning of an important dream to pursue, it was bothersome to be asked about whether the Becks had ridden to town the day before or the month before. Young Ned was too impatient, too caught up in the things of the day, things that would soon pass and be forgotten.

What Sully wanted Ned to understand was that he was not casual about the movements of the Beck clan. He had once paid them little mind, but since T. Spade Beck had shot at him, he had taken severe precautions in regard to the rest of the Becks. He did not mix up days and months, not when he was dealing with people who were inclined to shoot at him. Spirit time was always there; he could make trips in it in times of safety. He had seen the Becks yesterday, and had only just managed to scrunch down behind a big log to avoid being spotted.

"I seen them yesterday—don't be vexing me," Sully said. "It's bad enough I fell out of that tree."

"Somebody killed a white marshal in Tahlequah yesterday," Ned informed him. "That's why I was asking so particular about the Becks."

"Oh," Sully replied, "why didn't you say so?"

"Because I was waiting to see if you'd broke your neck," Ned said. "I was in town all day yesterday. A lot of people are probably going to think I killed that marshal. You might have to talk for me in the courthouse, if it gets that far."

Sully did not answer. His neck was not broken, but he felt a little dim in the head. A good nap in the cornshucks with his big rattler would be nice. He had come to think of the big snake as his protector. He slept better when he knew the snake was there, rustling around. If the Becks came after him in the cornshucks, the snake would get them.

"Does that horse ride double? I need to get to Zeke's," Sully said.

"He rides double," Ned said. "Zeke's is where I'm headed. Is he home?"

"No, Zeke's on the scout," Sully told him.

Ned helped the old man on the horse, and hurried on to Zeke's place. It was a disappointment to hear that Zeke was gone, but at least Becca would be there. He had a taste for her cornbread; she was his mother-in-law now, and would not mind cooking for him. He could give her news of Jewel. Jewel had sent word to her mother about the baby and had asked her to visit, but the word might not have reached her.

"How is Becca?" he asked Sully. "We don't hear much news over on the Mountain."

"Becca? She keeps to herself," Sully said.

When he knocked and then stepped into Zeke's house, Ned was surprised at how clean the place looked. When Zeke was home, he sowed confusion in the household arrangements. The table was usually covered with tobacco pouches and traps and ammunition. Zeke was always mending harnesses, or working on a mule collar, or cleaning a gun. He preferred to do the work at the big kitchen table so he could enjoy family life while he was working. He liked to drink chicory coffee with plenty of whiskey in it. If Zeke was a little tipsy, he might sing ditties to the triplets, or play an old fiddle he kept handy by the fireplace. Ned always enjoyed visiting Zeke, because things were lively at Zeke's house, in contrast to his own house, which had been rather dank and dull until he persuaded Jewel to move in with him.

Now Zeke's house was silent as a church. Ned had spotted the triplets, up in the barn loft, and had tried to gobble like a turkey to lure them down. The triplets did not like his gobble as well as they liked Tuxie's, and so they did not come down. Pete was not around to bark at him, either—that was unusual, considering how barky Pete was.

"Hello, Becca. Any grub?" Ned asked, when he stepped through the door. Becca had been knitting, but she immediately got up and began to poke at the fire. Her look was not unfriendly, but it was cautious. Ned knew he ought to try and get on an easy footing with Becca, for Jewel's sake, but he did not quite know how to go about it.

"There's taters and greens," Becca said. "I'll warm up a pot. What's the news from Jewel?"

"We sent word, didn't you get it?" Ned asked. "There's a baby coming."

"No, I didn't get it, I don't get much news here, not with Zeke gone," Becca said. She turned her back to Ned, and busied herself at the stove. For a moment she felt weepy, and she did not know why. Of course when a woman went off with a man, as Jewel had with Ned, it was to be expected that babies would be coming—that was nature. Becca was not sorry for her daughter; it was just that *her* life had taken a lonely turn of late, with things as they were between her and Zeke. She had no man in her bed, and no daughters in her house, either. She had the triplets, but the triplets led a life of their own, and Becca hardly saw them from dawn till dark. Now Jewel was about to have her own family, in a house such a distance away that visiting was not easy or practical. Even Liza had left, and seemed to be in no hurry to return. Becca lived in loneliness; for a moment, Ned's news made the loneliness deepen.

By the time the food was hot, she had caught herself. It was not Ned's fault that she had decided to live separately from Zeke. She served Ned taters and greens, and put some plum preserves on the table to go with his biscuit. He looked tired, but when she asked if she could spread a pallet for him, Ned shook his head.

"I'd better be going on home," he said. "Jewel don't like it when I'm gone at night. There's trouble in Tahlequah. I need to see Zeke, if you know where to find him."

"What sort of trouble?" Becca inquired.

"Two dead white marshals," Ned told her. "I imagine I'll be accused of killing one of them."

Becca asked no questions. She found it better not to question men any more than she felt necessary. The moment of sadness she had felt when she heard about the baby came back to her suddenly. Jewel's little child was not even born, and yet Ned, its father, would most likely be accused of a killing—the killing of a lawman. It meant he would be hunted, and that he would have to run. Zeke was running even now, but Zeke did not have a young wife who would soon have a child. It meant hard times for Jewel, who had always been the cozy one, needing her mother and sister and Zeke.

Jewel feared darkness and had never liked to be alone. But now, if Ned was accused of the killing of a white marshal, he would have to run, and run hard and far. Jewel's child would be coming; she might even have it alone, and raise it alone.

Becca looked at Ned, who was eating taters and greens as if he were starving. She wondered if she ought to ask him to allow Jewel to come home until the trouble passed—*if* it passed. Becca did not know Ned very well, but she liked him. It was on the tip of her tongue to ask; but she did not. Something in his manner warned her away from the question. He looked, to her, like the kind of man who would want to keep his wife at home—keep her at home, come what may.

"So where is Zeke, do you know?" Ned asked, between bites. Becca had been looking at him closely, so closely that it made him a bit uncomfortable, though he supposed it was a mother-in-law's right. Twice she had seemed to have a question in her eyes, but she did not ask it.

Just as he spoke, Sully Eagle limped in, reeking of grease. Sully used grease as a remedy for all ills, and falling out of a tree was ill enough to warrant good greasing, in his view.

"She don't know, and I don't, either," he said, in response to the question about Zeke. "He was at the Cave, but he left. Too much company."

"Well, I need to see him," Ned said. "If he comes by, tell him to get word to me. I'll meet him on the Mountain somewhere."

"He won't come by," Becca said, looking out the door. "You'll have to go track him if you want to see him."

Something in her tone, and the way she stood gazing at the hills, caught Ned's attention. Zeke was her husband; and yet, she had spoken of him in a faraway tone, as if he were merely a friend—someone she did not expect to see again. It was an unusual way for a woman to speak of her husband. Then he remembered that Liza said Becca had left Zeke for a while, and gone to live with her people. It was puzzling, but he was hungry and in a hurry. He looked at Becca, to see if she had anything more to say about Zeke. But she was staring out the door, looking at nothing he could see. The way she stood, with her feet planted wide apart, reminded him of Jewel. The urge to get home and hold Jewel in his arms came back to him with a rush. He had a sudden urge to start being a better husband to Jewel. He did not want the day to come when Jewel would speak of him as distantly as Becca had just spoken of Zeke, her husband.

It might be that Becca had reached a place so far away from

Zeke that she could not come back, no matter how loud he played the fiddle, or cut up with the triplets. Inside her, she was gone to the hills—or that was how it seemed to Ned.

Sometimes Jewel had gotten far away from Ned in her spirit. Those moments had frightened him, too. He remembered the first time it had happened: it was when he had taken her from her home to be his wife. They had been riding together on his horse and had stopped for a short rest. Ned helped Jewel down off the horse, and she stood staring back at the way they had come, looking as if she were no longer there with him. She stood that way for more than a minute. Ned finally had to walk around and stand directly in front of her to get her attention back to him. When she allowed her spirit to come back to where they stood together, Jewel looked startled—as if Ned had slapped her. Then, turning shy, she looked down at the ground, as Ned helped her back onto the horse.

Jewel's faraway look had been a worrisome thing to Ned. It had concerned him then; and now, seeing Becca, he reminded himself that he did not want Jewel drifting off to the hills in her spirit, the way her mother had just drifted.

Ned rushed through the rest of his meal, so as to get on home to his Jewel. The grease on old Sully was smelling up Zeke's house so bad that it was spoiling the taste of Becca's food.

When Ned finished, Becca followed Ned outside to his horse. She had one or two things more on her mind, but Ned had suddenly gotten impatient, as men would, and could hardly sit still another minute.

"Have you and Jewel got married proper yet, Ned?" she asked, once he was astride his horse.

Ned looked abashed—of all things for Becca to ask, when he badly needed to be on his way.

"That's why I went to town," he told her. "I went off to find a preacher. You know Preacher Williams died, before he could marry us. Jewel sent me off, she's anxious to have a preacher come before she has the baby."

Becca felt a sudden anger. This man who could hardly wait a minute after his meal was finished, had taken her daughter away. With no warning, he had ridden in and taken her off. Though he had not meant to, he had ended up taking both her daughters, for Liza could not stand being without her sister.

She knew the anger she was feeling was unfair—what Ned had done was nature—but she still felt the anger, like a slow burning in the middle of her chest.

"You do proper by my Jewel!" she chided, suddenly. "You find a preacher, and do proper by her . . . she ain't your whore!"

"And you stand by her, too!" she added. "She's just a girl. You stand by her, Ned!"

"Why, Becca . . . I mean to," Ned said, astonished and a little frightened by her vehemence.

"I mean to stand by her," he said, again.

But Becca Proctor did not hear him. She burst into tears, turned, and hurried back toward her house.

19

WHEN DAVIE BECK LEARNED THAT HE HAD MISSED A CHANCE to kill Ned Christie, he immediately ran outside the mill and began to beat his brother Willy as he would beat a cur. White Sut Beck had pounded his runaway bear with a fence post until the fence post broke in two. Davie Beck picked up half the post, and laid Willy out with it, looked upon by Frank Beck and Little Ray Beck and old Roy Tagus, the trader who had brought the news. Old Roy traveled around the District selling sewing needles and sharpening kitchen knives. He also sharpened harrows, rakes, axes, posthole diggers, hatchets, and any other tool that needed to have a sharp edge in order to perform as it should. Old Roy was almost as old as White Sut, but he was far less wild, and the sight of Davie beating his brother with a fence post caused his stomach to churn.

"He was right there asleep under a bush!" Davie yelled. "If you'd kept your eyes open, we could have caught the son-of-a-bitch and cut his head off."

"White Sut offered me a dollar for the head," he reminded Willy bitterly, who did not hear the reminder.

"Well, that's what they say in Tahlequah, at least," old Roy said. "I didn't see Ned myself."

He was wondering if it had been wise to call at the Beck mill. He had once done a brisk business with Polly Beck, but Polly was dead, and her in-laws unpredictable. Davie Beck was not the sort of man to worry about whether the knives were sharp; he would be just as happy to stab an enemy with a dull one, if the enemy was handy.

Now he had caused a flood of blood to pour out of his brother's nose, due to the fact that an enemy *had* been handy, but had got away.

"You should have kept your goddamn eyes open!" Davie yelled, standing over Willy, whose eyes were closed at the moment, due to the unfortunate fact that he was unconscious. White Sut's bear, far back under the porch and still smarting from its own walloping, began to whimper. It was afraid it would be the next one beaten, though its master, White Sut, was not present, having ridden off the day before without a word.

Davie did not beat Willy as long as he normally would have, because the hand he liked to wield the post with, his right hand, was sore from having been bitten by the irate badger a few days before.

"I don't know why you're so mad at Willy," Frank Beck said, once Davie's temper had subsided a bit. "At least you killed a marshal.

"It's not every day you kill a marshal," Frank repeated, hoping the thought would lift Davie's spirits. It was not that Frank Beck particularly cared whether Davie was happy; it was just that when Davie was *not* happy, violent fits were apt to slop over from Willy, the usual target, to anyone who happened to be nearby—and Frank was nearby.

"Kilt him, and got away with it," old Roy put in.

That aspect of the matter had not occurred to Davie Beck.

"What do you mean, got away with it?" Davie asked.

"They think Ned Christie done it—at least that's the opinion in Tahlequah," old Roy said. Davie was looking at him out of his crazed red eyes, looking at him so fiercely that Roy Tagus wondered if he had been wise to speak at all. For a moment, he thought he might have to repel Davie with his boot knife, a thin blade pointed as a needle that he had concealed in the sole of his right boot. If attacked, he could kick a man in the shin with the boot knife. The pain of a shin stab was so intense that Roy would usually have the leisure to escape or else inflict other, more serious injuries on his opponent.

The shin stab worked with normal men, but Davie Beck was

not a normal man—old Roy thought he might have to poke a scissor's blade into the man's jugular, if he charged. In close encounters, he had found scissors to be a more effective weapon than bowie knives. Many men did not even notice scissors; they would think they were winning the fight until they discovered they were bleeding to death. The sight of a bowie knife, on the other hand, might cause some opponents to resort to firearms, and firearms could quickly lead to fatalities.

Old Roy sought no fatalities—fortunately, Davie Beck liked the thought that he had gotten away with killing a white marshal.

"What's that? Are you sure?" Davie asked.

"Why, yes. The talk in Tahlequah is that Ned Christie probably killed that marshal," old Roy repeated.

"That's good news, Dave," Little Ray Beck said. He squatted down by Willy, and rolled back one of his eyelids. Willy's eyeball began to twitch, a sign that he was not dead, but merely insensible.

"They think Ned did it," Frank said. "That means you won't even have to kill him yourself, Davie. You can let the law hunt him down and hang him legal."

That line of reasoning might have convinced most men, but Davie Beck was not so easily swayed. He had his mind set on killing Ned Christie himself, and was not sure he wanted the law to do it—though of course, that would be the convenient approach. In his opinion, personal vengeance was one of the most satisfying things in life, and Ned Christie was the only man ever to shame him or defeat him. He was of no mind to let an Arkansas court cheat him of what was his.

"They can think what they like. I mean to kill Ned Christie myself," Davie said.

"Besides," he remarked a little later, "if I let 'em hang him, I'd lose that dollar White Sut offered me for his head."

"No, you wouldn't, Davie," Little Ray, the younger brother, protested. "You could still dig him up and take his head off.

"White Sut didn't say you had to kill Ned personal," Little Ray added. "He just said he'd give you a dollar for the head."

Davie Beck considered the argument picayune. He meant to kill Ned Christie himself, and was still annoyed with Willy for not spotting Ned when he was asleep under a bush, and easy to take.

Old Roy Tagus, convinced that there was little chance of selling needles or getting the Becks to allow him to sharpen anything, mounted his black mule and rode away. He meant to travel to Dog Town and try his luck on Belle Blue.

As old Roy was leaving, Willy Beck roused himself enough to crawl under the porch with the bear.

20

WHEN JUDGE PARKER HEARD THE NEWS ABOUT DAN MAPLES, he immediately closed his chambers, saddled his brown mule, and began the long ride into the Blue Hills to inform Wilma Maples that she was a widow. Mart was hoeing in the garden, as the Judge rode off. He waved at her, but Mart did not welcome distractions, and did not interrupt her work to wave back—once Mart took a notion to garden, there was no stopping her.

The Judge did not send death news by messenger, if there was a widow or a family involved. He felt he owed it to the families to deliver the news himself. As he rode, he chastised himself for allowing a whore-minded young man such as Buck Massey to accompany Dan Maples on the trip. Two steady marshals could have faced down the Becks, or any assembly short of a mob. But young Buck Massey had been so far from being steady that, if reports were correct, Dan Maples himself had had to kill the man. Now, the Judge reflected sadly, his own error in judgment had cost Dan Maples his life and had left Wilma a widow. Wilma was Mart's second cousin, too.

"You ought to send the army to Tahlequah," Chilly Stufflebean suggested, as the Judge was leaving.

"I'm a judge, Chilly—I don't command an army," the Judge informed him. "I don't even command two good marshals . . . if I'da had two, I would never have troubled young Massey to leave his whore."

Along the shadowy trail into the Blue Hills, the Judge met Cracky Bolen. One of his feet was in the stirrup as it should be, but the other—black, shoeless, and too swollen to fit in a stirrup—swung by the horse's side.

"That foot looks bad, Cracky," the Judge observed, pausing to give the black foot careful attention. "What bit you?"

"Why, a copperhead," Cracky said cheerfully. "I come on it in the henhouse, eating an egg. It was a big egg, too. I went to stomp the copperhead. It never occurred to me that it could bite me when it had an egg in its mouth. But the dern critter bit me, right through my shoe."

"A snake with an egg in its mouth is still quicker than a human," the Judge pointed out. He did not like the looks of the swollen foot.

"I had better not detain you in idle conversation," the Judge said. "I expect you better lope on into town and find the doc."

"My wife thinks it's too late," Cracky said. "She wanted to chop off my foot with the hatchet, but I wouldn't let her."

"Why not?" the Judge asked. "I admit it's drastic, but then it looks to me like you're drastically snakebit."

"I guess I didn't feel up to having no foot chopped off," he replied.

He was sweating profusely, and his blue shirt was as soaked as if he had fallen in a pond. His voice, though, was calm.

"I expect I'm a goner," Cracky said. He tried to hold up his foot, but the effort made him grimace. "I ought to have just sat on the porch till the angels came for me. It would have saved a doctor bill."

"Are you sure it'll be the angels, Cracky?" the Judge wondered.

"Oh, I expect," Cracky Bolen said, nodding his head. "I ain't sinned a whole lot."

He reflected on the matter a moment, studying his swollen foot as if the black appendage belonged to someone else.

"How would a person sin, Judge, up where I live?" Cracky asked. "I cuss a little now and then, but that's about the only form of sin available to me."

"Well, you're probably right . . . I expect it will be the angels. But they might delay their visit if you get on in to the doc," the Judge allowed.

"I've rarely seen you on this trail, Judge," Cracky remarked. "What brings you to the Blue Hills?"

"A sad errand," the Judge admitted. "Dan Maples was killed in Tahlequah."

"Now, you don't say," Cracky said. "Who killed him?"

"An assailant or assailants unknown," the Judge told him. "I have come to inform the widow."

"Wilma? Didn't you hear?" Cracky asked.

"Hear what?" the Judge said.

"Wilma lost her mind," Cracky said. "She lost it the day Dan left, right after that crow came and lit on his shoulder. I wouldn't go in that house, if I were you, Judge. Wilma might come at you."

"She's my wife's second cousin," the Judge revealed. "She won't come at me."

"She's got herself mixed up with that dern crow, Judge," Cracky said. "She sits on the roof, cawing the whole livelong day. I seen it myself."

"I expect she knows Dan's dead," the Judge said. "Women know things. Mart would know it if I died, even if I was in China at the time."

"Yep . . . I expect she knows," Cracky agreed.

"Good luck with your foot, Cracky," the Judge said. "You need to hurry, or them angels will be visiting you."

Cracky rode on. He was sorry Wilma Maples had lost her mind. She had been a fine neighbour to him, in happier days. The last time he had gone to check on her, she had ripped most of her clothes off. The fine womanly figure he had admired in secret for so long was mostly exposed, and yet the sight had only made him feel the sadder for her. She had rolled off the roof at some point, and was black with bruises. Her hair was tangled, and she kept up a wild cawing.

The sight of her had unnerved him badly. He had wanted to help her, but when he began to dismount, she ran into the woods and hid. There was not much he could do anyway, though he did chop a week's worth of firewood for her, just to be neighbourly.

As Judge Parker rode on into the Blue Hills, the shadows began to fall across the narrow trail, from the trees that lined the steep slopes. The Judge was a man who liked sunlight. It was a pleasure to him, when he walked home to lunch at midday, to see the hot sun shining on the surface of the Arkansas River. The water was green in the sunlight. A fish would leap now and then, and water birds skimmed the surface, hoping to grab a minnow or a water bug. Cloudy days cast a pall on his spirit, and so did shadows.

But the fact was, much of life's work had to be done in the shadows of death and doubt, like the work he was now about. Cracky Bolen would likely die of his snakebite; Wilma Maples had lost her mind; Dan Maples, her husband, was dead, as was Judge B. H. Sixkiller, a respected jurist.

The shadows that fell across the road into the hills were only mimicking the shadows of life. He knew he ought to pay no attention to them, but a gloom was on his spirit from the thought of what a hard business life was. He wished he could be more like Mart—if Mart had a garden to hoe, she was happy. As a general rule, she kept too busy to notice the shadows of life; or, if she did notice, she was too busy to comment.

When the Judge approached the Mapleses' farmhouse, a half-naked woman with tangled hair, her body black with bruises, rushed out the door. The Judge was shocked by her appearance. He would hardly have recognized her as Wilma, his wife's second cousin.

"He's kilt, ain't he?! He's kilt!" Wilma shrieked. Then she began cawing wildly, as Cracky had said she would. She spread her arms like a bird, and ran around in front of the house, cawing.

"My Lord," Judge Parker murmured to himself. He found what he was seeing hard to credit. The last time he had run into Wilma in town, she had been a cheerful, appealing woman. He had always felt better after a chat with Wilma, and he was not the only one to feel that way. Yet, here she was, so demented as to be almost unrecognizable, cawing like a crow in front of her own house, a house she had kept neat and clean for many years. Other women lost their husbands without losing their minds; he was at a loss to know why Wilma was so afflicted.

Perhaps it was the crow that lit on Dan's shoulder as he was leaving. The story was all over Fort Smith. The general line was that Dan had been a fool to attempt a dangerous assignment after such a warning. But why would such a thing make Wilma go crazy before she even knew her husband was dead?

It was a mystery the Judge did not expect to find an answer to, but here he was—he had to do something. If he rode off and left her second cousin in such a state, Mart would not be pleased.

"Wilma, it's the truth—Dan's dead," he said. "I expect you best get some of your things and come on to town with me. I'm afraid you might come to harm if you stay here grieving like this."

To his surprise, Wilma stopped cawing when he spoke, and looked at him submissively. When he took her arm, she did not resist. She let him lead her into the house, which was a chaos. Wilma had broken most of the glasses and smashed the plates. The Judge did not like being inside the house, not in the state it was in. It spoke of the disorder that could befall the human spirit, a disorder he dealt with every day in his work. When possible, the Judge preferred to banish it from his family life.

But he was made a little hopeful by the fact that Wilma had quieted down. Perhaps somewhere in her, part of the old, cheerful Wilma survived. Perhaps with good treatment, her mind could be reclaimed.

He looked at her again, standing a few feet away, docile.

"Would you like to get some of your things, Wilma?" he asked.

"I don't know what to get," Wilma confessed, simply. "I been up in the sky, looking for Dan. He's mad at me because he thinks I'm selling eggs . . . but I ain't sold no eggs. I need to find him and let him know, so he'll come back home."

Wilma made the speech as sensibly as if she were ordering flour at the general store. It was what she felt: Dan was in the sky somewhere, angry about the eggs.

When Wilma had realized that Dan, her husband, was gone, such a loneliness came on her that she could not bear it. She began to take off her clothes and climb the roof, trying to be a bird, so she could find Dan and bring him back. She could not bear the loneliness, and it caused something to break inside her. Seeing the Judge now seemed to be helpful; she was glad the Judge was there.

The Judge thought he had better not try to do too much. Keeping Wilma docile was the main thing. If he could just keep her level awhile, maybe the sensible, competent Wilma would come back. There were things that crazed women, or broke them, in the frontier life; there were things that crazed men, too. But maybe Wilma Maples had not really crossed the border into madness. Maybe she could be coaxed back.

The Judge rummaged until he found an old cloth coat, which

he managed to put around Wilma's shoulders, buttoning it in front to shield her bosom.

"I expect we best wrap up and go on to town," he said. He was careful to move slowly, and he avoided looking Wilma in the eyes. In her eyes, the wildness still lurked, and he had learned through long experience that it was never wise to look wild things in the eye—not mad dogs, and not grief-crazed women, either.

By talking in a soothing tone and proceeding slowly, he managed to ease Wilma outside and up on the mule. She was craning her neck and searching the skies, as if she were expecting the crow to appear again.

"He's kilt, he's kilt!" she said again, with her head craned up to the sky. But she did not caw, as she had when he rode up. The Judge thought that was a sign of improvement.

"I think Dan's in the sky," Wilma said, in a more normal voice, when they were a mile or so down the road.

"No, he ain't, Wilma," the Judge said. "Dan's in a grave over in Indian Territory. He was killed by an assailant in Tahlequah, while carrying out his duty.

"Dan was a man who never shirked a duty," he added gently. He saw no point in encouraging any more talk about the sky, since he believed Wilma might take it into her head to caw again.

For the rest of the ride to Fort Smith, Wilma Maples did not look at the sky. The trail was in deep shadow by then. Several times the Judge came upon deer, grazing by the path. For a time, he attempted to hum a hymn. He had a good baritone, and often sang in church, if not too far behind on his judicial paperwork. He hummed "Rock of Ages," and then a few other hymns he liked. He wanted to keep Wilma soothed until he could get her to Mart. Maybe Mart would know how to turn her grieving back onto a normal path.

"I'm gonna be lonesome, ain't I, without my Dan," Wilma said, at one point.

"I expect so, honey," the Judge said.

"I don't know how I'll stand it, being so lonesome," Wilma said. Her voice cracked, when she said it.

The Judge was not skilled at talking to women whose lives had been bent crooked by sudden death, and so he did not answer. Yet, sudden death lay all around them, like the shadows cast by the hills and the trees. He himself had been shot at seven times in his years on the circuit court. Fortunately, poor marksmanship was almost as common as death, or Mart would have been a widow long before. In those days, he had traveled with a law book and a bottle of whiskey in his saddlebags. The fact that seven men had missed him was not definitive, either; an eighth man could always come around the corner, and the eighth man might be a better shot.

When they were nearly to Fort Smith, he felt Wilma's head rest against his shoulder. Then he felt a wetness on his shirt, and knew that she was crying. He kept on humming his hymn; it was all he could do. Let her cry, he thought—crying was the normal thing for a woman who had just lost her husband.

A little later, he noticed from her regular breathing that Wilma was asleep. From then on, the Judge took care to hold the mule to a steady gait, hoping he could get Wilma all the way to Mart before she woke again. Mart had dealt with many griefs in her life. She had already lost three of her sisters, one brother, and several cousins. If he could just get Wilma to town without any more trouble, he felt confident that Mart, his vigorous wife, would know what to do.

As the Judge rode into Fort Smith, Wilma sound asleep against his shoulder, he saw several men gathered around something in front of the saloon. Two of the men had lanterns; it looked like a body on the ground. The Judge rode over to have a look. If some drunk had gotten himself shot, he wanted to acquire a few of the facts before they got muddied up with exaggeration.

But it was no drunk—it was Cracky Bolen, stone dead.

"His mule brought him in, Judge," one of the men said. "He was dead when he got here. We don't know what it was he died of."

"Snakebite," the Judge said succinctly, annoyed that sudden death had once more made the operation of his court more difficult. Cracky had been a reliable messenger, one of the few he had who traveled regularly into the Blue Hills.

"Snakebite? Why, snakebite don't kill a man, usually," the fellow said. "I guess it was a big old rattler."

"No rattler," the Judge said, turning his mule. "It was a goddamn copperhead with an egg in its mouth."

21

TEARS CAME INTO ZEKE'S EYES WHEN HE RODE UP TO NED'S place and his girls came running out. Tears came into Jewel's eyes, too—she had never seen her father looking so poorly. He was skinny and gaunt and filthy. When he hugged her, he hugged so hard her ribs almost cracked. He hugged Liza, too. Then Liza started yapping, trying to tell him all the things that had happened since she came to stay with Jewel and Ned. Jewel knew she would not be able to get a word in edgewise, not with Liza yapping, so she took his horse to the barn and unsaddled it.

The horse was so lame she had to lead it at a slow walk. Zeke had been walking, leading the horse, when he arrived. It was worrisome to Jewel, for her father had always taken pride in his horses, seeing to it that they had the best of everything. It was unlike him to show up on a horse so lame it could barely walk. The other worrisome thing was that there was no sign of Pete.

Zeke was unprepared for the feelings that came to him when he saw his girls. He did not realize how much he had missed them until he was holding them in his arms, looking at them, smelling their smells. He had been with those two girls most of the days of their lives, and had not thought much about them, day after day. But his recent loneliness made him see them in a different light.

Then Liza told him Jewel was going to have a baby, which surprised him so that at first he did not believe it. In his mind, Jewel was a baby herself, or at most, a little girl. But when he looked at her, hastily shucking corn by the back door of her house, he saw a rounding to her belly that had not been there before and knew that it must be true: she was going to be a mother.

"Pa, what happened to your horse?" Jewel asked. "It's so lame, it can barely walk."

"I come over a trail that was washed out," Zeke said. "He got his foot caught between two rocks. I expect he'll recover, but I don't know when."

In fact, he was annoyed with himself for being so impatient during his trip over the Mountain that he had allowed the horse to lame himself. Now if he had to go back on the scout and had to go quick, he would have to go on foot, unless he could borrow a horse from Ned, or from Tuxie Miller. Ned seldom kept more than one or two horses, and Tuxie Miller rarely owned one that was worth borrowing, which meant Zeke was in a fix or certainly would be, if the law came.

"Where's Pete?" Jewel asked. "I'm surprised you'd go off without Pete."

Zeke kept quiet. Jewel turned from her shucking, and saw that her father was looking at her with tears in his eyes. When she saw the tears, she immediately thought something bad must have happened to make him tearful—maybe something bad had happened to Pete. It was only when he was drunk, or playing the fiddle, or remembering his dead brothers, that she had ever seen him cry.

"Jewel, no one told me about your baby," Zeke said. "I been on the scout. I had no way to get the news."

Jewel was touched that her father cared so and was showing it. She went over and hugged him again.

"Ned thinks it's a boy, but I'm figuring on a girl myself," she said.

Jewel had always had a sweet smell, Zeke remembered. He hugged her again hard, dripping a few tears on her hair. Holding her close, smelling her sweet smell, he felt a flash of anger at Ned Christie, who had ridden up one day and taken advantage of the fact that Zeke had been drunk. The next minute, it seemed like, Ned had ridden off with Jewel.

"It'll be your first baby, you ought to get your way!" Zeke growled, getting angrier as he contemplated how their lives had changed since Ned had taken Jewel away from home.

Up until then, the Proctors had been a family. He and Becca had their falling-outs and their ups and downs, but that, too, was normal. He had a home to go to, and tasty grub on the table; he could carouse with his triplets every night; or play the fiddle till the wee hours; or just go up to the smokehouse and get drunk amid the hams and hindquarters.

It seemed to Zeke, in his unhappiness, that when Ned took Jewel away, it was as if he had pulled a plug out of a barrel. Their family happiness was the barrel: the minute Ned pulled the plug, it had started draining away, and it had drained away until he found himself without any more family happiness. Becca was no longer a wife to him; both girls were gone; he never saw his triplets; and according to Sully Eagle, even Pete was keeping himself scarce, no doubt embittered at having been left behind.

Now his family happiness had thoroughly drained away. He found himself sleeping in caves, with rough men, or else camping in the bushes, come wet or dry. In Zeke's mind, the business with Polly Beck was only an accident, though of course, an extremely unfortunate accident for all concerned. The real trouble started, in Zeke's mind, when Ned took away Jewel. It was not for nothing that he and Becca had named her Jewel; she had been their jewel, rare and precious, and they had laughed at her and cuddled her when they themselves had been happy.

Now here she stood, with a swelling belly, shucking corn. If he and Becca ever managed to get any happiness back, they would clearly have to do it without their Jewel.

Her father looked so gaunt that Jewel's first thought was to feed him. He was so weary that he nodded off at the table while Jewel was boiling the corn.

"Pa's tired—make him a pallet, Liza," Jewel told her little sister.

"What if the law comes? Where will we hide him?" Liza asked. She had only been to Tahlequah twice in her life, and had never even seen a lawman other than Sheriff Bobtail, who sometimes came by for supper—but in her imagination, the law was everywhere. She had had a powerful dream once, in which a lawman with cold, black eyes was quirting her with a stinging quirt. The sight of her father, so weary and so weak, made her apprehensive that the law would show up at any time.

"The law ain't gonna come, just make a pallet," Jewel said. She cooked her best meal and Zeke roused himself enough to eat heartily.

"Where's Ned?" he kept asking. "I supposed Ned would be here.

"He went off to find a preacher," Jewel told him. "If he brings the preacher back with him, maybe we can be married while you're here.

"I hope he finds one," Jewel added. "I'd like to be married by the preacher while you're here, Pa."

"What about Ma?" Liza asked. "Ma ought to be here, too, if there's going to be a wedding."

"Who would go get her?" Jewel asked. "Pa's horse is lame."

"Your ma's taken against me, I doubt she'd come, even if I went to fetch her myself," Zeke confessed.

The memory of Becca's cold refusal the last time he had been home still angered him. He wished he had boxed her ears a few times, instead of just dragging her by the hair. At the same time, he wished none of it had happened at all. He wished they could just be together again, simply—as man and wife. Jewel's belly was swelling; they were going to be grandparents soon, which in his view was all the more reason why they should resolve their differences and be together. But he did not know if Becca would take him back—she had put herself at a distance from him, and he did not know what he could do about it.

Liza fixed a nice pallet, and Zeke gratefully lay down on it. Though he was weary in the extreme, he could not sleep. He kept his pistol in his hand, and sprang up at every sound.

"When do you think Ned will be back?" he asked, several times. "I need to see Ned."

"I guess as soon as he finds that preacher," Jewel told him. Then she went on up to bed.

Upstairs, as sleepless as her father, Jewel had her own doubts to wrestle with. She lay down and stared out her bedroom window. The moon shone in, lighting up the livestock pen and the path that led away from their house. It would be easy for a horseman as skilled as Ned to ride home in the bright moonlight. She listened and listened for the sound of horse hooves approaching. Jewel had an ache just under her breastbone, a deep ache, she missed Ned so. But she could not help remembering, now that she lay in their bed together all alone, the hasty way in which Ned had taken his leave. He had saddled his horse, muttered a few words about a preacher, and left.

Jewel did not know, now, if she believed the part about the preacher. Ned had not said anything about a preacher for more than a month; then all of a sudden he blurted out something, and was gone. To her, it seemed like something in him just did not want to stay. She took care of him the best that she could; she embraced him whenever he wanted her, and eagerly; and she was as good to him as she could be, hoping that the part of him that did not want to stay would just dry up and blow away, like feathery dandelion flowers gone to seed.

Jewel looked out the window again. The moon shone bright, lighting the bedroom as if it were daytime. Though she was safe in their bed, with their baby inside her, she shivered—for Ned was gone, the bed was empty, and she was alone.

22

IT WAS THE MORNING MINNIE SQUASHED THE BULLFROG WITH the rock that she found the dead skunk. The little bullfrog hopped too far from the pond, and got in some weeds that kept it from hopping properly. The triplets surrounded it, and began to try and hit it with sticks.

"Hit it, Willie!" Minnie commanded. She normally gave the orders when the triplets were playing, and they were always playing.

"I done hit it," Willie pointed out. In fact, he had hit the bullfrog three times, but the bullfrog just kept up its ungainly hopping.

"That stick's too little, get a bigger one," Minnie instructed. Then she happened to see a big, flat rock, and smashed the bullfrog just in time. One more hop, and it would have been back in the pond.

"Look—its guts came out," Willie said. He was annoyed that his sister had seen the rock first. If he had seen it first, he would have smashed the bullfrog even harder, and even more guts would have come out.

"I'm going home," Linnie informed her brother and sister.

"Why, are you a sissy?" Minnie asked.

"No, but I didn't tell you to kill this bullfrog," Linnie said.

Linnie was the fastidious triplet. She did not like offal or blood. She liked to invent stories about the Little People. It was said that Little People looked just like Cherokees—they even spoke Cherokee—except that they stood only one or two feet tall, roaming the woods and sometimes snatching children who wandered off where they did not belong. Minnie and Willie were afraid of the Little People, but Linnie was intrigued by them. Her father had told the triplets how they ought to keep an eye out for one another when they were off playing, because the Little People were known to take children who were not watchful, or who strayed too far from home. When her father was around, the two of them would carry a saucer of milk out every night and leave it near a toadstool, for the Little People to drink.

"Is a saucer enough?" Linnie asked Zeke once, as they were putting a saucer near a toadstool.

"It's enough," her father assured her. "They're little people, Linnie. Why, some of 'em ain't no bigger than baby rabbits."

Now, every time Linnie saw a baby cottontail, she thought of the Little People. She wished her father would come home, so they could put the milk out for them again. Her mother did not like her putting out the milk; she thought it was wasteful.

"The Lord will take care of the Little People, like he takes care of all of us," her mother told her.

Linnie did not see what it hurt to put out a little milk, just in case the Lord got too busy and forgot about the Little People. But she did not argue with her mother. Her father would come home soon, she was certain, and they could put the milk out again, together. It was more fun to do when her father was home, because they could talk about the Little People, and how they lived. Her father said there used to be one in the barn— he claimed he could see it, now and then. Linnie looked and looked, but she never saw the one in the barn. In their talks, her father had often told her that the Little People were very shy. She was sure the one in the barn was just too shy to show itself to her. Sometimes, sitting in the barn, trying to be very quiet, Linnie would imagine that the one who lived there was nearby, just out of sight behind a pile of hay, peeking at her under a heap of harness.

Since her father had been gone, the fact that there was one of the Little People in the barn was a comfort to Linnie— knowing it was there made her feel a little less lonesome. She did not know exactly what they ate, but she thought they might like watermelon. When the melons in the field began to be ripe, Linnie would sometimes sneak down to the barn and leave out little pieces of ripe red melon. The melon would always be gone the next day, or at least bits of it would have been nibbled away, which made Linnie all the more certain that one of the Little People lived in her barn.

The frog Minnie had killed was a shiny green. Minnie was jiggling it up and down, trying to make more guts come out of the frog's mouth. Willie was jealous that Minnie had killed the bullfrog. He ran back to the pond with his stick, hoping to find another frog to whack.

"Let's make a fire and cook this frog," Minnie suggested. "Let's eat his toes."

"No, his guts are coming out, I don't want to eat him," Linnie said. "You should have let him be."

Minnie, suddenly changing her mind, whirled the frog around her head and threw it out in the pond as far as she could throw it.

"I guess an old turtle will eat it," she said, watching the dead frog float on top of the brown water. Patches of yellow pollen swirled around the frog, having fallen from the willow trees that hung over the edges of the pond. Several dragonflies were hovering over the pollen—to Linnie, the dragonflies looked a little like how she imagined fairies would look. She wondered if fairies could turn into dragonflies; it was one of the many questions she meant to ask her father as soon as he returned home.

It was while Linnie and Minnie were looking for plums, over by a little seeping spring where wild plum bushes grew, that Minnie spotted the dead skunk. She saw something black, over by a clump of rocks. At first, she thought it might just be a shadow. But when she looked again, she saw it was the remains of an animal with black fur.

"Look, Linnie. What's that?" Minnie inquired, moving close to her sister. Minnie had been bold when she smashed the bullfrog with the rock, but the sight of the black fur caused her to lose some of her boldness.

"I think it's something dead," she said to Linnie.

"Maybe it's a skunk," Linnie suggested. "Skunks are mostly black."

When they crept closer, they saw that Linnie was right: it was a dead skunk. Its eyes were open, but it was dead. Green bottleflies swarmed all over a big hole where its belly had been. Something had bitten off one of the skunk's legs, which lay a little distance from his body.

"What if a bear got him?" Minnie said. "Let's run!"

She was seized with such a fright that she could barely breathe, though she began to run as fast as she could toward their house. When Willie saw her running, he began to run, too, though he did not know why his sister was in such a hurry. From the look on her face, he thought she might have seen the bogeyman, a giant with hair all over him who lived in a cave and ate little children, if he could catch them. Sully Eagle had told them about the bogeyman. Willie himself did not want an old, hairy giant to catch him and eat him, so he ran as fast as he could. Neither he nor Minnie slowed down until they were at their house.

When they felt safe enough to stop, they looked back for their sister Linnie, and saw that she was still standing by the seeping spring.

"What if the bogeyman gets Linnie?" Willie wondered. "He'll take her to his cave, and eat her!"

It occurred to Minnie that if the bogeyman *did* eat Linnie, her ma would probably let her keep all of Linnie's things, including a rag doll that was better than Minnie's own rag doll.

"Go back and get her, Willie," she suggested. "Hurry and get her before the bogeyman gets her."

"I ain't going, he might get *me,*" Willie protested.

Privately, he thought that if Linnie was not smart enough to run, it would serve her right to be taken to a cave and eaten by the bogeyman.

"No, he won't, he only eats little girls—Sully said so," Minnie lied. The fact was, Willie had a slingshot and a stick horse she wanted—if the bogeyman ate Linnie and Willie, she might get the stick horse *and* the slingshot *and* the rag doll.

"You go," Willie ordered.

Minnie just ignored him. She crawled under the porch to a secret hideout she had made for herself. From her hideout, she could watch everything that was happening in the meadow and by the barn.

Willie ran inside the house. The more he thought about the big, hairy bogeyman, the closer he wanted to be to his ma.

From her hideout, Minnie watched, hoping to see the giant bogeyman run out and grab Linnie, who was poking at the skunk's remains with a stick.

Minnie could not figure out why her sister would want to

take a stick and poke at a dead skunk with it, particularly a dead skunk that was covered with green blowflies.

Then, to her disappointment, she saw Linnie walking slowly back toward the house. Minnie waited breathlessly, hoping at any moment to see the big, hairy bogeyman run up and grab her sister. But alas, no bogeyman appeared.

When Linnie was nearly to the barn, Minnie suddenly scrambled out of her hideout and raced into the house. She meant to get Linnie's good rag doll and hide it in the smokehouse. That way, even if the bogeyman did not get her sister, Minnie could keep the rag doll hidden for a few days and play with it herself.

23

JUDGE ISAAC PARKER DISLIKED VARYING HIS HABITS. VARIAtion was unwelcome at any time of day, but particularly unwelcome in the morning, when his pleasure was to take a leisurely stroll by the river on his way to work. In sunlight or cloud, the river was always interesting. He had been born and raised on the Ohio, and since childhood had never liked to live far from moving water.

Once in his office, the Judge invariably took a small tumbler of whiskey, to limber his brain. Then he read a few lines of Milton, from a small volume of poetry he kept in a drawer with his six-shooter.

After his brain was thoroughly limbered, he would prop his feet up and look out the window for twenty minutes or so, surveying the broad street to see if there were any miscreants in sight that needed arresting.

The morning after the Judge returned to Fort Smith with Wilma Maples, he had scarcely got to his chambers, downed his whiskey, browsed through his Milton, and propped his feet, when disruption struck. The first thing he saw when he looked out the window was Emil, the telegraph operator, hurrying up the street at a speed he would have been hard put to match if a bear had been chasing him. In his hand was a telegram, and he was headed straight for the courthouse.

Old Emil had delivered many telegrams to the courthouse,

but always at his own pace—a pace which meant that he was apt to take anywhere between two hours and a half day to make the delivery. Now he was jerking along at a gait that resembled a trot, or else a man afflicted with St. Vitus's Dance.

"Uh-oh," the Judge said to Chilly who had stepped in for a moment, to return a law book he had borrowed overnight.

"Why, it's Emil, what's his hurry?" Chilly asked.

"It's that business in Tahlequah," the Judge said. "I expect the big court's heard about it . . . or maybe the President."

"What big court?" Chilly asked. He had heard about Washington, D.C., but had only a vague notion of what went on there. He knew the President lived there, but could not recall the Judge ever mentioning a big court.

"The Supreme Court, Chilly!" the Judge said, impatient. "It's the highest court in the land."

Though usually brisk in spirit, the Judge felt a sag hit him. It was depressing, in the first instance, to have a bailiff so inattentive that he had never heard of the Supreme Court. Second, it was even more depressing to see old Emil jigging along with a telegram clutched in his fist. A telegram so important that old Emil felt he had to deliver it at a trot was not likely to contain news that was peaceful. Judge Parker had endured much conflict in his life—the long agony of the Civil War, for one thing— and he was more and more appreciative of the peaceful life, a life that would allow him time to walk the shady banks of the Arkansas River, or even permit him a few minutes now and then to tip back his chair and sample the great poet Milton.

The telegram that was on its way to him would more than likely confirm that which he already knew: substantial force would have to be used against the man or men who killed Marshal Dan Maples. The federal government did not ignore the wanton killing of its marshals, nor should it. And if it was proven likely that the killer of Dan Maples was a Cherokee, then nation would be pitted against nation—the small nation of the Cherokee Indians versus the large nation whose judicial representative was Judge Isaac Parker.

"Reach out that window and have him hand you the telegram," the Judge directed. "Emil don't need to climb them courthouse steps."

Chilly complied, though to effect the transfer Emil had to strain to hand the telegram up high enough so that Chilly could reach it. Chilly immediately handed the telegram to the Judge, who saw that it was from none other than Ulysses S. Grant, the President of the United States.

"You ought to have looked at that telegram before you handed it over," the Judge said.

"Why?" Chilly asked. "I figured you'd be in a hurry to read it, Judge."

"It's from the President of the United States," the Judge informed him. "It ain't every day you stick your hand out a window and come up with a telegram from the President of the United States."

"My Lord," Chilly blurted—for a moment, he felt so faint that he thought he might need to ask the Judge if he could sit down. He knew enough of politics to understand that General Grant had become President Grant, and as such was the highest officer in the land. That he had himself touched a piece of paper that contained the words of the President made him weak in the knees with awe.

"What does it say, Judge?" Chilly inquired.

The Judge looked at the telegram, which was succinct:

THE HONOURABLE ISAAC PARKER
FEDERAL COURTHOUSE
FORT SMITH, ARKANSAS

I HAVE REPORTS OF VIOLENCE IN THE CHEROKEE NATION. A COURT PROCEEDING WAS INTERRUPTED AND A FEDERAL MARSHAL MURDERED. THIS CANNOT BE TOLERATED. I IN- STRUCT YOU TO SEND AN ADEQUATE FORCE INTO THE GOING SNAKE DISTRICT IMMEDIATELY TO ARREST ALL PAR- TICIPANTS IN THESE DASTARDLY DEEDS. I RECOMMEND TEN MARSHALS, WELL ARMED. SEE THAT THERE IS NO SHORT- AGE OF HANG ROPES MADE AVAILABLE. THIS RASCALITY MUST BE DEALT WITH SHARPLY, ELSE IT WILL SPREAD. THE TREASURY WILL SEE ABOUT YOUR EXPENSES.
YOURS,

ULYSSES S. GRANT, PRESIDENT
UNITED STATES OF AMERICA

The Judge reflected on the telegram before formulating an answer to his young bailiff. Though President Grant was known for his directness, he had not been overly direct about the aspect of the matter that concerned Judge Parker the most: that is, his expenses. Ten marshals would cost the court a handsome sum, and a sum not immediately available. It was all very well for the President to say that the Treasury would "see" about his expenses—but when would they see, and how much would they allocate?

"I expect I'll have to deputize Tailcoat Jones," the Judge said.

"Tailcoat Jones?" Chilly responded, in surprise. He had heard that Tailcoat Jones, a tall, grizzled fellow who had once ridden with Quantrill's marauders up in Kansas, had done a little marshaling. But Judge Parker had refrained from employing him, at least during Chilly's time with the court.

"I heard Mr. Jones is mean," Chilly added.

"You heard right, then—he's mean," the Judge said. "He's also expensive. But what's my choice? Dan Maples was my best man, and he's dead. I'd send Bass Reeves, but I've already sent him after the Starr brothers."

Judge Parker was referring to the famous black deputy marshal who had few rivals in his ability to catch and bring in desperadoes anywhere in the Territory.

"Maybe Bass will catch the Starrs and get home quick," Chilly opined.

"I doubt it. The Starrs had too good a lead. Bass will catch them; Bass always catches them. But it won't be quick enough for my purposes over in Tahlequah," Judge Parker said.

"Get a move on, Chilly," the Judge added. "The President wants results, and he wants them quick. Do you know Beezle?"

"Who?" Chilly asked.

"Beezle. He's Tailcoat's man," Judge Parker said.

"I ain't acquainted with him, Judge," Chilly said.

"You soon will be," the Judge informed him. "I just saw him go in the saloon. He's a short stump with red hair, and he wears his pistol with the handle pointed forward. Go stop him and tell him I need to see his captain."

Chilly was not eager to come within speaking distance of Tailcoat Jones, or his red-headed underling.

"Tailcoat Jones prefers to lay up with whores. He has his whiskey brought to him," the Judge added. "I expect he sent

Beezle to fetch him some, which is why Beezle's in the saloon. If you hurry, you might be able to catch the man in the street."

Something was nagging at Chilly's mind. Despite his awe at having handled a telegram from the President of the United States, Chilly had remembered that he himself had a dislike of General Grant.

"Wasn't it President Grant that helped the Yankees beat us?" Chilly ventured. "I remember he was their best general."

"One of the best, yes," the Judge conceded. "He had a fair hand in the outcome, but that war's over, Chilly. General Grant is President now. You need to be letting all that war stuff drain out of your mind."

"What if it won't drain?" Chilly said. "I knew there was something I didn't like about the President. He helped the Yankees win the War."

The Judge sighed. Some days, it was hard to get the simplest request acted upon. Chilly, who should have been fifty yards down the street by then, was still standing in his office, upset about the Civil War.

"Chilly, I asked you to go do an errand," the Judge reminded him. "I have to see Tailcoat Jones, and I have to see him now. I ain't got time to fight the Civil War all over again, just because you're aggrieved."

Chilly saw the crease between Judge Isaac Parker's eyes deepen. He knew it was time to get a move on.

"I'm going, Judge, right this minute—didn't you say his man was red-headed?" Chilly asked, as he went out the door.

24

NED RODE MOST OF THE NIGHT GETTING HOME.

All night, riding homeward, Jewel was the only thing on his mind. He wanted to slip in the door and slide under the covers with Jewel before she got out of bed. He could imagine how warm her body would feel, and how soft her skin. Her breath on his lips would be sweet, when he kissed her to let her know he was home.

That plan was spoiled, although Ned rode in well before dawn and quietly put his horse in the barn. Even before he got in the door, he heard coughing—it did not sound like Jewel's coughing, or Liza's, either.

When he stepped in the house, Jewel looked at him with worried eyes. He only caught a glimpse of a smile, in the light of the lantern. She was bending over Zeke Proctor, who lay on a pallet by the fireplace, coughing hard, clearly sick. Jewel was putting a mustard plaster against her father's chest.

"Hello, Zeke . . . I guess you're poorly," Ned remarked. "At least you got a pretty nurse."

Jewel raised up, hugged Ned, and let him kiss her. Then she made him feel her father's forehead.

"Zeke, you're hot with fever," Ned said, concern in his voice. "You sound kind of wet in your lungs, too. Where have you been to get so poorly?"

"On the scout," Zeke said, his voice weak. "I stayed too long in that dern drippy cave. If it ain't the pneumonia, I'll be better tomorrow."

"I'll make you coffee, Ned," Jewel said. She went off to the stove to heat the water, leaving Ned by her father's side.

"It scares me when you ride at night," she whispered a little later, when Ned came over to get his coffee. He felt her belly, to see how much the baby had grown.

"I meant to get here in time to slip in with you," Ned whispered back. "I didn't know Zeke was visiting."

Jewel smiled when he said it. Earlier in the night, she had had a dream in which Ned came home and slipped in with her. In the dream, she rolled over, and there he was, warm beside her. Then her father's coughing woke her, just when the dream was sweetest.

"What's the news from town, Ned?" Zeke asked, in a weak voice.

"Bad news," Ned admitted. "Marshal Dan Maples got murdered —another marshal, too. They say Dan Maples killed the first marshal himself in an argument, but the white law may not believe that. All they'll believe is that two marshals are dead in an Indian town."

He came and squatted by Zeke for a moment, to take a closer look at him. Zeke's chest was heaving with every breath—he was struggling mightily to get air in his lungs. Then, when he did manage to get a breath, he coughed, a cough from so deep inside him that it seemed to come out of his bowels. Ned had scarcely been home five minutes, yet Zeke already appeared sicker than he had seemed when Ned walked in. It was a worrisome situation, made more so by the knowledge that both of them might need to be seriously on the scout within a day or two.

"Who kilt him, the Becks?" Zeke asked.

"I don't know who killed him," Ned replied. "I went to your place looking for you. Sully claims the Becks were in town the day the marshal was killed, but I never saw them."

"Who's the suspect, then?" Zeke asked.

"Why, me, I guess, Zeke," Ned said, with a quick glance at Jewel. He knew his wife would be horrified by that revelation, but she was going to have to hear it sooner or later.

"Ned . . . you should have come right back home!" Jewel said.

Ned started to mention the fire in the Senate building, but decided against it. He had already been married to Jewel long enough to know that the more information he gave her, the more she would find to pick about.

"That's bad," Zeke said. "Whoa . . . that's real bad. They won't chase you too hard for killing a Beck or a Squirrel, but they'll chase you to hell and back for killing a lawman."

"I expect so," Ned said quietly.

"Did you see the marshal?" Zeke asked. It occurred to him that maybe Ned *had* killed the man, but did not want to alarm Jewel by confessing.

"I never saw the man," Ned assured him, glancing at his wife again when he said it. "I did see his horse, though, tied down by the jailhouse."

"Well, that's no crime," Zeke said. Then before he could reflect on the matter further, he fell into a light sleep.

"Let's go upstairs while he's resting," Ned whispered to Jewel. "It'll be sunup pretty soon."

Now that he had Jewel close where he could touch her, he had a fever in him to equal Zeke's—only it was a different fever.

"I'll make Liza come down and watch Pa," Jewel said. "She needs to change those mustard plasters every hour."

Despite the sweet dream of a few hours earlier, Jewel could not stop being uneasy when she and Ned were under the covers. Outside it was pearly grey, mist hiding the treetops. The sun would be up soon, boring holes in the mist; but it was not the coming daylight that kept Jewel uneasy, even as she was in her husband's embrace. Fear had slipped up the stairs with them and gotten in between her and Ned. The fear made a coldness in her that would not leave, no matter how close her husband held her, or how hard she strained against him.

Jewel began to cry a little—she could not help herself. She wanted everything to be right for Ned, but the fear would not leave. Then Liza came back up the stairs, half asleep, and asked Jewel something about the mustard plasters. Ned was irritated. He thought Liza ought to have better manners than to interrupt them at such a time, although by then they were simply resting together in the quilts.

Then the sun bored through the mists, and they could hear Zeke coughing, from below.

"What if Pa's bad?" Jewel asked.

"I might have to find Old Turtle Man," Ned said. "He ain't so bad but what the healer can cure him. He cured Tuxie, and Tuxie was so far gone I even started digging his grave— remember?"

Jewel looked at him with a flash of anger when he said it. Ned remembered a fact he had come to appreciate: women never stopped being mad about things they were really mad about. Every time the subject of Tuxie and the half-dug grave came up, Jewel gave him a hot look.

Jewel got up then, and went downstairs to help Liza with the mustard plasters. Ned barely had time to yawn and turn over before she was back, a scared look on her face.

"Pa's real bad," she said.

Ned hurried downstairs. When he got a good look at Zeke, he realized immediately that Jewel had not been exaggerating. Zeke's eyes scarcely focused, and he had been seized by a deep chill. Ned built up the fire, and the girls piled blankets on their father, but Zeke still trembled with chill.

Ned accepted some coffee from Jewel, but he felt discouraged. Just when he needed Zeke's advice, the man had gotten too sick to give it. He had assumed, as he rode home, that the law would be the enemy he and Zeke would have to run from. But now, Zeke had been brought down by a more immediate enemy, an illness so severe that it looked as if it might kill him.

He felt a fool for having left home in the first place. He

should have stayed home and enjoyed his wife; now, when he wanted nothing more than to stay home and do just that, he would have to be off in search of Old Turtle Man. If he could not manage to find the old healer quick, the white law would not need to send more of its marshals after Zeke Proctor— Zeke Proctor would be dead.

"I'll go get Turtle Man, Zeke," he said. "You lay there and try to get warm."

"No . . . no," Zeke said, reaching up a weak hand. "I don't need Turtle Man."

"Yes, you do—he can cure you," Ned said. "He cured Tuxie, and he was worse off than you."

"No, Ned . . . I need Becca," Zeke said.

Both girls came and stood behind Ned, listening to their father. Liza began to cry when her mother was mentioned. With her father so ill, she realized that she missed her mother badly.

"Zeke, Becca's at your place," Ned pointed out. "I just come from there. It's thirty-five miles. I could have Old Turtle Man here in three hours, if I catch up with him early."

"No, Ned . . . I need Becca," Zeke insisted. "I done Becca bad. I need to see her and make it right . . . if she'll let me."

His feverish eyes fixed Ned with a look he could not ignore. It was the look of a man who might be dead before the day was out. The request that had been put to Ned was not one he could refuse.

"All right, then, Zeke . . . I'll go for Becca," Ned said. "My horse is tired, though, I rode him all night."

"Mine's lame, or you could take him," Zeke said—then he took such a fit of coughing that he could not speak for several minutes. He coughed and coughed, rolling on the pallet. At one point, he coughed so hard Jewel had to stop him from rolling into the fireplace.

Ned went outside, stripped off, and poured a bucket of springwater over himself, to get himself better awake. Jewel came out while he was dripping wet. She brought him a clean shirt and pants, and helped him dry off. The thought of the seventy-mile ride to Zeke's place and back made Ned feel disheartened.

"I mean to stop off at Tuxie's and see if he'll go fetch her for us," Ned told Jewel. "Tuxie might not mind making the trip, if Dale will let him go."

"Then I could go look for the healer," he added.

"Jewel, Pa's coughing bad," Liza yelled from the doorway. Then she saw that Ned did not have his pants on yet, and ran back into the house.

When Ned rode away, Jewel stood watching her husband until he was out of sight. Though she was way down by the well, she could hear her father coughing. The sound made her afraid—and so did the sight of Ned leaving again. When Ned got home, the fear inside her left; but this time, the fear had stayed.

"Jewel . . . come inside, he's bad," Liza yelled again from the doorway, in a panic.

Jewel turned, and hurried back toward her house, wondering if there would be a time in her life when she did not have to be afraid.

25

TAILCOAT JONES WAS RESTING IN BED WITH TWO YOUNG whores, when Beezle knocked on the door.

Both whores were plump and cheap, which was the way Tailcoat liked his women. It irked him to pay cash money for the use of a skinny woman, and he rarely did so, unless desperate. Bony hips were a particular affront to him. Fortunately, the two young whores in bed with him, both stout girls from Alabama, had hips as wide as boats, amply covered with flesh. He could pleasure himself with them at length, and never get jabbed by a hip bone.

"I've a thirst, hurry on in with that whiskey," Tailcoat said. "You took your goddamn time fetching, I'll say that."

Beezle had knocked softly, and then—as a prudent move— had taken a few steps back down the hall. It was not wise to stand squarely in front of the door when delivering whiskey, or anything else, to Tailcoat Jones. Once, during the War, Tailcoat had been surprised while in bed by a contingent of Yankees, one of whom shot him in the collarbone before Tailcoat killed him and two of his comrades. The collarbone had never healed properly, and the fact of that surprise left Tailcoat with a nervous attitude about doors. Often as not, he would put a shot or two through the door when someone knocked, just to be on the safe side.

Beezle believed in being on the safe side, too, which was why he usually trotted back down the hall a few steps after knocking on Tailcoat's door.

"Don't shoot, I'm comin' in," he said, edging back toward the door.

Nelda, the younger of the two whores in the bed with Tailcoat, pulled the covers up over her eyes when Beezle stepped in to bring Tailcoat his whiskey bottle. Nelda had an aversion to Beezle because of the thick, bristly red hairs which stuck out of his nostrils and his ears. The hairs in Beezle's nose and ears seemed like pig bristles to Nelda. She did not like seeing stiff little pig hairs sticking out of a man's nose, and did her best to keep under the covers when Beezle was in the room.

"Judge Ike wants to see you," Beezle said, handing Tailcoat two bottles of fresh whiskey.

"Well, I'm home, let him come," Tailcoat said.

Beezle had been woman-shy all his life, and he did not enjoy having to palaver with Tailcoat when the man had two fat girls naked in his bed. One of the whores had the good sense to cover her face, but the other, Darcie, had so little shame that she was lolling half under the covers with her bosoms exposed. Beezle had to hand the whiskey right over her bosoms in order to pass it to Tailcoat.

"I did not speak to Judge Ike myself," Beezle admitted. "His man came running up to me in the street and said the Judge was in a hurry to talk to you.

"I think he needs a marshal," Beezle ventured.

"Cover up, Darcie. Beezle can't afford you, so you oughtn't to be tempting him," Tailcoat chided. He pulled the quilt over Darcie's generous young bosom and sat up in bed in order to sniff the whiskey Beezle had just brought him. In country towns such as Fort Smith, he found it wiser to sniff whiskey before sipping it. There was whiskey to be had in the more raw parts of Arkansas so strong that it could render a man temporarily blind, or permanently insane. With a lucrative marshaling job to be had, Tailcoat did not think he could afford either state.

273

"I expect it's them killings, over in Indian Territory," Beezle suggested. "I imagine Judge Ike wants us to go round up the killers."

"This whiskey smells mighty fresh," Tailcoat said, wafting his hand over the open jug so as to get a proper whiff of its contents. "Why don't you go downstairs while I drink it? Darcie and Nelda might have some work to do yet. We can go see Judge Ike this afternoon."

"What'll I do while I wait?" Beezle asked.

"Well, you could traipse over to the hardware store and see if they have any new Winchesters," Tailcoat suggested. "If we have to deputize a posse and go after violent Cherokees, we might have to invest in some new rifles."

As soon as Beezle left the room, Nelda lowered the covers a little. It had been hot under the covers, but being hot was better than looking at a squatty man who had red pig hairs sticking out of his nostrils. She looked over at Darcie and saw that Darcie was having one of her blue spells. Nelda felt as close to Darcie as she would have if Darcie had been her own sister. She would have liked to hug Darcie, and help her with her blue spell, but she could not hug her because Tailcoat Jones, an old, sour-breathed man, was between them in the bed.

"I don't know if I ought to drink too much of this whiskey," Tailcoat commented. "It smells strong enough to take the paint off a board."

Then he spat the cork from the first bottle halfway across the room, and began to drink the whiskey anyway.

That was fine with Nelda: smelling strong whiskey was better than smelling Tailcoat Jones's old sour breath.

26

THE MORE JUDGE PARKER THOUGHT ABOUT THE PRESIDENT'S telegram, the more out of sorts he became. The President had as much as ordered him to hire ten marshals, which in practical terms meant hiring ten outlaws and sticking badges on them. When the President had still been a general, he had mainly operated in theaters where he had an abundance of able subordinates—a luxury the Judge did not enjoy, as he made plain to

Chilly Stufflebean, when Chilly came back to report on the situation with Tailcoat Jones and his man, Beezle.

"The fact is, Chilly, there ain't ten able lawmen left for hire in the whole Territory," the Judge said. "If I had the entire Treasury to spend on this matter, I wouldn't be able to find ten competent men to employ.

"It's mostly crooked timber we've got left down here in Arkansas now, when it comes to lawmen," the Judge reiterated. "Tailcoat Jones is a case in point. He's little more than a killer himself—he has yet to come before my court to answer for one of his killings, but if he ever does I expect I'll hang him..

"In fact," the Judge added, "if I had my choice I'd rather hang him than hire him. But I don't have my choice. I ain't the President, and that's that."

Chilly had rarely seen Judge Parker in such a continuous state of distemper. Three times in half an hour, he had watched the Judge take his whiskey bottle out of his drawer, pour himself a tumbler full, and drink it straight down. Of course, court was not in session; the Judge had always been more prone to repair to his whiskey bottle in times of boresome idleness than when he was holding court. But three tumblers of whiskey in half an hour was an exceptional rate of whiskey drinking, even on an idling day.

"His man said he'd be here this afternoon," Chilly said. "I asked him why not this morning, and the man didn't answer."

Personally, he considered Tailcoat Jones to be a disrespectful person, for making the Judge wait. Of course the Judge frequently made people wait, if he happened to be reading his Milton, or poking through his lawbooks trying to locate a statute or a law of some kind. But the Judge was the Judge—if he made people wait, it was in the interest of eventually producing better law.

Tailcoat Jones, in Chilly's opinion, had no excuse. He was making the Judge wait for no better reason than whores and whiskey, which was rudeness, pure and simple. He knew there was such a thing as contempt of court and wished the Judge would lay it on Tailcoat for dawdling and insolence. Chilly himself did not go so far as to suggest it, however. Judge Parker rarely welcomed suggestions about the law, or about anything, unless he specifically asked, and he welcomed even fewer when he was freely imbibing whiskey. Chilly had enough sense to know that any man's temper would be at a simmer after inhaling three tumblers full of whiskey. In Judge Parker's case, a little more whiskey or an ill-timed suggestion would be sufficient to bring his temper to a full boil, a condition Chilly wanted to avoid if at all possible, since he himself was the one most likely to be scalded if the Judge's temper boiled over.

About midafternoon, with the sun blazing down on the street, the Judge saw Tailcoat Jones, wearing the long, dusty coat that had given him his nickname, come out of the hotel and saunter toward the courthouse. His man, Beezle, soon fell in beside him, leading Tailcoat's grey horse. Though it was not more than seventy-five yards from the hotel to the courthouse, Tailcoat Jones evidently decided that the walk might be oppressive. He mounted the grey and came trotting along briskly, riding right under the window where the Judge sat watching the broad street.

Tailcoat Jones was a man with a personality exactly like his demeanor—and he looked arrogant and hard. He had no more feeling for his fellow human beings than he did for a stick of firewood. He was but one of the many unrestrained ruffians who prowled the border states after the War, ruffians who thrived on robbery, rape, and murder. The necessity of employing such men to do the work of honest lawmen disturbed Judge Parker to the point of indigestion, and on this particular day it had caused him, already, to drink far too much whiskey. The Judge had no doubt that Tailcoat Jones was worse than most or perhaps *all* of the men he was sending him after—he was a practiced killer, whereas most of the trouble in Tahlequah had only been caused by erring humans who had let their passions get the best of them. They deserved apprehension, and if convicted, punishment. In the Judge's opinion, however, it was unlikely that they deserved Tailcoat Jones.

"He's a hard-looking sort, ain't he?" Chilly remarked, after Tailcoat had ridden past the window.

"Yes, but President Grant ain't met him," the Judge said. "The President's used to better help than we got down here in Arkansas."

A moment later, Tailcoat appeared at the door of the Judge's chambers. The Judge did not rise to greet him, but he did gesture for Chilly to leave. He did not want his youthful bailiff to have to witness such a sordid transaction as the one he was about to conduct. He did not want Chilly to go sour on the law; he wanted the boy to believe that the law was a thing of dignity, or even majesty—and such a view might not survive too much palavering with the mercenary who stood in the doorway.

"Hello, Your Honour, what's the chore?" Tailcoat inquired.

The Judge had spent the morning preparing his charges from a mass of gossip and wild accusation about the Tahlequah killings. He had winnowed out five names that he thought might warrant indictments. These he had carefully printed on a single sheet of tablet paper. The names were Willy Beck, Frank Beck, Davie Beck, Zeke Proctor, and Ned Christie.

"Am I welcome to a seat, or am I expected to stand like a goddamn nigger?" Tailcoat asked, from the doorway.

The Judge gave the man a sharp look.

"If you'll avoid vulgar profanity, you can sit, Mr. Jones," the Judge said, in his stiffest tone. It was a tone that would have cowed most men, but if it made any impression on Tailcoat Jones, the Judge could not tell. He strode in, jingling his military spurs, and took a chair. Then he struck a match on his boot-heel, fished the stub of a cigar out of a pocket in his long coat, and lit the stub.

Once the thick cigar smoke drifted away from Tailcoat's face, the Judge faced him squarely. He did not offer the sheet with the five names on it.

"I was about to offer you a commission from President Grant," the Judge said. "If your aim is to be disrespectful to this court, then I won't offer it."

Tailcoat despised the old judge. In fact, he despised *all* judges. He would rather have sawed the old man's throat open with a dull knife than listen to a minute of his sass; but financially, he was not in a position to act on his impulse. A simple-looking stagecoach robbery north of the Natchez Trace had failed to come off as planned. A resilient posse had appeared out of nowhere and had hung on tenaciously in pursuit, chasing them nearly fifty miles and wounding three of his men in the process. All three of the men died, leaving Tailcoat, Beezle, and a gaunt renegade named Jerry Ankle to flog their tired horses to safety in Arkansas. Not a cent had been earned in the process, and the future for random robbery did not look bright.

Though Tailcoat had boldly sent Beezle off to the hardware

store to see if there were enough new Winchesters available to equip a force of deputies, the action had been a bluff. He did not have enough money to buy a box of cartridges, much less a fine Winchester rifle. So far, all of his whoring and drinking in Fort Smith had been done strictly on credit. His reputation still intimidated pimps and saloon keepers, but there was no likelihood that this state of matters would last forever. Several worms had turned on him in his time, and one or two of the worms had been surprisingly hard to subdue.

It was mainly for reasons of finance that Tailcoat felt he ought to take a mannerly approach to Judge Ike Parker, at least until a few expense chits were signed and in his possession.

"I didn't mean to rile you, Judge," he said. "It's just that I prefer to take the weight off my ankles, whenever I can."

"Understood," the Judge answered. "It's the profanity I grudge you, not the chair. You've heard about the troubles in Tahlequah, I expect?"

"No, I prefer not to fill my head with slanderous gossip," Tailcoat said. "Beezle said some Cherokees shot off their guns in the courthouse. That's all I know."

"Twelve men died on that occasion," the Judge informed him. "I sent Dan Maples to arrest the known culprits, and somebody killed him."

"It must have been quite a fracas, if it's got Ulysses S. Grant stirred up," Tailcoat remarked.

"*President* Grant," the Judge corrected. "He's stirred up enough that he's ordered me to send ten deputies into the Going Snake District to apprehend the suspects."

Reluctantly, he handed the sheet of paper with the five names on it across the desk to Tailcoat, who glanced at it briefly.

"Ten deputies for five men?" Tailcoat said, lifting an eyebrow. "They must be scrappers, Your Honour."

"Know any of them?" the Judge asked.

"Well, I met this Zeke Proctor once or twice during the War," Tailcoat said. "I recall that he liked to race horses, but I don't think he was much of a shot. Of course, shooting in a courtroom is close-range shooting."

The fact that the killer sitting across from him had been so rude as to call the President of the United States by his first name irked the Judge considerably, once he thought about it.

He felt his indigestion getting worse, from the mere fact that the man was taking up space in his chambers.

"These men are the suspects that interest this court, Mr. Jones," he said. "They may be innocent men, for all I know. Your job is to arrest them—that's all. There's been too much gunplay already. More would not be welcome."

"I wouldn't welcome it myself, Judge," Tailcoat said. "There's men over in that country who don't welcome arrest, though . . . what if I meet up with one or two of those?"

"I'll repeat what I've already told you," the Judge said. "I will tolerate gunplay only as a last resort.

"The next question is, do you think you can locate ten able deputies?" he asked.

"If the President can afford it, I can," Tailcoat admitted. "I ain't had my breakfast, Judge, and it will soon be sundown. Let's strike a deal. Then I'd like to go eat a good thick beef-steak, at Ulysses S. Grant's expense."

"*President* Grant—I told you to watch your tongue, sir!" the Judge said, sharply. He noted a flicker of amusement in the killer's eyes when he said it, a fact that did not help his indigestion.

Nonetheless, he was acting on presidential orders. Within the next half hour, he struck a deal.

27

"NOPE. TUXIE AIN'T GOING ON ANY LENGTHY ERRANDS," Dale Miller said firmly, when Ned showed up to ask if Tuxie would go fetch Becca Proctor to her husband's bedside.

That was the response Ned had expected, but it annoyed him anyway. The most annoying thing about it was that Tuxie himself merely sat there, not even trying to pretend he was the boss of his household—Tuxie just looked at Dale, and smiled.

Ned himself would have loved to give Dale Miller a good shaking, but she was Tuxie's wife, not his.

"Dale, I just come from there, only I didn't know Zeke was sick," he said. "Why can't Tuxie go fetch her?"

"Because Davie Beck might drop out of another tree and

saw his other leg," Dale said. "I ain't risking it, Ned, and that's that!"

Tuxie was friend enough to loan him a fresh horse, at least, though it did little to improve Ned's mood. While he was saddling up, he could not restrain himself from complaining to Tuxie about Dale's high-handed behaviour.

"Why, you're no better than a slave, Tuxie," Ned remarked. "That woman tells you when you can butter your biscuit, and when you can't."

Tuxie did not care to argue the point. He knew his friend thought he ought to be a more forceful husband, for they had debated this same problem several times before.

"I nearly died, Ned," Tuxie reminded him. "Dale's right to try and keep me off the roads. You may be a match for Davie Beck, but I ain't—and we got nine little ones to think of. I'd go fetch Becca for you if the roads were safe, but they ain't, and they won't be while Davie's on the prowl."

"I hope I see that fool. I'll draw his damn fangs, if I do!" Ned replied.

He left the Miller farm in a high lope, annoyed by the difficulties women could create for a man. He could not recall his own mother ever making such difficulties for his father. She worked hard, kept to her place, and said little. Ned could not imagine her being so bold as to tell his father he could not go someplace he might need to go.

Now, though, he himself was constantly being jerked about by the obstinacies of women. His own wife had thrown a cup of scalding coffee at him, for no better reason than that he had proposed to leave. Dale Miller's balk where Tuxie was concerned meant that he had to ride thirty-five miles over a road he had just traversed, in order to try and persuade yet another obstinate woman to come to her own husband's bedside.

Ned had not forgotten Becca's chilly response when he inquired about Zeke, on his recent visit. Becca had exhibited no concern, and no curiosity, either—though Zeke was her wedded husband. Ned did not suppose that Zeke was a perfect mate; no doubt he slipped out with women, and more than likely had been slipping out with the Beck woman before he accidentally killed her. Ned did not approve of such behaviour himself, but he was realistic enough to know that these were the ways of men.

Though Ned loved his Jewel and was eager for their child to come, he wondered for a few minutes, as he set off up the long trail north, if he had been wise to marry into Zeke Proctor's family. It meant that he had to deal not just with his pretty Jewel, but with her chilly mother and her yappy sister as well. That was three women right there, to be drains on his energy and his patience—and Dale Miller made a fourth. Dale was not an in-law, but she was a neighbour and the wife of a close friend. Just neighbouring with a woman as strong-willed and direct-spoken as Dale could be a wearying thing.

Ned soon worked himself up into a lather of irritation, at the thought of how put upon he was by naggy womenfolk. He pushed the horse as hard as he could, eager to get his errand finished and behind him.

When he was about three miles from Zeke's place, he came upon Sully Eagle once again. This time, Sully was not falling out of a tree; he was sitting on the ground, playing with a stack of bones.

"Dern if you ain't always on the road, Sully," Ned said. "A fellow would think you lived out here and slept in a thicket. Is Becca home?"

"She was last time I looked," Sully replied. "You're back quick, Ned. What's the news?

"Zeke's taken ill, he's at my place," Ned said. "I'm here to fetch Becca, if she'll fetch."

Sully was studying the stack of bones, and did not seem eager to comment about Becca.

"Do you think she'll fetch?" Ned asked, finally. He was nervous about Becca, now that he was so close to the Proctor homestead, and would have appreciated a word of help from Sully.

"Becca's working in the garden . . . I don't know about the fetching," Sully admitted. He had no intention of commenting on Becca's willingness to go tend to her husband. Of course, he knew Becca was on the outs with Zeke at the moment, but he did not suppose that meant the condition would be permanent. To Sully, relations between husbands and wives were like the weather—some days good, some days bad; some days better, some days worse. He himself had seven wives, over the course of his life, all of whom had often been on the outs with him, though they had each and every one stayed with him until they died. His last wife died over two years ago—a cold stretch of time to be womanless—but he was too poor to afford another wife. Sully was optimistic, however, and still had hopes that an affordable wife might turn up. Meanwhile, he was sleeping in the cornshucks with the big rattlesnake. The last thing he wanted to concern himself with was Becca's problems with Zeke, or Zeke's problems with Becca.

The fact was, Sully had his own problems with Becca Proctor, the main one being that she expected him to work in the garden all day and some of the night. Sully did not mind gardening, up to a point—but he had other things to do with his life, such as think about the bear bones he had stumbled onto up on the hill. It was rare to find bear bones laying out on the grass, for bears usually went underground to die. Sully had located quite a few of the bones from the bear's paws and had them spread out on the ground before him, trying to fit them together so he could get a sense of what the bear had been like when he was alive. It was slow work—he had to concentrate on the bear, as he arranged the bones on the grass before him. And it was important work, too—bears were powerful, and needed to be understood. The bear who had left his bones on the hill might have descendants or kinsmen close by. Sully could not be bothered with pulling weeds out of Becca's garden when he should be thinking about the bear, so he had run off for the day. He did not mind young Ned Christie stopping and palavering for a moment, since he liked Ned. But he did not intend to deflect his attention from serious study of the power of bears, in order to speculate about Becca and Zeke—a pair of stubborn, contrary humans.

"If you see Zeke, tell him his dog's pining for him," Sully said. "Pete just lays there under the porch all day. He won't hardly even eat."

"I have to get on and fetch Becca," Ned said. "I ain't got time to worry about Zeke's dog."

When Ned rode up to Becca, she was on her knees in the garden, planting spuds.

Becca was badly startled to see Ned Christie back so soon. Her first thought, when he rode up, was that Zeke might be dead, or else captured by the white law.

In the time since her husband had been gone, Becca had had many lonely nights in which to probe her feelings, and inside, slowly, her heart was changing in its feeling for Zeke. She had studied her Bible, particularly the part that said a husband and wife should cleave to one another. Reading the Bible had left her with a feeling of guilt; Zeke had been wrong, but she had not been a perfect wife to him, either.

The ghost of her caring for Zeke had come back to haunt her. She had gone to bed every night for the last week hoping that Zeke himself might come home.

She was the wife he had taken vows with, and he ought not disrespect her. Still, she had come to recognize that she had been sour with her husband—and, after all, men were only men. She thought she might manage a change of heart, if he would only come home to her again. The sight of Ned caused a sharp fear to stab her. What if Zeke was dead? He would never know her forgiveness, and she would be left forever with the knowledge that her sourness had driven her husband away, to die alone.

"Is he dead?" Becca asked at once, her fear rushing into her mouth.

"Well, no, Becca," Ned said. "He is bad sick, though. He's at my place. I believe you better come, if you don't mind."

Becca dropped the spade she had been digging with, and started immediately toward the house.

"Would you saddle me that sorrel mare, and catch the little mule, Ned? We'll have to take the triplets over to Zeke's sister Susan, on the way," she said, as she passed him. "Susan will look after them. I can't leave them with Sully. He's so old he loses track of them a week at a time."

Ned scarcely had time to catch the mare, saddle the little mule, and water Tuxie's gelding, before Becca was back with her things. The triplets trailed behind her, and she had Pete in her arms, a look of surprise on the dog's face.

"Is his fever high? If Zeke's poorly, we don't want to linger," she said, as they rode off. "He always runs them high fevers when he's sick."

"It was up when I left," Ned said. "Maybe the girls have got it down by now."

"I'll get it down myself," Becca said, in a determined tone. Ned was surprised by the change in her manner, and much relieved. He had not relished the thought of having to face Zeke without her, when Zeke was so sick. Pete rode in front of her saddle, his tongue lolling out as they moved along.

"I expect seeing you and Pete will cheer him up," Ned commented.

Becca did not answer. She urged the mare into a high trot, ready to go heal her husband, and bring him home.

28

OLD MANDY SPRINGSTON DID NOT LIKE MEN TO BE RATTLING her door in the middle of the night. Her temper shot up at the sound, and she crawled out of bed with a mouthful of curses ready to spew at men nervy enough to disturb her rest. She meant to deny them whiskey, whoever they were; the time for selling whiskey was before her bedtime. Most of the drinkers in Tahlequah knew that and bought their whiskey by sundown, or a little bit after. These strangers would soon find out, too—Old Mandy meant to give them a tongue scalding they would not soon forget. What right did they have to be milling around in her yard, shining lanterns in her window, when it was too late for even owls to be making noise?

"Noisy fools!" she said, when she flung her door open. It was as far as she got with the tongue scalding.

Jerry Ankle stood there, a hard killer from the Natchez country. The men behind him, in their long coats, silently holding lanterns, looked just as hard if not harder. Bill Pigeon, at the moment dead drunk on her back porch, had once raided with Jerry Ankle. According to Bill, Jerry Ankle had once taken against a whore in some shantytown in the Arkansas Flats. He had tied her to a wild mule, and chased the mule through cane thickets until the whore was dead.

Now Old Mandy was facing not only Jerry Ankle, but seven or eight more silent men. She forgot about cursing the intruders; she was too scared even to talk. When hard men with long coats showed up in the middle of the night, it was best to walk small.

"We need Bill Pigeon," Jerry said. "If you got him, rout him out."

"What do you want with Billy? He's drunk," Old Mandy said.

A tall man stood a little ways back from Jerry. She could not see his face. All that was really visible was the red end of the cigar in his mouth. She heard a clicking sound—a gun was being cocked, and uncocked.

"We're marshals of the law," the tall man said. "We need the man, and we need him prompt."

Old Mandy did not want them to take Billy. Though he had done a few bad things in his life, he was not a killer—he was soft, compared to the men who stood in her yard. She was afraid that if they took him, he would die on the trail and she would never see him again. Her one hope was that Billy would be too drunk to be of any use to the men. Though all he did was lay on her back porch and drink all day, he was *her* Billy. Without him, she would be bereft, just an old woman who sold whiskey out of a chicken-house.

"I expect he's on the back porch," she told them. "I don't know if he'll wake up—Billy's hard to rouse, when he's heavy drunk."

"We'll rouse him," Jerry Ankle said.

They *did* rouse Billy Pigeon, but not quickly.

"Who's that? I'm asleep," Billy said, when they yanked him off the porch, trying to get him on his feet. A short stub of a man cuffed Billy soundly three or four times, but the cuffing had no effect. The moment the men turned loose of him, Billy's legs went out from under him and he fell full out in front of them, snoring loudly.

"Why, the damn sot—he's worthless. Let's leave him," Jerry Ankle said.

"No. I want him along," the tall man said. "These dern Cherokees all look alike to me. I don't mind shooting Indians, but I'd rather shoot the Indians we're getting paid to arrest. It's the practical thing. We need this fellow to point out the men the Judge wants."

"But he won't wake up," Jerry Ankle said. "A dern sot like this will slow us down, Tail."

The tall man strode over and looked down at Billy. Old Mandy began to whimper, afraid the tall man was going to kill Billy for sleeping too hard. Instead, the man took a whiskey bottle out of his long coat and poured the liquid liberally over Billy's legs.

"This liquor tastes like kerosene. Let's see if it'll burn as good," he said. "Strike a match to him, Beezle. If he don't wake up, we'll just cook him. He looks like a damn fat sausage anyway."

"Don't burn Billy," Old Mandy said, but one of the men backhanded her, and knocked her onto the woodpile. Her head spun, and her lip poured blood. The stubby man named Beezle lit the match. In a second, blue flames shot up from Billy's pants legs. Billy snored on, but then he sat up abruptly, looked down, and realized his legs were on fire.

"I'm afire, boys!" he screamed. "Put me out!"

No one moved to help him, so he jumped up and ran for the horse trough, twenty yards away. Several of the marshals' horses were watering at the trough, but Bill Pigeon shoved right through them and jumped in the water.

"That'll teach the damn sot to snore at me when I'm in a hurry," the tall man said.

Old Mandy ran over to Billy, who was moaning loudly. His pants had stopped burning, but his legs were badly scorched. As soon as Mandy helped him out of the horse trough, two of the men grabbed him and threw him on a horse. Pieces of his scorched pants were stuck to his legs.

"I'm burnt, Mandy . . . where are they taking me?" Billy asked. He assumed he would soon be murdered.

He started to moan again, but Jerry Ankle rode up to him, cuffing him hard.

"Shut up that whining, we don't want to wake the whole town," Jerry said.

"Who's that man who burnt me? I swear he's a hard one," Billy said.

Jerry Ankle was silent.

Soon Billy was gone into the darkness. All Old Mandy could do was cry.

29

JEWEL WORKED ALL DAY TO KEEP HER FATHER FROM DYING before her mother could get there. She remembered that when Tuxie Miller's fever was high, Dale had instructed that he be laid in the creek so the chill water would cool him. She and Ned had done it twice, before Dale got back with Old Turtle Man.

They did not have a creek, and she and Liza could not have carried Zeke to it anyway, but the water from Ned's well was cool enough. Jewel bathed her father in it frequently, and kept the mustard plasters fresh.

"I've smelt so much of this mustard that I doubt I'll ever be able to smell proper again," Liza complained—but Jewel paid her no mind. She kept working on keeping her father alive. She had observed Dale Miller closely during her five-day struggle to save Tuxie, and was convinced that Dale had saved him mainly by paying attention. Dale had not wandered off, not even to make water—Jewel made Ned fetch her a bucket just for that purpose. She did not sleep, or eat, except to sip a little coffee occasionally. Dale never looked off long enough for Tuxie to slip away from her and die.

Jewel meant to be as careful with her father. She helped him to sit up; he did not cough quite so hard when he was upright. His abdomen was swollen, and he complained that his bowels were stopped up. Jewel remembered a prune syrup that Ned's mother had left with her, in case Ned had such a complaint. Jewel gave a few spoonfuls to Zeke, and the syrup worked; by the middle of the afternoon, Zeke took a turn for the better, enough of a turn that he was able to walk to the outhouse with her and Liza's help. He stayed in there so long that Jewel grew worried—she thought he might have worsened, and died. She was about to go peek in on him, when he opened the door and stumbled out. He was moving slowly, but he no longer looked like a man on the verge of death. When they got back in the house, Zeke sat up on his pallet and asked for his guns and some rags. He began to clean the guns, now and then humming a little tune while he worked. His fever had dropped, and an hour later he announced that he felt his appetite coming back. He asked Jewel to kill a hen, if she could spare one. He took off his filthy clothes and asked Liza to wash them. Jewel gave him one of Ned's nightshirts to put on until his clothes dried.

The hen was promptly killed and plucked, and while Zeke was eating it, Jewel remarked that Ned ought to be back with her mother pretty soon. Zeke, who had been eating with a good appetite, suddenly lost it. It occurred to him that Ned had probably told Becca he was at death's door. When Ned had left to go fetch her, it was quite true—he had never felt so sick in his life. He had not expected to ever look upon his wife's face again. While he knew he would not be at full strength again for a few days, he was not dying, not with a good bellyful of his daughter's chicken and taters. Becca, who was suspicious by nature, was likely to think she had been chicaned.

"I don't know what your ma's going to think, Jewel," he said. As soon as he finished his meal, he got back on the pallet and practiced coughing. When Becca walked in, he wanted to look as sick as he could.

"Don't be frettin', Pa," Jewel said. "When she gets here, me and Liza will tell her how bad you was."

"I expect I just needed to get out of the wet and see my girls," Zeke said. "I hope this trouble with the white law blows over. I'm too dern old to go on the scout."

"You ain't old, Pa," Liza protested. "I bet you're still the best dancer in the District."

Zeke nodded. He had always been wild in the dance. In his youth, he could dance down three or four ladies—in plain fact, he had danced down Becca the night he met her.

He decided Liza was right in her opinion: he was not old. Sully Eagle was old, and White Sut Beck, too. He himself was forty years younger than either man, well short of age. But another truth fitted with that one—the truth that he was not young, either. Going on the scout had once been nothing to him; cold or hot had been nothing to him; and likewise wet or dry. He thrived in whatever weather befell him, but that had changed. Now, three weeks in the damp had nearly killed him. Hunted men sometimes had to stay out months until the white law forgot about them, or lost interest in their crimes. Zeke did not believe he could make it for months out in the elements. It was not a prospect he relished. Thinking of it caused his fever to come back a little.

When Becca walked in and took a close look at her husband, she knew immediately that the crisis had passed. But she also knew, from his hollow cheeks and dull eyes, that there had been a crisis—a severe one.

"Hello, Bec. I've been poorly," Zeke said. "Jewel's fed me up, and I'm gonna live now, I guess." Pete, who walked a little wobbly after his long ride in front of the saddle, did his best to run up and lick Zeke's face.

Becca saw the fearfulness in Zeke's eyes, and it touched her. She smiled at him, and felt his forehead. It was the first time she had felt like smiling at him since the trouble between them began.

"It's good you're fed up, Zeke," she said. "We need to be going home as soon as you're able. The garden's weedy, and the livestock are running all over the hills."

Jewel looked downcast.

"Ma," Jewel said. "You just got here and you've had a hard ride. You ain't even hugged me, and I'm gonna have a baby."

With that, Jewel burst into tears at the thought that her mother had only been there a minute and already wanted to leave. She had not seen her mother since Ned came and took her away. Ever since she learned she was pregnant, Jewel had yearned for some time with her mother. Now that she had her here, she wanted a proper visit.

Becca turned quickly, and hugged her daughter, knowing she had been rude to speak of leaving so soon. Jewel seemed more grown—so tall, and womanly—a wife now, and almost a mother. Becca felt she scarcely knew her daughter anymore. She knew she ought to settle in for a spell and counsel Jewel —sit in her house, watch her be a wife, get to know her tall husband a little. That would be the proper thing. Yet she felt distracted from propriety by the need to recover her own husband and get on with her marriage again, and the sooner the better.

"I'm a homebody, Jewel—that's all it is," Becca told her daughter.

She laughed a little at herself, as she dried Jewel's tears.

"I don't know how to be in nobody's house but my own," she confessed.

It was true, too. She had not spent a night away from home in the seventeen years she had been with Zeke, not until the trouble came, when she left him to return to her people. She doubted she could sleep in a strange house, although this house was her own daughter's home.

"Pa's a lot better, Ma. We cooked a hen and he et like he always does," Liza said, just as Ned walked in the door. He had been unsaddling the horses, tired from having ridden seventy miles to fetch a wife to a sick man.

But instead of a sick man, he saw Zeke Proctor sitting by the fireplace with his guns piled around him, a shine in his expression. He did not look sick enough for Ned to have ridden seventy miles for him, or seventy feet, for that matter.

"Why, Zeke . . . you rascal," Ned said. "When I left, you had one foot in the grave. Now you're up eating cobbler and taters."

He said it in a testy tone, testy enough to provoke a snappy reply.

"Why, I'm sorry I didn't die, just so you wouldn't waste a ride, Ned," Zeke said, with a feisty look.

"I didn't want you to die . . . I'm just hungry," Ned said.

He knew his irritation was unseemly. After all, Zeke had been sick enough to die. It was just that he had been spending his life lately riding between his own place and Zeke's, when he ought to have been getting some useful work accomplished.

There was not much of the chicken left, either, just taters and greens. Jewel saw that her husband was brooding. She offered to cook him some hog back, but Ned was in such a mood, he denied that he was even hungry anymore.

"It's good you're better, Zeke. I expect we'll have to be back on the scout in a day or two," he said.

Jewel opened her mouth to protest, but her father beat her to it.

"Not me, I'm going home with Bec and try to get my place back under control," Zeke pronounced. "Bec says I've got livestock running all over the hills. Some damn rustler's liable to drive 'em off if I don't get home and look to them."

"I feel the same, but it's hard to work a farm with a posse of marshals apt to show up any minute," Ned said.

"If they show up at my place, they better show up blasting," Zeke said, looking around at his arsenal. "I've just put my weapons in order. I figure I can hold a posse at bay for a while, if I can just get on home."

"We'll get home, Zeke," Becca assured him.

She took her daughter upstairs, sat down on the bed, and had a good, long talk with her. She wanted Jewel to be well informed, when her time came. She also meant to do some sewing for the baby when she got back home. Jewel was grateful her mother took the time to visit, though she was disquieted by this new, distant manner her mother took with her now. She did not know what to say. She was still her mother's child, yet not a child. They were two women now, and their menfolk were in the same predicament.

"Ma, I don't like it when Ned's gone at night," Jewel admitted. She had to express that fear while her mother was with her.

"I'm afraid men might come . . . I'm afraid of what they might do!" she said.

"You got that from me, I guess," Becca said. "I've always been afraid some rough men might come while Zeke's gone."

She looked at her daughter, not knowing what to say. There would always be things to fear, if you lived in a wild place.

"Keep a heavy bar on the door. And be sure you have a gun inside with you, when Ned's away. I don't know what else you can do, Jewel," she said.

Zeke and Ned were downstairs, smoking. Pete was asleep under a chair. Ned had gotten over his annoyance at Zeke for his quick recovery and was dozing by the fire. Zeke kept looking upstairs. He wanted Becca to come back down. Now that his wife was in a friendly mood with him again, he was jealous of her time. He knew she needed to visit a little with her girls, but he kept looking up the stairs, hoping she would soon be coming down.

When Becca finally did come down, the mood took them both to head on home, though it was nighttime.

"It'll be cooler traveling for the horse," Zeke said.

The fact was, he and Bec wanted to be to themselves, and there was no place they could be to themselves in Ned's house, not with Ned and both the girls.

"Easier traveling on what horse?" Ned asked, when he got awake enough to realize that Zeke and Becca wanted to set out for home immediately. "I've got Tuxie's horse, and he's rode down. Becca's mare is rode down, too. Your horse is lame. All that leaves is a slow mule."

"We'll take the slow mule, then, if it ain't too much bother," Zeke said at once.

"It's a passel of bother," Ned assured him. "Becca's rode thirty-five miles with no rest. Thirty-five more on that slow mule will take you all night, and most of tomorrow."

Ned could not believe his ears, or his eyes, either. Only a few days before, he had tried to coax a good word out of Becca Proctor about her husband, but she had looked at him as if he were asking about a stranger. There was such ice in her expression that he had felt tongue-tied, and gave up trying. Now she was sitting by Zeke as if no cloud had ever passed between them. All Zeke had on was a borrowed nightshirt, with a blanket around his middle. How could he be planning to set off on a long ride, at night, no less?

"Zeke, you ain't even dressed," Ned pointed out. "Why can't you stay with us a day? Becca and the girls can wash your clothes, and we can send you home clean. Becca's mare will be rested up by then, too."

"Stay, Ma. You ain't even seen the place in the light," Jewel urged. She had come as a bride to a rough bachelor house, and had taken pains to clean it up and make it pleasant. She had a good, well-weeded garden, although she did want to ask her mother's advice about planting tomatoes and squash.

Mainly, she wanted her mother to understand that she was a good wife, and had done the correct things to make her husband's life healthier and happy. She wanted her mother to know that, despite her fears, she was doing things in the proper manner. How would her mother know that, if she did not stay long enough to see her new home in the daylight? Jewel wanted to show her mother the smokehouse, and where she did the laundry, and the barn, and the garden, and the milk-pen calf. Her mother owned a good, solid cradle, the one the triplets had slept in—Jewel was wondering if she could borrow it for her baby.

But those questions did not get asked, nor would Becca consider waiting for daylight to start home.

"I ain't sleepy. I'd just as soon make a start," Becca said. "We've got a world of work to do when we get home," Becca said, several times. She meant it, too. She had put things right with her man, and now she wanted to get him home.

Zeke let Becca do most of the talking. Ned was arguing, and Jewel was pleading, but he knew they ought just as well save their breath. He had a line of stubbornness in him, but it was nothing compared to Becca's line. Nobody was likely to out-stubborn Becca.

The one problem they faced was clothes. Zeke's were so filthy that Becca would not consider letting him put them back on.

"You'll be needing a good delousing when I get you home, Zeke," she said, throwing his old clothes in the fireplace. All he was left with was his coat, his gunbelt, and his boots. Ned finally gave in and loaned him a pair of pants. They were too long in the leg and too tight in the waist, but Zeke solved the waist problem by only buttoning the bottom two buttons.

The mule was named Pelican, because he had a long, droopy jaw. He was not happy to find himself loaded up in the middle of the night, with two heavy people and a black dog. He bit Ned's finger twice during the saddling; Ned had to cuff him to get him to stand. It was, on the whole, a vexing business. Jewel and Liza stood there holding a lantern, crying because their mother was leaving without even spending a whole night with them. Zeke was trying to pretend he had never felt better in his life, when in fact he was still coughing and spitting on a regular basis. Becca gave her girls a hug and Ned a handshake, before climbing up behind Zeke. She was all business. It reminded Ned a little of how Jewel became when she threw all her passion into some kind of work—scouring the pans, or clean-ing out the fireplace. Jewel's jaw even jutted forward as Bec-ca's did—the sign of stubbornness, Ned thought. He wondered a little uneasily if Jewel would get more and more like her mother as she got older. Would his own wife get so out of sorts with him someday that she would walk out the door and go home to her folks?

Soon, Becca and Zeke were out of sight. Ned heard Pelican, the mule, snort a few times from somewhere in the darkness; then, after a moment or two, he heard nothing.

"Now that's what I call a short visit," Ned commented.

Jewel and Liza were too weepy to reply. As they were walk-ing to the house, Ned put his arm around Jewel to comfort her.

Jewel immediately clung to him, squeezing him tight, so tight that it suddenly occurred to him that there might be a bright side to the fact that Zeke and Becca had taken themselves away so abruptly. If they had stayed, there would have been little chance for him to slip in with his own wife. He would have had to bunk on a pallet, or even outside. But now there was only Liza left with them, and Liza would soon cry herself out and be asleep.

"I wish Ma had stayed," Jewel whispered. "Just till mornin', at least. I miss Ma."

"Now, Jewel, they had the livestock to think of," Ned pointed out gently. All of a sudden, the Proctors' departure seemed a lot more sensible than it did when he had had to rouse himself and go catch the mule.

"It's still two hours to cockcrow," he whispered back to Jewel. "Let's slip into the covers."

Jewel was thinking that she was not going to have her mother very much anymore, the mother who for so long had watched her every day and helped her with the problems of life. Her mother lived thirty-five miles away, and she had the triplets to finish raising, a husband to care for, a farm to tend. Jewel knew she would have to learn for herself the things she needed to know to be a mother, or a gardener, or whatever she might need to be, now that she was gone from home. Her mother had her own duties; she would not be coming to visit much. It gave Jewel a lonely feeling, even more lonely than when she had first gone away with Ned. She wished now that she had paid better attention, or talked to her mother more in the years when she had still been at home.

When they were nearly to the house, Ned suddenly cursed and jumped aside. He had stepped right on a snake. Jewel saw a flash of coil in the lantern light.

"It's a dern snake! Shine your light on it, I might be bit," Ned said. Jewel managed to locate the snake, just before it slithered under the house. It was just a harmless old blacksnake, one that was usually to be found by the woodpile.

Ned was still shaky from the scare, when they went up the stairs. He was fumbling at his own buttons, as if his fingers would not work properly. It amused Jewel that her husband could take such a scare from an old blacksnake. She undid his buttons for him, to keep him from getting impatient and popping them off, which would mean a passel of sewing if he did.

"I do despise stepping on reptiles in the dark," Ned said. "That dern snake should stay by the woodpile, where he belongs."

His legs were wobbly, those strong legs that took such a long stride. Besides his eyes, one of the first things Jewel had noticed about Ned was his long stride. She liked to watch him walk. He walked much more gracefully than other men.

It touched her that he was shaky. For a moment, it was Ned who was weak, too unsettled to get his clothes off. Jewel's confidence rose, for now she was the strong one. Ned stood patiently and let her undo his buttons, as trusting as a child.

"There could have been a rattler there, too. Rattlers and blacksnakes have been known to coil up together," he told her. "Shine the lantern on my legs—I want to make sure I ain't bit."

"You ain't bit, Ned, though I might bite you myself if you don't hush up about that snake," Jewel said, with mock annoyance.

"Shine the light," Ned insisted.

Instead, Jewel blew out the lamp.

Then she did bite him, and kept biting him until she got him safely in bed.

30

AS ZEKE AND BECCA WERE MAKING THEIR SLOW WAY IN THE dark across a grassy meadow on the mule Pelican, Zeke thought he saw a spot of light in the forest above Tuxie Miller's farm. He saw it just for a moment—it was as if a lantern flickered, high on the wooded ridge.

"What's that? Did you see it, Bec?" he asked, stopping the mule.

Becca, more tired than she had wanted to admit at Ned's house, had been nodding against her husband's shoulder. Before they had ridden a mile on the slow mule, Becca realized that she had been a little foolish for insisting that they leave, when she could have taken a short rest with her girls. Seventy miles on horseback and muleback was hard on the bones, though she felt a driving urge to get home and did not much regret her haste. It was hard to keep her eyes open, though, with the mule plodding along at a walk. Now Zeke was talking to her about lights on a hill, even stopping the mule to watch.

"I had my eyes shut, Zeke," she confessed. "I didn't see nothing."

"I swear I saw a lantern flash, near the top of that ridge over toward Tuxie's," Zeke said.

"Who'd be out with a lantern this time of night?" he asked, as much to himself as to Becca.

Just then, a shooting star arched down through the dark sky.

"Maybe that's what you saw," Becca said. "Maybe it was just a shooting star."

Zeke was not convinced.

"A shooting star is white," he replied. "What I saw was yellow. It looked like a lantern light, to me."

Becca expressed no further opinion. She put her head back against his shoulder and closed her eyes, thinking a little sadly of what a fine grown woman Jewel had come to be. That was the purpose of being a mother—to turn daughters into fine young women. Becca knew that, but still felt a little sad. She would not be seeing very much of her Jewel, now that her daughter was grown and soon to be a mother herself.

Zeke was troubled by the light on the ridge. He had only glimpsed it once, out of the corner of his eye, but the light had been made by a lantern, of that he was sure. Who would be up in the hills with a lantern, in the hour before dawn? Coon hunters usually gave up and went home well before this time —and if it was coon hunters, they would have hounds. He heard no hounds.

"It might be possemen," he said, but Becca did not respond. From the way her head lolled against his shoulder, he knew she must be asleep. Like Becca, he began to regret leaving Ned's so abruptly. At the time, it had seemed vitally important to get started for home; but now, it seemed only a silliness. Why had they not just rested for a night on a pallet? Then if it was a posse on the hill and the posse showed up at Ned's house, he and Ned, with their combined firepower, could put it to rout.

That opportunity was lost, for he was two miles gone from

Ned's, on a slow mule. A well-mounted posse could beat him there and have Ned shot or captured or hanged long before he could be there to help.

It was still a good mile to Tuxie Miller's place, and he could not get there in time to send a warning to Ned, even if the argumentative Dale Miller would allow Tuxie to take a warning. Besides, Tuxie's tired horse was still over at Ned's, a point Zeke just now came to realize.

If there was somebody up there with a lantern, it would more than likely flash again. Zeke sat where he was, watching the hills for ten more minutes, stroking Pete so he would not bark.

But no lantern flashed. Zeke began to wonder if he had really seen a flash; perhaps Becca was right. Perhaps he had only seen a shooting star. Mounted as he was, with a sleeping wife on a slow mule, he could not easily go investigating.

Then Zeke remembered Old Turtle Man. The old healer was known to travel at all hours. He might be up on the ridge, on some errand of healing.

The thought did not quite still his worries, for he could not get the notion of a posse out of his mind. He tried to persuade himself that he had been seeing things, but the flash nagged at him. He just was not sure.

No second flash came, and his eyes became tired from scanning the hills. Finally, he kicked the mule with his heels, and he and Becca headed on toward home.

31

IN THE DAYS AFTER THE DEPUTIZING OF TAILCOAT JONES, Judge Isaac Parker began to exhibit signs of an uneasy conscience. Martha Parker, who had often been the person who made the Judge's conscience uneasy, was quick to note the indicators. The Judge, a solid sleeper who would normally be unlikely to wake up if the house was burning down around him, ceased to sleep well. He began to toss and turn, muttering curses in his restlessness. Once Mart heard him say "owl," though no owls had been around to bother them. Another time, she distinctly heard him say "Mr. President," though he appeared to be asleep.

Besides being a solid sleeper, the Judge was also an accomplished eater. He could readily dispose of several eggs at breakfast, as well as a sizeable intake of steak, bacon, pork chops, or whatever meats might be available. He preferred his coffee scalding—instead of sipping it as most folks would, he blew on it a time or two, and then drank it down like water.

The morning after Mart heard him say "Mr. President" in his sleep, he came plodding downstairs and requested a single egg for breakfast.

"Fry it hard, I might want to bounce it," the Judge said. He was usually neat at breakfast, but this morning, his suspenders were unsnapped, and his shirttail out.

"Are you sick? Tuck your shirt in," Mart said, crisply.

"I'll answer the question—no, I ain't sick—but I won't obey the command," the Judge said, sitting down at the table, his shirttail not tucked in.

"Ike, are you ornery today, and if so, why?" Mart inquired. "Are you sure you only want one egg?"

"You'd never make a lawyer, Mart—you can't keep to the subject at hand," the Judge informed her.

"I ain't trying to make a lawyer, Ike, I'm bein' a wife," she told him. "I'm trying to find out what's the matter with you."

"I guess I'm like a preacher who's decided to sin with a deacon's wife," the Judge said. "I've reached the point where I'd rather break the law than enforce it."

Mart cracked his egg, and dropped it in the skillet, a frown on her face. She did not like to hear mention of the sin of adultery, at her breakfast table or anywhere else. Her husband knew that, plain and clear.

"I don't know what you're talking about, but I'll thank you to clean up your mouth," Mart admonished.

The Judge was so taken aback by the sudden reprimand that he sat in silence and listened to the egg sizzle in the skillet. When Mart served it, it certainly looked hard enough to bounce.

"Many thanks," the Judge said. "And for your information, it is a fact that preachers have been known to be taken in sin with wives of deacons."

"You can eat your dern facts for a while, and see how you like it," Mart said.

Conversation choked off for several minutes. Then husband

and wife commenced apologies at the same time. Neither heard the other's apology, and both left the table with a sense of grievance. It was not until the Judge was correctly dressed and about to go out the door, that Mart tried again to find out what was bothering him.

"It ain't like you to toss in your sleep and call out names," Mart said. "What's wrong?"

"It's that business in Tahlequah," the Judge said, looking down the hill at the swollen Arkansas River. It had rained somewhere upstream, and the river was in a flooded state.

"Ike, the President himself told you to do what you did," Mart said.

"Yes, and I should have told him I resign," the Judge confessed. "Now I've deputized a bunch of hard killers. I'll be surprised if more honest men don't die before this is over."

Then he gave Mart a peck—he did not want her to think he was hopelessly ornery—and headed down the hill. He wanted to have a walk by the old, muddy river before he opened court for the day.

32

LYLE MILLER WAS TEN, AND PRONE TO DISOBEDIENCE. HE slipped out of the house before daylight, while his mother, Dale, was nursing the new baby. He raced down to the livestock lots, caught the colt, and was about to ride down to the creek to a place where there was a mess of crawdad nests, when he happened to look up and see the lights on the hill. Lyle enjoyed poking a stick down the crawdad holes. Sometimes the old crawdads would grab the stick with their pinchers, and he could pull them up. He carried an old can that he kept the crawdads in. His favourite trick to play on his sisters was to put crawdads under their covers. His mother had whopped him several times for doing it, but Lyle was determined to get back at his sisters for all the mean things they did to him.

Seeing lights on the hill made him forget the crawdads, for he had never seen lights on the hill that early before. It made him feel strange. It was still misty; Lyle could not see the top of the ridge because of the mists. Once in a while, the old healing man, the one who had saved his pa when his pa had been so sick, would wander the hills with a lantern. But these lights were not made by one old man; several men with lanterns were shuffling around up in the hills among the trees.

He heard a horse nicker, and his colt nickered back.

Then his mother was there. Somehow she had slipped out of the house and caught him with the colt. He knew it meant a licking for sure. She still had the baby with her. She had slipped along so fast that the baby had lost the breast. His mother's breast was still oozing milk. Lyle was shocked at the sight, since his mother was always careful to cover herself with a shawl when she was nursing the baby.

"Ma, I was just gonna . . . ," Lyle said, before his mother grabbed his chin, and pulled his face close to hers.

"Do you think you can find your way to Ned's house?" she asked him, in a low tone.

"Yes," Lyle answered. "Me and Pa, we've been there a lot."

"Riding a trail with your pa and riding one by yourself are two different things, Lyle," his mother told him. "I wouldn't make you risk it if I had a choice, but I don't. You need to slip out the back of the barn and ride down the creek a ways, before you turn back to the trail."

Lyle felt scared all of a sudden. He had only meant to go poke at crawdads with a stick. He did not understand why the lights were in the hills, or why he had to go to Ned's, or why his mother had squeezed his jaw and whispered to him in a serious tone. He had never ridden very far without his pa— what if he got lost, and a bear ate him?

"There's some men on the hill," Dale said. "I expect it's a posse from Arkansas. You've got to go to Ned's and tell him the posse's coming, Lyle. If they take him by surprise, they'll kill him."

"But they ain't at Ned's, Ma . . . they're here," Lyle pointed out.

"They're here, but they won't stay," Dale explained. "You need to leave by the back door of the barn, and you need to leave now—before it gets any lighter, else they'll see you."

"What'll I say if they stop me?" Lyle asked. "They might take me to jail."

"No, they won't . . . you're a boy, and you ain't done nothing," his mother said. "I doubt they're bad enough to disturb ten-year-olds. Now get!"

"I wish Pa could go," Lyle said. But he said it to himself. His mother was already slipping back toward the house, holding the baby to her breast as she moved along.

Lyle took the colt back into the barn, and then out the back door before he mounted. He was not worried about the trail, or about the men up in the hills—he was only worried about bears. He did not believe the colt could outrun a bear; he began to regret contemplating the crawdad hunt at all. Now he might get eaten, and all because he wanted to get back at his sisters.

But his mother had told him to go, and he did not dare linger. The one thing that cheered him a bit was that Ned Christie's new wife made good flapjacks. Maybe when he got there, she would make him some, for being so brave about the bears.

33

DALE MILLER STOOD AT HER KITCHEN WINDOW, BURPING HER newborn baby, Sarah, as the possemen came slowly down the hill toward her house. There were ten riders in all. The lead man was a short, red-haired fellow riding a pinto. He wore an old grey jacket that looked like it had once been part of a Confederate uniform. The other men wore long coats, and carried rifles across their saddles.

"It's ten of them, Tuxie," she said. "They've raised a force to take Ned."

Tuxie had just saucered his coffee. He had looked forward to a peaceful breakfast, but it looked as if peace was over. He sipped some coffee anyway, since the posse was still a good fifty yards away.

"If it's only ten, I doubt they'll take Ned," Tuxie replied. "Ned will shoot five or six of them, and the rest will run."

"Yes, but then they'll come back," Dale said. "When they come back, there'll be twenty of them, or thirty. I doubt it will end until he's dead."

"Oh, now . . . ," Tuxie said. He did not believe it would go that far.

Dale was thinking of Jewel. The girl had no idea what it

meant to be a mother; she was only just learning what it meant to be a wife. Now a posse of ten riders had come looking for her husband—and they looked to be a rough bunch, too.

"All this is because Zeke Proctor couldn't be content with his wife," Dale said. "He slipped out with a woman, and now there's war."

"Well, but that wasn't Ned's fault," Tuxie said. He was hungry for sausage, but the posse was nearly there.

"Ned went to court with him—*that* was the fault," Dale said. "He should have stayed home and let Zeke worry about his own foolishness.

"It's when you don't mind your own business that things like this get started," she added, with a pointed look at Tuxie.

Then she started outside to face the posse. Tuxie got up to come with her, reaching for his big shotgun as he rose.

"Leave that gun, Tuxie," she ordered. "There's ten of them. I don't want you to give them a reason to shoot you."

Tuxie reluctantly left the gun. The only person he recognized, when he stepped out the door, was Bill Pigeon—and he looked an awful sight. His pants seemed to have been burned off him, and his bare legs were blistered and raw looking. Bill was shivering and shaking, as if he had the chills. They had tied him to his horse.

The red-headed man in the old Confederate jacket rode over to parley. He rode so close that Tuxie had to turn his head or else have the horse slobber on him.

"We're U.S. marshals," the redhead informed him. "We've come for Ned Christie. Bring him out."

"Oh, Ned don't live here," Tuxie informed the red-headed man. "This is the Miller farm."

The redhead glanced at Bill Pigeon, who was shivering as if he had pneumonia.

"Bill Pigeon says that's his horse in the lots," the redhead said. "If his horse is here, I expect he is, too."

"Nope, he ain't," Tuxie said. "His horse was rode down, so he left it with us and borrowed one of ours to go on a trip."

A lank man broke from the group, loped down to the lots, rode into the barn, and loped back. Tuxie did not like the lank man's looks, or the redhead's, either. He was building up a little irritation from having to stand so close to a slobbering horse. But it was his farm, and he did not intend to back up just because the man was rude and rode his horse too close to a person. He thought Dale had been wrong not to allow him to bring the shotgun. The red-headed Reb probably would not have ridden the horse right into his face if he had been armed with his shotgun.

Dale herself had not said a word, which was unusual. She stood beside him silently, keeping her eyes to herself. She still had baby Sarah over her shoulder, trying to get her to relieve her belly with a good burp.

"We ain't got grub enough to offer you breakfast, but you're welcome to water your horses, if they're thirsty," Tuxie said, in an effort to be polite.

The lank man rode up beside the redhead, and a third rider, the tallest and roughest of the lot, joined them.

"Did you find the colt?" he asked, looking at the lank man.

"No colt," the lank man answered. "Just that grey horse, and two plow mules."

"Did you find the colt's tracks, then?" the tall man asked. One of his hands rested on his pistol butt. He took the gun out of its holster, and began to click the hammer.

The lank man looked startled.

"You didn't tell me to track it, Tail," he said. "It ain't in the barn, though—I looked."

"There was a colt in that barn earlier today," the man clicking the pistol said. "I heard it whinny. Now if I send you to locate a colt, and it ain't there, tracking it would be one way to locate it, wouldn't it, Marshal Ankle?"

"I believe that would just be common sense, wouldn't it?" he added, in a tone as sharp as a rattler's fangs. "I don't like to lose track of a colt when we're trying to arrest a dangerous criminal. For all I know, Ned Christie could have caught that colt and ridden off on it. Get out of the way, Beezle."

The redhead looked agitated.

"What?" he asked.

Just as the redhead turned to look at the tall man in the dusty black coat, the man backhanded him with the pistol, right in the face. The redhead did not fall off his horse, but when the pistol hit his face, it made a sound like a tree branch cracking in a heavy wind. Blood began to pour out of his mouth, along with a goodly number of the man's teeth.

"Clean out your ears so you can hear an order when I give

it. I despise having to repeat myself," the tall man said. "And the order was, get out of my way!"

The redhead immediately jerked his horse backward, enabling the tall man to lean over and backhand the fellow who had been remiss in not tracking the colt. The pistol barrel caught the man across the forehead, knocking him backward off his horse. The blow had been a hard one; the lank man did not so much as twitch, once he hit the ground.

Tailcoat Jones then turned his attention to the Millers, smiling an icy smile.

"Excuse my manners," he said. "It's deuced hard to get competent help in Arkansas. Was it Ned Christie took the colt?"

Tuxie was startled to hear that the colt was gone. He had supposed the animal had merely wandered into the barn.

"No, Ned ain't here, and he ain't been here since he borrowed that horse," he explained. "That colt belongs to our boy Lyle. If it ain't there, Lyle must have slipped off early."

"Slipped off and went where?" Tailcoat inquired. He believed the Indian. He looked too honest to lie.

But then there was the white woman. No woman, white or Indian, was too honest to lie, not when a friend was involved —or a child.

"Crawdad fishing, I expect," Tuxie said. "There's a big patch of crawdad nests about a mile down the creek. If Lyle ain't on his pallet, then I expect that's where he's gone."

He started to ask Dale if she had seen Lyle that morning, but thought better of it. The man on the ground still had not twitched. His forehead had been sliced open by the blow from the gun barrel, so clean that Tuxie could see his skull-bone. The tall fellow who complained of poor help had whipped the pistol around so quick that Tuxie had not really even seen it, though he sure heard the barrel hit. A man could die from a lick that hard, delivered right to the forehead. In such circumstances, Tuxie thought he should leave his wife out of the discussion.

Tailcoat Jones looked at the woman. Though she had not spoken, she had an impudent stance. His suspicion was that she had slipped out somehow and sent the boy off to warn Ned Christie. He had a notion to take her over by the woodpile and have her horsewhipped for her treachery.

He considered whipping her, for a moment. He particularly hated to be interfered with by some damn sly female with a brat at her teat. But if he whipped the woman, he would have to shoot the husband, and he did not want to start the day by shooting the husband, whom he had nothing against.

"That's a fine brat. Do you have others?" he asked the woman, who had yet to raise her eyes.

"We've been blessed with ten children, all healthy," Dale said, in as neutral a voice as she could manage.

"That's a passel of blessing," Tailcoat said pleasantly. "I'd advise you to get 'em out of the house promptly, so they can keep their health."

"Why?" Tuxie asked, puzzled. "It's barely sunup. Most of them are still asleep."

"Hush up, Tuxie, do as the man says," Dale said. Then she went on in the house and began to gather up the children. Tuxie followed her inside, flustered. He wanted to grab the shotgun and fight, but when he had the gun in his hands, Dale yanked it away and told him just to get the children and not forget any —she knew they must not forget a single one of them.

By the time they were all back outside, the marshals had already fired the house. The man with the split-open forehead had revived and was on his feet, wandering around by the well, moaning that he was blind.

Dale noticed that one of the raiders was missing. She could only count nine. She hoped the other one was too slow to catch her Lyle. The colt was fleet, at least; if Lyle had not pussy-footed too long about leaving, she considered that he had a good chance of making it to Ned's.

Tuxie was stunned when he saw that his house was afire. He knew white law could be capricious, but he had not expected a bunch of marshals to ride up in the morning and set fire to his home. He and Dale had built the house themselves, with the help of Ned and their neighbours. He had expected to live his life in this house, and someday, die in it. Now it was blazing, sending smoke high into the heavens. The tall man who was so expert at pistol-whipping sat watching, a cigar in his mouth.

"Why, hell, I never even had breakfast, and now you've burned me out!" Tuxie said.

The man with the cigar just glanced at him, cold as a January dawn. The children were all whimpering. Dale took Tuxie's arm, and shook it hard. She had counted the children three times, to make sure they were all safely outside. She wanted the men in their long coats to go, while all her family was still alive. With the children outside, her only worry was Lyle.

"Hush, I said," she whispered. "Don't talk. Let it burn, then maybe they'll go."

"It's our house, Dale!" Tuxie protested. "I guess I can cuss the man that burned it down, at least."

"Mind me, now," Dale demanded, in a fierce whisper. "Don't cuss him . . . don't say a word. You saw him nearly kill two of his own men, over Lyle's colt. That tall man ain't just crazy, like Davie Beck. He's a pure killer. He won't bother sawing at your leg—I expect he'll kill you, and maybe our children, too, if you cuss him."

Tuxie was restive, snorting through his nostrils, something he rarely did.

"Tuxie, be still," she said. "What's burning is just a house . . . it's just lumber. You and me built it once, and we can build it again. Hold steady, and maybe none of us will get killed. That's the main thing.

"We're all alive, and we're healthy—that's the main thing," she repeated. She made Tuxie look her in the eye. She did not want him doing anything fatal, just because he was in a bad temper.

Tuxie looked at the tall man in the dusty black coat—looked at him, and held his tongue. He wanted to cuss the man, and cuss him hard, but he held his tongue. He knew his wife was right: the house was just lumber. They could build it again. They were all healthy, and alive. That was the main thing.

The children continued to cry and wail, but Tuxie did not say a word.

While the house was burning, the men in long coats rode off along the trail toward Shady Mountain, and Ned Christie.

34

NED AND JEWEL WERE IN THE BARN, CUTTING A SHOAT, WHEN they heard the horses running.

Ned was not fond of cutting pigs. He tended to put the task off until the shoats were big enough to have developed a fearsome squeal. Jewel was holding the shoat's head, and Ned was working between his legs.

"They say a pig can squeal high enough to scare off bears —hurts their eardrums," Ned said, trying to get a good grip on the young pig's slippery little testicles.

"Hurts mine, too, Ned. I'll be deaf for a week if you don't hurry," Jewel said. She wished there were some way to squeeze her ears shut, but there was no way.

It was when the pig was catching its breath between squeals that they heard the horses running. The sound took them by surprise, for the shoat had been squealing so loud and so long that they were braced for pig squeals and did not at once know what to make of the running horses. It was all the two of them could do to hold the squirming shoat, so they could not easily go take a look.

"Now who's that coming so fast?" Ned asked, a little vexed. If he let go of the slippery testicles, the pig would suck them back up into his body and he would have most of the work to do over again, coaxing them out. Jewel was sitting on the pig's head. If she stood up to go look, the shoat would get up despite him, and they would have to chase it around the pen for half the morning just to catch it and complete the job.

Still, two horses running had to mean something. They were coming from the direction of Tuxie Miller's, which could signify an emergency of some kind. Tuxie was accident prone, due to clumsiness.

"Maybe Tuxie fell out of the loft, or let the plow run over him. It'd be just like him," Ned said.

Then they heard a gunshot, and another. To Ned, it sounded like a .44 pistol being fired. He shot .44 pistols himself, and knew the sound.

"Ned, there's shooting!" Jewel said, just as the pig caught its breath and began to squeal again.

There was no talking over the squeal, but Ned and Jewel both knew that gunshots could not be ignored. Ned's rifle stood nearby, propped against a wheelbarrow. He looked at Jewel, and Jewel looked back. Jewel jumped up, as Ned released the shoat. He took the rifle, and hurried outside.

"Why, it's Lyle," Ned said immediately. "Lyle on his colt."

The boy was riding bareback, bent low, clinging to the colt's mane. Fifty yards back, a man in a long, brown coat, well mounted on a tall bay gelding, was trying to overtake the boy. He held a heavy pistol, and as they watched, fired a third shot at Lyle—it went wild.

"Ned, why would he shoot at Lyle?" Jewel said.

Liza popped out of the house just then, having heard the shots, and stood in the doorway, watching the chase.

"I guess he's a posseman, or some kind of villain," Ned said, raising his rifle. Lyle's colt was spent from the race. Though young and fleet, he was no match for the posseman's bay. The posseman was rapidly closing the distance between himself and the boy. He had missed with three shots, but he might not miss with a fourth. A heavy .44 bullet would do dreadful damage to a skinny boy like Lyle Miller, even if it only struck him in the shoulder or the leg. And the posseman was pulling closer with every stride to the boy on the exhausted colt. Ned started to shoot the man's horse, but decided it was too risky. Unless he made a perfect shot, the bay would keep on coming, as White Sut Beck's big gelding had, enabling the posseman to get off a fatal shot.

Ned saw the posseman cock his big pistol, preparing to shoot at Lyle Miller a fourth time. The colt was stumbling now, and the posseman was not more than thirty yards back.

Without further hesitation, he swung his rifle and shot the posseman clean out of his saddle. Lyle Miller jumped off the winded colt, and came running for the barn. Ned levered another shell into the chamber, waiting to see if the posseman would rise and make a fight of it.

But the posseman did not move. He lay dead where he had fallen. Lyle Miller was so badly scared when he got to the barn that he could not talk, at first. His eyes were wide with fear, and his teeth were clenched. Jewel talked to him soothingly, and Liza came down to help, but it was a few minutes before Lyle could unclench his young jaw enough to talk.

While the women were calming him, Ned walked over and looked down at the dead posseman, a sallow fellow with a long scar along his jawline. He wore a nickel badge. That fact did not surprise Ned, but it saddened and sobered him. All he had been doing was attempting to castrate his shoat. Then, the white law had chased an innocent boy right into his hen yard. He had shot to protect his neighbour's son, as any fair man would. What it meant, he knew, was that the battle had been joined between himself and the Arkansas law. It had been joined—and who knew where it would stop?

Ned's bitter regret was that Zeke Proctor had taken himself off so prematurely in the middle of the night. Zeke would not have been involved with castrating a shoat, and he might have been able to run out and deflect the posseman before matters had reached a fatal juncture. But that opportunity was lost. Zeke had left, just when he might have been helpful.

When Ned got back to the barn, Lyle Miller was past the worst of his fright and was able to give a fair account of his morning.

"I was goin' to poke crawdads, but Ma sent me off," Lyle said. "There was lights in the hills. It was men coming."

"Yes, and one of them got after you," Ned commented.

"I was nearly here before he caught up with me," Lyle said. "I was scairt of bears, but I didn't see no bears."

Lyle looked anxiously across the hen yard to where the man who had chased him had been, but he did not see the man— only the man's horse, grazing.

"He got after me back at the turn," the boy said.

Then a new anxiety struck him. He turned his eyes to Ned.

"I hope they didn't shoot Ma and Pa," he said. "There was lights in the hills. Ma told me to go out the back of the barn and come tell you."

"They wouldn't shoot your ma and pa," Ned said, hoping he was right. "I expect they saw that nag I left with your folks. Somebody might have told them it was mine. It's me they want, not your ma and pa."

He saw Jewel watching him with fearful eyes. Liza had even stopped yapping, from the shock of seeing the man in the long coat shot down.

"You should run, Ned," Jewel said. "Run before they get here.

"They won't find you, once you're on the Mountain," she added. Suddenly her worst fear was for Ned. A man had been killed in her hen yard—a lawman, maybe. The whites would want a death for his death. It was not fair, for Ned had only shot to protect a boy. But the whites would want a death, fair or not. Her fear of being alone and at the prey of men was a small fear compared to her fear of losing her husband forever.

She wanted Ned to go. If he was on the Mountain, he would be safe. The whites would never find him in the woods and rocks. She wanted him to go, and go quick, before the men came who had made the lights in the hills above the Millers' farm.

Ned knew Jewel was giving him good advice. He ought to go while he still could. He had no way of knowing how large the posse was; all Lyle knew was that there had been lights in the hills. But Dale had sent the boy to him, knowing that there was risk to her child. Dale Miller was not a woman who would be apt to risk the safety of one of her children unless she felt the matter to be desperate to the extreme. And if Dale thought it was desperate, then Jewel was right: he ought to go on the scout and go at once. On the scout, he could survive. The posse might be too big for him to beat back. If he stood and fought them, he might not survive.

Yet it felt wrong, leaving. He was on his home ground, with his pregnant wife and her sister. He had killed in the courtroom only to protect innocents. He had not even seen, much less killed, Marshal Dan Maples. And he had killed this morning only to protect his own neighbour's ten-year-old son.

Bad men sometimes rode for the white law, men who took the law's money but practiced whatever lawlessness took their fancy, and did it under the name of the law. If he left, he might be leaving two women and a boy at the mercy of such men. The possemen would surely be enraged that the prey they sought had escaped them. They might vent their fury on the women—beat them, outrage them, even kill them. Jewel's worst fear might come true on this bright, sunny day. She might find herself in the hands of rough men—merciless men.

Though Ned wished he knew how many men he would have to fight, he knew he could not leave. He had better stand with his woman, on his own ground. If the posse only numbered five or six, perhaps he could turn them back. Then he could take Jewel and Liza to Zeke's, leave them where there was a chance they would be safe, and prepare himself for a long time on the scout.

"It's too late to leave, Jewel," he said. "There's a dead man laying in the hen yard, and I expect the rest of the posse's on the way."

He saw protest in her face, and spoke firmly to quell it.

"Don't fight me on this," he said. "Our best bet now is to turn them back. If it ain't but four or five of them, I expect I can do it. Then we'll go to your ma and pa's, where you and Liza will be safe."

"What if there's more than four or five?" Jewel wondered. "What if you can't turn them back?"

"Why, I can't say—I don't know the answer to everything right now," Ned admitted. "I just know I ain't leaving. Take Lyle and get to the house. I've got to tend to this dead man, and quick."

Jewel was both scared and glad. Maybe Ned's way would be best. If anyone could turn back an Arkansas posse, it would be her husband.

Lyle Miller, meanwhile, was over his scare, and he was hungry. He was confident Ned Christie could take care of the bad men if they showed up.

"Got any flapjacks this morning?" he asked Jewel. "I ain't et breakfast. I sure would like some flapjacks."

Ned laughed—a boy had to eat, even if there was going to be a war. The fact was, he could use some flapjacks himself. The shoat they had started to castrate was standing over by the trough, eating slop. Maybe there would be time for a little breakfast before the posse came.

Jewel looked at him doubtfully, but Ned gave her a smile.

"Fix us some flapjacks, Jewel," he said. "We might as well eat while we wait. Liza, you gather up a few eggs, if you can find any, and bring a hen or two into the house. If they try to lay siege to us, it would be nice to have a chicken on hand."

Liza went off and soon filled her apron with eggs. Jewel and Lyle went to the house, and Ned found an old wagon sheet to wrap up the dead marshal.

The shoat kept grunting at Ned. It had cleaned out the slop, and wanted more.

"Don't be grunting at me," Ned said to the pig. "Just because you got away today don't mean you'll get to keep your nuts. You ain't hefty enough to be no boar."

Then he took the wagon sheet and went back to the hen yard, to wrap up the dead killer from Arkansas.

35

TAILCOAT JONES WAS LECTURING HIS TROOP WHEN THEY SAW Everett Dane's big bay horse come trotting up the trail toward them. They were within three miles of the Christie farm when the bay came trotting back with Everett Dane's body. Tailcoat was in a foul mood, and did not trouble to hide it.

"Dern, there's a body roped to that bay," Jerry Ankle said. "I expect it's Ev."

Beezle could not talk, due to a badly swollen mouth. He loped over and caught the bay. The body roped to the bay was indeed that of Everett Dane, the man Tailcoat had dispatched to catch the missing Miller boy, a mission that had obviously failed. All Ev Dane had caught was a bullet, and upon inspection the bullet turned out to have been well placed.

"Right in the heart," Jerry Ankle said nervously. "I expect he was shot at close range."

"This fool wasn't shot at close range, but *you* will be if you don't improve your tactics," Tailcoat informed him. "Some of you other marshals will be shot at close range, too, if you keep stumbling around in the morning, shining lights for people to see."

He had his pistol out, and was clicking the hammer in vexation. The men hung well back, and kept their eyes down. They only had to look at Jerry Ankle's forehead to see what could happen when Tailcoat Jones grew vexed enough to click the hammer of his gun. The six-inch slice across Jerry's forehead had been hastily stitched up with a darning needle and some heavy thread. Jerry himself had stopped complaining of blindness, and now complained of double vision. It did not require double vision, however, to tell that Tailcoat Jones was in a dangerous mood.

"I'm glad somebody shot this lagging imbecile," he said, after a brief inspection of the wound in Everett Dane's body. "He couldn't even catch a boy on a colt."

"I guess the boy had too much of a start," Jerry ventured.

"Yes, a fine start," Tailcoat said. "You boys lit up the hills like Christmas with your damn lanterns and your coffee fires. That damn impudent woman saw the lights and slipped that boy off. Christie's probably gone on the scout by now—we may have to chase him for a month, and he still might get away."

Tailcoat proceeded on at a high lope. If at all possible, he wanted to catch Ned Christie at home. The prospect of having to pursue him deep into the woods and thickets did not appeal to him.

When they finally came in sight of the Christie farm, Tailcoat called a halt. The Miller boy's colt was grazing in plain sight, but the boy was not in plain sight, nor were any other humans.

"All right, now, watch what you do," Tailcoat instructed. "They say Christie's such a fine squirrel hunter that he don't even hit the squirrel when he shoots—he hits the limb under the squirrel, and just picks the varmint up when it falls. Saves meat. All you boys are a lot bigger than squirrels. If he sees you, I expect he'll hit you—if he chooses to fight, that is."

"Why wouldn't he fight?" Dick Sabine asked. Dick hailed from Little Rock, and had hair the color of straw. He carried a shotgun rather than a rifle. He was so shortsighted that he had once shot his own horse by mistake, after which he gave up trying to use a rifle.

"Why, he might believe he's innocent and prefer to take his chances in a courtroom," Tailcoat said. "Otherwise, the odds are nine to one."

He angled off into the woods above the farm. Ned Christie, from what he had heard, was the most formidable of the five men he had been sent to arrest, which was why he had come after Ned first, before his force became depleted in battle. Now the depleting had already begun.

Once Tailcoat's men were well spread out among tree

stumps and logs, Tailcoat himself settled down behind a thick oak stump and watched the house for a while. It soon proved to be a boresome tactic. Nothing stirred in the farmyard, except a bloody shoat, a few chickens, and the Miller boy's colt. No one came out of the farmhouse. Somebody would usually be stirring around on a farm; chopping firewood, mending harness, plucking a chicken. Tailcoat had a spyglass, which he took out and trained on the windows of the farmhouse. He hoped to catch a glimpse of Ned Christie, or one of his women, but he saw nothing. If the house was inhabited, the inhabitants were being careful to stay away from the windows.

An hour passed, and the situation did not change. Though bored, Tailcoat was patient. He had been a sharpshooter in the War, and spent many a day watching and waiting for an enemy to reveal himself. In this case, the only vexation was flies, which swarmed with a vengeance in the heavy woods. They had to be continually swatted away.

Beezle had not been born with the gift of patience. He hated to spend a day sitting in the hot underbrush swatting clouds of flies away from his bloody, wounded mouth. He had already sucked in several, which irritated him so that he put aside caution and approached Tailcoat Jones.

"I've swallowed so many flies I'll soon have a bellyful," he informed his captain.

"Well, that'll save grub," Tailcoat said politely.

"Why can't we just go arrest the fellow, and not do all this waiting?" Beezle inquired. He wheezed a little when he talked, due to a swollen tongue.

"Because he's a competent rascal," Tailcoat said. "He might resist."

"But there's nine of us," Beezle said. "I doubt he'll try to whip nine of us, if he knows there's that many of us."

"Oh, he knows—that is, he does if he's home, and I suspect he's home," Tailcoat said.

"One of the boys says he's got a pretty wife," Beezle said. "If he ain't home, we could whop her till she tells us where he is."

Tailcoat had heard about the pretty wife from other sources himself. Before the posse left Fort Smith, Judge Parker had specifically warned him to go easy on the womenfolk over in the Going Snake District. The warning had been so sharp, in fact, as to verge on insult.

"You're to leave the women alone," the Judge said pointedly, as he looked over the rough posse he was about to dispatch. "I just paid for three new hang ropes. If I hear of any raping, I'll be ready to do some hanging."

"Why, Judge—is that a threat?" Tailcoat had asked.

"Not a threat, sir—that's a verdict," the Judge answered, before turning and walking away.

Now, through the sultry afternoon, as Tailcoat Jones lay behind the oak stump swatting black flies and watching the farmhouse below him, his thoughts began to dwell upon the pretty woman that was said to be married to Ned Christie. He had already let one woman off easy on this trip, the insolent wife of Tuxie Miller, who deserved a good horsewhipping for her treachery. If Ned Christie's wife was as pretty as she was said to be, he might let the men have some sport with her— though not, of course, until her dangerous husband was thoroughly dead. It would be a way of showing the old judge how little he cared for his orders, or his verdicts.

Jerry Ankle came over, as the afternoon was tending toward dusk. He, too, was much vexed by the flies.

"I don't think he's there, Tail," he said. "I expect that boy warned him, and he went on the scout."

"Well, then, why don't you just go knock on the door, Marshal Ankle?" Tailcoat suggested, in a dry tone. "Knock polite, and ask if the master of the house is in."

"What?" Jerry said, puzzled. It was not the response he had expected.

"You heard me—just go knock," Tailcoat repeated. "You'll find out soon enough who's there and who ain't. If you're lucky, he'll just crack you across the noggin a time or two, like I done—you can enjoy a few more stitches."

"You think he's there, then?" Jerry Ankle asked.

"Yep," Tailcoat replied. "I think he's there, and I would bet that his rifle's loaded."

"It's going to get dark pretty soon. It's shadowy here in these hills," Dick Sabine remarked. He had crept over to join the parley.

Tailcoat Jones said nothing. He was bored with the company, but comfortable behind his stump. Waiting had never bothered him; in point of fact, he enjoyed it. Patience was a necessary quality in a sharpshooter. Sooner or later, most men got restless and showed themselves. Tailcoat did not get restless. His concern, though, was that his opponent, the squirrel hunter Ned Christie, did not appear to be the restless sort, either. Most of a long day had passed, with no movement from the house.

Tailcoat watched closely. He had a sense that Ned Christie was watching back, perhaps just as closely.

Jerry Ankle, after some deliberation, decided that he did not want to go knock on the Christie door. He was still seeing double, and felt that it would be foolish to risk another lick on the head.

"What's the plan, then, Tail?" Beezle wondered.

"Spread our pallets, and wait till morning," Tailcoat informed him.

"You mean make camp?" Beezle asked.

"No—no goddamn camp," Tailcoat said, a little annoyed. "Just spread your pallets, and wait."

"You mean we ain't to eat?" Jerry Ankle said. "No coffee, even?"

"Not unless you can milk it out of your teat," Tailcoat said. "I don't want no fires or no lanterns, this time. No lights at all. I plan to forgo my smoke, and I expect the rest of you men to do the same."

"We ain't even to smoke?" Beezle said, appalled at the dismal prospect that lay ahead. Tobacco smoke put the black flies off; without it, they could expect a night of terrible buzzing.

"You can't even smoke," Tailcoat said. "Just rest, and think —if you *can* think."

"Then what?" Jerry asked. "What if the man sneaks off in the night?"

"He won't sneak off," Tailcoat said. "I doubt he'd want to leave that pretty wife."

"What are we going to do?" Beezle asked, impatient. "Just sit here until the man decides to go milk his cow?"

"Why, no, Beezle . . . no," Tailcoat answered, calm. "I expect to spend a restful night, and I hope you do the same. Along about daylight, we'll all whip up and go pay Mr. Ned Christie a visit in his home."

36

NED WATCHED THE POSSE FILE INTO THE HILLS FROM A TINY crawl space he had constructed at the top of his house, just under the roof. He had removed the chinking from between two of the logs, to allow himself a nice peephole. He could shoot through it, if necessary, though nothing that drastic had ever been necessary. His father, Watt Christie, had urged him to leave the little space just under the roof. Watt Christie's belief was that the Cherokee people could not be too careful. It was always better to have a space in your house where you could watch the trails without being watched yourself.

The space was so small that Ned had to slide into it and out of it, flat on his stomach. He could not raise up or turn, but it was so cleverly hidden behind a beam that a person would have to know it was there to find it.

"Be a good place to hide children in case there's war," his father had said, after taking a look at the crawl space. Watt Christie could only look; he had grown too bulky to fit into the space himself.

What Ned saw as he watched the posse convinced him that he had been right not to leave the women. The men in long coats looked hard—every single one of them. And their leader, the tall man in the dusty long coat, looked the hardest of all.

The men seemed well armed, too, which was worrisome. Ned saw the stocks of new Winchesters protruding from their rifle scabbards. Somebody—the government, probably—had put up the money to equip a force of professional killers, and the posse had not stinted on weaponry. Of course that did not mean all the men could shoot. Ned felt confident that he could outshoot most of them, for his own guns were excellent weapons, and well maintained. In his opinion, the low death count in local conflicts was mainly due to the fact that half the guns involved would not discharge with any regularity. He knew he could not count on that advantage with this posse.

He stayed in his crawl space most of the morning, watching the posse position itself among the stumps and logs on the hill above his house. It surprised him a little that the men had not simply ridden up and demanded his surrender. After all, they were nine to one, and the tall man in the dusty coat had not looked like the fearful sort—why was he waiting?

The nine men were hidden by foliage, but by careful watching, Ned was able to establish the position of most of them. He watched the birds, and saw the spots they avoided. Also, the men were restless—no doubt, the flies were a vexation. Now and then, one would stand up to swat or scratch, revealing a hat, or an arm. The only posseman Ned could not locate with some exactness was the leader. That man had ridden up the hill, and vanished. He did not stand up. If he scratched, he did it with a minimum of movement.

In the afternoon, when the crawl space got so warm he was soaked with sweat, Ned slid out backwards and went down to Jewel and Liza. He had instructed them both to stay well away from the windows. He did not want so much as a shadow or a flicker of life to be visible to the men on the hill. Jewel and Liza were scrunched up by the fireplace with fearful looks on their faces. Lyle Miller, his stomach full of flapjacks, slept peacefully on the floor.

During his time under the roof, Ned had noticed what looked like smoke far away to the west toward the Millers' place. Of course, it could have been smoke from a lightning-struck tree; trees were often ablaze on the ridges of the hills in the time of summer storms. But it might be smoke from the Millers' house itself—a somber thought. If the posse had burned the Millers out, it would explain why Dale had not showed up, wanting to make certain her boy was alive and safe.

The fact was, the Millers themselves might not be alive. The man in the dusty coat had looked plenty capable of raw murder, and worse.

He did not mention that possibility to the women. They were already frightened enough. Jewel wanted to stir up the fire and cook a meal for them, but Ned forbade it.

"I don't want that posse to see smoke coming out of the chimney," Ned told her. "I expect they know we're here, but let's keep 'em guessing as long as we can. Let them think they've staked out an empty house."

"What about the milk cow?" Jewel asked. "Her bag's going to swell, if we don't milk her soon."

"One night won't hurt her," Ned assured her. "I expect this matter to be settled in the morning."

"I wish Ma and Pa hadn't left," Liza said. "They wouldn't dare bother us if Pa was here."

The comment reminded Ned that he was vexed at Zeke. He thought Liza overrated her father's reputation. The white law would not be likely to turn and ride off, just because Zeke Proctor was in the house. Very probably they had an arrest warrant for Zeke, too. But Liza was Zeke's daughter, and it was natural for her to think her pa was the most fearsome man in the land.

As soon as Lyle Miller woke up, he began to whine to go home. When Ned informed him that he could not go back just yet, a fit of homesickness took the boy—a fit so severe that he burst into tears.

"But I miss Ma, and it's getting night," Lyle whimpered. "I've always slept where Ma's at. I'm gonna be scared, sleeping away."

"One night won't hurt you, Lyle," Ned told the homesick youngster. "Maybe Jewel will make you some more flapjacks in the morning."

Jewel put her arms around Lyle and tried to comfort him, but the boy continued to sob, somewhat to Ned's annoyance.

"Dale's tied that boy to her apron strings so tight he's afraid to spend one night away from her," Ned whispered to Jewel. "When I was his age, I was camping all over the Mountain by myself. If I kilt game, I'd be gone for a week at a time sleeping out."

"Everybody ain't independent like you, Ned," Jewel reminded him. "I never left my ma till I came here . . . Liza, neither."

They made a light supper on some potatoes and a little cold bacon left over from breakfast. Ned kept his rifle in his lap throughout the meal. Afterward, he took a jug of whiskey and went upstairs. When Jewel came up, he was sitting by the window, sipping from the jug.

"Ned, don't you be getting drunk, with those white men nearby," Jewel said. She seldom quarreled with him about his drinking. But this was a serious situation—if he had to face the white law and possibly submit to arrest, she wanted him to be dignified and sober, as a Cherokee senator should be.

Ned smiled at her. Mostly, he was tolerant of Jewel's efforts to keep him on the straight and narrow. Trying to keep men on the straight and narrow was a woman's task. But he was facing an army up on that hill. On this night, particularly, he wanted his liquor—it would put the lightning in him, if a fight came. Ned rarely thought of death, though he had seen a good deal of it. But he knew now that death lay around them. The men on the hill had lit no fires and had swung no lanterns. He had not seen even the flicker of a cigar. What that meant to him was that they were disciplined killers—or their leader was, at least. The whiskey he was sipping would not make him lax, it would make him ready.

Now and then, from the meadow, the Millers' colt whinnied. It was confused, like Lyle, who whimpered intermittently until he finally fell asleep again. Liza was too afraid to sleep by herself. She crept into Jewel and Ned's bedroom, and made a pallet by their bed. It vexed Jewel a little; Liza knew Ned liked his privacy. He only wanted his wife in the bedroom.

But on this night, Ned was so preoccupied with his watching that he hardly noticed Liza. The more he thought about the smoke to the west, the more convinced he was that the Millers had been burned out. He did not want someone sneaking off the hill and firing their house; they would be caught cold if they were driven out of their shelter. The possemen would kill him for sure, and the women would suffer hard handling.

In the deepest hour of the night, Ned thought he heard movement on the hill. He could not identify the sound, but he was certain the possemen were stirring. The night birds had grown silent. He would usually hear foxes up on the Mountain, but no foxes yipped this night. Jewel and Liza had fallen into nervous sleep behind him. In the deep, silent darkness, Ned came close to losing his fighting spirit. Though he considered himself a decent fighter, he was not so self-impressed as to suppose himself a match for nine men—not if the men were led by an experienced leader, as these men were—a leader who could keep them sitting all night without even tobacco smoke to help them ward off the flies and mosquitoes.

He wondered, for a time, about surrender. It might give the women a better chance. But he did not wonder long. If death was to be his lot, he wanted it to be a fighting death. He was not going to let the white men handcuff him, put a hood over his head, and drop him through a hole in the floor, so he could die at the end of a rope.

He bent all his energy to staying alert. Once the women were asleep, he began to rove through the house, upstairs and down, checking all the windows. It was a large house, a better house than most brides were brought to by men his age. The matter of the preacher crossed his mind; he knew he had been neglectful in that regard. Now a violent situation had caught them, one they might not survive. Jewel and he were still not married, not by a preacher with a Bible in his hand. It was a lapse on his part, one he intended to make up to Jewel if only they got out of the present scrape alive.

Back up on the second floor, he heard the sounds from the hill. They were faint, but he knew what they were: horses were being saddled; stirrups creaked; men were mounting. The darkness was just beginning to grey, but it was still more dark than grey. Ned strained his eyes, but could not see the men who were making the sounds.

He felt the same disquiet he had felt in the courtroom, when he had gone striding for his guns. Something was about to break out upon them, from up on the hill. He quickly shook Jewel and Liza awake, and rushed them downstairs. There was a small root cellar behind the kitchen, under a little porch where buckets and ropes and every sort of thing got stacked. Ned grabbed up Lyle, and got the two women and the boy into the root cellar. Lyle Miller started to whimper again, but Ned shook him gently and shushed him.

"You got to be quiet now, all of you," he said firmly. "Stay in the root cellar and don't come out till I tell you."

Ned had scarcely gotten back from hiding the women and the boy, when a voice called out from the hill. Ned could not see the speaker in the darkness; no doubt the man was still protected by foliage. But he knew it belonged to the tall man in the long, dusty coat.

"Come out and surrender, Christie—we're offering you one chance!" the man yelled. "*You* come—or else *we'll* come!"

Ned felt fight rise up in him, at the man's insulting tone. On impulse, he fired one quick shot at the sound. It was a thing he had practiced when he was a boy. If he heard a squirrel chatter, or a wild turkey gobble, he would flash a shot at the sound. Often as not, a branch or a cluster of leaves would deflect the shot, but not always. Usually, he walked home with a squirrel, a partridge, or a mallard. Once, in the rain, he had even killed a young deer on the run, by merely shooting at the sound.

Immediately after the shot, there was silence up on the hill. The silence stretched on and on. Ned put a new shell in his rifle. He wanted a full magazine, in case the men came on. He had shot, and now the battle was joined. At least the possemen knew he would not be carted off to Fort Smith in order to be hung at the end of their hang rope.

"My God—he's hit Tail!" someone said, from the hill.

It gave Ned a jerk of satisfaction. His old skill had not left him, and the hard leader in the long coat had an answer to his insult.

Ned had only a moment to enjoy the sense that he had dealt the first blow. A second later, rifle fire poured down on him from the hill. He stretched belly-down on the floor and crawled behind the bed. Soon, all the window glass shattered. Though the house was of solid log, now and then a bullet ricocheted off a windowsill, and into the room. The rifle fire was continuous. Ned saw a mounted man start down the hill, and promptly shot him out of his saddle. It was not a fatal shot; Ned saw the man crawl away.

The firing was so thick that Ned felt cautious about even raising his head. He crept to a west window, and shot another posseman—the fellow had been standing by a bush, in plain sight. It was grey now, the darkness receding, and Ned could see a good deal better what he was shooting at. The fellow who had been standing by the bush did not crawl away, and Ned considered that he had one less opponent. He had hit three, counting their leader, but could only be certain that he had eliminated one killer. The rider he had only hit in the shoulder; he had no way of knowing how seriously he had injured the tall man named Tail.

Ned started up to his crawl space. It meant leaving one side of the house unprotected, but it was the safest place to shoot from and provided the best view of the hill. He could see anything that moved.

Before he could get to it, he heard the sound of hooves. The whole posse was charging now. He thought he saw seven riders, which did not accord with his count, but he had no time to check. He stood by the nearest window, and fired. He knocked off two riders before the posse made it to the house. One man jumped off his horse and ran in the door. Ned had reached the stairs by then, and he shot the man before he had both feet in the door.

Horses and men were all around the house when, suddenly, Lyle Miller appeared.

"Ned, I'm scairt!" the boy cried.

"You ought to have stayed put, Lyle!" Ned said. He shot another posseman through the window, but Lyle's appearance had rattled him—he only hit the man in the leg. The man clung to his horse, and disappeared. There was so much dust from the horses that Ned could not see clearly. He grabbed the boy, and carried him back to the second floor.

Before he got to the crawl space, he smelled fire. One of the possemen must be expert at firing structures, to get a fire going so quickly and in the middle of all the shooting, Ned thought.

Ned did not know if he could squeeze into the crawl space with Lyle. He felt a powerful duty to his friend Tuxie to protect his son, and so stuffed Lyle in first. Then he heard something behind him—turned—and shot a man who had followed him upstairs. The man had a gash across his forehead, raggedly sewn up. The man fell backward down the staircase—dead, Ned felt sure.

"You get in there and you stay put, Lyle," Ned ordered. "You can't be popping out, with all this shooting going on."

Smoke was already curling up the stairs by this time. Ned did not immediately fear the house flaming up—it would take half a day for the stout logs to burn through—but he did fear smoke. He hastily ripped off a piece of quilt to make rags to cover his nose. He handed one to Lyle, though he knew it would take a while before the smoke penetrated to the crawl space. He thought of the women in the root cellar, Jewel and Liza, but did not feel he could risk going back down the stairs. It might be filled with possemen already, and one of them might surprise him and end the battle. Besides, the smoke would rise. The women would be safe enough in the root cellar, unless the floor collapsed, and that was not likely to happen for hours. Surviving the battle was the task he had to accomplish. He thought he had accounted for half of the posse—if not killing them, then disabling them sufficiently to keep them from wandering around in a smoky house looking for him.

Before scooting into the crawl space, Ned turned for a moment to look out a window. He knew the riders were still milling around outside. He heard the nervous horses whinnying; horses never liked fire. He thought he might be able to shoot down on the men, perhaps killing or disabling one or two more. If he could, maybe they would give it up and leave. It seemed there was at least a chance of that, since he had hit the leader early. Then it flashed to him that he had seen the leader, Tail, in the charge. Though well to the rear, he had been the seventh man.

Or so Ned thought; it was hard to be certain of what exactly he *had* seen, in the few seconds the men were racing down on him. His worry now was that he had only dealt Tail a small wound, when he shot at the sound of his voice. It was a troubling thought, dashing his hopes that without their leader to force them on, they might not have the stomach to continue such a deadly fight.

Just as Ned edged to the window, something struck his face, right by his nose. It spun him around, causing him to drop to his knees. He was looking directly down at the floor, but could not see it—in fact, he could not see anything. His vision had gone. The world was black, with just a distant spot of light, at the center of the blackness.

Oh Lord! Blind, he thought—blind, finished! He had a Colt .44 in each hand, the guns his father had given him, but he could not see to fire them. The moment at the window had been incautious. Now he was hit, and he was blind. Any one of the possemen could finish him, if one happened to be bold enough to come up the stairs.

Ned stayed on his hands and knees for a moment, in a black world, no vision at all. He felt a weight in his head between his nose and his eyes; he knew it must be a bullet, and wondered why he was not dead. He wanted to sneeze out the weight, but could not.

He began to cough from the smoke. He still had the rag in one hand and quickly put his face in it to stifle the coughs. He did not want to give his position away. He could smell that the smoke was billowing thicker, which was both good and bad. It would hide him, discouraging the possemen from climbing the stairs—but it would also choke him and finally kill him, if he did not move to get out of it.

Ned had whirled when the bullet struck. He had to reach out with one hand and touch the bed to know which way he faced. His upper teeth ached; he wondered if the bullet could have struck his teeth and gone up his nose, but he knew he had no leisure to worry about the wound. He was blind, but he was still alive—he had to get to his crawl space before the smoke choked him, or a posseman found him. He tucked one pistol inside his shirt and kept the other in his hand, as he inched across the floor. Though blind and wounded, he took care to move quietly. If the possemen heard him, they might shoot him through the floor. As he crawled, he wondered who had shot him. He had only shown himself at the window for a second, and yet had been shot in the face. It must be that the posse had a sharpshooter with them.

It troubled Ned that he had let go of his rifle when he fell. He wanted the rifle, but knew he could not take the time to locate it, blind as he was and with the smoke getting thicker. At least he had his pistols. He would have to shoot at sound if anyone came at him.

The smoke thickened so that Ned thought he would die before he made it to the crawl space. Even with the rag at his face, the smoke got into his nostrils when he tried to draw a breath. It stung his nostrils, and made his eyes water. He could not see, though his eyes teared.

When he got to the crawl space, weak from the smoke and from the weight in his head, he whispered to Lyle Miller. He wanted to hand the boy his pistols, afraid he might damage one of them crawling into the small space. He whispered, and got no answer. He reached into the crawl space, fearing the boy might have passed out from the smoke, or from fright—but Lyle was not there. It stunned him for a moment. He had put Lyle in and told him to stay, only a few minutes before—had he bolted again? Had the posse found him? Was he on the roof? They were all questions Ned was unable to answer. All he knew was that the crawl space was empty. Lyle Miller had disappeared.

Ned had no time to ponder the mystery. He carefully eased himself in, and closed the little flap of wood concealing the space. In the little hollow, he could breathe again, without the smoke burning his nostrils. The flap kept most of the smoke out, or did so far; Ned inched along until he could put his face up to the small peephole to the outside. He could breathe pure air and ease his lungs. He heard the sound of horses milling in the backyard. He hoped Lyle Miller had managed to wiggle off and get away. He would never be able to face Dale and Tuxie, if the boy was hurt.

Then he heard Liza screaming: they had found the women! If they had Liza, they had his Jewel, and here he was, shot in the face and blinded, unable to help. Ned felt a rage that pained him far worse than his aching teeth. Men had come to his farm —bad men—they had shot him, fired his house, and now they had his women. Jewel was carrying their child, and yet he was too wounded to fight for her or the child. He felt he had been wrong to snap off that first shot, when the man had asked for his surrender. He had been wrong to try and fight so many. Better to have surrendered and then tried to escape on the road to Fort Smith.

But it was too late. Liza was screaming, and then he heard someone hit her hard—but not with a hand—and then the screaming suddenly stopped. He longed to hear Jewel's voice, even if she was fearful, so he would know she was still alive. But Jewel made no sound. She might have fought the men when she came up from the root cellar; she might be dead.

Ned had a hard time keeping consciousness, the pain in his head was so bad. He wanted to fight, and yet, he was blind. That was the main fact he had to act upon: he was blind. Inside one eye was a piercing, painful light; and yet it was not a light that showed him anything. It was as if a tiny sun were shining inside his head. The light was a bright circle, intense as fire. It was painful, and yet Ned was glad of it. It offered him the hope that he might not be blind forever. Old Turtle Man had saved Tuxie when the last breath of life was about to leave him. Perhaps Old Turtle Man would understand what the light was. If he could survive, perhaps Tuxie or Dale would fetch the old man to him. If the house did not burn up completely, he could survive in the crawl space until the old healer came.

The light was only in one eye, which meant that the other eye might be lost. Even if that was so and he had to fight with one eye, Ned meant to recover. In his mind, he tried to be sure he remembered the face of every posseman, although he had only glimpsed them briefly as they charged. He intended to survive his blindness, or half-blindness. His woman might be dead; his unborn child dead, too. There might be nothing left for him but to be a warrior. If so, he meant to be a fierce one, a warrior the whites in Arkansas would never forget.

He heard the horses leaving now, and he could hear flames crackling on the north side of the house. The posse must think he was dead, cooked amid the burning logs of his home. They must be so sure he was dead that they were not even going to wait to search the house for his body—to take an ear, or a finger, to show to the court. Such things had happened to Cherokee men, warriors who fell in battle with the whites. His father had told him the stories, and his grandfather.

But this posse was lazy, and the logs of his house were solid. They would take all day to burn. Ned lay in his crawl space, the little sun burning in one eye, and tried to determine by listening how many horsemen were left. He wanted to know how many men he had killed, and how many were left to fight, if he had to fight them again. But he could not tell. Maybe the whites were taking the bodies of their fallen home for burial —nine horses had come; nine were leaving. He held onto consciousness until they were out of earshot, trying to count. But he could not be sure of the number.

He wanted his Jewel to come. Maybe she could blow the painful little light out in his eye, as she blew out the lamp at night before she came to him in bed. The light shone too brightly, searing his brain, making a heat in his head. He touched his face and felt a bullet, wedged at the top of his nose just under the skin. He pushed and the bullet moved; he pushed again, and it came out, followed by a rush of blood.

Ned did not mind the blood, for there was space in his head again, hazy space. The little sun inside his head grew dimmer and dimmer, until finally he could sleep, holding the spent bullet between two fingers.

37

"NED'S DEAD . . . NED'S DEAD," LYLE MILLER SAID, TO THE red-headed man who kept shaking him and cuffing him. "I seen him on the floor when I run out."

Lyle did not want to be dead himself, as Ned was, and Liza. One of the possemen had hit Liza in the head with a stick of firewood, to make her stop screaming. After he hit her, Liza stopped screaming—and also stopped moving, or breathing. Lyle saw her body by the woodpile, as the men were moving them out.

Jewel was not dead. The possemen put him and Jewel on the same horse. Jewel kept quiet, and so did he.

Lyle was sorry he had to say that Ned was dead, for Jewel began to cry when he said it. The men had stopped by a little creek and made a fire. Several of them were wounded and bleeding, and wanted to wash their wounds.

Before the fire was even hot, the red-headed man began to shake Lyle and cuff him. Lyle was very afraid. He did not want them to hit him with a stick of firewood and leave him dead, like Liza, so he did not cry out, or scream; he told them about Ned being dead on the floor. Jewel did not cry for long. After a while, she sat looking down at the ground. The men stood around the fire, waiting for the water in the pot to boil. Some had their shirts off, or their pants, examining their wounds. Except for the red-headed man, they paid little attention to Lyle, or to Jewel. The red-headed man was rough—he shook Lyle until Lyle's neck popped.

The tall man who wore the dusty coat was wounded in the shoulder. He had taken his coat off, and his shirt, too. He held a little pocket mirror in one hand, using it to inspect his wound, which was not bleeding much.

"I'm luckier than I was when those Yankees shot me," Tailcoat said. "The bullet went through and missed the bone. I'll be damned if I would have enjoyed another smashed-up collarbone."

"I still don't know how he hit you," Beezle said. "You was well hid, Tail."

"Well hid, but I opened my goddamn mouth," Tailcoat said. "I ought to have known better. He shot at the sound, and he didn't miss by much."

"Not many men can hit a feller just by aiming at his sound," Beezle marveled.

"I could, when I was sharpshooting," Tailcoat informed him. "I wounded several Yankees just because they were fools and talked too loud."

Then the tall man said something that surprised Lyle.

"Why have you brought that boy?" Tailcoat asked Beezle. "Let him go."

"Why, he's the one says Ned Christie's dead," Beezle said. "I was just giving him a good shaking to make sure of the information."

"He'll be a nuisance to travel with . . . let him go," Tailcoat said. "I shot Ned Christie through a window. He didn't leave the house, and the house is afire. If he ain't dead from the bullet, I expect he'll burn up."

"Well, but that's not sure, Tail," Beezle conjectured. "Judge Parker likes marshals to be sure about things like that."

Tailcoat Jones was galled as it was. Despite much evidence of the excellence of Ned Christie's shooting skills, he had lazily underestimated the man and got himself shot through the left shoulder. He wanted to hurry on to Fort Smith to get the wound treated by a doctor. Over the years, he had developed a profound fear of infection from having seen many men die from serious infections in wounds such as his, during the War. He did not want to sit around all day waiting for the heavy log house to burn down, just so he could locate Ned Christie's bones. Four of his men had been killed outright, and three more were wounded. Only two of the ten possemen had escaped from the conflict unscathed.

Under the circumstances, one thing he did not intend to tolerate—from Beezle, or anyone else—was a lecture about what Ike Parker liked or did not like. He would, of course, have preferred to bring Ned Christie's body back to Fort Smith as evidence of the success of the raid. But a burned body would be a stinking thing to travel with, and in any case, Ike Parker was so contrary he might well consider the posse a failure and dock their pay. After all—he had requested five criminals to try—being given one who was past trying might only irk the man.

"Oh—so you're afraid Ike will be irked?" he said to Beezle, who promptly released the boy.

"I just know that he likes his marshals to be sure of what they did," Beezle repeated, cautiously.

"I'm sure we have four dead men and three wounded," Tailcoat said. "Go home, boy . . . get!"

Lyle was happy to obey. He missed his mother badly. He missed his pa, too—he even missed his sisters. He knew he would have to walk it, since his colt was still back at Ned's—but that was better than being hit with a stick of firewood, as Liza had been hit.

Lyle's only worry was leaving Jewel. She was not tied, but there were men all around her. She would not have much of a chance, if she ran. He thought she might ask the tall man if she could leave with him. With the two of them traveling together, there would be that much less danger of bears. But Jewel would scarcely raise her eyes to look at Lyle; she did not look at the tall man at all.

"I'm afraid I'll get lost, unless Jewel comes with me—she knows the way," Lyle said. It upset him to leave Jewel, even though he was anxious to be home with his ma and his pa and his sisters. These men were bad. They had killed Ned, and Liza. He was afraid they might kill Jewel, if he left without her.

Jewel looked up quickly then, and motioned for Lyle to go.

"Go on home, Lyle, it's an easy trail," she said, in a low voice. She did not look at him when she said it. She kept her eyes lowered.

"Go on, boy—get!" Tailcoat said again.

Nobody seemed inclined to let Jewel go with him, and Jewel herself made no move to get up, so Lyle reluctantly walked on out of the camp. He was scared, but Jewel herself had told him to go.

Once he was out of sight of the camp, his fear of bears came back, and he broke into a trot. He knew he could not outrun a bear on foot, if one came at him, so he figured he better try and get on the trail home as quickly as he could.

Jewel tried to believe that Ned was not dead. It was only two miles from their house to the creek where the men had brought her. Over the treetops, she could see the smoke rising, as her home burned. Seeing the smoke made her hopes crack; they cracked, and then split. If Ned had been badly wounded, he could be in their house right this moment, burning up. She had to choke down a sob that was fighting to rise in her throat.

But then she remembered how strong Ned was, and how clever. He had shown her his crawl space; maybe he was still in there, in his little hiding place, merely wounded. If only the men would let her go, she might be able to rescue him yet. She knew he must be badly wounded, or he would have come to her aid. But then Tuxie Miller had been badly wounded himself, and now he was well. If only the possemen would not kill her, she could nurse her husband back from any wound—if he was alive. She would do what Dale had done: sit by him, day and night; make her water in a bucket; hold his finger and press it, to remind him that she was there with him. She would endure whatever the men decided to do with her in order to stay alive and help Ned.

Jewel kept her eyes down, but she could feel the men looking at her—they were looking at her in a way that made the hair raise on the back of her neck.

She knew they were men without pity. One of them, a stout one with broken teeth in his mouth, had smashed in Liza's skull because she was yelling in fright. Jewel had a deep fright, too, but she managed to stay quiet. It was her worst fear—that rough men, strangers, would show up and look at her in that way—or do worse than look. In her frightened imaginings, it had always happened at night. Ned would be gone on an errand, and men would come and grab her when her husband was not around to protect her.

Now it was happening, not at night, but in broad daylight. If she ran, they would catch her—and when they caught her, they would be even angrier than they had been with Liza. She knew her only hope was to try and be as small as possible, to try and shrink inside herself. If she was quiet enough, maybe they would get to talking of other things and not notice her. Some of them began to drink whiskey, to dull the pain of their wounds. Maybe they would get so drunk they would go to sleep, and she could slip off.

But the red-headed man—the one who had been cuffing Lyle—was not drinking. He was the one who had pulled her out of the root cellar, tearing her dress in the process, right in front at the bodice. Jewel was holding the dress together with one hand.

The red-headed man kept looking at her.

"Tail . . . here's his squaw," Beezle said. "We took his squaw."

Jewel had never been called a squaw before now. It shocked her. She knew it was the word white men used to shame Indian women. But the few white men she saw when she was growing up had always treated her with respect. No one had ever called her a squaw, not until this moment. Though it was only a word, the way the red-headed man said it sickened her—it felt as bad as it had felt when he tore the front of her dress, pulling her out of the cellar.

"I see her," Tailcoat replied, indifferently.

In fact, he had not taken time to look at Jewel, until that moment. His wound had preoccupied him. He had been a young man when the Yankees broke his collarbone, and it had taken him a year to recover. One shoulder still drooped, from the way the bone had healed. The thought that another bone might be broken, and in almost the same place, concerned him more than any squaw. He could ill afford another slow recovery.

After examining himself, he came to the conclusion that the bullet had missed the bone. If he escaped infection, getting shot by Ned Christie would leave him not much worse for wear.

He looked over at the squaw, and saw that she was tall and shapely, though no more than a girl. She was keeping as still as possible, which demonstrated intelligence on her part. She was the woman of a formidable warrior—a warrior who, fighting alone, had decimated his own well-equipped force. But the warrior had fallen; now, she was in the hands of his enemies. Keeping still was about all she could do, but keeping still would not save her.

"I see her sitting there, Beezle—what's your point?" Tailcoat said, again.

Beezle was infuriated by his leader's indifferent manner. What did the man think his point was, with a ripe young squaw sitting there, her dress already torn open?

"We want to take her up the hill," Beezle said. "Back where the bushes are thick."

"Why?" Tailcoat asked. "What can you do with her up on the hill that you can't do right here by this creek?"

"Well . . . he killed half of us, and wounded most of the rest," Beezle said, looking at the woman.

"Yes, I know that, Beezle. I'm one of the wounded," Tailcoat informed him, in a tone that made it clear he considered his assistant hopelessly simpleminded. "What's that got to do with the squaw?"

Beezle hated it when Tailcoat played talk games with him, just to confuse him. Tailcoat could outtalk him by a long shot.

In fact, he could outtalk anybody, excepting maybe Judge Parker. Why did the man have to be so hard to get an answer from, when all they were talking about was a Cherokee squaw?

"We want to do her," Beezle answered curtly. "We'll hold her, if you want to be first."

Jewel tried to keep herself still, though she wished she could stand up and run as fast as she could—away from this place by the creek, with these rough white men who called her squaw. Three of the men had moved closer to her, as the conversation between their leader and the red-headed man went on. She could feel them, just behind her. One of them was a heavy man—she could smell his sweat, as he stood behind her.

"Nope, I'm a whore lover," Tailcoat said. "I'll pass."

Beezle looked around at the rest of the men. They were waiting impatiently, their lust rising. He himself was confounded with Tailcoat Jones, and a little nervous. Why would Tailcoat refuse to do the woman? It would make all of them feel easier about the matter, if their leader would go first.

"But she's free, Tail. It would save cash," he pointed out. "We'll put her on a blanket, if that's what you need."

The moment Beezle said it, he realized he had made a mistake—though he was not exactly sure how.

"I don't need anything I can't buy," Tailcoat said, in his chilliest voice. "You don't make no enemies when you buy a whore. But you make at least two, when you rape a woman."

"Two?" Beezle repeated, puzzled.

"That's the count—two," Tailcoat said. "One's the woman, the other's her man."

"But this one's man is dead," Beezle reminded him. "You heard the boy say so."

Tailcoat put his shirt on, and lit a cigar.

There was a long silence. Beezle looked at the men. Then he looked at the squaw. He had seen her young breasts that morning, when he tore her dress pulling her out of the root cellar. Some of the other men had seen them, too, and they were not in a mood to relent and ride on, just because Tailcoat Jones preferred to pay for a woman.

"Well, but you don't care . . . do you? If we take her up the hill?" Beezle ventured, attempting a conciliatory tone. "You're still welcome to go first, if you change your mind."

Tailcoat puffed a little smoke Beezle's way.

"Beezle, if you want me to order this rape, you're wasting your time and mine," he said. "I don't order it, and I don't forbid it. It's a free country. If you're disposed to have this woman, and you're all men enough, then do it."

Beezle waited a moment. No one spoke.

"I guess we'll take her up the hill," Beezle said, finally.

"Why bother with the walk?" Tailcoat said, again. "Have her right where she sits, and save yourself the stroll. I ain't a deacon. I won't pray at you."

Then he turned his back on them all, and opened his pants to tuck in his shirttail. When he finished, he took his gun out of its holster and clicked the hammer a few times. Every man took a step back, when he started clicking—injury usually accompanied Tailcoat's clicking his gun hammer.

But when he turned back to them, he was grinning.

"Just seeing if my gun hand still works," he said.

"You boys are slow," he continued, sitting down on his saddle. "I've rode with gangs that would have spread this little squaw all over the place by now."

"I think we'll take her up the hill," Beezle said, a fourth time. Hot as he was for the squaw, he felt it would not be wise to handle the woman in front of Tailcoat Jones, not with Tailcoat in his present mood.

As they were walking Jewel up the hill, the large man who stank suddenly caught her dress and ripped it away. Other men started grabbing at it, too. The only thing she had left to cover with, when they finally threw her down, was the little piece of bodice she had been holding together all day.

Jewel clutched the scrap of cloth tight, and was still clutching it when, three hours later, the men left her on the hill and rode away.

38

"I SUSPECT HE AIN'T DEAD—AND EVEN IF HE *IS* DEAD, HE ain't," Judge Parker said. Tailcoat Jones, his shoulder freshly bandaged, had come to the court to give his account of the expedition against Ned Christie. The Judge was visibly irked with Tailcoat Jones, for the man had been back in Fort Smith for a night and half a day before showing up at his courthouse to report. He and his men had spent last evening in the saloon, and from the information relayed to Judge Parker by his bailiff, Tailcoat Jones's report today would contain little, if any, good news.

The Judge sat looking out his window, displeased, a fact that did not surprise Tailcoat.

"I suppose I'm dense," Tailcoat said. "I don't follow your reasoning."

"I wasn't reasoning," the Judge informed him. "You were in the War, were you not?"

"I was right in the thick of the War, yes," Tailcoat admitted. "I enlisted the first day."

"I don't care to hear your war stories," the Judge said. "Have you encountered people who believe that Stonewall Jackson is still alive?"

"Why, yes—a few," Tailcoat said. "I guess folks don't want to admit old Stonewall's gone."

"Because he was a hero," the Judge pointed out. "And now you've made Ned Christie a hero, whether you killed him or not. If he's dead, there'll be Cherokees who won't believe it. They'll fight in his name, dead or not."

"They can, but I doubt they have his ability," Tailcoat said. "*I* don't have his ability, and I'm a goddamned good fighter."

"Don't swear in my courthouse, sir," the Judge ordered. "Not unless you want to spend a few days locked up."

"You're a hard old cud to get along with, I'll say that," Tailcoat complained, annoyed by the reprimand.

"I've heard that opinion before," the Judge said. "Let's get back to your report. You fired the man's house, but you don't know if you killed him?"

Tailcoat nodded. "A neighbour's boy claimed to have seen him dead inside the house—under the circumstances, that was good enough for me," he said.

"Under what circumstances?" the Judge inquired.

"Under the circumstances that he already killed four of my men outright, and had wounded three more—me included," Tailcoat said. "I only had two able-bodied men left. If I'd sent them in and he was hiding, he would have killed them, too. I didn't choose to risk it."

Judge Parker took a deep breath, to calm himself before asking the next question.

"I understand a girl was killed. Why?" the Judge asked.

"She was yapping and yelling. To keep her quiet, one of the boys tapped her with a stick of firewood," Tailcoat said. "I guess he tapped her a little too hard by accident."

The Judge had been whittling a willow stick, but he stopped abruptly and put the stick and his pocketknife back in the drawer. Prolonged exposure to Tailcoat Jones was making him want to get down to the river and smell a fresh breeze.

"You've made a disgrace of this, and I'm disgraced for hiring you," he told the man. "You could have brought me some Becks, and left Mr. Christie for last. Poor strategy, I'd call it."

"Well, the Christie place was on our way," Tailcoat said. "I expect the Becks are tame compared to Ned Christie. We can round 'em up at your convenience."

"My convenience is to dismiss you on the spot!" the Judge hissed.

"I'll have my pay, then," Tailcoat said, considering one of his fingernails.

"You don't have to pay for the dead men—that'll save you some cash," he added, with just a shadow of sarcasm in his voice.

"We'll determine the issue of pay, once I'm sure who all's dead over in the Going Snake," the Judge informed him.

With that, he got up and walked out, leaving Tailcoat Jones in the act of striking a match on his boot-heel.

The day was cloudy, and the river was grey—but the Judge took a long walk anyway. He did not pause to chat with the fishermen, as was his wont, for this was one of those times when the sorrows of life weighed heavily upon him.

Across the river, toward the Indian lands, it was raining on the dark hills. He was reminded of the grief of women who had lost their men before their time. Wilma Maples, Mart's second cousin, had become entirely demented, and had been sent away to an asylum. Now Ned Christie's young wife—the great-granddaughter of the late Judge B. H. Sixkiller, a decent and respected Cherokee, and a fine judge himself—had probably lost her husband, too. What other degradations had she suffered as a result? And what about the girl who had been hit too hard with a stick of firewood, all because she had been too frightened and too young to know she was in the hands of ruthless mercenaries—the known killers he himself had sent to catch men who had only been suspected of being killers. Had that been the wise course?

An old black woman, Ellie Bratcher, came walking up from the river with three perch on a string. Ellie's husband, Isaiah Bratcher, had been a slave owned by a prominent Cherokee family who had come up the Trail of Tears back in 1838. Soon after arriving in their new homeland, Isaiah's Cherokee masters had realized they would barely be able to provide for themselves, and so they gave Isaiah both their blessings and his freedom. Isaiah moved to Fort Smith, Arkansas, where he found a job and Ellie. During the Civil War, when a contingent of Rebs accused Isaiah Bratcher of stealing one of their horses, he had been lynched from a tree behind the hardware store where he worked. The horse Isaiah was supposed to have stolen trotted up to the Rebs' camp a few hours after Isaiah was hung. Ellie, his widow, could be seen fishing at the river almost every day since.

"Why, Aunt Ellie," the Judge said. "Nothing but them bony little perch biting today?"

Ellie Bratcher stopped, and held up her three small fish.

"Nothing but perch, Judge," she said, shaking her head. "I reckon I'll just have to watch out for them bones."

BOOK THREE

NED'S WAR

AS TOLD BY EZEKIEL PROCTOR

Show me a hero, and I'll write you a tragedy.

F. Scott Fitzgerald

1

NED CHRISTIE'S WAR BEGAN THE DAY ME AND BECCA RODE home on that slow mule. That same day, the white law came over the Mountain from Arkansas, burned Ned's house, killed our Liza, took turns with our Jewel, and shot out Ned's left eye.

It was Ned's war; yet I fault myself for it some. I seen that light on the Mountain, and I had a feeling, then, that it might be a posse. I ought to have waited and made sure, but I had Becca with me, and because I wanted my wife home and happy, I put it out of my mind.

In the evening of that same day, I got her home. Ned's mule was a balker; the trip was terrible slow.

"I can walk faster than this mule," Becca said, at one point. Becca was ever impatient. She got off, and walked five miles, taking Pete with her—she and Pete got way ahead of the mule, too. But then she wore out, and had to get back up and let the mule carry her the rest of the way.

Frank Beck was waiting on our porch when we got home. From the looks of his horse, he had ridden hard.

"Now what is he wanting? We didn't invite him," Becca said. She was put out with all the Becks. It went back to Polly, I guess.

But Frank Beck was decent. Even Pete hardly barked at him, when he got down from in front of my saddlehorn. The minute I saw Frank, I had the fear that he had come with bad news . . . mostly I felt it for my not making sure about that light.

"Hello, Zeke . . . it's terrible news," Frank said.

When he told it, Becca began to cry to the saints. Her cries rent the air so that all the chickens ran out from under the porch and hightailed it. Pete crawled under the porch, and we didn't see him again until nighttime. Becca fell down on her knees, from grief.

"We lost our Liza, Zeke!" she shrieked. "We lost our Liza!"

"I know, Bec . . . ," is all I said. There was no comfort I could offer her. One moment I felt like crying myself; then the next moment, I wanted to jump on my horse, find Tailcoat Jones, and kill him. He was a raider and a raper in the War, and he's a raider and a raper still.

"I had better be going, Zeke," Frankie Beck said, after Becca sank to her knees.

"I would offer you a meal if I had one, Frank," I said. "I thank you for taking the trouble to come. . . ."

I wanted Sully Eagle to pasture the mule. I had Rebecca to tend to.

"Have you seen Sully anywhere?" I asked Frank.

"Sully? He's dead," Frank informed us. I don't really think Becca heard him, when he said it.

"Dead?" I said, still stunned by his account of the attack on Ned's place. "Dead of what?"

"Just dead of death, I guess," Frank replied. "He's in the corncrib."

"Well . . . I swear," I said.

Frankie's information was accurate: Sully was dead in the corncrib. The big rattler that lived in the shucks was coiled on his chest when I went to look. The rattler rattled at me till I was of a notion to shoot it. But finally, the old snake just crawled away.

Sully hadn't died of snakebite, either. He had just died of death, like Frankie Beck said.

The fact that the rattler had coiled on his chest I considered an omen of war.

2

I DIDN'T CLOSE AN EYE THAT NIGHT, AND NEITHER DID BECCA. She rocked all night in the rocking chair, holding one of Liza's dolls, Pete laying beside her the whole time.

"I ought to go see if Ned's alive," I told her, come sunup. "If he's dead, I'll be needing to bring Jewel home. Do you want to come?"

Becca kept putting the little rag doll against her face. She had cried till the doll was soaked.

Finally, she shook her head.

"You go on, Zeke," she said. "I don't want to be leaving our place again—not till I'm put in my grave."

"I better get moving. There's no telling what kind of shape Jewel's in, even if Ned's alive. I got to bring her back here, and then go get the triplets. But I hate to leave you with no company, Bec," I said. "I don't want you to grieve yourself to death."

Rebecca didn't answer. She just sat there, rocking with Liza's doll.

"I fault myself for this," I confessed. "I ought not to have ridden off without seeing about that light."

Becca looked old, then—as old as if she'd lived a thousand years. From the look in her eye, I had the fear that she might be losing her mind. I was afraid if I left, I'd come back and find her demented.

But I misjudged my Becca. While I was stabling the mule and saddling a horse, she went inside and cooked me up some bacon. I was surprised that there was any bacon, but she told me she and Sully had slaughtered the only pig they could catch. The rest had gotten loose and gone wild.

"It's a long ride back. I want you to eat," she said. "Don't be talking to me about faulting, either."

"Why not?" I asked.

"Life's but a quilt of faults, and I patched the quilt, same as you," Rebecca told me. She was wrapping me some meat to take on the trip, when she said it.

"If anybody comes by, see if they'll bury Sully for us," I

told her, just before I left. "If Sully's left out much longer, there'll be buzzards on the barn thick as fleas."

Becca looked irritated, like she used to look if I woke her up before she got her sleep out. Only now, it was her grief I was waking her up from, I guess. But it was a practical concern; Sully was dead in the corncrib, and I had to hurry to Ned's.

"I'll tend to him, Zeke, you go on," she said. "Jewel's the one needs help now."

"He might be too heavy for you to carry," I proffered.

"Then I'll drag him with the mule, if he is," Becca said. "I've dug graves before—I buried my own father. I'll get to it in a minute, before it gets too hot."

I didn't say more. Becca was a woman of her word. I put the bacon in one saddlebag, and filled the other with ammunition. My packing the bullets didn't sit right with Becca. She gave me a look, and it wasn't the look of a woman who was losing her mind.

"Who are you planning to shoot with all those bullets?" she asked.

"Why, I don't know who I might shoot," I told her. "I expect I'll shoot the goddamn cur that killed our daughter, if I see him."

"I thought you were going to see about Jewel and Ned," she said. "I didn't know you were going off to fight."

"I ain't going off to fight," I said. "But I want to be ready, if it comes to that."

Becca got up, put the doll in the rocking chair, and picked up a spade that was leaning against the porch. The chickens had returned, and were clucking. The chickens had always liked Becca. When she was cheerful, she kept corn in her apron, to scatter for them. She wasn't happy now, but she tolerated the hens anyway.

"I come home to be a wife to you, Zeke," she said. "I didn't come home to be a widow."

She looked at me, while the hens clucked.

"I'll dig a grave for Sully," she said. "I don't want to have to be digging a grave for my husband, not after losing our baby girl."

"The bullets are just a precaution, Bec," I said. "There'll be a war now. I don't want to be caught without bullets."

Becca looked at me. Then she walked over by her garden, looking for a place to dig Sully Eagle's grave.

3

ON THE ROAD PAST TAHLEQUAH, I MET SHERIFF CHARLEY Bobtail.

Charley had a little place where he grew corn and sweet potatoes. Charley was known to have a big appetite for sweet potatoes. He looked fearful when he spotted me. I guess he thought I was going to shoot him for having been my jailer. Charley was renowned for the sweet potatoes, but not for good judgment; I always wondered how he made sheriff over in Tahlequah.

Those jail days in Tahlequah seemed a long time ago. Worse troubles had come, and they had probably come to stay.

"I guess you heard about the raid," Charley said, when I rode up. "Are you going for vengeance, Zeke?"

"I'm going to Ned's, if he's still alive. I need to see how my daughter's doing," I told him.

"They say Ned's blinded—that's about all I know," Charley volunteered. "Tuxie was burned out, too. It's an outrage to the District, burning farms out like that."

"Well, I've got to hurry, Sheriff," I said. "I expect you need to weed your corn."

Charley Bobtail had been scared to see me come; now he seemed as scared to see me go. I guess he thought Tailcoat Jones might show up and shoot him or hang him, or at least burn up his corn crop. Tailcoat had burned the Millers out for no reason. He just might enjoy hanging a Cherokee sheriff for no reason, too.

4

MY THOUGHT WAS TO STOP BY THE MILLERS' ON MY WAY TO Ned's. I wanted Tuxie's opinion on what had happened, and what we ought to do.

But when I got there, there were no Millers, and no house, either. Their home had been a frame structure; it had burned all the way down to its foundation. I didn't see a soul, but I heard banging down at the barn. The barn wasn't burnt, but it wasn't much of a shelter, either, not for a family of twelve. Dale rode Tuxie day and night, but she hadn't ridden him hard enough to get him to fix the barn roof, which had holes you could throw a mule through.

I thought Tuxie must be pounding something on the anvil, which was on the far side of the barn and out of sight. I approached him cautious, thinking he might be jumpy, but the man pounding the anvil was Rat Squirrel, who jumped nearly out of his skin when he saw me, despite my cautious approach.

Seeing Rat was a big surprise. He was not known to be friendly to the Millers, or to anybody else. He was trying to straighten a horseshoe on the anvil, but he seemed drunk. He was only striking the horseshoe about one lick out of three. I suppose he thought he was welcome to the use of the anvil, since Tuxie wasn't home.

It was the first time in my life that I had seen Rat Squirrel without his brothers, a fact I mentioned to him at once, hoping to put him at his ease.

"Why have you wandered off without your kin, Rat?" I inquired. "I've never seen you in your life apart from your kin."

"I didn't wander, Zeke . . . it was my dern brothers who wandered," Rat said.

"Wandered where?" I asked.

"Jimmy went up to Kansas and married a wild slut with buckteeth," Rat said. "He brought her home, but she didn't like Moses, 'cause you shot off his jaw and got him surly."

"Moses was surly long before I shot off his jawbone," I informed him. "And I wouldn't have shot it off if he hadn't been planning to hang me."

"Anyway, that buck-tooth gal ran off, and Jimmy's chasing her. He says he can't get enough of buck-toothed women," Rat said.

"Where's that damn surly Moses?" I asked.

"Went to Little Rock," Rat said. "There's a doc in Little Rock who is supposed to be able to make jaws."

Rat kept looking at me, and then at the trail, while he attempted to straighten the horseshoe. I expect he was worried about the posse, too. Everybody was worried about them.

"What have you heard about the posse?" I asked him.

"I heard Ned killed about half of it," Rat said. "Our best mule ran off, that's why I'm here. I want to find that mule and get on home before the next posse shows up."

"Well, good luck in your search, then," I said, before I rode off.

Despite his villainy, I felt a little sorry for Rat Squirrel. He was a man with no friends, and no abilities, either. Rat would be easy pickings for a posse, or for anybody else who came along and wanted to pick him.

It made me hot, thinking about the posse. A bunch of white ruffians rode over the hill, armed with the white court's authority, and plenty of firearms. They burned out two families, killed one of my daughters, and done Lord knows what to the other one. I decided then and there that if Ned Christie could see at all, I'd talk him into helping me get up a militia.

There were hellions among the Cherokee at that time, but most Cherokee people were decent and law-abiding. They didn't deserve to live scared, jumping every time a horseman rode up to the barn. The more I thought about it, the more I took to the idea of a militia. It would need to be well armed, and well mounted, too, so the men could gather quick in case of attack. Twenty men who could ride and shoot might be enough. The white law would likely think twice before challenging twenty Cherokee fighters.

I meant to talk to Ned about it, if he was well enough to talk when I got there.

5

ON THE RIDE UP THE MOUNTAIN, I BEGAN TO THINK OF OUR Liza, and my spirits started sinking. The shock had wore off, and the fact was there: our Liza was dead. Our Jewel was a real sweet daughter, but she was never much of a talker—Liza was my talky girl. I could sit her in my lap and yarn to her for hours, about her Grandma and Grandpa Proctor; about my traveling the Trail of Tears when a mere boy; about meeting Becca and marrying her; and my talky girl always had something to say about the yarns. We used to joke that Liza would only stop talking the day she died. It seemed a cruel joke, now that a posseman from Arkansas had quieted Liza forever. The dead were piling up now, in the hills, but I never expected my sprightly little girl to be a part of the pile. Frank Beck said he heard it was an accident, but you don't hit a girl with a stick of firewood by accident. If the man that done it could be identified to me, I meant to see that he died in his turn. But it might be I would never see the man.

Whether I found him or not, there would be more killing. The whites hadn't wanted the Cherokee in Georgia; now, they didn't want them west of the Arkansas River, either. I figured out why, finally: whites have always been scared of Cherokees, because they don't understand them. My ma and pa loved Georgia; they loved the streams and valleys, the hills, the woods, their friends and families, their home and their land. They were rooted in the very soil they planted their crops in, and that held the bodies of our dead loved ones. White folks don't understand or respect those things like Cherokees. They jump around from one place to the other like frogs in a hailstorm. Indians ain't wanted anywhere, but they're a pure fact of life. Forming a militia would let the white law know we Cherokees meant to stay.

I started thinking of things I could say to Ned about it. It took my mind off our dead girl.

6

TWO OF THE WALLS OF NED'S HOUSE WERE STILL STANDING when I rode up. The roof had fallen in, smoke still rose from the ashes, and several of the big logs still smouldered. I remembered the house from when Ned and old Watt Christie built it. I helped out with the roofing for a day or two. It was sad to see such a fine house reduced to two walls, both of them still afire, and with nothing but smoky ashes where Ned and Jewel had lived.

Of course, in the War, burned-out houses were a common sight. It was common then, too, to see families living in the open until they could rebuild. But that War was over. It was only meanness now, when a family's home got burned out.

Ned sat on a saddleblanket under a tree, with a piece of wet sacking over his eyes. Tuxie Miller sat by him, whittling a stick. I suppose Tuxie was whittling to distract his mind from the fact that he had ten younguns now, and no roof to shelter them.

From a distance, it looked as if the Christies and the Millers had been merged together by the troubles. Five or six of the Millers' active tots were scampering around by the barn—it takes more than tragedy to keep active tots from scampering. Just seeing them made me miss my triplets, off with my sister Susan, who wasn't half the cook that Becca was. I knew the triplets would be wanting to come home soon, and eat some of their ma's good grub.

Ned recognized me by the creak of my saddle, I guess. He took the sacking off his eyes and turned his head my way, but I couldn't tell whether he was seeing me, or just hearing me. He had a raw wound on his cheek. I got down and shook his hand. He jumped a little when I took it, but he squeezed my hand hard.

"Can you see at all, Ned?" I inquired. I thought I best not mention my notion of a militia, if Ned was too blinded to join up. Ned would want to be with the fighters, and I knew it would discourage him to have to sit at home and rock in a rocking chair.

"Zeke, I wish you hadn't left when you did," he said. "I believe we could have stood them off, if you'd been here."

I knew then that he faulted me as much as I faulted myself. He was right, too. Between us, we could have fought back the posse; at least we could have spread out and kept them from sneaking in and firing the house. Ned would be sitting by his hearth now, not on a saddleblanket under a tree.

I didn't blame him for faulting me. Still, I couldn't bring the yesterdays back. I had been thinking of getting home with my wife, as any man would have in the same situation. All I could hope was that Ned wouldn't let it be a bitterness between us. I had a dead child; I could see her grave down west of the garden. I didn't want a bitter friend.

"I regret leaving you, but it's done," I told him. "It's done, and it will have to stay done. What's the news about your eyes?"

"I can see a pinprick out of the right one," he said. "I seen the sparks fly up, when the roof fell. It's like I'm looking through a keyhole, only it's more like a pinhole."

Tuxie Miller had ashes all over his shirt, and on his pants legs, too.

"You look like you've been wading in an ash dump, Tuxie," I said.

"Ned's anxious about his rifle," Tuxie said. "I tried to look for it in the ashes, but the dern ashes are still too hot."

"I am anxious about it," Ned confessed. "If I could just get a little more vision in this right eye, I believe I could sight a rifle.

"I'd like to be able to sight a rifle if that posse comes back," he added. He had both of his .44 pistols on the blanket with him. His voice was cracky, no doubt from swallowing smoke.

"I see a grave. Is it Liza's?" I inquired.

"That's her, Zeke—Lyle and me dug the grave," Tuxie told me.

I took my hat off, and walked over to the grave to pay my respects to my little girl. Tuxie went with me, but hung back a little. I had no words to speak, and neither did Tuxie. Liza could have outtalked the both of us a hundred times, had she still been alive. I stood there for a while, remembering all the times Liza had listened to me yarn.

"You're a lucky man, Tuxie," I said, finally. "You fathered ten tots, and haven't had to bury a one of them. It ain't right to have to be burying your own child."

A buck deer came out of the woods and stood looking at us, in easy range of a rifle, but neither of us had brought a rifle with us. The buck grazed a few minutes and stepped back into the brush. Tuxie's younger children were making a racket down by the barn.

"At least Ned's got a barn he can stay in," I said. "You can't house your family in your barn, because you've neglected the roof."

Tuxie only sighed. I guess he had more on his mind than a barn roof with a hole in it you could throw a mule through.

"Jewel's in the barn, Zeke," he said. "Dale's tending to her. Dale was hoping you'd come."

I knew Liza was dead. I thought I was prepared for it, but seeing the fresh dirt on her grave brought it home harder than I had expected. It wasn't that I didn't want to go to Jewel, but for a moment, I felt too weak-legged to walk to the barn. The same weakness came over me that I felt that day in the courtroom, the same weakness when the Squirrels cornered me and tried to tie me with Rat's suspenders. Ned's wheelbarrow was nearby. I plopped on it and cried. My crying embarrassed Tuxie, I guess, because he went back over to Ned.

When the weakness left me and I went on down to the barn, what I saw shocked me near as bad as the sight of Liza's grave. Jewel lay on a saddleblanket, too—saddleblankets were the only blankets the Millers and the Christies had left.

Jewel began to cry the moment she saw me. Besides being outraged, she had been beaten black and blue. Dale later told me one of the marshals beat Jewel with a heavy stick because she didn't submit quick enough to suit him. From the look of my Jewel—one of her eyes was swollen shut—if the stick had been a little heavier, I'd have two daughters dead and buried.

Dale Miller looked weary. Who could blame her? She had a newborn baby at the breast, Jewel to nurse, nine other children running around like banshees, and only Ned's barn for a house.

"She lost the baby, Zeke," Dale told me at once.

"Oh, Pa . . . ," Jewel sobbed. When I hugged her, I could feel how weak she was. She could barely lift her arms to put them around me, and it was a long time before she could say anything more.

It was all I could do to control myself, when I looked at my Jewel, so beaten and weak. I felt a seizure coming, I was so angry at the ruffians who would treat a woman—my own beloved daughter—so bad. If the bunch of them had been brought before me then, I feel I would have strangled them all.

But they weren't there, and Jewel was, white as death except for the bruises on her face and arms. Dale said she was bruised from head to toe, but I didn't look. I'd seen enough to prompt some hard strangling, if I ever caught up with the men who used her so rough.

In my arms, Jewel cried and cried. I think she wanted to tell me about losing the baby, but she couldn't get it out. I noticed that her feet were coated with mud, and asked Dale about it.

"She burned her feet bad, getting Ned out of his hiding place," Dale told me. "I guess the stairs were on fire when she got back here and found him. The mud from the pigpen's all I have to soothe her feet.

"She saved him, though," Dale added. "He'd have died when the roof fell, if Jewel hadn't made it back here, walked up the stairs, and pulled him out."

"I don't see how she did it," I said, and I didn't. "She's so weak now I doubt she could stand, much less pull Ned out of a fire."

"That's from the bleeding," Dale told me. "We almost lost Jewel from the bleeding last night, Zeke."

For a minute, Dale had that thousand-year-old look—the same as Becca had, when she was rocking on our porch. Maybe it came to women from seeing young ones die, or almost die. Dale was stout as a post, but for a moment she looked as if she might be having a spell of *my* weakness. She was ashy, too, like Tuxie. When I asked her about it, she said she had been trying to salvage a pot or two from the kitchen.

"It's hard, what Jewel went through," Dale said. Jewel seemed to doze, and we walked outside.

"Hard what you went through, too," I told her. "First Tuxie's leg, and then now this."

Dale looked at me as if to say that I didn't know what hard was, and shouldn't be presuming to talk to her about it. She looked as if she wanted to peck me like a hen pecks a bug.

But she didn't.

"Yes, it's hard on all of us," she said. "Hard—but your Liza's the only one of us who's dead, Zeke."

"That's right," I said. "Ned might get his sight back, and Jewel might have another fine baby yet. My Liza's the one that won't be among the living no more."

Dale looked at me hard again, as if she wanted to say more. But the baby was fussing at her—I expect it was wanting the breast—and Dale turned away.

Maybe she figured that whatever she had to say to me could wait, which was my opinion, too.

7

JEWEL GOT WORSE IN THE NIGHT. WE BROUGHT NED DOWN TO sit by her, which helped a little. Jewel got so weak we thought she was going. Ned persuaded Tuxie to go off looking for Old Turtle Man, though none of us had any confidence that Tuxie could find him in time, or find him at all, for that matter. Unless the moon was bright, Tuxie Miller was hard put to find his way home. Mainly, he relied on his horse for direction.

I offered to go. I knew the hills better than Tuxie, but Jewel didn't want me to leave.

"Stay, Pa," she whispered. And that was all she said.

Ned couldn't see her; he had no idea how bruised and torn she was, though he did know that she had lost the child. Later, when she was better, Jewel told me that she was glad Ned was blinded when she walked home and pulled him out of the house. The possemen hadn't left her a stitch, and the only clothes she could find were an old pair of overalls that Ned hung on a nail in the barn, and only wore when he had to cut a calf or a shoat, or do other bloody work.

She had been wearing the overalls when Dale and Tuxie found her, laying by Ned under the tree. There was so much old blood on the overalls that it took Dale a while to realize there was new blood, too—Jewel's blood.

That's when she knew the child was lost.

"Zeke, what if she dies?" Ned said to me several times in the night. "What'll I do, if she dies?"

"She won't die," I told him. I was trying to believe it myself.

"Well, but why won't she? Dale says she's bled out," Ned said.

"Jewel's strong. She won't die," I told him.

It was a hope, mostly. I knew I would nearly die myself if I had to go back to Becca and tell her our Jewel was gone.

My hope was not to fail. It was a good hour after sunup before Tuxie got back with the old healer, and by then the crisis had passed. Dale was feeding her brood chicken soup out of a big kettle Ned kept in the barn to render lye. Dale cleaned the kettle, and threw a chicken in it every time she could catch one. Jewel even took a little nourishment; I spooned her a few swallows of soup myself. The spoon was burned black from the fire, but it still held soup.

The old healer stayed for two days. He made a poultice that dried up Jewel's bleeding, and another that he tied around Ned's eyes. One problem was a shortage of pots. Dale refused to give up the big kettle. She needed it to feed her brood. Old Turtle Man had to brew his potions in a bucket, which didn't suit him. He fussed at Dale, and she fussed back. Finally, Tuxie rode home and brought back the Millers' big kettle, which settled the dispute.

Old Turtle Man made Ned lay flat on his back. He bound the poultice tight around his eyes, and told him to leave it that way for a week. Jewel was to change it twice a day.

Ned was vexed at the order.

"I can't be doing without my eyes for a week," he announced, but the old man lectured him soundly. No doubt he had heard patients complain before.

The upshot of it was that Ned lost the sight in his left eye forever. Old Turtle Man thought the other eye would recover, if Ned was mindful.

"You better mind him, Ned," Dale told him. "If you lose that other eye, Jewel will have to wait on you hand and foot for the rest of your life."

"I despise being waited on," Ned said. Except for his eye, he had not suffered a scratch, which made it hard for him to keep still. I couldn't blame him; I like to be up and doing myself.

Jewel began to get some of her strength back, enough that she could help Dale a little with the tots. But a sadness had settled in my Jewel's eyes—no doubt she had seen sights no woman ought ever to see. She lost the sparkle in her eyes, up on that hillside.

Jewel's only hope and joy was Ned Christie. She sat by Ned all day. When his poultice needed changing, she changed it; if he requested grub, she brought it. I don't suppose I've ever seen a closer couple than my Jewel and her Ned.

8

IT WAS THE NEXT DAY I SHOT THE BUCK DEER THAT WANDERED out of the woods while I was grieving by Liza's grave.

Tuxie Miller skinned it out, and we had venison that night. Everybody was hungry for meat. It was a small buck, and fifteen of us eating, but we got our fill. Tuxie Miller hadn't said two words since I arrived—I think he was shocked that he no longer had a house—but at least he was healthy in the appetite department. He ate most of that deer's hindquarter all by himself. Tuxie was a noisy eater, too. Ned got tired of listening to him chomp.

"Sounds like you're eating it bone and all," he complained. "A pig could eat quieter than you, Tuxie."

Tuxie was too busy chomping to reply. Dale Miller was slicing the deer guts into sections; I expect she was planning to make sausage. Dale was a worker, I'll say that for her. The rest of us would wear ourselves to a nub, and Dale would still be working.

That night, when things had settled down, I noticed that Ned was wakeful. He kept sitting up, which he wasn't supposed to do, twisting his head around toward the Mountain. Ned was said to have exceptional hearing; I wondered if he heard something I couldn't hear. I suppose that posse could have taken on reinforcements and be headed back to finish Ned.

"Is it horses?" I asked.

"No horses," Ned said. "I'm just smelling the air."

I thought since he was awake, it might be a good time to mention my notion of a militia. The posse might not be on its way that night, but posses would come again, and keep coming until we showed them we wouldn't take it.

But Ned hardly listened to my talk of a militia. He kept craning his head around toward the Mountain, though he had the poultice tied around his eyes and couldn't see.

"You can get up a militia if you want to, Zeke," he said. "I expect it would help the folks down in the flats, if you did."

"It would help you, too, if it was a strong militia," I told him.

"Nope. What I need is a fort," he said. "I aim to go as high up the Mountain as I can, and build one for me and Jewel. I aim to start the day I get my eyesight back.

"I won't be burned out again," Ned declared. "I aim to get some land on top of the Mountain and build a fort with walls so thick the white law can't burn it—not unless they bring fire from hell."

I saw his mind was set. I didn't say more about the militia. We shared some tobacco and sat on the grass, not saying much. Ned was in no mood for sleep, and neither was I. I wanted to get home to Becca and my triplets, but I felt I mustn't run off hasty again—not with Ned blinded, and unable to shoot.

If Tuxie Miller could have shot as well as he ate, he could

have held off any amount of law. But the fact was, he couldn't shoot a fence-post at five feet.

I passed a week with Ned and Jewel and the Millers, helping out as best I could. Jewel's bruises healed, and she got most of her strength back. Jewel was quieter than ever, and she scarcely left Ned's side, unless it was to help Dale Miller with some chore. The sparkle was still gone from her eyes.

Long before the week was up, Ned wanted to yank the poultice off, but Dale Miller fussed at him so hard, he let be.

When he did take it off, he could see as good as ever, though only out of the one eye. To prove it, Ned and Tuxie and me went squirrel hunting, high in the woods. Ned's rifle had been found, no worse for wear. His shooting was no worse for wear, either. One-eyed or not, he shot the limbs out from under six tasty squirrels, not missing one time. Tuxie and me popped away at squirrels all afternoon, and only killed two.

When finally it was time for me to go home to Becca, Ned walked up to my horse and told me he had taken a vow never to speak the English language again. The bullet had left Ned's nose twisted a little to the side, and he wasn't quite as handsome as he used to be. But he was still a great warrior in the eyes of the Cherokee Nation. He had survived attack, and so had my Jewel, his wife; he wanted me to spread the word among our people. He wanted them to know that he would never speak the enemy's tongue again. Becca was fluent in Cherokee and English. Being that the Cherokees were the only Indians with a written alphabet, Becca had made certain Jewel learned how to speak and write in both languages, too. She had crooned all our babies to sleep by singing hymns to them in Cherokee, and Jewel knew most of the words to those songs herself. I figured, rightly, that Jewel would be able to keep up with Ned in the language department.

To my knowledge, Ned Christie kept his word: he only spoke the Cherokee tongue for the rest of his life.

9

BECCA HAD THE TRIPLETS THERE, WHEN I GOT HOME.

From the look of the new grave, Sully had been well buried in back of the garden. I guess that big old rattler didn't care to stay, with Sully gone. I never saw it again.

Pete was whimpering when I came in; Willie had stuck Pete's tail in the fire. When they saw me, the triplets came at me like a swarm of honeybees. I was about wore out from my trip to Ned's, but I tussled with them and yarned with them all till bedtime.

Becca was quiet during supper. She didn't want to talk about the troubles in front of the triplets.

We were in bed and had blown out the lantern, when Becca finally got around to asking about Jewel and Liza.

"Liza's buried in a pretty spot," I told her. "The grave's at the edge of the trees. It's grassy all around it."

It was a few minutes before she asked about Jewel. I thought she might have fallen asleep, but she was just laying there in the dark, thinking about our Liza, I'm certain.

"Was Jewel poorly, Zeke?" Becca asked, in a whisper.

"Yes . . . they were rough on her," I admitted. "She lost the baby, and I was afraid the first night that we were going to lose her, too, Bec. But Old Turtle Man came, and she got better. She was up and doing, when I left."

Becca got quiet again. She didn't say another word, not for a long time. It made me uneasy, Becca being so quiet for so long. Sometimes the quiet can seem louder than noise, late at night.

"Jewel's a young woman," I reminded her. "She's but seventeen. She's got Ned, and she's got time to heal up and get over this."

Becca shifted around a little in the bed, before she answered me.

"There's some wounds time can't heal, Zeke," Becca said. "You ought to know that by now."

10

THEN THE NEWS CAME THAT TAILCOAT JONES HAD DROWNED, unexpected news for sure.

Rat Squirrel brought it. He was perplexed by the disappearance of his best mule, and came by to ask if I had seen any fresh mule tracks. I hadn't; then Rat came out with the news about Tailcoat Jones.

"Drowned?" I said. "Why was the man in the water?"

"All I heard was that he went out in a boat with a whore, and they got caught in a bad storm," Rat said. "Maybe the storm turned the boat over—nobody knows."

"Why take a whore out in a boat? There's better places to take a whore," I remarked.

"I don't know," Rat confessed. "I hope a dern storm didn't drown my mule. It'll be hard to get the plowing done, without that mule."

11

THE NEXT WEEK, I WENT IN TO TAHLEQUAH AND MADE A speech in the Cherokee Senate about the need for a well-equipped militia. I had hoped Ned would be able to come, but he couldn't. He felt it best not to leave Jewel just yet.

That being the case, I felt free to speak for him. Chief Bushyhead was annoyed that I had let Pete come in the Senate building with me, and he picked Pete up by the scruff of his neck and threw him out in the street. Pete sat under the window and whimpered for the rest of the session, making it difficult to hear the speeches, but Chief Bushyhead didn't care. He was too deaf to hear much of the speeches anyway. Chief Bushyhead knew what he thought about most of the questions before he even called the Senate into session. Speechifying made little impression on him.

"A militia will only aggravate the white people and lead to more fighting and bloodshed," he told the Senate—whereupon the notion was promptly voted down.

The fact that my notion had been voted down so promptly riled me, I have to admit. Also, I didn't appreciate having my dog thrown out the door. There was no rule on the books saying personal dogs couldn't attend Senate sessions.

While riled, I made my speech.

"You are a bunch of goddamn cowards," I said. "Ned Christie, our noble warrior, has taken a vow never to speak the English language again. There have been depredations visited on our land and our people, so many I can't keep count anymore. Our women have been mistreated and murdered, valuable structures have been burned, and livestock have been lost, as a result. I say we band together into a militia and smite our enemies, next time they show up to burn and rape."

I thought I made a fair speech, but I might as well have been talking to the chickens, for all the good it did. The old deaf Chief got his way.

All right, then, I thought, I'll raise my *own* damn militia. By sundown, I had ten men, only two of them drunk. Arch Scraper, Tail Sixkiller, Blackhaw Sixkiller, John Walkingstick, Thomas Walkingstick, George Beanstalk, Duck-Wa Beemer, Jesse Still, Ned Still, and John Looney were the men. They all promised to avoid horse races and stay out of gambling halls, in case the white law showed up in force.

Later, as I was about to head home, well pleased with my militia, Sheriff Charley Bobtail informed me that my name was one of five on Judge Parker's arrest list, along with Ned Christie and three of the Becks.

"He'll play hell arresting me now, unless he's got most of the United States Army over there in Fort Smith," I said.

Charley Bobtail had no opinion about the matter. Charley had looked a little poorly ever since the big shootout in the courtroom. In my view, Charley Bobtail had too mild a disposition to be a sheriff, besides which he couldn't cook worth a damn. A sheriff who's expected to keep the health of his prisoners ought to be able to cook, in my view.

"Why don't you resign, Charley, and avoid all this hell?" I asked, before I rode off. "You could just sit there on your farming place, and grow sweet potatoes for the rest of your life."

Charley got a gleam in his eye, when I mentioned the sweet potatoes.

12

THE NEXT NEWS I HEARD OF NED CHRISTIE WAS HE HAD bought a steam engine, and a fine pair of mules. I expect he borrowed money from his pa for such a purchase. The mules were to drag the logs for his fort; the steam engine was to power a little sawmill he used for the cutting. Frank Beck brought me that news.

Frank Beck was turning into a fine neighbour. He said Davie had left the Territory, planning to find a gold mine in Colorado. I could only suppose with his wild brother gone, Frank wanted to be shut of the bad blood between us.

Frank didn't mention White Sut, and I didn't inquire.

"If he's got a sawmill and two big mules, I guess he's building his fort," I told Becca later. "Ned's a good builder. Jewel will be safe, once he gets that fort finished."

Becca was churning butter. I don't know if she didn't hear me, or if she wasn't convinced, but she didn't say a word.

13

IT WAS BECAUSE OF THE MILITIA THAT I ENDED UP GETTING my amnesty from President Ulysses S. Grant himself. I would never have supposed President Grant would be required to take notice of me at all, or of our militia, which we called the Keetoowah Militia, because most of the boys in it belonged to the Keetoowah Society and did their best to keep to the old Cherokee ways and customs—ways that our people had practiced in the Old Place, before the white men came and inflicted their ways upon us.

The only reason I ended up with an amnesty from President Ulysses S. Grant was that two white marshals from Little Rock let a whiskeyseller get away. The whiskeyseller was one of Belle Blue's sons, Zacharias Blue, or Zack for short. Zack was young and reckless and sold whiskey openly at times when he should have been amusing himself by whoring or fishing.

Zack's whiskey was not the pure stuff Belle Blue concocted; the two marshals came to know about him because a man had gone blind, from drinking Zack's whiskey.

The fellow, whose name was Johnson, disliked being blinded by the liquor so much that he took recourse to the law. The marshals sent to arrest Zack were named Lee Chaney and Cephus Washburn. They were dispatched from Little Rock instead of Fort Smith because Judge Ike Parker's wife had died suddenly of a tumour, and the Judge had closed the court for a month, to wrestle with his grief.

If Judge Parker had been running his court at the time, I doubt the trouble in Dog Town would ever have happened. Ike Parker would have had better judgment than to send two men who couldn't shoot, and who could barely ride, to Dog Town to arrest one whiskeyseller.

I guess the judge in Little Rock thought any fool could arrest an Indian or a whiskeyseller. It was a mistake quite a few judges make, in my experience.

Marshal Chaney and Marshal Washburn rode right past Zack Blue, when they rode into Dog Town. Zack put his hat over his eyes and pretended to snooze as soon as he saw the marshals coming, and the marshals bought the bluff. Zack waited until they were well past him, and then slipped off into the hills.

There was a fine meadow about a mile north of Dog Town, popular with people who liked to race horses. I was there with a dozen or so militia men, matching some two-year-old horses run against each other. We were not racing serious, just running little hundred-yard matches, when the two marshals rode up.

There had been no disturbances recently, and I had about forgotten that I was a candidate for arrest, when Marshal Lee Chaney discourteously rode up to me while I was adjusting a stirrup and shoved a six-shooter rudely into my ribs.

"By God, if you're Zeke Proctor, I'm taking you to Fort Smith," Lee said.

"Oh—I ain't Zeke," I replied. "Zeke's my younger brother. That's him on that sorrel filly."

The man on the sorrel filly was actually Looney. He was ten years younger than me, and looked nothing like me at all. You would think even the dumbest lawman would see through such a trick, but it convinced Marshal Chaney.

He took the six-shooter out of my ribs, and as soon as he

did, I whistled up the militia. In less than a minute, the two marshals were in the middle of twelve Cherokee militiamen, all armed and competent.

"Whoa now, boys—this is a damn crowd," Marshal Chaney observed, as the horsemen crowded around him.

"A peaceful crowd, except when some fellow pulls a gun for no reason," I told him. "I'm Zeke Proctor, and this is the Keetoowah Militia. If I were you, I would state your business, and leave."

Marshal Chaney had managed to get it set in his head that John Looney was me, for no better reason than I had just told him so. He was attempting to puzzle out who was who, but evidently could not think clearly while in the midst of a bunch of mounted horses.

"No, that one on the sorrel is Zeke," he told his companion, Cephus Washburn.

"No, it ain't, Lee—*this* one is Zeke," Marshal Washburn said, pointing a bony finger at me.

"It don't matter anyways, because we didn't come to get Zeke Proctor," Marshal Washburn added. "We come to get Zacharias Blue. He's the one selling the whiskey that blinds folks."

My militia boys kept quiet—real quiet. Twelve Cherokees being quiet at the same time amounts to a passel of quiet; it's like that quiet at night that seems louder than noise. I believe it unnerved the marshals more than if we'd all gabbed at once.

"Whichever he is, Zeke's wanted, too," Marshal Chaney declared. "He's wanted for that shooting in the courthouse. Judge Parker mentioned him to me himself."

Marshal Cephus Washburn knew he had serious trouble on his hands if he didn't behave, a fact his partner had yet to figure out.

"Lee, I ain't worried about no old disputes," he asserted. "Just put up your weapon, and let these boys get back to racing their horses."

"We're just testing our colts," I said. I was trying to be sensible, and so was Marshal Washburn. I was hoping the matter could end without gunplay, and it might have, if Marshal Chaney had a better holster. Once he took his pistol out of my ribs, he tried several times to shove it back in its holster, but the holster was tight and the gun wouldn't go in, which fact meant the marshal still had his pistol in his hand. It was a hefty pistol, and a small holster. I suppose the marshal had been in a hurry when he left, and had gotten his guns and holsters mixed up.

I soon regretted that I had ever mentioned John Looney. Confusion leads to wildness, and Marshal Chaney was bad confused. He looked at me, and he looked at John, and his eyes got wilder every time he switched from one of us to the other.

"Hell, one of them's Zeke, let's take 'em both in. The jury can sort it out!" he said.

"Maybe you didn't hear me, sir," I said. "This is the Kee-toowah Militia surrounding you. We can police this part of the country without your help. We'd all be better pleased if you'd put away that gun and leave."

"That's fine, but we'll have the whiskeyseller if you'll point him out to us," Marshal Cephus Washburn said. "We've ridden a long way, and have our expenses to consider."

We weren't going to tell them Zack Blue had just scampered into the timber. Marshal Washburn's horse had nearly stepped on the boy as the two men were riding into town. It would have made them look more foolish.

And they *were* foolish. But it would be wiser to let the Judge tell them that—they weren't holding no gun on the Judge.

"You're welcome to the whiskeysellers, if you come up on them, but I'd approach them careful, if I were you," I said. "There's six or eight of them, and they ain't low on bullets."

Of course, it was a leg pull; there weren't any eight whiskey-sellers in the whole Territory. If there had been, I'd have likely been drunk all the time. There was just Zack Blue and his mother Belle, and Old Mandy.

The leg pull didn't matter. Neither did my effort to be sensi-ble, or Marshal Washburn's, either. The other marshal, Lee Chaney, was fast coming to a boil. I saw it, and so did Marshal Washburn. I waved for the boys to move back. I thought maybe if we gave the man air, he'd calm down.

"Whoa, Lee . . . best not be reckless," Marshal Washburn said, just before Marshal Chaney hit the boil point and started shooting. I was three feet away, but with no weapon on me. I had been running my colt, and had wanted to dispense with the weight.

"Throw me a gun!" I yelled, expecting to be shot before a weapon arrived.

But Marshal Washburn made a lunge for his partner—trying, I suspect, to get him under control before they both got mowed down by the Keetoowah Militia. It was the sensible thing to try, but it failed due to the crowded conditions. Lee Chaney's first shot hit his partner in the left kneecap, rendering him a cripple for life. That kneecap exploded like a crabapple would explode if you shot it with a buffalo gun. Marshal Washburn turned white from surprise.

"Goddamn, Lee!" he yelled, and then his horse reared from nervousness, and he went off the back of his saddle.

Arch Scraper was nearest to me, and had the composure to hand me a pistol.

"Marshal, stop!" I commanded. "You just shot your own man!"

I doubt it registered with Lee Chaney, though. He was in such a state of wild confusion that he was determined to shoot somebody.

I saw him swing the pistol toward John Looney, whom I had foolishly said was me. The boys were packed together so tight, they could barely pull their guns.

"Hold off!" I yelled, as loud as I could.

Lee Chaney shot one shot at John, but all he hit was the sky. His eyes was like a crazed cow's. If I had a crowbar, I might have stopped him with it—that, or a sledgehammer, but I didn't have a crowbar *or* a sledgehammer. John Looney wasn't much more than twenty feet from Marshal Chaney. Even a man who had gone cow-crazy might hit his target, if given enough opportunities.

"Marshal, don't shoot no more—*I'm* Zeke!" I protested, but it still didn't register. Lee Chaney took aim at John Looney again, at which point I shot him dead.

It was a poor end to a pleasant day. I had only wanted to run some two-year-old colts on a grassy meadow with good footing. That was all the militiamen had wanted, too—a little horseracing, and maybe a swallow or two of liquor.

But now we had one dead marshal, and another wounded so painfully that he could scarce draw a breath without moaning.

"I wish one of those whiskeysellers you were sent to catch

would show up," I told Marshal Washburn. "Whiskey's about all there is around here that would be likely to ease your pain."

Marshal Washburn looked weak and white. No doubt, he was thinking what a long, painful journey it would be back to Arkansas. I wasn't a doc, and I didn't know much about kneecaps, but a brief look at his wound convinced me that Marshal Washburn would be walking on crutches for a good, long time.

Although I enjoy my whiskey, the events of the day made me take against the whiskeysellers. There was trouble again in the Going Snake District, all because Zack Blue was too lazy to make whiskey healthful enough that it wouldn't turn a man blind. If I could have caught young Zack while I was in my rage, I would have given him a licking he would be a long time forgetting.

The deed was done, though, and the horseracing was over. What I couldn't figure was why the white law couldn't produce even two marshals who knew how to behave. Marshal Chaney had no reason to be poking a gun in my ribs, even if he did think I needed arresting.

"Lee was hotheaded," Marshal Washburn admitted. "Many's the time I've asked him not to be so quick to draw his gun. Once you point a gun at a man, there's apt to be shooting happen."

"I expect we'd have got through it without gunplay if he'd had a bigger holster," I said. "He couldn't get his pistol put away, so he fiddled around and shot you in the knee."

"Yes, the dern fool," Marshal Cephus Washburn said.

14

I THOUGHT ABOUT THE MATTER CONSIDERABLE, AND DECIDED to take the dead marshal and the wounded one back to Arkansas myself. I knew Becca would be dead set against it, so I didn't go home to argue the matter. I sent John Looney to explain; loaded the corpse on one horse; and with the help of Belle Blue, borrowed a small wagon to cart Marshal Washburn. I didn't think the man would survive a horseback trip to Fort Smith, much less Little Rock. Every time the horse's hoof hit the ground, that shattered kneecap would pain him. Taking a dead body all the way to Little Rock would have been a damn nuisance, since Fort Smith had a fine cemetery anyway, and was a sight closer besides.

Marshal Washburn seemed a frank man, so I put a frank question to him that night, when we camped.

"According to this dead fellow, I'm still a wanted man," I said. "Do you think they'll lock me up and hang me, when I show up in Fort Smith with you and the corpse?"

"Not over this," the marshal said. "That damn hotheaded Lee Chaney caused this. It's a terrible aggravation, but I will not tolerate them hanging you for it. You were only looking to your stirrup, and Lee poked you with his gun."

"I thank you for your honesty," I said. "I hope Judge Parker respects your opinion."

"The Judge lost his missus. He's in a sad state," the Marshal informed me.

"I have heard they were a respected couple," I told him.

We heard a pack of coyotes yipping, whenever the conversation lagged.

"Did Marshal Chaney have a wife?" I inquired.

"Yes—a fine one," Marshal Washburn told me. "I'll be surprised if I don't marry her, now that Lee's gone.

"I'm a widower myself," he added. "It's too dern lonesome at night, when you're a widower."

"Agreed," I said. "I've been a married man myself, since I was a youth."

It was grey in the morning, and grey when we came to the Arkansas River. A man named Lonnie Vont, whom I knew slightly, ferried us over to the Fort Smith side. Lonnie was known to be a gossip; I suppose it's boresome, pulling the same boat over the same water, day after day.

"Who's in the wagon sheet?" he asked. We had wrapped Marshal Chaney up as neatly as we could.

"That dern Lee, the hothead," Marshal Washburn replied.

"Oh—I expect Zeke shot him?" Lonnie said. "Zeke's shot a passel of folks, I hear."

Idle remarks like that one had always irked me. I walked over and picked up Lonnie—he wasn't large—and heaved him out of his ferry.

He bobbed up after a moment, looking surprised. Marshal

Washburn, though in pain, laughed out loud. He enjoyed the sight of Lonnie Vont flying out of his own ferryboat.

We were about halfway across the river, when Lonnie made his vexing remark. It was still a good distance to the Arkansas shore, and the water was choppy and cool.

"Reckon he can swim it?" Marshal Washburn asked. He craned his neck for a look at Lonnie, who was already a good fifty yards behind us.

"I hope not," I said. "I hope the river washes the goddamn rattlemouth clean out to sea."

"Out to sea?" the Marshal asked. "Does the old Arkansas go that far?"

"It goes to the big Miss, and the big Miss goes that far," I informed him. "It's because fools like him start yarning about killings in the District that causes men like yourself to get their knee bones exploded."

The next minute, I was sorry that I had used the word "exploded." The marshal might have forgotten his wound for a while, in his amusement at the plight of our gabby ferryman. No sooner had I said the word than he began to look peaked again—peaked, and scared.

"If that's what it looks like, I guess I'll be a long time on a crutch," he said. Marshal Washburn didn't speak another word on the rest of the crossing, and quickly lost interest in whether Lonnie Vont sank or swam.

When I docked the ferry and drove the wagon onto land, Lonnie was still visible, though he had drifted a far ways downstream. His head, on that big water, looked as tiny as the head of a turtle.

I decided I didn't dislike him enough to want him washed out to sea, but I meant what I said to the marshal. Every Cherokee killing got talked about by the whites until it wasn't just one killing, anymore. Pretty soon, it turned into six or eight, ten or twenty. Then some judge felt he had to call out the marshals; then the Indians outshot the marshals, unless the marshals broke into fighting among themselves before they located the Indians they were supposed to arrest. That had happened twice recently. Marshal Maples shot Marshal Massey; Marshal Chaney shot Marshal Washburn—and in between those fatal encounters came Ned's battle. I still have no accurate sense of how many marshals Ned killed, but I believe it was at least four. Tacking that four onto Massey and Chaney made six marshals dead or wounded, all because some white judge listened to wild talk.

I got a little worried about Lonnie, at that point. His head had disappeared. I thought maybe I had drowned the fool, which was more than I had intended. But it was too late, by this time, to go dive for him. If he was drowned, he was drowned.

Then, to my relief, I saw him wading ashore about 150 yards downstream. He was making slow progress, too—it looked like he had found a nice gummy patch of Arkansas mud to wade through. Four people were waiting for the ferry. If Lonnie didn't speed to shore, he would soon be losing business.

I hoped it would teach him a lesson, but I doubt it. Rattlemouths have a hard time changing their ways.

15

IN THE STREET NEAR THE COURTHOUSE, I MET THE TALL, skinny fellow who had tried to be a bailiff the day the courthouse in Tahlequah got shot up—the day of my trial. I had forgotten his name, if I ever knew it, but I was glad to see him.

"Uh-oh," he said, when he saw we had a body wrapped in a wagon sheet.

"Uh-oh is right, and this other marshal's shot in the knee," I informed the man. "First, I need the doctor—and then, I need the Judge."

"I think this one's dead, too," the tall, skinny man said, peering into the wagon. "We're using up a passel of marshals, over there in Indian Territory."

Unbeknownst to me, the marshal had passed out again. I knew he wasn't dead; I could see his chest moving when he breathed. Evidently, the young bailiff was nearsighted. I wasn't disposed to be testy with him, having recalled that this bailiff had shot T. Spade Beck, a fellow who wanted to kill me in the worst way. I was unarmed at the time of the killing, too. The least I owed the youngster was a little patience.

"I guess I can take this marshal to the doc for you," the bailiff volunteered.

"I'd be obliged if you would. What about the Judge?" I asked.

He pointed up the hill, to where a man in a dark coat was chopping wood with an axe.

"There's the Judge," he said.

"If he's a judge, why is he chopping wood, this time of day?" I inquired, though it was not my business, really.

"I can't speak for Judge Parker, and I would be a fool to try," the bailiff told me. "I guess he figures he might need the firewood."

He kindly took the wagon from me, and found a doctor for Marshal Washburn. Later, I heard that the marshal had to be hauled all the way to Little Rock at government expense. I think the same doctor that made Moses Squirrel a new jaw tried to make the marshal a new kneecap, only it didn't work. I happened to encounter Marshal Washburn some years later, and he was still using a crutch.

Judge Parker didn't stop splitting his firewood until I was about twenty feet away from him. He wore a dark coat, and a string necktie, neatly knotted. From that fact alone, I took him to be an unusual man. Very few people in Arkansas, or in the Cherokee Nation, either, put on a string necktie when they need to split a little firewood.

It was a sultry morning, and the Judge was perspiring some, though the heat didn't seem to tempt him to remove his coat.

"Hello, I'm Ezekiel Proctor," I said, at which point the Judge looked at me severely and put down his axe.

That was all he did: just looked. He didn't say a word.

"Pardon my curiosity," I said, "but do you always wear your frock coat when you need to split a little wood?"

"No, just since my missus died," the Judge said. "I promised her I'd dress proper, and not become a slouch.

"It's a promise I mean to honour," he added. His voice broke when he said it, and I believe I saw tears in the man's eyes.

"Why, I'm sorry, Judge," I said at once. "I see that I've intruded on the memory of your wife."

"Sir, it would be hard not to, I have such a passel of memories of her," the Judge said. At that point, he took out a cotton handkerchief and carefully wiped his eyes.

"Forty years' worth," he added, tucking his handkerchief back in his lapel.

"Your bailiff was kind enough to help me," I told him. "I brought back two marshals—one dead, and one crippled."

"Who killed the dead one?" the Judge inquired.

"I did," I admitted. "He was shooting recklessly into a crowd of people. One of the people he shot was the other marshal. In fact, the other marshal was the first person he shot."

"It's a poor record, ain't it?" the Judge said. "I sent a pair up recently, and one of them shot and killed the other.

"If there's a moral, I don't know what it is," he added, shaking his head.

"I hear Tailcoat Jones drowned in the river," I said.

"He drowned, and his whore, too," the Judge told me. "Mr. Jones washed up in about a week, but the whore has never been found."

The old Judge looked weary and sad. I knew his reputation, and had braced myself for a quarrel, but I don't think he had the spirit for a quarrel.

"Have you come here to give yourself up, Mr. Proctor?" he inquired.

"No, I ain't—because I ain't guilty of nothing, though I did shoot the woman by accident," I said. "I admit that—but I didn't start the fight in the courtroom, I was an unarmed prisoner at the time."

"Sir, I'm chopping wood, not trying cases," the Judge reminded me. "If you're disposed to surrender, you'll have to look up the Sheriff. I've closed down my court for forty days, and I don't want to hear of these matters in the meantime."

"Forty days? Why that's as long as the Flood lasted," I told him. "There'll be so many crimes committed in that length of time, you'll be hard pressed to catch up."

"I expect you're right," the Judge said. Then he heaved a big sigh. "But my court's closed anyway. My wife Martha was a help and a comfort to me for forty years. I figure I owe her a day of mourning for every year, and she's gonna get it."

He turned, then, and headed for his house. But he stopped after two or three steps, and looked back at me.

"I will ask you one question, since I am unlikely to have another opportunity," he said. "I don't believe Mart would begrudge me a question."

"What's the question?" I asked.

"Is this man Ned Christie a decent man, or is he a killer?" the Judge asked.

"Ned? Why, he's as decent a man as the Cherokee Nation can boast," I said. I was glad for the chance to say it, too.

"You're certain about that, are you?" the Judge asked.

"Damned certain," I told him. "He's a senator, and a fine upstanding fellow. I wouldn't have allowed the man to take my oldest daughter for his wife, if that weren't the honest truth.

"My daughter's but little more than a girl, and those goddamn marshals you sent outraged her to a point where she was hard put to live!" I added. My temper flared up sudden, at the thought of Jewel's ordeal.

"And my other daughter was killed outright!" I reminded the man. "You've got a grief, and I've got two. You ought to try those goddamn killers you hired, when you start your court up again."

The Judge just looked at me.

What could the man say? He knew I was right.

"I'm much obliged for the information about Mr. Christie," he said, finally.

"It's accurate information, Judge," I assured him. "Ned Christie's an honest citizen."

"I expect he is, but I doubt it will save him," the Judge said.

"Why, it ought to save him!" I declared. "Why won't it?"

"It would take a prophet to know," Judge Parker said, "and I ain't a prophet. I'm a judge, and a slow one, at that. I've spent forty years trying to separate right from wrong, and I'll tell you, sir—it's a damned hard task.

"I could hardly do it when I had Mart, and now I don't have her and never will have her again," the Judge said, as he turned toward his house.

I stood, and watched him go. It was clear from the shuffling way he moved that Judge Isaac Parker was a brokenhearted man.

16

I PROWLED THE SALOONS FOR AN HOUR, HOPING TO LOCATE one or two of Tailcoat's men. I would have done some fine strangling, if I could have found one or two, but the word was they had all gone back to the Natchez country. I didn't choose to follow; Mississippi's too swampy for me. I went there once, to hunt bear. I had a cough for a month, from sleeping in mouldy clothing.

In one of the saloons, there was a newspaper fellow of some sort. He had a long-winded name, and was drunk as a pup. He said he had been in Fort Smith for a month, waiting to meet me, or Ned.

"Why, you could stay here for a year and never meet us," I told him. "The reason for that is we don't live here. I just came today to deliver a dead man."

The fellow had three initials to his name and was so drunk, if you hung him up and drained him, nothing but whiskey would come out. He claimed he intended to come to the District and get the facts about me and Ned.

"Come a-flying, then," I told him. "I'll tell you some fine, true yarns. I can't vouch for Ned—I expect you'll have to learn Cherokee if you want to talk to him."

"Cherokee? Why's that?" the fellow asked, in some surprise.

"Because Ned Christie has took a vow never to speak the English tongue again," I told him.

I guess that news excited the fellow. He pulled out a little tablet and started scribbling before I even got outside.

Lonnie Vont was in his underwear when I got back to the ferry. He had his clothes spread out on some barrels, hoping they would dry. He looked nervous when he seen me coming in the wagon. I felt duty bound to return the vehicle to Dog Town, even though it was far out of my way.

"Howdy, Lonnie—have a refreshing swim?" I asked, once on board.

"It's a wonder there's any river left, Zeke," Lonnie replied, in humble tones.

"Why's that?" I asked.

"Because I feel like I swallowed about half of it," Lonnie said. "Besides that, I lost both shoes in that gummy mud."

"I trust that will teach you not to gossip about my gunplay, Lonnie," I told him. Lonnie looked like an old muskrat who had nearly drowned in his own hole.

He winched that ferry across the Arkansas as fast as he could winch. I guess he figured if he took his time, I might lose my temper and heave him back in the river again.

17

As I RODE BACK THROUGH THE HILLS, NED CHRISTIE AND MY Jewel were much on my mind. I would have dearly liked to go see them. But Dog Town, where I was obliged to return the wagon and the place on the high part of the Mountain where Ned had built his fort, were in opposite directions. Plodding up the Mountain to Ned's place would be slow work, and I'd have to journey all the way back to Dog Town, once I had my visit out.

My other concern was Becca, who had been low and weepy since the news came of Liza's death and Jewel's abuse. Becca didn't shuffle through her days quite as slow as the old Judge, but the fact was, she had lost a daughter and was broken-hearted, too.

I stopped feeling at ease in my mind when I was gone too long from Becca. My fear was she might slide down so low in her feelings that she would bog in megrims and melancholy, never able to enjoy the sunlight again, or take a little pleasure in scattering corn for her hens.

As I was passing through Tahlequah, I had the good fortune to notice Arch Scraper, waiting at the blacksmith's. If he was at the blacksmith's, he was very likely waiting. The blacksmith in Tahlequah was known to be slow as Sunday meeting. It was Arch's brother's team I was driving. Petey Scraper had been enjoying the horserace, but had headed for the timber at a racing pace himself when Marshal Chaney started firing his pistol. I had borrowed the wagon and team with Arch's permission, and thought I could save time by asking him to take it home to Petey.

"No, I ain't speaking to Petey," Arch said, with no more than a glance at me when I made the request.

That was no surprise. The Scrapers stayed on the outs with one another almost as often as the Becks, though no Scraper of my acquaintance was near as cranky as Davie Beck, or old White Sut, either. The Scrapers worked a farm together, but that didn't stop them from quarreling.

"Arch, I didn't request that you hold a conversation with him," I pointed out. "All I want you to do is take his team and wagon home. I have an important errand up on the Mountain, and Dog Town is ten miles out of my way."

"Don't care if it's a hundred miles out of your way," Arch retorted. "I ain't driving Petey's team home."

"Now, why would that be such a goddamned hard chore?" I inquired. "You're going to the farm anyway."

"What if one of them horses went lame on the way?" Arch said. "Petey would claim it was his prize racer and charge me fifty dollars for the sprain."

"Now, Arch," I said. "Just use your common sense. I drove this team to Fort Smith, Arkansas, and it didn't go lame. Why would it go lame between here and your farm?"

Arch Scraper was always chewing on a twig. He kept several twigs in his shirt pocket, just for that purpose. I have never known him to chew tobacco; twigs are what he likes to chew. Once or twice when he was excited, he's been known to swallow the twig he was chewing on, but he didn't swallow it on this occasion.

"I got no interest in common sense," he said. "What I go by is *my* sense, and *my* sense is that I'd be a damn fool to touch Petey's team. He wouldn't like it."

"Arch, you're the one loaned me the team," I reminded him. "I'd think he might thank you for bringing it home safe."

"Think what you like, Zeke—I ain't doing it," he said.

"Would you do it if I paid you a quarter?" I asked. "You're going home anyway. Why not go home a quarter richer?"

The one thing I knew about the Scrapers was that they liked cash money. I thought a quarter in cash money would bring Arch around, but the fool argued me all the way up to a dollar and a half, before he gave in. By then, I was so determined that he'd drive the team home, I would have offered him $100, if that was what it took. I was about ready to curse him when he finally gave in.

"If you ain't stubborn, I don't know what stubborn is," I told him.

Arch just took my money, and chewed another twig.

All the way up to the Mountain, I was disquieted in my feelings about Becca. I had squandered a dollar and a half, just to persuade Arch Scraper to drive his own brother's team home so I could go pay Ned and Jewel a visit; and yet, I couldn't stop thinking about Becca, which was an odd thing. A year ago, before the tragedies started accumulating, I could ride off on a hunt, or go to a horse race, or gamble a little, and never give Becca a thought, even if I was gone two weeks. I had to do my roaming and get my mind clear of family duties from time to time. It was the right of a man to roam with a free mind. Becca had a fine house and ample food for our young ones. She had her chores and her children, and I never doubted her ability to keep the place up, and the children well tended to.

Since the troubles, though, I couldn't roam with a free mind. I kept thinking about Becca. It seemed she had filled up so with sadness, since Liza's death. I didn't know how to drain the sadness, either. She never smiled, even at the triplets. I had been thinking lately of hiring a young cousin of Becca's, a spry girl named May, to come and live with us, just so the triplets would see a happy face and hear laughing in the house once in a while.

What I couldn't get out of my mind was an old neighbour woman of ours named Louisa Faulks. Her old man and her only son died within a year of one another. I liked Louisa, and after her men died, I offered to let her come live with us and help with the triplets. But she just wouldn't come. She lived alone with a milk cow and two cats. She dipped a little snuff, and ate mostly turnip greens, so far as I could tell. I called her Mother Faulks and went by to visit with her whenever I passed near her shack. Sully Eagle courted her a little, after her old man died, but Mother Faulks wouldn't have Sully.

One day, Mother Faulks's milk cow got the bloat and died. Mother Faulks took the cowbell off the old hussy, found a sturdy post oak limb, and hanged herself with the strap that had been on the cowbell. I noticed some buzzards circling over the poor old woman's shack, and was shocked to find her, black in the face, hanging from that post oak limb.

I guess coyotes or foxes got the cats. I intended to bring them home for the triplets, but couldn't locate either one of them.

It was old Mother Faulks I had on my mind, as I trotted up the Mountain. It would be a dreadful thing for the triplets if Becca took the hanging path. Of course, it would be a terrible thing for me, too. I hadn't wanted to associate with anyone but Becca since she came home with me from Ned's and Jewel's on that slow mule of his. I still liked to watch young horses run, but except for that, most of my pleasures were home pleasures. Becca and I could sit on the porch together for hours, rocking but not talking, and listening to the triplets chatter, if they were in earshot. Maybe I'd play my fiddle a bit. Even with the sadness on her, Bec was the only companion I sought. It was unusual—most of my life I had enjoyed the company of men—rowdy men, too, usually. But now, I preferred to stay home with my wife.

I wavered in my mind, but I kept going toward Ned's. Every traveler brought tales of the fort Ned had built, high on the Mountain. None of them said much about Ned himself, other than to say that his nose was a little twisted. No one so far had mentioned Jewel, and Becca wouldn't ask.

The fact was, I had expected to despise Judge Parker, but in fact, I had liked the look of the man. It might be that he would falter under his grief and give up the court, but I didn't really expect it. He wore that tie to chop wood; probably he would face up to his loss and go on with his duties. I thought the old Judge might give us a fair hearing, and was hopeful I might talk Ned into going with me to the court. It was a better gamble than gunfights.

The moment I came into the clearing where Ned's fort was, I knew the courthouse approach was not to be. The trees had been cleared for 150 yards all around the house. That was because Ned didn't mean for anyone to come sneaking up on him again. I had thought people were mainly exaggerating, when they said Ned was building a fort. People *do* exaggerate in the District—they've had me slipping out with more women than I ever slipped out with—so I figured when they talked of

Ned's fort, they meant he had built himself a well-fortified house.

But for once, the gossip was accurate: the structure I saw when I rode into the clearing was a fort—not a house. There were no windows on the second floor at all, just slits for firing rifles. There were no windows on the ground floor, either—just thick log walls.

Right away, it made me feel sorry for Jewel. The house that got burned up, the one Ned brought her to as a bride, was big and roomy, with glass windows that let in the light. There was usually a breeze through the windows or the door, if it was muggy and close. There was a fireplace big enough to cook a pig in, and a wide hearth for relaxing. When I was younger—of course, Ned was younger then, too—we used to sit by the hearth and try to whistle tunes. Ned's whistling made me jealous. He made whistling tunes seem as easy as breathing. I couldn't whistle half the tunes that he could, and my whistling was so thin he practically had to be sitting in my lap to hear it. The fireplace cast enough light that a woman could sit and sew by it, or even thread a needle if she needed to.

That house had been a place to encourage enjoyment, and that was far more than I could say for the building I was looking at in the clearing Ned had made to prevent sneaks from sneaking in close to him.

The new house was a fort, and forts weren't made for enjoyment, unless what you enjoy is killing and dying.

My Jewel stepped outside just then. I expect she saw me through one of the slits on the second floor. She didn't run to me, as Liza would have, but then Jewel had never been a child who would rush up and hug me. But she did remember my stiff knee, the one I injured years before in a fall from a ladder, and came out to hold my stirrup steady so I could easy my boot out.

"Hello, Pa," she said.

"Jewel, is that your new house?" I asked. I was hoping, at least, to see the sparkle back in her eyes, but it wasn't there. She was pale as a salamander, too. I guess the color had bleached out of her from living in such a dark place.

"Yes, Ned built it himself," she said, once I had dismounted.

I hugged her and hugged her. Jewel didn't cry, but I could feel the sadness in her, just from the hugging.

"Jewel, why would Ned want to put you in a place like this?" I said, walking around and studying the walls. "How would the sunlight ever get in such a house?"

"We keep the lamps lit," Jewel said. She didn't really look at me directly, when she said it; she looked away, as if she was afraid of what I'd see if she looked me in the eye.

When Jewel took me inside, I saw that the walls were two logs thick. Ned had poured sand between the logs. That was careful planning, but the house was dark as pitch. The night animals might have enjoyed being inside it, but I didn't. I like a little light when I'm inside. I get surly as a badger if I have to sit around in a pitch-dark place.

Becca didn't like to waste kerosene keeping the lamps lit, but I was always at her to change the wicks and keep things bright, especially if it was a cloudy day and I had to be inside. I hate a dark house, and Jewel was like me in that way. Now, her own husband had put her in a house that was nearly as dark as a cave.

While I was stumbling around trying not to fall over a bench or a churn, I heard a pig grunt. A shoat came walking over to me.

"What's this? Why would you keep a pig in the house?" I asked. Jewel had never been expected to live in any house that harbored swine before. Swine belonged in the pigpen, not in the house.

"Ned's got water stored," Jewel said. "He brings the goats in at night, too. He says if we have animals inside, we could hold out a month if the white law comes again."

I was getting bothered. I wanted to talk to Ned. My girl was accustomed to doing chores with the livestock, but not in the house. She looked pale and poorly; she had fallen off in her face, too. I know what was done to her by those white rascals was terrible—some women would have died from it. But I would rather Ned had taken her away to Texas or someplace farther west, than to stick her in a fort and have her smell pigs and goats at night. In the old times, after the Trail of Tears, some folks kept their livestock in with them to protect the critters from bears and wolves—but now, there were very few bears, and almost no wolves.

"Where is Ned, Jewel?" I asked. "I've come from Fort

Smith. I've seen the Judge. Maybe there's a way to head off this war, so you can live in a regular house again."

I saw that Jewel didn't believe me. She had accepted her husband's way. I don't expect Jewel believed that she would ever live in a regular house again, or be happy, either.

"Ned found a honey tree," Jewel said. "He went off with the axe and the wheelbarrow and some buckets. I guess he'll be back when he's cleaned out the honey."

Impatience is one of my failings. I'd rather be on the go than wait. But Jewel asked if I'd stay the night, and I said I would.

"Did he go east or west?" I asked. "I know he couldn't go up because we're on top of the Mountain. I want to talk to him as quick as I can, Jewel."

"Why, he went west, Pa," Jewel said, and I was soon out the door. The sound of an axe striking a tree carries a long way. I figured I could locate Ned and be of some help.

I located him, but not quick. I kept going west and kept going west, until I was less than a mile from Tuxie Miller's. I was wondering if the bees had stung Ned so bad he couldn't chop. I was a wily honey robber myself, having robbed many a bee and slipped off unstung, but Ned did not have my experience. I saw a swarm of honeybees overcome a boy, once. It was Charley Bobtail's youngest boy, and the bees worked him over so bad the boy was a whole week getting back on his feet. I thought maybe the same had happened to Ned, but just as I was about to ride on toward the Millers—they had rebuilt their house and were living there now—I heard the axe.

When I found Ned, he had roped himself to the trunk of an old, half-dead sycamore tree. He was twenty feet up, bees swarming all around him. He had made himself a kind of cigar out of leaf tobacco and was puffing smoke at the bees as best he could, while he worked with the axe. He already had a wheelbarrow full of honey, and a bucket of comb, but he was still chopping away.

"Ned, that's enough honey for three winters," I told him. "Come on down."

"I might not find another bee tree for three winters, either," he said. "There's more honey in here—I mean to have it, before I quit."

"You're only a half a mile from Tuxie's," I reminded him. "Why didn't you get him to help you?"

"Let him find his own bee tree," Ned said. "You can help, if you're anxious to be useful."

We ended up with three buckets of comb and a wheelbarrow so full of honey buckets we could barely push it. It was dark honey, so strong it would make you cough. I couldn't resist licking a fingerful now and then, but Ned didn't touch it.

"You're welcome to a lick because you helped," he said. "I'm putting the rest in a barrel."

"Is that for the same reason you're keeping a pig in your house?" I inquired. "Are you *that* determined to fight?"

Ned had got grave, since his injury. He looked at me solemn.

"The white law's determined to kill me," he replied. "I *have* to be determined to fight."

"Now, maybe not, Ned," I informed him. "I was in Arkansas yesterday."

"Yes, I heard," he said. "Taking another goddamn dead marshal home."

"That's right," I agreed. "I saw Judge Parker myself."

Ned got a stony look on his face. We took turns wheeling the wheelbarrow, which was heavy. When it came my turn, I had to keep my mind on where I was going. If I hit a rock or a root and turned the wheelbarrow over, it would be a terrible waste of all that honey.

"Ned, you oughtn't to fight if you don't have to," I told him, next time it was his turn to wheel. "If it'll die, let it die on its own, without no more bloodshed."

"What makes you think it will die?" he asked. "The marshals that come after me were well trained enough not to kill one another. I had to do all the killing, and I killed four. Why in the world would it die after all that?"

"Because sometimes things just die," I told him. "There's only so many marshals to be hired, and crimes are happening every day. The Starrs are robbing everything that moves over to the west. Maybe they'll send all their marshals after the Starrs and just forget us here in the Going Snake."

"Maybe—but what if they don't?" Ned asked. "If they don't, I'll have to fight, and I want to be ready."

"I saw Judge Parker. His wife died," I told him. "And Tailcoat Jones drowned, along with his whore."

Ned just kept wheeling the wheelbarrow. News didn't seem

to affect him. He had chosen his path, and he meant to keep on it, whatever the news.

"Didn't you hear me?" I said. "Tailcoat Jones is dead, and he was the leader of that bunch what attacked you."

"He let them ruffians take turns with my Jewel," Ned replied. "I had expected to kill him myself, but if he's dead, I can't. So that *ain't* good news, to me. I didn't know the Judge or his wife, so I got nothing to say about that."

His tone with me was so stiff, I felt myself getting riled. Ned and I had been friends for years, and I had just helped him fill several buckets with honey. I had lost my touch with the bees, too. I got stung four times while I was trying to be helpful. I didn't appreciate the man talking to me as if I was a stranger or a fool, but I thought it was important to try and argue Ned out of armed conflict with the authorities. So, I held in my temper.

"The point about this judge is that the loss of his wife has just about broke the man," I said. "He's so grieved, he's closed his court for forty days."

"She must have been a good wife," Ned remarked.

"Well, the Judge thought so," I said. "If we was to go there and talk to him on the day he opens his court back up, I believe he'd be fair. He might call this thing off, if you could talk to him face-to-face."

"Does the Judge speak Cherokee?" Ned asked. We had just come into the clearing where his fort stood.

"I don't expect so, no," I replied.

"Then we can't talk, and I see no point in the trip," Ned said. "I'll be talking Cherokee and nothing else, till the day I die."

"You're too goddamn stubborn to associate with, Ned," I told him. "If talking a few words of English to a weary old judge would save your life and maybe Jewel's life, too, why wouldn't it be worth doing?"

Ned got that eagle look then.

"No," was all he said.

Jewel came out, and began to take the buckets from the wheelbarrow.

I knew from the way Ned Christie looked that nothing now could turn him from the warrior path.

18

THAT NIGHT, JEWEL MADE ME A GOOD CORN MUSH AND SOME flavorful beans with a little pork rind in them. It was an old recipe of her mother's. Ned allowed a little of the honey to be used to sweeten the mush, but he put the rest in a barrel and nailed the lid on. He had a good potato pit, and a great pile of corn stored. I could see he was preparing for a long siege.

But the meal had put us in a friendly mood and I let the quarrel go, for Jewel's sake. We brought out the checkerboard and played several games, though the house was too dim for fine concentration on checkers. The fireplace didn't cast much of a glow, and Ned would allow only one lamp.

Jewel stood behind him, and rubbed his head while we played. One reason for the dimness was that Ned's one good eye was variable. He saw bright lights in his head, and got headaches and cramps in his neck. Jewel had a little oil of some kind that Old Turtle Man had given her. She rubbed the oil on Ned's neck, while I lost three checker games.

"You ain't the checker player you used to be, Zeke," Ned remarked.

"No, because I ain't an owl or a bat," I said. "I play better checkers when I can see the board.

"I can't even see my hand," I added. "I might be making moves I don't want to make, for all I know."

"I have to save this one eye," Ned explained, in an easier tone. "I can see sharp and shoot fine, but it waters up if I strain it. I like to rest it, when I can."

"All right, but what about your whistling?" I asked. "Learned any new tunes while you're sitting around in the dark?"

He hadn't. Ned still bested me at whistling—always had—but it still didn't keep me from attempting a tune. My whistling was so paltry that Jewel smiled. It was the only time I saw her smile, during our whole visit.

What I noticed as we sat by the fireplace was that Jewel and Ned were close now. Before the battle, my feeling was that the two of them had not quite settled into the married life yet. They were nervous, and rarely stood near one another, or touched in public.

Now, it was the opposite: they were seldom out of hand's reach of one another. Ned had taken to smoking an old pipe. Jewel brought him his tobacco, and drew on the pipe a time or two herself, while she tamped it for him. Before they went up to sleep, she soaked a rag and laid it over his eyes for a few minutes. Ned was always reaching out to hold her hand for a moment, and Jewel didn't draw away. I guess adversity had brought them close together, only it seemed to me that too much damage came along with the closeness.

I would rather they could have stayed nervous, and spared them the wounds. They would have settled into the married way, once they got a little older. Time—not raping and shooting—would have brought them closer.

After we gave up whistling, the two of them went up to bed. Jewel held the lamp. At the top of the stairs, she turned. Just for a moment, I saw her white face looking down at me. It was just a glimpse; Jewel soon followed Ned on to bed. But seeing her face like that haunted me so that I couldn't get to sleep. I sat by the fire in Ned's fort, watching the embers cool, until the roosters began to crow and the day birds flutter.

I was not one to talk much to my children, I guess. I yarned with them, and sung them songs, but I left most of the talking to Becca.

That night, though, I waited, hoping Jewel would come down a minute, so we could chat. It wasn't one thing in particular I wanted to talk to her about, and I don't know if there was anything in particular Jewel wanted to say to me. I just know that her look, from the head of the stairs, unsettled me. For years after, when Jewel's face came to me, whether in day thoughts or night dreams, it was that look I remembered.

The next morning, Ned took me through his fort and showed me the rest of his preparations. He had acquired plenty of rifles, and enough gunpowder and bullets to have fought the Civil War all over again. He had even dammed a little stream and rechanneled it, so it would flow through the fort. He had barrels to catch rainwater as well, and had rubber hoses attached to them so he could siphon water inside.

Ned had prepared careful, but I got melancholy seeing all the fortifying he had done.

"You ain't just ready for war, Ned—you *want* war!" I told him. That was the point that troubled me.

Ned didn't deny it. He had the eagle look again.

"I was a farmer till the whites done what they done," he said. "Now I'm a warrior, and I intend to be a fine one."

"I expect you will, Ned," I told him.

Jewel got upset when she saw me getting ready to leave.

"I wish you could just stay one more night, Pa," she said.

"I can't, hon—your ma's poorly," I told her.

Jewel looked sad. On impulse, I asked her if she was with child. I don't know what feeling brought those words out of my mouth—but Jewel just shook her head.

Later, riding away, I wished I hadn't asked, for she got the distant look when I did. She looked past me, and shook her head.

Jewel was not yet eighteen. I don't know what I thought the hurry was for her to have a child, especially after the bad business with Tailcoat Jones and his gang of white ruffians.

Ned wore a big-brimmed hat in sunlight, to shield his eyes. He was practicing shooting, when I left. He had walked over to the woods and was shooting crabapples off a tree. He didn't miss a one, not while I was looking.

19

TUXIE'S WAS ON THE WAY HOME. I THOUGHT I'D STOP AND get his opinion and Dale's about Ned's war. They were his close friends, and I thought maybe they'd want to speak to him, too, about the possibility of squaring things with the old judge.

But I arrived at a bad moment. The Millers had just buried their baby girl Sarah, the one who had been at the breast the day they were burned out. Losing babies was common, in that time; but it was the Miller family's first loss, and they took it hard. The children were all howling, and Tuxie was so upset he could barely spade the dirt over the little grave. Dale didn't speak at all. She was staring away, like Jewel. Tears had made ruts in her cheeks, from heavy crying.

"I swear, Tuxie. What did the tyke die of?" I inquired, speaking soft.

"I don't know, Zeke. She just didn't wake up this morning," Tuxie said.

"Well, I swear," I said, again.

There was not a thing I could do for a family with such a fresh loss. I left them to their grief, and rode on home.

Years later, Dale Miller mentioned to me that the baby's digestion had never been good, after the raid.

"She spit up my milk, couldn't hold it down," Dale said. "I expect she got too scared, with me trying to nurse her while I was chasing around."

I guess that baby girl was one more victim of Tailcoat Jones and his raid.

20

WHILE THE OLD JUDGE WAS IN MOURNING, THE GOVERNOR OF Arkansas, evidently an old fool, sent five marshals after me for the killing of Marshal Lee Chaney.

I guess the Governor hadn't heard about the Cherokee Militia, when he sent those marshals after me.

After the outrageous affair at the horserace in Dog Town, with Marshal Chaney blazing away for no reason before he even produced a warrant, there was a boom in recruiting. Before I knew it, the Cherokee Militia numbered over thirty men. Partridge McElmore joined up, and three of his brothers. Victor Horsefly volunteered, and so did Edley Springston. Then there was Cooley Silk and his brother Arley, and Lightning Boles, along with several Cherokees I scarcely knew.

I was particularly proud to have got Victor Horsefly into the Militia. Victor was so big, he was an outcast. He weighed so much—over four hundred pounds—that he had to be weighed on a cattle scale. The only horse in the District stout enough to carry him was a draft horse he had journeyed all the way up to Wisconsin to purchase. Victor was a quiet fellow who didn't rage often, but when he did, snapping a spine would be no more to him than snapping a twig. He once kicked the whole front off a saloon in Fort Smith, after which he swam the river and walked home. Nobody said a word about arresting him, although the saloon had to be totally rebuilt. When they ran over to the courthouse after Victor kicked down the front of the saloon, Judge Parker took one look at Victor out his window, and promptly ruled that saloons were beyond the protection of the law.

"A man that large is best left to his own devices," the Judge said—or at least that's what was reported to me.

The leader of the marshals the Governor sent to arrest me was named Coon Rattersee. Coon was fresh from a raid against the Starr boys, and was said to have wounded two Starrs in a chase that went on for fifty miles.

It was rainy the day Coon and his deputies rode into Tahlequah in their yellow slickers. I only had about three hours' notice that they were coming, but I was able to put twenty-five well-armed militiamen in the street to greet him.

I was at the head of them, armed with a ten-gauge shotgun. Seeing what a shotgun had done to Sam Beck that day in the courtroom convinced me that the fowling piece should not be scorned as a weapon.

Coon Rattersee had convinced himself that he was the equal of the Starrs, which he wasn't. I knew him slightly. We had once hunted turkey together, but we quarreled because the rash son-of-a-bitch claimed an old gobbler *I* shot. Now here he was in Tahlequah, in a yellow slicker.

I don't believe he had expected resistance—at least not to the extent of twenty-five armed Cherokees.

"Now, what's this, Zeke? A goddamn war party?" he asked. He started to ride over to me, but stopped when he saw the ten-gauge.

"It's the Cherokee Militia, Coon," I informed him. "It's our task to keep order in the Going Snake."

"Why, I expect it'll be orderly enough, once you're arrested," he declared.

"You'll not arrest me today," I told him.

Coon reddened in the face. He had done the same, when I refused him the gobbler he tried to claim.

"My warrant is from the Governor of Arkansas," he said. "I don't suppose you're wicked enough to disobey the Governor of Arkansas, are you, Zeke?"

"I don't live in Arkansas, don't know the Governor, and

don't care to," I said bluntly. "The marshaling profession has lost seven men in the Going Snake lately. I'd hate to see it lose five more, but it could happen, if you don't turn around and go home."

Milo Creekmore trotted up to Coon, at that juncture. Milo was a deputy marshal of some experience who had the good sense to tread lightly when faced with a broad disadvantage in numbers.

The other three marshals were just young sprouts. They looked green as sycamore leaves.

"Hold up, Coon. Let's stay nice and calm, while we talk this over," Milo said.

"That's good advice, Milo," I agreed.

Coon Rattersee, though, was full of bluster. He didn't appreciate Milo's advice.

"You can go home if you're so goddamn interested in staying calm," he said. "I was sent here by the Governor of Arkansas to arrest a felon, and there he sits."

Coon pointed a rangy finger at me. But being a man of experience, Milo had encountered bluster before. He had a chaw in his mouth the size of a turkey egg. When he spit, a man didn't want to be anywhere near him, unless he fancied tobacco splatter.

"I see him, Coon," Milo said. "There he sits. And then what?

"Them boys with him don't seem friendly toward us," he added. "If I had known we was up against twenty-five men, I would have ordered my coffin before I left home."

"We hope not to shoot you, Milo," I said.

"I hope you don't neither, Zeke," Milo agreed. "Why don't you just surrender, and make Coon happy?"

"I don't care whether the fool is happy or not," I said. "He has ridden in here on a foolish quest. As you can see, you're considerably outnumbered. A quick trip home would be what I'd advise."

Coon Rattersee swelled up and got red—so red, that I leveled my shotgun at him, hoping the threat of a chest full of buckshot would keep him from going for his gun. If Coon started shooting, the three green boys would think they had to back him up, in which case my militiamen would cut them all down. There'd be a bunch more bodies to pack off to Fort Smith.

"Why, goddamn you! You're a worse rascal than I thought," Coon said.

I held my peace, but I didn't lower my shotgun. Coon had ridden up a little too close when he thought he could cow me. At such a near distance, a shotgun blast would go right through him, just as it had through Sam Beck. Coon Rattersee knew it, too.

He frothed, but he didn't try for his gun.

"When did you get up your militia, Zeke?" Milo asked, in a mild tone of voice. I think he considered the crisis over, and wanted to engage in a little neighbourly conversation to cool the atmosphere.

"We've had it awhile, Milo," I replied.

Coon, now that he had decided not to make a fight of it, blustered a little more, mostly for the benefit of the young marshals, I guess.

"Now goddammit, Zeke. What am I gonna tell the Governor of Arkansas?" he asked. "He's the Governor. He expects cooperation, when he sends a troop of marshals to place suspects under arrest."

"I don't care what you tell him, Coon," I said. "I guess you can tell him the Cherokee Militia stood you down."

"Now, Coon," Milo said. "Now, Coon." I think he was afraid there might be a flare-up yet.

"Who said you could get up a militia anyway?" Coon asked. "You look like a bunch of goddamn pea farmers, to me."

"Well, Coon, be that as it may," I said, "we're the Cherokee Militia, and that's that."

There wasn't much more to talk about. The little posse of marshals in the yellow slickers milled around a little on the other end of town. While they were milling, Victor Horsefly walked down to the blacksmith's and pitched the anvil out into the middle of the street. Then he picked it up again, and pitched it back. In idle moments, Victor liked to pitch anvils around. It was his favourite pastime. He was far too strong just to pitch horseshoes, like the rest of us did. When Victor pitched a horseshoe, that was the last you saw of the horseshoe. He could sail a horseshoe halfway across the District, he was that strong.

Just before the marshals rode away, Coon Rattersee came loping back to where I sat with the Militia. We intended to wait until the men in the yellow slickers rode on out of town.

"Zeke, I have this to say," Coon told me. "We will not take you with us today, but you're to consider yourself a prisoner at large."

"A prisoner at large? What's that?" I inquired.

But Coon had already turned, and was loping away. I guess he thought making me a prisoner at large was a clever way to save face, or maybe he thought it would help him with the Governor—I don't know.

What I *do* know is that was the last attempt the white law ever made to arrest me. I guess I remained a prisoner at large for the rest of my life.

21

OUR TURNING BACK THE MARSHALS IN TAHLEQUAH DID NED Christie a bad turn, I believe. It may have built up antagonism in the marshaling forces. It wasn't but a week before Coon Rattersee struck again, and this time, he struck at Ned.

Coon probably figured we couldn't get twenty-five men high up on the Mountain where Ned lived, and he was right. But what he hadn't reckoned with was Ned himself. Coon came back with Milo Creekmore and the same three green boys. No doubt, Coon was surprised when he rode into the clearing and saw Ned's fort. Ned yelled a warning, but Coon didn't react quick enough. Ned shot Milo Creekmore and two of the green boys before the party of marshals could get back to the cover of the forest. Milo Creekmore didn't die, but Ned's bullet shattered his hip. He walked with a limp for the rest of his life.

Milo was better off than the young marshals, both of whom were shot dead. Coon Rattersee was so hot that he wouldn't leave, which any sensible posseman would have done, considering that he had two young men dead on the ground and his most experienced marshal crippled for life. He stayed in cover all day, shooting at Ned's fort. Of course, he had no chance of hitting Ned, and the bullets made no impression on the logs.

They say Coon Rattersee was down to four rounds of ammunition, when he gave it up. He picked up the bodies under cover of night, and rode back to Fort Smith in the dark.

Milo Creekmore almost died on the trip back.

22

THAT'S WHEN NED'S WAR BEGAN IN EARNEST: WITH COON Rattersee's foolish raid. Ned had taken the warrior path, and no one could turn him from it. After that day, with Milo Creekmore wounded and the two young marshals killed, I don't suppose anyone tried.

From that time on, through four years of raids, the peaceful farming life was lost to Ned, and to our Jewel, too. They lived and fought together—the warrior, and the warrior's woman. Even Tuxie and Dale Miller, their near neighbours, saw little of them after that.

Each posse that came—and I believe there were seven in all —was a little larger than the last. Nobody, not even the Millers, wanted to be drawn any deeper into Ned's war. The Millers had twelve children by then, and they had been burned out once. I believe they would have stood up for Ned in a court. But a posse ain't a court; it's more like a firing squad.

No one could blame the Millers for not wanting to get lined up and shot.

Two weeks after the standoff in Tahlequah when the Cherokee Militia sent Coon Rattersee home, who should race up to my house but that skinny bailiff from Fort Smith? I wouldn't have been much more surprised if an angel of the Lord had lighted on my porch.

The man—I believe his name was Chilly—looked scared, mighty scared. He was twisting his head every which way, and shaking like a leaf.

"I just seen something terrible, Mr. Proctor," Chilly said.

"What might that be, sir?" I asked. "Has that ugly boar of mine got loose again?"

"No. I seen a head in the road," he said.

"Well . . . a head off what?" I asked, thinking he meant an animal head of some kind.

"Off White Sut Beck. I think that's his name," the bailiff said. "Wasn't he that old man who charged the courthouse and picked up that man you choked?"

"White Sut Beck's lost his noggin?" I said. I doubted the story, at first.

"Yep. His head's in the road, about two miles back," the bailiff said.

The bailiff looked so scared it made me think the story might be true.

"Maybe that wild Davie sawed it off with that saw knife of his," I suggested. "The old fool was hard to get along with. It wouldn't surprise me if Davie done for him."

"Well, I didn't see Davie," Chilly said. "All I saw was that head."

He declined to ride back down the road and show me the head, even though I offered to let him carry my ten-gauge for the trip.

"I don't believe I better," he said. "I'm going to be having bad dreams about that head, as it is."

So I left the bailiff with Becca and her cousin May. I had invited May into the household to bring a little merriment. She brought the merriment, and was a fine little cook, as well. She was feeding Chilly pork sausage and blackeyed peas when I left. The triplets, shy around strangers, were staring at him as if he was as dangerous as a panther.

Chilly Stufflebean wasn't as dangerous as a panther, but something that dangerous or worse had torn off old White Sut Beck's head. It was laying right there in the road, just where Chilly said it was.

I had Pete up with me in the saddle. Before I even spotted the head, Pete's hackles rose, and he began to snarl like he'd snarl at a badger.

I had to backtrack nearly a mile from White Sut's head before I found his body. It had been laying dead a day or two, at least, and there were bear tracks everywhere.

I studied the situation for an hour or more, trying to puzzle out what had happened. Pete was quiet during this period, you can believe. He could smell the bear and had sense enough not to do much barking and growling, not with a bear in the vicinity. Pete wouldn't even make a good bite for a bear, and he knew it.

As best I could figure from the tracks and the signs, old White Sut must of got himself tangled up in the chain he used to chain his bear. Probably the old man was drunk, or maybe he was beating the bear. He was known to pound on it with a post, if he didn't like its behaviour.

Somehow, he must of got the bear chain wrapped around his neck. When he did, the bear spooked and run off with him, and then kept running until the old man's head came off. How the head got a mile from the body was a mystery beyond my powers of reckoning. Maybe the old bear was sorry he had popped the head off his master, and dragged White Sut's body around for a while, hoping the old fool would come back to life. White Sut had that bear for years; it's likely that the beast had become attached to him, despite the beatings.

I put the head with the body, and piled some rocks on them to keep the varmints off White Sut for another night. They had torn him up some, but there was still enough of the old man to bury. I meant to go find Frank Beck, with whom I had become quite friendly, and get him to help with the grave digging in the morning.

Chilly was asleep in the rocking chair when I got home. He must of been the victim of a terrible fatigue, to sleep so soundly with the triplets shrieking and screeching from the porch. Becca had put a blanket over the man.

"Don't wake him," she said. "He's rode all this way to bring you an amnesty."

"A what?" I said.

"An amnesty. It's like a pardon. That's what the man said," Becca told me. "It's from the President himself. It means they won't be coming after you no more."

Becca's eyes had a bit of sparkle in them, when she mentioned the President. I was dumbfounded: Becca's eyes hadn't shined in a year, and here she was, talking about a pardon from the President. She had tucked her best blanket around the man who brought the news, too.

"The President? You mean Ulysses S. Grant?" I asked.

"Why, I don't know, Zeke . . . I think that's him," Becca said. She paid little attention to politics, living back in the hills as we did.

It was an unexpected bit of news. I couldn't remember what I had done that I would need a pardon for, unless it was the accidental shooting of Polly Beck. It was all I could do to restrain myself from waking up the bailiff and requiring him to explain.

But Becca made it clear she wouldn't tolerate any interference with the man's sleep, so I did the next best thing, which was to take my fiddle and go out in the smokehouse to celebrate. I played the fiddle and drank, while the triplets chased fireflies down by the pond. They finally wore down and went to bed, but I was keyed up by the news and drank most of the night, before visiting Becca in bed. She was still shining at me, too—another surprise. Becca hadn't brought her shine to bed in many a long month.

We fiddled and faddled to our hearts' content, but I was up with the dawn, to question Chilly Stufflebean.

Chilly wasn't up with the dawn, though. It took a while to get him awake, and then he didn't recollect where he was for the first few minutes. Finally, he went down to the well and sloshed water on himself, until he was in his right mind and ready to tell me about the amnesty.

"It's because you got that militia up that the President granted you that amnesty," Chilly informed me. Water was dripping off his hair.

"Hold on, now. What is an amnesty, just so I'll be clear on the matter?" I asked him.

Chilly was silent for a while, after I asked the question. I don't believe he was too clear about what an amnesty was, either—or it may have been that he just couldn't think clearly when his head was wet.

"Well, it means the Judge ain't going to send no more marshals to arrest you," Chilly said.

"All right. But what made him decide to stop?" I asked.

"Your new judge, I reckon," Chilly said. "I know he sent over names of all the militia you had with you at the Dog Town fight. Judge Parker looked over the list, and decided he couldn't scrape up enough marshals to arrest all of you. So he wrote a letter to the President, and told him the facts. I guess the President decided just to call it off."

Chilly pulled a letter out of a little oilskin pouch, and handed it to me. I could read Cherokee like a tribal elder, but the letter was written in legal English, most of which made no more sense to me than a chicken track. I could read names pretty well, though, and there was the President's name, right at the bottom: *Ulysses S. Grant.*

"I hope whatever killed that old man don't catch me on the way back," Chilly said.

He was a good deal more interested in getting home safe than he was in the fact that I held right in my hand a piece of paper signed by the greatest general that ever fought a war. Just seeing the name made me proud: I had been a loyal soldier of the Union army, and here I stood with an amnesty from my commander-in-chief.

Becca and May cooked Chilly Stufflebean a fine breakfast —there were biscuits, and corn on the cob, and ripe persimmons. Becca even gave him a big dish of clabber with cinnamon on it, as a special treat. But the cooking and the cinnamon was mostly wasted on Chilly. The thought of having to ride down the road where old White Sut's head was disturbed his appetite to the point that he could scarcely eat.

Then another lucky thing happened, which was that Frank Beck rode up with some mail in his saddlebags. He looked so relieved when I told him White Sut was dead that I thought he was going to cry from happiness. It annoyed Bec. She was of the opinion that you ought to mourn your kinfolk, no matter how rascally they were.

Later, though, Frankie told me that White Sut had threatened to kill him three times in a week, because Frank had poisoned his buzzard. Frank had recently taken up with Edna, who had been left at the mill when his brother Little Ray ran off with a younger whore. Edna particularly despised the buzzard; I guess the scabby old thing had taken to roosting on her windowsill. She told Frank she was leaving unless he did something about the buzzard, so Frank shot a possum and mashed some strong strychnine up inside it. When the buzzard ate the possum, it soon fell off its roost and died.

Once he figured out what had happened to his buzzard, White Sut laid plans to kill Frankie—a fact which he informed him of several times.

"White, he didn't make no idle threats," Frank told me. "I 'spect if that bear hadn't yanked his head off, I'd be dead by now."

His relief was so great that he offered to go dig the grave himself, leaving me with an idle morning before me. Even though all the facts were explained to him, Chilly Stufflebean was shaking so hard he couldn't cinch his saddle on securely. Finally, I told him I'd ride along with him to Tahlequah, to get him over the worst part of the road. I rook a rifle with me. White Sut's old bear was a free bear now, and bears can be cranky.

"I hope I don't have to serve no papers over here again," Chilly Stufflebean said, when we were nearly to Tahlequah. "The first time I come, there was that shootout. This time, I seen that head. I believe I'd prefer to live out my life in Fort Smith, Arkansas, if nobody minds."

The bear did not appear.

A month or two later, I heard that a bear with a collar on showed up in Mobeetie, Missouri, and run a bunch of Sunday folks out of a church. The bear ran off, and eluded all pursuers.

I thought to myself it must have been old White Sut's bear.

23

I FOUND OUT THAT BELLE BLUE, A PRACTICAL WHORE IF there ever was one, had written down the names of all the militiamen who stood up with me when the two marshals interrupted the horseracing that day in Dog Town. I guess in her business, she thought it was good policy to keep track of names. Whores have to do their best to stay in good with the law.

After Coon Rattersee's first raid on Ned Christie, Belle gave the list to Bird Doublehead, who was the new Cherokee judge in Tahlequah. I liked Bird Doublehead; he was a reasonable man, if a little slow in his thinking. If you ran into Judge Bird Doublehead when he wasn't expecting to see you, it would take him a minute or two just to think to say hello.

Bird Doublehead had some plain sense. He took the list of names over to Judge Parker himself, and the two judges agreed that an effort to arrest the whole militia wouldn't work. Most of the militiamen had brothers or sons who would feel the need to avenge them if they were fatally interfered with. Killing would follow killing, until the hills would run dark with blood.

So, the old brokenhearted Judge wrote to President Ulysses S. Grant, and the President decided to amnesty me. I guess he was afraid that if I ever got loose with the Cherokee Militia, I might try to refight the War.

Later, Belle Blue fell on hard times. I suppose most whores do, though some I've known have retired and married respectable. She lost most of her teeth, got religion, and took to singing at camp meetings. I sometimes helped her out with a dollar or two, if I happened to be in Dog Town.

After all, if Belle hadn't wrote down those militia names and taken them to Bird Doublehead, I wouldn't have my amnesty from President Ulysses S. Grant, who later died himself.

24

NED'S FORT WITHSTOOD THE FIRST SIX POSSES THAT CAME AT it. The marshals would make a big show, and shoot up most of their bullets on the first day. Then they'd camp in the woods for two or three days or a week, and yell at Ned to surrender. If they tried to approach too close, accurate rifle fire drove them back. Ned killed no more marshals—they soon learned to hide better—but he wounded several. A good percentage of the marshals around Fort Smith had knocked-down shoulders, or busted hips, from incautious behaviour while assaulting Ned's fort.

Every time I heard that a posse had gone after Ned, I felt like I ought to go and help him. The fact that me and the rest of the militia boys had got amnestied meant that the white law had more time to concentrate on Ned. In time, after they had suffered a few bad defeats, Ned became about the only person in the Going Snake District that the white law really wanted. Even the whiskeysellers seldom got harassed, in the years of Ned's war.

Finally, I went to Judge Bird Doublehead myself, and asked him what the chances were that President Grant might give

Ned an amnesty, too. After all, he was costing the government a whole lot more in marshaling salaries than I ever cost them.

Judge Bird Doublehead didn't have to think long about *that* matter.

"The President does not want to be bothered with any more news from the Going Snake," he told me bluntly.

"Well, how would you know that? Is your name Ulysses S. Grant?" I asked. It riled me that Bird Doublehead, whom I had often fished with, felt confident that he could speak for the President of the United States.

"No, it ain't, but I'm still in the right about this matter," Bird said.

"Why, I suppose," I replied. "You're a judge, and a judge can't be in the wrong."

"They can be wrong when the law's cloudy," Bird Doublehead informed me.

"What's cloudy about this situation?" I asked him. "Ned Christie is a fine citizen, and you know it."

"Yes, I like Ned," the Judge agreed.

"Then you ought to put in a word for him with the President," I told him.

But Bird Doublehead wouldn't do it. And that was that.

25

SEVERAL TIMES, I STARTED TO GO VISIT NED AND JEWEL. BUT Becca held me back.

"No. You stay away from Ned's," Becca told me.

I had just decided on the trip a few minutes before. I walked down to the lots and noticed my new bay mare looking frisky. The notion of a trip came to me, and visiting Ned Christie was the first thing I thought about. I saddled the mare, and walked back to the house to inform Bec of my plans. Then she hit me with the "no."

"What?" I asked, thinking I might have misheard. Maybe I had given her the impression that I was off on a drinking spree.

"No. You stay away from Ned's," Becca said, again. Not only did she use the same words twice; she used the same tone, too. Never before in our marriage had Rebecca given me an order, flat out. I didn't like the feel of it.

"Don't be telling me what I can't do," I told her, steaming a little. "Ned's my Keetoowah brother. If I want to go visit him, I will.

"Besides, our Jewel is married to him," I reminded her. "Why wouldn't I want to go visit my own daughter?"

Becca looked at me with a chill in her eye.

"Ned's in trouble, Zeke," she told me. "But you ain't, anymore. You're pardoned. Nobody's coming 'round trying to shoot you or hang you or arrest you. We're living here in peace. I'd like to keep it that way."

"Well, I'd like it, too, Bec—but Ned's a fellow warrior," I told her. "I can't desert him in his hour of need, and I can't desert our daughter."

"You got three children here. What about them?" she asked me, still with the chilly look.

"I'm not going away forever, I'm just going on a visit," I repeated, trying to keep my tone polite.

"If you're killed or hung, you'll be gone forever," she said.

I stopped talking, and so did Becca. We just stood there, looking at one another. I was set to go, and would have liked a word of good-bye, but Becca wouldn't soften. I got tired of looking at her, and mounted the bay mare. The mare acted like she might crow-hop if I wasn't careful with her.

Then Becca stepped off the porch, and caught my bridle rein. That was another thing she had never done.

"If you leave, *I* leave," she said. "I'm too old to be having the worries I have, when the law's after you and you're on the scout. I'm too old, Zeke. I won't have it."

I was dumbfounded. I never expected Becca to threaten me in that way. Then I remembered that she had left before.

"I won't come back, this time," she told me. "If you go to Ned's and get yourself mixed in this trouble again, I'll take the triplets and go. You can batch forever, if that's your mood."

I couldn't think of what to say. On the one hand, I was riled, though she was right about the law. They would be after me again, if I mixed in Ned's conflict. But Ned was my Keetoowah brother, and Jewel was my daughter—Becca's, too.

"What about Jewel? Just tell me that," I said. I thought if anything would turn her, it would be mention of Jewel. But

Becca's will, once she decided something, was like bois d'arc wood: you couldn't cut it, you couldn't break it, and you couldn't wear it down.

"Jewel chose the path of her husband," Becca said. "She's cleaving to her husband, like the Bible says she should. She's got the Lord, and she's got Ned. She don't need you, but *I* do . . . and so do the triplets."

"So you'd just leave her be?" I asked. "We lost one daughter up on that Mountain. Do you want me to stand by when there's a risk of losing another?"

"Yes," Becca informed me. "Jewel chose her man. Let her man care for her. You've got three children right here. They need you."

We stopped talking. Becca still held the reins of my mare.

"That's a damn stiff line," I told her. "Turn loose of my goddamn bridle."

She turned loose of the bridle, and walked back up on the porch. I was trying to decide whether she meant it or not; it might just be a bluff. But Becca went right on in the house, without looking at me again.

I sat on the mare about ten minutes, thinking Becca might come back out and continue the discussion. But she didn't come back out. Finally, I dismounted and went inside. Becca sat at the table. She didn't look up at me. The more I studied her, the less I thought she was running a bluff. Becca didn't play cards; it was against her religion. She didn't bluff. If she said a thing, she meant it.

"I don't enjoy taking orders from my wife," I told her. I sat down at the table across from her. She looked at me, and suddenly her eyes filled with tears.

"I can't bear it, Zeke! That's what I'm telling you!" she cried. "It ain't like I'm ordering you to go milk the cow, or telling you what harness to buy. It ain't . . . a thing . . . like that!"

I deplored a situation in which my wife would sit there crying at me, though that was the plain fact of the matter: there she sat, crying.

"I can't stand the fear of you dying," Becca said. "I'd rather live away from you, than have that fear in my mind every day."

I let Becca cry some, before I answered. When she was calmer, I tried to take her hand. But she yanked it away.

"Death's always a neighbour, Bec," I said. "I could walk up the creek to fish, and get et by White Sut's bear."

Becca tightened her lips, and got up from the table.

"You might kill a bear, but you can't kill all the marshals in Arkansas. That's the difference," Becca said. "You can't, and Ned can't, either."

"I don't know, he's killed a passel of them already," I told her. But she was gone out the back door, to her garden.

The last thing she said was the truest: I couldn't kill all the marshals in Arkansas, and neither could Ned. I pretended to dispute it, but I knew it was true. Sooner or later, Ned would have to give up to the white law—or else die by the gun.

That night on the porch, Becca said another thing that surprised me. Becca had taken to dipping a little snuff. Though it was against her Bible teachings, she did it anyway. The triplets were in the lots, trying to ride the milk-pen calf; Pete was snoozing next to her rocker.

"Ned Christie don't want your help, Zeke," Becca said, out of the blue.

"Of course he wants it. What would make you think he don't?" I asked.

"Because he's the kind of man that wouldn't," Becca said. "He's got that pride."

I tried to get her to explain what she meant, but she wouldn't. She dipped snuff, and rocked in her chair until the moon came out.

26

THEN, IN THE THIRD YEAR OF NED'S WAR, WHEN HE HAD crippled five posses and was a hero to all the tribes in the Territory—to the Seminole and the Chickasaw, the Cherokee, the Choctaw, and the Creek—she died on me, my Bec—died delivering a stillborn child.

It was the hardest blow of my life.

From the moment she knew the child was in her, Bec was afraid.

"I'm too old, Zeke," she told me. "It'll kill me, unless I'm lucky."

Rebecca wasn't lucky, and neither was the tiny little girl she carried. The birth came during a sleet storm; no doc could get there. May and me did our best, but still my Becca died. I believe the shock of the baby's death was what finished her, finally. When May told her the baby was stillborn, Becca just slumped back in the bed, and gave it up.

Linnie was so upset, she ran off into the woods and nearly froze. Minnie sat in the corner near the fireplace, and cried and cried. Willie cut his foot bad with an axe the very same day. He was cutting firewood, and the log was icy.

The ground was frozen too hard for grave digging, and so we had to put Becca and our baby girl in the smokehouse until there was a thaw.

It was in February when it happened.

I have been moody in my spirit, in the month of February, ever since.

27

IN THE SPRING OF THAT YEAR, NOT MORE THAN A MONTH after Becca died, a sixth posse from over the hills came at Ned. Old Judge Parker didn't order it; he had left the bench at the turn of the year. The new judge was named Josiah Crittenden, and I suppose he was a terror. He didn't like the notion of a lone Cherokee warrior defying the white law, so he sent fifteen men after Ned.

Luck was with Ned Christie, though, for a bitter blizzard struck. Ned and Jewel were snug inside their fort, but the possemen were exposed. Then, a second blizzard struck before the first one had time to thaw.

The Mountain was nothing but a ridge of ice. Seven or eight of the possemen lost toes to frostbite, and one even lost a foot. The possemen banged away at the cabin for over a week, accomplishing nothing. Ned fired three shots and wounded two of the possemen, one of them through the lung. The weather refused to moderate, and the posse finally gave up. Ned Christie had turned back the white law again.

When the weather did moderate, and the blooms of spring began to color up the meadows, I buried my beloved wife and daughter, and then decided I better go visit Ned and Jewel. I had sent word to Jewel about her mother, of course, but it was a terrible hard winter, and travel unpredictable, as that posse had found out.

Besides, people were afraid to get too near Ned's fort. I gave the news of Becca's death to several men, hoping one of them would eventually make the trip. I told Hunter Langley and Bic Acorn and Scot Mankiller, hoping one of them would run into Ned. But I had no sure report on the matter, and finally decided I better go myself. Jewel had a right to know that she had lost her mother, and I suppose I wanted to be with my oldest daughter and grieve a bit. The triplets were still young; they had each other, and had already bounced back, mostly, as children will.

But I wasn't young. I wanted to sit with Jewel, and talk about Becca. Jewel and me had memories we could share. I never spent much time remembering Becca when she was alive; there was always too much to do. Of course, there's always too much to do on a farm. When Bec was alive, I might skip out for a day or two, but I generally got the planting done when I needed to plant, and kept up with the work pretty well, with the help of old Sully Eagle.

With Becca gone, it was harder. Some days, I'd set out to do a chore and end up not doing it at all. I'd sit by the fire and smoke, or go up to the smokehouse and drink whiskey. On those days, the memories came over me like a flood.

Rather than drown in them, I decided to go see my Jewel. I had hired Bill Dutch to be my handyman while I was gone, and left the triplets with May. May had as much energy as they did, and could keep them corralled better than I could.

It wasn't just Jewel that I wanted to see—I had a serious hankering to see Ned, while I was about my grieving. I wanted to see what his thinking was on his situation, now that he had turned back six posses. The Cherokee Senate was due to start its new session in a couple of weeks. I wanted to talk politics with Ned, and then see if there was any way the Cherokee Nation could muster its forces and help him in his fight.

I stopped in Tahlequah on the way, procured the loan of a stout mule, and loaded it up with every kind of provision I could think of, including a few ribbons and a bright swatch of cloth for Jewel. With Ned not leaving the Mountain, I figured they might be running low on thumbtacks and baking soda and such.

By good luck, Tuxie Miller happened to be in town, getting a tooth pulled. It must have been a pretty bad tooth—Tuxie's jaw was as black as if someone had hit him with a brick. He yelled a good healthy yell when the dentist yanked the tooth out, too. It wasn't until he yelled, that I knew he was in town.

"If that mule wasn't loaded to the gunwales, I'd pile on a barrel of molasses," Tuxie said, when he walked up to me. "The younguns have been pestering me to bring home some sweetening, but I ain't got no way to carry a barrel of molasses."

"I guess you could rent your own mule," I suggested.

"Nope, Dale would never stand for the expense," Tuxie said, and he was right about that. Dale was known to keep a close clutch on the family purse.

"I'm surprised she let you squander money on a dentist," I told him. "She could have pulled that tooth by herself. All she would need is a good pair of pliers."

Tuxie ignored that point. He was the sort of man who didn't allow much jesting at the expense of his wife. I remembered that the old fool who ran the store had some sugarcane stalks stuck in a barrel—I suppose they had come up the river from Louisiana. I went back and bought twelve of them, for the Miller young ones. Sugarcane stalks were a lot easier to fit on my mule than a barrel of molasses would have been.

"I guess I ought to buy a stalk for Dale," Tuxie said.

"Why, no—buy her ribbon, Tuxie," I said.

The thought just made him look doubtful.

"What would Dale do with a ribbon?" he asked.

I let the matter drop. Twelve children, and the man still didn't know that women like ribbons. I wanted to talk to him a bit about Ned's situation on the ride up the Mountain, but the dentist had neglected to pack the tooth hole adequately. Every time Tuxie tried to converse, blood poured out of his mouth. He spent most of the ride home spitting.

"Dern, Tuxie. If a stranger picked up our trail, he'd think somebody gored an ox, from all the blood you're spilling," I told him.

"I wish I owned an ox. It would ease the plowing," was Tuxie Miller's reply.

28

THE MILLER YOUNG ONES GNAWED UP THAT SUGARCANE LIKE beavers in a lumberyard. By the time we got home, Tuxie had bled all over himself, a sight that annoyed Dale.

"Get them overalls off, I've got to wash them or that blood will never come out," she said. The tooth hole was still bleeding, but Dale soon stopped that by poking cotton in it with a knitting needle. The woman gave me but a scant hello. I believe she meant to hold Polly Beck against me until the end of my days. But she set me a place at the table, when suppertime came, and allowed me to share the meal, which was beefsteak and gravy. They had built themselves a log house this time, but hadn't quite finished chinking the logs. That was how Dale occupied herself after supper, while Tuxie and me smoked. The children were as bright eyed as little coons, and every single one of them took after their mother.

Dale finally softened a little, when I told her of my loss.

"That's hard, Zeke," she said. "And just as you two were getting back to being married folks again."

"Yep, just as we were," I admitted. "I don't know if Jewel knows Becca died. Do you ever see her or Ned?"

Tuxie had nodded off by this time, tipped sideways in his rocking chair. I guess having that tooth pulled wore him out.

"They're living a hell, Ned and Jewel," Dale told me. "If there's to be any heaven in it for them, it's not in the here and now."

"I mean to petition the Senate to find some way to get the law to leave them alone," I told her. I rarely discuss Senate business with anyone, but the circumstances were desperate—and Dale Miller was forceful in her thoughts—more forceful than her husband, who was asleep anyway.

"You better see Ned about it first," she told me.

"Why, I will, Dale, if he'll see me. That's one of the reasons I came," I replied.

Dale didn't answer, nor did she explain her remark. She was still chinking logs when I finally stretched out by the fire and went to sleep.

29

THE MILLER CHILDREN WERE MANNERLY. DALE AND TUXIE had seen to that. Every single one of them thanked me for the sugarcane, before I rode off the next morning.

Dale was dipping her chickens in a washtub. She had procured some solution that was supposed to rid them of mites. The chickens didn't appreciate her concern. The ones that had been dipped were running around squawking, and the ones that hadn't were doing their best to elude the children, whose chore it was to fetch them over to Dale.

"Many thanks for the supper, Dale," I said, walking over to the washtub. Dale was dipping chickens two at a time. She had two hens in each hand, when I approached her, but she looked up at me as if she might have an opinion to convey.

"You ought to bring Jewel out with you, if you can," Dale said.

I was startled by the comment. Dale Miller was all family, and it was a surprise to have her tell me I ought to persuade Jewel to come out. I remembered what Becca said when we had our quarrel. Jewel had chosen her path; it was her duty to cleave to her husband, as Dale had cleaved to Tuxie—twelve children's worth.

"It'll come to that anyway, Zeke," Dale said. "There's talk that they're bringing a cannon, next time they come after Ned."

"A cannon? Up here?" I asked. "Now it would take some fine mules, and not a few of them, to drag a cannon up this rocky old hill."

"Mules ain't scarce in Arkansas, Zeke," Dale said. She looked sad when she said it; I expect Dale had come to care for my Jewel.

"Why bring a cannon after one man?" I said. "It's a dern long way to drag a cannon. That would mean a passel of expense."

Even as I said it, though, I remembered the War. The generals on either side—Lee, or Grant, or Sherman—took cannon where they wanted cannon. Terrain didn't daunt them.

The shock to me was that the white law would go to such trouble and such expense for one man: Ned Christie.

Tuxie ambled over, a little pale from his tooth removal, and I sounded him on the rumour.

"There's a marshal named L. P. Isabel who led that last posse," Tuxie said. "They come by here on their way out, hoping Dale would help them take off their frostbit toes."

"And did she?" I inquired.

"Why, yes. She took off twelve toes, mostly with the sheep shears," Tuxie said. Dale was too busy dipping chickens to contribute to the discussion.

"Good Lord! Twelve?" I said.

"Yep—a dozen toes," Tuxie told me. "Frostbit toes smell worse than putrid meat. But old Isabel was riled. He vowed to get Ned if it was the last thing he does. He said he was coming back, and aimed to bring a cannon."

"Good Lord," I said, again. It made me understand why Dale thought I ought to bring Jewel out. Cannonballs are no respecters. They'll smash women as well as men, if a woman happens to be in the vicinity when the cannonball hits.

"Do you think Ned's fort can withstand a cannon?" I asked Tuxie. In the War, Tuxie had been at Vicksburg, and I supposed he had ample experience of cannon from that siege.

"Well, one cannonball won't knock it down," he said. "But if they bring a wagon full of cannonballs, I expect it's the end for Ned."

"Maybe he'd best slip out," I said. "Ned's a fine woodsman. An army couldn't find him if he went on the scout."

Tuxie just shook his head.

"Ned ain't like he used to be, not since they shot out his eye and abused Jewel," Tuxie said.

Tuxie choked up after he made that statement. I didn't know whether his tooth had bled into his throat, or whether some memory had caught him—maybe a memory of happier days, when he and Ned had hunted together and roamed the hills near their boyhood homes.

"Ned's all fight now. It's what he waits for," Tuxie said. "He won't be leaving that fort, unless they blast him out."

"I guess Dale's right, then," I said. "If they're planning to bring a cannon up the ridge, I expect I ought to try and bring Jewel out, till this lets up."

Tuxie shook his head, turned around, and walked over to pick up a jug that had once contained Dale's mite-killing liquid.

"It won't let up," he said. "And Jewel won't come."

"I'd better go see for myself, then," I told him.

The Miller children were scattered all over the hill, trying to chase down the last dry chickens, when I rode away.

30

NED AND JEWEL WERE PLANTING THEIR GARDEN, WHEN I came into the clearing. They had plowed a big circle around the fort, so they could get to cover quick, if a posse showed up while they were planting. What it meant, too, was that fresh food would be handy, just a few steps out of the fort, if they got besieged. They could always sneak out at night and gather beans and spuds, or pull a few ears of corn.

It was a smart arrangement, and yet, the sight of it chilled me. Tuxie had been right: Ned and Jewel were not likely to leave. They had water and food and a good strong fort; it would take a determined posse with time to spare—several months' time, probably—to flush them out.

My Jewel was pale, and had lost considerable more flesh since last I had seen her. The young curve of her cheek was gone; she reminded me so much of her mother that it gave me a start.

I guess Ned sniffed me or something, for he had his Winchester in his hand, waiting when I rode into the clearing. He was gaunt as a hawk, and his sightless eye had filmed over. Jewel's eyes lit a little when I rode up, but neither of them smiled. I guess they were through smiling, Jewel and Ned, which was a pity. Ned had such a fine, deep laugh, in his carousing days.

"I'm glad I ain't the one that will have to weed this garden," I told them both, when I dismounted. "My back don't bend as easy as it used to, and a garden this big will require a passel of bending."

Jewel hugged me, and Ned shook my hand. But after that,

we just stood there, not knowing what to make of one another. Jewel was my own daughter, and Ned my oldest friend—and yet, we seemed all but strangers, the two of them were so changed.

I suppose it was living with just themselves that made Jewel and Ned awkward to visit with. They knew what to do with enemies, but had stood distant so long from family and friends that they could not enter back into the normal round of life: a life where goods were bought and sold, and horses raced, and babies made and born, and quilts patched by womenfolk and such.

I can josh most folks into some little kind of conversation, but I had hard going with Ned and Jewel. It was as if they were braced together in silence, like saints of the church. I remembered what Becca had said about Ned not wanting my help, and realized, now, that she had been right. Jewel did her best to be polite; she asked me if I wanted coffee. Ned gave me the Keetoowah greeting; then he propped his rifle against the wall of the fort and went back to planting spuds.

I accepted the coffee, mostly as a means of getting a private word with Jewel.

"Jewel, did you know about your ma?" I asked, when we were inside.

Jewel nodded, and looked down.

"Scot Mankiller told me," she said.

"That's Ma gone, and Liza, too," she said. "I expect I'll soon be seeing them in heaven, if those white men don't let Ned be."

Jewel looked grave when she said it, but she didn't look scared.

I saw, then, that it wasn't going to be the kind of visit I had hoped for. Ned hadn't offered to unsaddle my horse; Jewel hadn't asked me if I planned to spend the night. It wasn't meanness in their attitude. It just seemed like it hadn't registered that they had a visitor.

I thought I ought to speak my piece, at least to my daughter, while I had her alone. Her eyes kept looking out the door, seeking Ned—she seemed anxious that something might happen if she let him out of her sight.

Riding along the ridge from the Millers' on the way to

Ned's, I was full of words I meant to say to my Jewel, and I had another set of words I wanted to say to Ned.

But now that I was standing three feet from Jewel, looking her in the face, all the words I had been thinking of saying blew out of my thoughts like leaves in a dust devil. Jewel was a woman now, and she was doing exactly what her mother thought she ought to do, which was to cleave to her husband. News of the cannon that might come with the next posse wasn't going to matter to her. She could hardly be at peace, unless she could locate Ned with her eyes.

I couldn't ask Jewel to leave with me. She would think I was daft. I felt like a fool for having come with such an expectation. It seemed like a reasonable hope when I was still in town, or at the Millers', or even at my place. But Ned and Jewel were at war now, and ways of living that normal people expected didn't mean a thing to them. I had been in the War, myself; when I was a fighting Bluecoat, I forgot the normal things, too, except for drinking whiskey. Stuck way off on some guard post in the fog, with one or two boys for company, I'd forget the horseracing, and the baby making, and the quilt patching, and the like. All I could think about at such times was the Rebs. Were they coming? And if they weren't, when *would* they—and how many?

But I volunteered for that War, because I wanted to fight the Rebs. It was bastards from Georgia and Carolina and the South that herded up the Cherokees and the other Indian people, and marched them along the Trail of Tears, where my ma died, and many another. I had good reason to fight the traitors and the killers that herded us away from our homes and our farms, taking away nearly everything we owned, breaking our hearts and our spirits, and causing us to die by the thousands on that march.

Jewel had no such reasons for being in a war. She had come home with her husband to bear children and care for a family. She hadn't courted trouble, but here she stood, in a fort, of all things, with boxes and boxes of bullets stacked against one wall. My daughter Jewel seemed farther away than her own mother—and her own mother was dead.

"Jewel, I don't know that I could bear it if I lost you, too," I blurted.

A sag came on Jewel, when I said it. She looked down again,

and turned away. She started for the door, but she stopped and turned back, taking my hand for a moment.

"Ned got Preacher Joe to come," she said. "The two of us are married proper now, Pa."

"Well, that is one good thing, honey," I said.

But she was already gone out the door.

31

I WAS RAISED TO BE USEFUL, SO I PITCHED IN WITH THE PLANT-ing. Ned looked a little startled when I got myself a shovel and joined in the work.

"You ain't the only man in the world who knows how to plant a spud, you know," I said, when he threw the startled look at me.

Ned kept a milk cow staked to a long grazing rope, moving the stake every day so the cow would have fresh grass. I didn't see any pigs; I guess they butchered them and salted them down, so they would have plenty of meat inside if the whites showed up in force.

Ned seemed to prefer to work in silence, so I obliged him for a while. I unsaddled my own horse and put him out to graze by the milk cow. In the afternoon, we walked over to the creek, washed the dirt off our hands, and took a long drink. I didn't mind the working, but I felt like I was going to bust if I didn't say something about the situation Ned was in.

So, I just came out with it.

"They say they're bringing a cannon, next time a posse comes," I informed him. "I'm surprised the authorities would drag a cannon this far, but I guess that L. P. Isabel is a deter-mined fellow."

"He froze three toes himself, I expect it riled him," Ned replied. "Dale Miller cut them off with the sheep shears."

He nearly broke down and smiled, at the thought of the marshal's discomfort, and Dale's brass.

"Are you determined to die, then?" I asked. I knew I had best seize my chance for a discussion while enjoying a cool drink of water.

"Nope, ain't aiming to," Ned replied. "They've come at us six times, and not made a dent in this fort. They can't get close enough to burn us out, and I doubt these logs would burn, even if I let them build a bonfire."

"Yes, but what about the cannon?" I asked him. "They'll make a dent in the fort, if they bring a cannon."

Ned *did* smile, then.

"I'll worry about that when I see the cannon," he said. "I doubt they've got the patience to blast me out. Even with a cannon, it might take a month."

"Well, now, that depends on the cannoneer," I said. "I've known gunners that could put a cannonball down a chimney at six hundred yards."

"Yes, but I doubt any of them fellows are available in Arkansas," he said.

"I think it's a risk," I told him.

Ned shrugged, and started walking back toward the garden.

"These possemen ain't patient," he said. "They come hell-bent-for-leather, and shoot every gun they've got as fast as they can shoot, until they bust the barrels. Then they wait for a week, griping, and getting drunk. Then the weather gets cold, or else it gets hot, or else it gets rainy, and the whiskey runs out. About that time, I manage to wing one or two of them, which is usually enough to make them go on home."

"It might not be that easy forever," I told him.

"I don't know much about forever," he said. "It's been that way six times."

Ned almost started having a normal discussion again, and then he remembered that he was done with normal discussions. He drew back.

"You ain't going to live forever yourself, Zeke," he added, giving me a stern look.

I thought I might as well say my piece about the Militia, while Ned was at least listening.

"I've got up a fine militia, Ned," I told him. "It's Keetoowah brothers of ours that's in it. We put twenty-five well-armed men in the field the last time they sent marshals after me. The result was, it turned them back, and me and most of the boys got pardoned.

"They know they ain't got the manpower to arrest twenty-five of us," I went on. "So, they gave up. But there's just one of you . . . where you're concerned, they won't give up."

"I'd say they made a bad choice, then," Ned replied. "I

expect they could whittle down two dozen of the boys easier than they can take me."

"Why, Ned, that's vain," I told him. "What makes you think you can outfight twenty-five men?"

"The fact that I got a fort, and they ain't," he said. "A fort's proof against ambushes, and ambushes is what you have to fear."

That was the end of the conversation, as far as Ned Christie was concerned. I started talking about the Senate, and how I thought I could win a vote on an order for his protection. My plan was to have five or six militiamen take turns helping Ned guard the fort, but before I even finished describing my plan, Ned shook his head.

From the way he looked at me, I knew he'd had enough of my blab. But I'm a terrier, when I'm talking. I won't be shook off that easy.

"You should listen to me, now!" I told him, getting louder. "I'm not only your friend, I'm the father of your wife. The white law won't give up. It's got no reason to. There'll always be young fools willing to take a chance on killing a famous outlaw, and there'll always be governors or judges who'll deputize them."

Ned went back to his gardening, as if I wasn't even talking.

"Another thing is, they know where you are," I went on. "If you was willing to go on the scout, you might have a chance. These woods will hide you till you're an old man. Jewel can live at home, and you can slip in and see her when it's clear."

That seemed to anger him. He whirled towards me, with fight in his face.

"My wife will live where I live," he said. "I'll either protect her, or die in the effort."

A little later, I saddled my horse and got ready to leave. I think Jewel would have asked me to stay, for seeing me seemed to bring back memories of a time when families visited freely. But the memories didn't come quick enough—or strong enough. Jewel was half willing to ask me; maybe, if I hadn't irked him, Ned would have been half willing, too. But they had lost the habit of society.

When the shadows began to stretch out from the ridge and it was time to quit the hoeing, Ned and Jewel stood together again, and nobody asked. Ned shook my hand hard, as I was leaving, and Jewel hugged me hard, too. If I had asked, I'm sure they would have spread me a pallet for the night and made me a meal.

The truth was, I felt too peculiar to ask. One minute, I was glad I had come; the next minute, I regretted making the trip. I felt like I'd visited two ghosts. Tailcoat Jones had done a better job than he knew, before he drowned with his whore. He hadn't killed Ned or Jewel, but he drove them from the common walks, and the child they should have been raising in happiness was lost to a hillside rape.

I felt so peculiar about the matter that I rode all night, though I was dead tired from trying to show Ned that I could plant as many potatoes as he could.

I'd seen Ned and Jewel, but I hadn't reached them, not as I could have reached them before the Tailcoat Jones attack. I had to doubt that I'd ever see either one of them alive again; and that's a terrible doubt, considering that Jewel was my oldest living child.

"At least you tried, Zeke," Arch Scraper said, when I described the visit to him. I was eager to talk to someone, and Arch was the first person I met.

"Tried, and failed," I replied.

Tried and failed would be my feeling about that visit for many years to come. I told myself many a time that I ought to have done more.

Then I realized it was one of those hard games where you're beat before you start. Ned Christie didn't want my help, or anybody's help. Jewel didn't want it, either—not by then.

What they wanted was what they had: their fort, each other, and their war.

32

I RODE HOME, AND MARRIED MAY. SHE WAS BUT NINETEEN, and skinny-legged as a killdeer, but she made as merry a wife as any man could want. To the triplets, she was like a sister, before and after she became a wife to me.

I had taken to reading the Bible some, the same book Becca

had thrust on me in the Tahlequah jail. There was foolishness in it, and way too many names, but I noticed that all the old prophets and patriarchs had themselves wives. I felt it was no slight to Becca's memory that I took May as my new wife. I am not a monk, and cannot abide without a woman to lay abed with. Some would say May was too young to be made my wife, but I dispute that—and besides, there's nothing in Bec's old Bible about the age of wives, nothing that I could locate, anyway.

The proof is in the pudding, they say, and the pudding in our case was a fine baby boy May produced a mere nine months after I'd had Preacher Joe in to marry us.

To my surprise, May fought me to a standstill on the name. She wanted to name the baby William, after her grandfather, but I insisted on naming him Ned, after my friend Ned Christie, the great warrior of the Cherokee people. He had stood off the white law for more than three years, when our little Ned was born.

Then, to my vexation, May started calling the baby Billy anyway. May might have been young, but what a will she had! She would resist to the end, if she wasn't allowed her way.

"His name ain't Billy, it's Ned!" I told her, one day when I caught her using Billy.

"Don't you forget it, either, May Proctor!" I went on. I was getting fairly riled that she would be bold enough to defy me in such a matter.

"He's gotta have a nickname, don't he?" she asked. May tended to colour up in the cheeks when her temper flared. She was colouring up pretty good when she looked at me.

"His name is Ned, and that's his only name!" I insisted. "A Cherokee warrior don't need any other name but his own."

May didn't answer, but she was looking at the baby as if she was passing a secret to him. I knew she meant to call him Billy again, the moment I was out of earshot.

I went off my head for a minute, and shook May like a terrier shakes a rat.

"You'll call him Ned, by God!" I told her. "If I catch you calling him Billy again, I'll slap your cheek and give you old bully hell!"

But then the triplets started calling him Billy, and the hired help, too. Billy was the name that stuck—not Ned. I guess

May had her way that time, though it's a mystery to me how she got it.

By the time the boy was five, I was calling him Billy myself.

I've pondered it, and the only notion I could come up with was that the boy wasn't meant to have a warrior's name. He grew up to be so shortsighted that he couldn't count his own fingers, not with his arm stuck straight out in front of him. The glasses the eye doc fitted him with were thick as a plate. He was good with figures, though. He could do sums in his head that I couldn't have got correct if I had a month.

I held the name business against May. It was a bone we fought over time and time again, whenever either one of us felt cranky.

"I thought I ought to get to name my firstborn son," I told her. "But, by God, I didn't!"

"Billy ain't your firstborn son—Willie is," May reminded me.

"So thanks to your damn stubbornness, we've got two Bills in the family," I pointed out.

"Billy was *my* firstborn son!" May retorted. "I suppose I had as good a right to name him as you."

I took no part in the naming, after that. One of our girls was nearly six months old before May got around to telling me her name. I was sheriff of the Going Snake District by then, and was on the road a lot, rounding up various rascals who were trying to elude the law.

She was a bright-eyed little girl, too. She was just beginning to gum bones and try to crawl around, when I come in and happened to notice her on the floor, making straight for the fireplace.

"What's that little one's name?" I asked.

"Dorothy Ruth," May told me. She was cooking at the time.

"Why, that's two fine names wasted on one tot," I told her. "Why not save the Ruth for the next little gal that comes along?"

"Her name's Dorothy Ruth, Zeke," May informed me. And that was that.

33

THE FALL AFTER MY VISIT TO NED AND JEWEL, WHEN THE frost on the Mountain was hard enough to leave ice in the wagon ruts, the last battle of Ned's war was fought to its bloody conclusion. L. P. Isabel led fourteen marshals up the Mountain; a coloured man drove the mule team that pulled the cannon.

Rather than come through the Going Snake, where folks would have noticed them and given Ned the alert, the marshals dragged that blessed cannon nearly forty miles out of their way, in order to come at Ned from the eastern road, where there were fewer neighbours.

It was wasted effort. Arley Silk was up on the eastern reaches of the Mountain on a deer hunt, and saw the posse coming. He raced ahead of the bunch and informed Ned. The difference it made was that Ned had time to get his milk cow into the fort, along with sufficient fodder to keep her inside for a while.

Arley told me later that he tried to get Ned to run, or at least to let him bring Jewel out, from fear of what the cannon might do. But Ned and Jewel both refused to leave their home. According to Arley, the two of them were as cool as if they were on their way to a barn dance or a church picnic.

Ned did question Arley about how big the cannon was. When he heard it was just a small one, he shrugged off the threat.

This time, the posse didn't bother to request Ned's surrender before they started firing. They announced their arrival with a cannon shot. The ball sailed completely over the fort, and damaged a tree stump a hundred yards on.

Right then, the marshals realized what Ned Christie had suspected when he told Arley Silk to stop worrying about the cannon and get along home. The posse contained several men who had been around cannon during the War, but none of them were gunners, and their skills with the weapon were slight.

Besides that, they had only brought fourteen cannonballs. I guess they figured that if they could just thunk a ball or two into the fort, the walls would fall in and Ned would come stumbling out and offer himself to the hangman.

It was poor planning, of course. Six of the fourteen cannon-balls missed the fort completely. Several of them tore holes in Ned's garden—he had long since gathered in the vegetables by then—and a few just sailed on into the brush beyond the clearing. One I know of was found by a peddler nearly twenty years after the battle. It's on display in Tulsa, I believe.

Eight cannonballs hit some part of the fort, but most of them hit low. They dented the bottom logs a little, but made no impression on the structure. Three hit it square, and did some damage to the outer logs, but no wall fell or was penetrated. When the posse had used up its last cannonball, Ned, Jewel, and the milk cow were still inside the fort, snug as bugs in a rug.

So far, Ned had not even bothered to fire at the possemen. Respect for his marksmanship was one reason for the poor job the marshals did with the cannon.

Later, when I visited the site of the battle and saw how little damage those fourteen cannonballs had done to Ned's fort, I figured Ned himself must have had a good laugh at the antics of this last posse. Here they had dragged a cannon over one hundred miles, and yet had only thought to bring fourteen cannonballs, though more than half the posse—including Marshal Isabel—had been in on the earlier assaults and knew what a sturdy fort they had to try and knock down.

I have no doubt that L. P. Isabel and the rest were at their wit's end—the ones that *had* wits, at least. They were all anxious to reap glory by bringing in Ned Christie—or else bringing him down—and there they were, out of cannonballs, with Ned safe as ever.

The spirits of all the great Cherokee warriors must have been proud of Ned Christie, that day. Even the white man's cannon hadn't been able to blast him out of his fort.

34

MILO CREEKMORE, THOUGH A LIMPING CRIPPLE, HAD COME with Isabel and the others. It was a painful journey for a man with a knocked-down hip, but Milo made it because he was convinced that this time, the posse had the firepower to bring out their man.

"We didn't just bring the cannon," Milo told me. We were talking about the battle a few months later. "A cannon can go off in its aim, though L.P. didn't think so. He had himself a fine fit when we used up that last ball, and Ned was still inside."

"Who'd he cuss the loudest? The cannon, or Ned?" I inquired.

"The Judge," Milo said, which surprised me. "He's right, too. That new judge don't have no more sense than a beetsie bug."

"I wouldn't know about that, Milo," I replied. "I have had very few opportunities to converse with beetsie bugs, and so far, I ain't talked to that new judge at all."

"Well, it was Crittenden who forced us to bring the dern cannon," Milo informed me. "He thought if we made that kind of show, Ned would give up. I knew better, and L.P. knew better, and most of the boys knew better. None of us wanted to drag that heavy son-of-a-bitch along."

It was a story that would echo through the Cherokee hills for years. I'm an old man now, and I still hear it in barber shops and general stores: that posse dragged a cannon all over Indian Territory, and then had not a man who could shoot it accurate.

Many a Cherokee warrior has gone up against the white posses and won, but Ned Christie, to this day, is the only one to stand down a cannon. That's one reason his name will live forever among the Cherokee people.

"It's a dern good thing we thought to bring that dynamite," Milo went on.

"Yep. The dynamite finished it," I said.

"We'd have never took him without it," Milo replied.

"That's my belief, too," I said.

35

DONNY GREASE, AGED EIGHTEEN AND RIDING WITH HIS FIRST posse, was the man who got the job of planting the dynamite up against Ned's fort.

It was pitch-dark the second night of the siege. The cannon-balls had been used up, and L. P. Isabel was mad enough to bite a hydrophobic dog, but Donny Grease still didn't want to do the deed.

"I just come along on this posse because I owe money on a mule," the boy said. "This dynamite could go off any time and blow me to kingdom come.

"And if that don't happen, Ned Christie will shoot me," he added.

Milo Creekmore said the boy was shaking so hard he nearly dropped the dynamite when L.P. shoved the sticks into his hand.

"Son, it's so dark, an owl couldn't draw a bead on you," L.P. told him. "Wiggle on over there, and do it."

Donny Grease started off on his belly, and then realized he didn't have any matches to light the fuse. He wiggled back, and borrowed some from Johnny Copeland.

"It's a heavy dew," he said, when he came crawling back. "I'm as wet as if I crawled through the creek."

"You better keep that fuse dry, boy, or you *will* get shot," L.P. informed him. "Hurry up now, before it gets light."

The boy done his job, too. Milo said it was still dim when the dynamite exploded and blew the west wall off the fort.

Jewel had lingered in bed after Ned got up and went down-stairs to light the lamp. She didn't sleep well with white men on the Mountain; I expect she was too afraid that what had happened to her once might happen to her again.

She was halfway down the stairs, when the blast came. It was like a cyclone took her and flung her across the fort. Jewel didn't regain consciousness until the middle of the afternoon, at which time she couldn't hear out of either one of her ears. Her hearing finally came back in the left ear, but never came back in the right. She was deaf in her right ear for the rest of her life.

36

NED LIVED THROUGH THE BLAST—LIVED THROUGH IT, AND came running out of the hole in that fort, with his two .44 pistols blazing. The possemen were charging by then, and Ned was firing at them with both barrels. They say he raised a high Cherokee war cry, maybe in hopes of spooking the horses.

Donny Grease was crawling for dear life on his belly, trying to wiggle back to a patch of dry cornstalks, the only nearby cover that offered him any hope. The first he saw of tall Ned Christie was when Ned came racing through the gloom and smoke and jumped right over him, making for the same cornstalks. It's certain Ned didn't know he was jumping over a posseman, or Donny Grease wouldn't have lived to tell the tale.

Donny raised up his pistol, and shot. The bullet entered Ned's brain, killing him in midstride.

The great warrior of the Cherokees died in the dawn light, by his own corn patch.

Some of the possemen didn't accept that Ned Christie, the man they had hounded and hunted for four long years, was truly dead. Tuxie said when he and Dale got there, half the possemen still had their guns in their hands, twitchy smiles on their faces. When the coroner examined Ned's body in Fort Smith, he counted twenty-two bullet wounds. Twenty-one of them were shot into him after he was done killed.

Ned was stone dead, and propped up on a door—but the marshals still had their guns out. I guess the fools thought he might come back alive and attack them still.

L. P. Isabel asked Tuxie if the dead man was really Ned. One of the possemen even had the notion that Ned Christie might have escaped and made it into the hills.

"It's him, and you goddamn rascals killed him," Tuxie told them, tears in his eyes. The sight of his friend, shot by more than twenty bullets, caused a heavy sadness to come upon him. For a moment, the sadness was so heavy, Tuxie told me, he could scarcely lift his feet.

It was over: Ned was dead, just as they had all predicted.

But predicting it and seeing it with his own eyes were two different things.

"Ned Christie was my lifelong friend," Tuxie told them.

Donny Grease was practically in shock. I think it was a wonder to him, that he had been the one to kill the famous warrior.

"They shot and shot," Donny Grease told Tuxie, bewilderment in his voice. "I never shot but that once. The last thing I expected in my life was to be the man that killed Ned Christie." He would say it again, a thousand times, at barbecues and fish fries, to newspapermen and gossips and wide-eyed children, down the years, through the long course of his life.

Then Dale chimed in.

"Cover up his body. It's not a thing for his wife to see, if she's still alive," Dale told them, blunt as ever. "You done your job, now it's time to be respectful of the man."

The men of the posse were quick to heed Dale Miller's reprimand, you can bet. They covered Ned's body decently.

"Good Lord," Milo Creekmore said. "We're so dern het up, we plumb forgot about Mrs. Christie."

Later, Milo told me it was a thing that bothered his conscience for the rest of his life. He ran into the fort with Dale Miller, while the others put Ned's body in a wagon for transport to Fort Smith. They found Jewel unconscious on the floor. They pulled her out, and laid her on a blanket. But she had swallowed a lot of smoke, like Ned had in that first fire.

For a time, they feared for her life.

Dale Miller told me she first thought it was an earthquake, when the dynamite blast slapped across the hills that morning. She had been in an earthquake once, while passing through Illinois when she was a mere girl. Ever since, she had had a powerful fear of quaking ground. She was milking her brindle cow, and Tuxie was carrying a bucket of slops to the pigpen, when the big noise hit. The rooster had been crowing, the pigs grunting, and the morning birds making a racket. They had heard each of the fourteen cannonballs being fired the first day, but the sound of the dynamite made that little cannon pop seem like a firecracker. The dynamite was louder than a hundred cannons.

What Tuxie remembered was how the barnyard, always so

noisy at first light, with chickens complaining and pigs grunting for their slop, got quiet as midnight, the morning the Fort Smith posse used dynamite to blow up Ned Christie's fort.

The Millers' brindle milk cow was so affected by the blast that she didn't let her milk down again for three days.

37

NED CHRISTIE'S WAR WAS OVER. OUR BRAVE NED WAS NO more.

By evening, news of Ned's death had spread across the whole of the Going Snake District, and on into the rest of the Cherokee Nation. The Cherokee people knew that their warrior hawk had passed into the spirit land; men and women sat on their porches and cried. For years afterward, folks would talk about what they had been doing when they first heard the terrible news.

Frank Beck was the one who told me. I was in the middle of birthing a heifer calf at the time. My right arm was bloody to the shoulder from reaching in to try and turn the calf so it could slip on out.

Frank tied his horse, walked over, and told me Ned was murdered.

I felt like Victor Horsefly had pitched an anvil on me, when I heard that they'd finally got Ned.

"The goddamn marauders!" I said—but the moment was critical—I still had my arm in the cow, and could not stop my work. I felt a powerful need to sit.

"I'll take over the calving for you, Zeke. I know you're upset," Frankie Beck told me.

"Aw, hell, I'm already bloody," I told him. Though it was a fine, neighbourly offer, I never met a Beck who knew anything about livestock. I turned and turned, and then the calf slipped on out, healthy and soon on its feet. May came to the well with me, and helped wash off the blood.

Later, Frankie and me took a jug up to the smokehouse and drank far into the night. I told more stories about Ned Christie than I even knew I remembered, and the stories multiplied upon themselves as the night wore on.

We had some fine times together, me and Ned, in the short years of his life.

I was right in the middle of a story about me and Ned on a deer hunt—while hunting deer, Ned always insisted on using the bow and arrow—when, to my surprise, Frank Beck started to cry.

"It's Davie, Zeke. He's gone now, too," Frank told me. "If any more of us dies, I'll be a goddamned orphan!"

I hadn't given a thought to wild Davie Beck in a number of months.

"He was digging a mine somewheres in Colorado, and the dirt collapsed on him and smothered him out!" Frank said.

"Why, you mean Davie's smothered?" I said. I thought it best not to remind him that I had done my best to strangle Davie with a handcuff chain that day in the courtroom in Tahlequah. Frank was grieving for his brother, and I was grieving for my lifelong friend, shedding my own measure of tears.

It was no time to be bringing up them old disputes.

38

FRANK TOLD ME THE MILLERS HAD BROUGHT JEWEL HOME with them and were caring for her. The report was that she couldn't hear at all.

Jewel was deaf, but the sadder part was that she had come slightly unhinged in her mind. I had acquired a light buggy in a trade with Little Dan Bobtail, and I drove over to Tuxie's to fetch my daughter home.

Dale saw me coming, and met me down by the chicken yard. The Millers had enough chickens by then to start a hen business.

"Well, Dale, how is my girl?" I inquired.

"She's poorly, Zeke," Dale told me. "She ain't sleeping so good. She's laid awake the past two nights, tense as a wire. She may get over this, and she may not."

"But she's a young woman yet, Dale," I told her. "Young folks, they can get over most anything, if they live."

"I hope you're right," Dale said. She looked doubtful about the matter.

Jewel was sitting in a rocking chair, covered with a soft blanket, when I came in and bent over to hug her. She lifted her eyes to me, and recognized me right away. Tears formed in her eyes, but she didn't speak.

"We're going home, darlin'," I told her, hugging her tight and squeezing her hand. "Your pa's gonna take you home."

I felt a clench in my stomach when I looked into Jewel's face. Her features were young, but her eyes reminded me of my mother's eyes. I was but seven years old when we walked the Trail of Tears up from Georgia, but I'll never forget the look in my mother's eyes the day we were wrenched from our home by President Jackson's army. It scared me, seeing the same look in my own daughter's eyes, so many years later. My mother never recovered from that loss; I feared my own daughter wouldn't recover from hers.

When it was time to leave, Tuxie walked down with me to the pond and helped me water the buggy horses.

"Jewel can't hear a thing," Tuxie remarked. "I don't think it's soaked in yet that Ned's been killed."

"It ain't soaked into me either, Tuxie, and I heard the news plain from Frank Beck," I said.

I turned, and looked back towards Tuxie's house, where my sorrowful daughter waited.

"You have to give things like that a little time," I told him.

EPILOGUE

Later Years in the
Going Snake District,
As Remembered By
Ezekiel Proctor

ONCE THE WHEEL IS BROKEN, IT CANNOT AGAIN BE BOUND UP right, is a saying from the Book, I believe. But whether it's from the Book or not, it proved true of my Jewel.

I took her home that very evening in my new light buggy. She went back to the room she had resided in as a maiden girl and lived in it thirty-two more years.

Jewel's hearing came back a little, but her mind was off its hinge and could not be fixed. The fact that Ned Christie was dead never did soak in.

Whenever a horseman would ride up to the farm, Jewel would colour as if from a fever and run out the door, thinking it was Ned.

Over and over I explained to her that our Ned had been killed back on the Mountain by an Arkansas posse. Though it was the truth, in Jewel's mind it didn't take hold.

"Ned's on the scout, Pa," she would say to me. We might be in the chicken yard, or working in the garden, and Jewel would say it. I suppose in her mind, that was where he was.

The last time I recall her saying it was more than fifteen years after Ned was dead and buried.

★

"Hell, we all might be crazy, for all I know," Tuxie Miller said, when I spoke of the matter to him. "Dale believes there's angels up in the sky that play golden harps, but I don't. At least Jewel ain't the harmful sort, Zeke."

"Better than that. She's my comfort," I told him. And I meant it.

May's notion of mothering was much like a hen's—once her pullets got big enough to get around, May was ready to be shut of them.

I doubt any of my six younguns by May would have lived to be full-grown if Jewel hadn't taken a hand and been a good and dutiful half sister to them all. She was a fine help with the triplets, too. It was my Jewel that bathed them, and fed them, and seen that they done their lessons, once they were school age.

Jewel lived in her thoughts, mostly, but she looked after me kindly, as I got old, and was a fine nurse when one of the little ones got sick.

★

I lost my dog Pete scarcely a year after Ned was killed.

A pack of wild curs cornered Pete, and chewed him to a frazzle.

★

For want of better employment, I took up politics and was made sheriff of the Going Snake. The thing I liked best about being sheriff was that it kept me ahorseback. I have always enjoyed fast travel and a good lope on a fine horse.

I arrested a goodly number of rough scamps and harassed the whiskeysellers so severely that most of them moved out of the District.

Chief Bushyhead died about that time, and they come to me to be President of the Senate. It was a big honour, but I passed. I do not relish bookkeeping, which was mostly what the job entailed.

Chasing scamps on a good fast mare was more to my taste.

★

During my years as sheriff, I had occasion to arrest five of the Arkansas boys who had been in on the last raid on Ned's fort. Their names were Heck Tolbert, Dade Bruner, C. D. York, Lee White, and Charley Hare. The first two were bank robbers; C. D. York was a horse thief; and the last two committed murders in the course of desperate brawls.

Judge Crittenden had been shot down himself by this time, the killer being a white man, the father of a boy he hung for horse thievery. They had persuaded old Judge Parker to pick up his gavel once again. All five of the culprits were tried in his court. He hung the horse thief, and one of the murderers; I don't recall what happened to the other fellows.

It gave me some satisfaction to bring the scoundrels in. They hounded Ned Christie to death, took my Jewel's mind and happiness, and then turned criminal themselves.

★

Judge Isaac Parker never remarried. Every fresh widow in Fort Smith set her cap for him, but Judge Ike resisted them all. He remained a lonely man to the end of his days.

In the years when I was sheriff, I was in and out of his court quite a bit. Sometimes, if I was bunking in Fort Smith for the night, I'd go up and entice him into a game of rummy. He still wore his necktie when he chopped wood; his promise to his wife held good throughout the years.

Judge Ike was a blue streak when it came to card games. I rarely won a hand from him, and I'm no slouch at cards.

"Where'd that skinny bailiff go, the one that brought me my amnesty?" I asked him one morning, when he had allowed me to join him in his walk by the river, a walk he invariably took.

"Ohio," the Judge replied.

"Well, but why Ohio?" I asked. "What took the man there?"

"The Widow Silvers," Judge Ike told me. "Chilly's a married man now, and his wife ain't poor, neither. I imagine he's set for life, if he behaves."

Judge Ike had not lost his ability to cast stern looks. He cast one at me, right there by the Arkansas River, but I did not respond.

My guess is the Widow Silvers set her cap for the Judge, but couldn't get him.

So, she took the bailiff instead.

★

Judge Isaac Parker was found dead by his woodpile one morning, still wearing his frock coat and string tie.

I enjoyed a game of rummy with him, about a month before his death. He was drinking bourbon whiskey from a tin cup throughout the game.

Several times over the years that I knew the old judge, I started to ask him what he thought about Ned Christie, and the war that came about because he sent those posses after Ned.

But I never asked. Just didn't.

"You sure hung a bunch of men, Judge," I did remark, one day when we had both been sipping from the tin cup.

"Any regrets?" I added.

"If I was to start in with regrettin', Zeke, they'd have to send me to the asylum, I expect," was all the Judge said.

When he fell dead by the woodpile, he cut his head a little on the edge of his own axe.

★

My Jewel was long thought to be the best-looking woman in the Going Snake. There had never been anyone to hold a candle to her, in the beauty department. Her high cheekbones, her long, black hair, and her modest ways caught the eyes of most of the available men in the District. Before a year had passed, men started coming by our home, in the hopes of courting her.

They came and came, a stream of them, for nearly thirty years: good men, and bad; tall men, and short; loud men, and fellows so quiet you wouldn't know they were even alive, unless they belched.

I doubt that Jewel noticed the men coming to court her. In her mind, she was still Ned's wife. And that was that.

If a fellow was polite, she might offer him vittles—but nothing else.

Arley Silk, who was a very decent fellow, courted Jewel for over ten years. Ned had been dead twenty years by that time, and Jewel had done raised most of mine and May's kids.

I thought I'd put in a word for Arley, and I did, though I was mostly thinking of Jewel, when I did it. She was still a woman in her prime, and only a little unhinged in her mind now. She could have made Arley Silk a fine wife, and had a little enjoyment for herself, too.

But it was wasted breath, what I said to her.

Arley Silk finally had to give up, and marry his second cousin.

★

The week after my sixty-eighth birthday, that rascally little May ran off with a horse trader from Texarkana.

The devil came to sell me a gelding, and promptly ran off with my wife.

Of course, May would flirt with a stump, but I never expected her to leave me. I grabbed up my pistol and a horsewhip, and set off in hot pursuit. I meant to shoot the scalawag if he wouldn't stand still for a horsewhipping.

I chased them halfway to Wichita Falls, Texas, before it occurred to me that I was behaving like an old fool. May never cared for me, anyway—not like Becca did—and she spent my money on anything she could find to buy.

That horse trader could supply her with money himself, if he liked her so much.

So, I coiled up my bullwhip, and went home.

Six months later, May was back with some wild tale about the horse trader trying to sell her to the white slavers. She claimed he had slipped powders in her coffee, powders that made her unable to think straight.

"Scat, May, you ain't even a good liar," I told her.

But the next spring, my Jewel died of scarlet fever.

When the fall came, and the days turned gloomy, I got to where I couldn't stand the empty house.

I found my rascally little May, and took her back home for good.

★

Tuxie and Dale worked hard and prospered. They acquired Ned's acreage and set their oldest children to working it. The old fort was converted into a fine stable. Tuxie got better sense, as he got older; finally, he got so sensible that they made *him* President of the Cherokee Senate. He made a good president, too, although my suspicion was that Dale did the bookkeeping for him.

★

As the years passed, and then the decades, it seemed there was no end of interest in Ned Christie and his war.

It started the day of his death. That drunk Yankee newspaper fellow with three initials in front of his name met the posse at the ferry that brought Ned's body across to Arkansas. He got a story in the New York paper, and the San Francisco paper, and maybe a lot of other papers, too, for all I know. I heard the news even crossed the seas.

Over the years, the newsies kept finding me and following me home, always to ask about Ned. If I was drunk, I would usually talk to them; if I was sober, I'd chase them off.

I was sent quite a few of the write-ups, over the years, but I didn't study them much. I wasn't up to it. Whenever I'd see Ned's name in the papers, it would make me tear up.

That's how much I missed the living man.

I missed his joshing, and his sweet behaviour, particularly to my beloved Jewel. Except when he was riled and in a temper, Ned Christie was as sweet a man as there's ever been, or ever will be.

I even missed the way Ned twisted his neck around, when he caught a glimpse of a squirrel, high up in a tree. His rifle barrel would come up; there would be the shot; bark would fly from the limb the squirrel was on; then Mr. Squirrel would come sailing down.

He made it seem as easy as whistling, Ned.

Easy as whistling, was how Ned made it seem . . .

LARRY McMURTRY

Winner of the Pulitzer Prize

COMANCHE MOON

A NOVEL

THE FINAL VOLUME OF THE
<u>LONESOME DOVE</u> SAGA

**COMING SOON IN HARDCOVER
FROM SIMON & SCHUSTER**

SIMON & SCHUSTER